C000274771

The Memory Year

Christine Trueman

Grosvenor House
Publishing Limited

This book is published by
Grosvenor House Publishing Ltd
Link House
140 The Broadway, Tolworth, Surrey, KT6 7HT.
www.grosvenorhousepublishing.co.uk

This book is a work of fiction. Any resemblance to
people or events, past or present, is purely coincidental.

A CIP record for this book
is available from the British Library

ISBN 978-1-80381-234-2

In memory of our parents,
who gave us so much love and support.

November 2016

I am lying on a tiny settee, no bigger than a bathtub when I wake. My eldest son had dragged the settee along the road for me from outside a neighbour's house. Even when I have had money, I've remained a scavenger. Waste not, want not, a lesson learned from my grandmother who survived the hardships of the war by using newspaper as toilet roll and hiding her hair loss under a scarf – alopecia caused by the stress of raising four children alone.

When he left, the husband of thirty-or-so years, I floundered in No Man's Land beneath a duvet for a while. With a large family and a sudden plunge in capital, it wasn't possible to flounder for long.

In order to cover the cost of living, I had taken on five foreign language students. This is why I lie on a settee that's not helping my sciatica. I might be an old lady in Syria, I suppose: foodless, having to burn my furniture for fuel. Fortunately, the students are nice young men who try to keep the place clean and who wolf their dinner back in the evening, appearing to appreciate my on-a-budget slop. It cheers me up to have them there.

My youngest son, his partner and their little girl live on the top floor of the house. This is also where my son James is to be found. They want to move out but they don't have the money to do it. This is Oxfordshire, where house prices are as ridiculous as they are in London and young people cannot afford to buy their own homes.

On the floors above, my children, granddaughter and the students sleep; the student from Vietnam sleeps in what was our marital bed. I hope his dreams are happy ones. Towards the end of our marriage, mine were not.

I have a new partner; he lies upon the floor beside my scrounged settee. Jack the collie is the new man in my life. He is Harry's dog, a handsome and affectionate beast. I bought him years ago for fifty pounds from a Cornish farmer. Jack is obedient, but currently he seems a little confused about pack order. Once upon a time, I was at the top of the house while he slept in an old armchair downstairs. Then, all of a sudden, my income fell with my status and I started to sleep in his kennel. Jack's snoring is louder than my ex-husband's.

Last night Jack went too far. When I came into the room having cleaned my teeth to apply a layer of face cream, he was grinning at me devilishly from my settee.

"What the hell do you think you are doing?" I snapped, trying to restore order. He leapt off my bed instantly, slinking across the room to his chair.

I wake, looking from the bright stars still twinkling in the winter sky, to my mobile phone. I wonder why I am now waking regularly at five a.m. It could be the nicotine making my brain race, or the cheap Lambrini which tastes like fizzy pop (but is low in calories, or so my friends tell me). He left me with a hankering for wine. These things have to stop, but I'm not quite ready yet.

"Can you come and unblock the toilet?" Bleary eyed, I squint to read the text on my phone.

Oh, joy. Not again. I roll from the uncomfortable settee.

When the children were young, I was an early riser. I loved and appreciated a time of day when I could think my thoughts, plan my plans, catch up on housework – a time without the voices and demands of the children at home, swiftly followed by the voices and demands of the children at the school where I taught.

The days when I was pretty and my husband loved me. Not much use in dwelling upon that, now.

Perhaps the fact that I was waking earlier was a sign of recovery, or maybe a need to retrace problems and find solutions.

There were no solutions to some things.

Our mother was dying. Having got over the loss of him, it had hit me with a sudden rush of pain and panic that now I would lose her. She was, undoubtedly, my best friend. I could not bear to suffer the loss of her, to live without that unconditional love and that friendship.

As I put out the students' breakfast and wash the plates from the evening before, I think about Mum and last Christmas. In just over a month, it will be Christmas again.

I'd wanted to take our parents to Venice. They had never been to Venice. She would have loved it there. He was right about one thing, that life is too short.

Last Christmas, I had been morose, depressed. I did my best to hide this from our children. Although they are adults, they suffered their own heartache and insecurity at our parting. They lost faith and confidence and I worked very hard to show them that everything would be well in the end. But I did not manage, sometimes scarcely tried, to keep sadness from Mum, always my confidant.

Then, I had wrapped presents alone, for the first time ever, drinking cheap wine as I did so and watching an Agatha Christie murder mystery. I confess that I actually smoked in the living room in my large dark house. What did it matter? I told myself. He had gone.

The photographs of laughing family faces mocked me. I was afraid of my own movements in the house, afraid of my own shadow. Left creeping around my home in fear of... what? A ridiculous fear. He had stayed away often and yet I had never feared ghosts and burglars before this.

Knowing how miserable I was, my tiny mother, reduced by chemotherapy and lack of appetite to six and a half stone, said, "Let's go into Oxford, have a cup of coffee and a cake."

I hadn't wanted to go anywhere near Oxford City. When young and confident, I felt I owned Oxford, but now I was afraid of the place of my birth; afraid we might bump into someone who would ask how he was and that I would have to explain the situation.

We went on the pretence of buying presents that I had already bought. We went because she had cancer, because she wanted to go.

She walked beside me, her arm through mine, a tiny woman, now. She wore a scarf to cover the hair that had once been beautiful. She wore leggings beneath her coat and warm boots. In the face of death, she still cared about her appearance. She walked slowly, carefully, leaning upon my arm. I wore the camel coat that he had bought for me two years before.

We must have made a sad pair as the shoppers walked briskly past us, clutching their purchases. The likelihood was that nobody noticed us. We were like ghosts. She was the positive ghost with the beautiful, smiling face, the ghost who always carried herself with pride.

I pull on my boots and the same camel coat, mud spattered now, and I no longer care. I am becoming a different person, maybe the person I used to be, long ago. I would walk proudly through Oxford with my mother in a dressing gown, if need be. I am so proud of her, proud to be her daughter.

Walking around the field in the semi-dark with Jack, before the day's work, I read the text messages from Louise.

"Can Patrick come at four and take Ned to the park? Could you take the children to the dentist at 2pm tomorrow?" There were unread texts from the day before. "Could you have the kids overnight so I can go to the staff do?"

"Could I borrow some milk and bread?" Who the heck was that? Not our daughter. Now strangers are asking me for bread and milk.

When he loved me, he used to warn me not to walk around the field in the dark in case someone pounced on me. I took to carrying a short, sharp knife in my coat pocket. When I tried to imagine the instance of using it against an assailant, I knew I couldn't do that. By the time the ethical debate had taken place in my head, the mugger would have sent me sprawling in the mud. He, being a lawyer, had said, "I don't think you'd get away with it in court... unless you carried a piece of fruit with you as well, then you could say you used the knife for that purpose." He's very clever, oh yes.

For the first time in ages, my eyes are opened to the sunrise setting fire to the trees, to the early winter sunshine caught in the hedgerows of bright red berries, to the beauty of it.

I pick some of the branches to take to Mum.

When he left, I noticed nothing about the changing seasons of the year. Spring ran into summer and all I thought about was his going. I am waking up early again, noticing things. His grip on my heart is growing weaker at last. My love for her grows stronger, makes me stronger.

I reply "yes," to all of the messages, then shut the garden gate and chop up meat and vegetables in the kitchen to slow cook them in a casserole pot. I toss the remnants to the rabbits that I never wanted but inherited. I have thought about slow cooking them in a casserole pot at financial low points over the past year. Then I drive to Louise's house for the school run.

Louise thinks that she is not like me. She prefers to think that she's like her father. Once I preferred to think that about my father. Perhaps it's the way of little girls.

The most complimentary text she ever sent me, apart from 'I love you', of course, was a text that said, "I look like you, you're my Mum xx."

But she now does many things 'like me'. One of them is to keep chickens, although, unlike me, she will not go as far as to slide around in the mud of their pen in office shoes. On countless occasions, I have fed them and collected their eggs.

I kept chickens. My father kept chickens. That's where it came from, Bletchingdon, in the Oxfordshire countryside.

Dad's dementia has worsened and without Mum he is more anxious and confused than ever. My sister and I have taken turns to stay with him since she went into hospital. He forgets to eat unless one of us is there to tell him to do so. We take it in turns to prepare evening meals or to take him a pre-packaged meal. He forgets to have baths, to wash his hair and to change his clothes so we tell him to do this and many other things besides. He asks repetitive questions and it is cruel to try to prompt his memory with "Think about it, Dad; where do you think Mum is?" So, we try not to do that any longer.

He forgets what is wrong with Mum, forgets the countless hours spent in chemotherapy at the Churchill. He asks the same question five times in an hour and he is still deteriorating. Neither Marion, Howard or I want to see him in a home; he wouldn't cope. He knows us, but he is so lost. He is in a time machine that jumps forward and backward without remorse. We take care of him, but if we have to go anywhere for a short while, he will ring us repeatedly to ask when we are taking him to see Mum. It's the first time he has used the phone in two years.

What will he do when we can no longer take him to see her? He is so anxious and this will worsen.

If I develop dementia, I am determined to don a wet suit, get pissed and walk into the sea in Polzeath. I am not pro-suicide, but I don't want my own children to have to care for me with this horrible disease – with any horrible disease. We are our memories, and without them we are nothing.

Before Mum got cancer, diagnosed in 2014, and despite the fact that we saw our parents almost every day, we had no idea how bad Dad's memory had become. Mum would grumble about it and we would gently chide her for 'having a go at him'. But we had no idea how difficult it had become for her. She wanted his company, his physical help, but with the most active brain on earth, being with him had become a kind of torture for her. We simply didn't understand, then.

Sometimes she would be rude to him and we would tell her off.

"He'll forget it in a minute," she would say. Of course, he would, but it can't have been reassuring to be talked to like that. So much can be disguised from the world in a close relationship.

Dad is standing at the window of his house, waiting for me, waiting for someone he might recognise.

Marion has gone to work and he has made himself a cup of tea. He is dressed in a clean shirt and sweater. I let myself into the house and greet him with a kiss.

"Chris, tell me, where is Mum?" This is the first thing that he says to me.

"She's been moved to the care home in North Oxford, Dad."

"Ah, yes." A pause, I know exactly what he is going to say next.

"When do you think she'll come home?"

I kiss his cheek. Every time you tell him something he isn't going to want to hear, you hate yourself. But you can't lie, or perhaps you can, I don't know.

"She can't come home, Dad. She's too ill."

"Don't tell me that," he says for the millionth time. So, what can I tell him?

"Dad, we have to get used to it Mum will die soon and she knows that..." Is that what I must say? That she has rewritten her will? That she has told my ex-husband that she loves him? That she has seen a priest? That she has said she wants her ashes to be buried in the same plot as her father and mother?

Their living room is strewn with equipment provided by the palliative care team. Once we dreamed of her coming home, lying on a couch, watching the television programmes she loved with us. I dreamed of taking her to Venice. It was too late. Her daily care, lifting and turning her, meant that too many nurses would be involved. She would never see the home she loved and cared for again, never see her little treasures or photographs.

I start to cry, biting the inside of my lip to stop it. It would only distress him.

I make him a bowl of porridge with jam and he eats it. Then I help him into his jacket and we get into the car.

I have driven to one hospital or another two or three times a day, every day for four weeks, since she tripped over the chair and broke her hip. She had blood poisoning after the operation. That was when she gave up hope.

"Chris, remind me, where is Mum?" Dad asks, as he pulls on his cap and gloves.

Fine Day for a White Wedding

I went to a wedding in the February after he left, a family wedding to which my husband was invited. My family are all very fond of him, still. I don't know whether I feel that way; it's all a bit fresh in my mind.

I was reluctant to go in the same way that I had been reluctant to go to many events without him at first, with a feeling of being foolish, of being watched in some way. People were used to seeing us together. The fact that we were going to divorce left some people visibly shocked.

Paula once said, shortly before we married, "You're swopping one mother for another." It made no sense to me then, but it does now. She was right.

I drove us to the wedding, Mum and Dad and Aunty Steph, to my cousin's wedding. I had always been so enthusiastic about weddings and parties but this was so different to me, a hurdle that I had to leap across rather than the simple, pleasurable thing that it ought to have been.

The wedding would be lovely, I knew that. It was a chance to have fun with Mum, with my family. But I had been married to the same person for such a long time, and I was scared without being sure of what it was that frightened me.

I suppose that I could have made an excuse. I didn't for several reasons. I felt that I was being silly; that was the first reason. Secondly, I am very fond of all of my cousins and didn't want to hurt anyone's feelings. Thirdly, having avoided so many things that would have been fun for her, through sickness and exhaustion after long chemotherapy sessions, the idea of the wedding had kept Mum going. It had been something she could look forward to and she was excited about it, as though her cancer didn't exist.

She had dressed so carefully and looked lovely, had made her face up and was smiling, and in the rear of the car she laughed excitedly with her sister. How could anyone deny her this? If I had been prepared to stay all night, I think that she would have danced all night.

We drove into the Cotswold countryside and stopped at a pub on the way to ask for directions. We had plenty of time, so Dad suggested that we have a drink.

Just before pulling into the pub car park, I had started to feel cold. At first it was a small, hard lump of ice melting inside me and then gradually it spread through my veins. I said nothing. You tend not to complain about physical ill health when someone has endured session after session of chemotherapy.

As we waited for our drinks, I caught Aunty Steph staring at me. Mum asked, "What's happened to your nose?"

Putting my hand to my face, I could feel the swelling. In the bathroom, I examined my face in the mirror. The right side of my nose was swollen red; I thought there was a boil beneath the swelling so I tried to conceal it with some foundation.

Returning to them I was still shivering and I ordered a whisky. I hadn't drunk whisky since I used to gargle with it as a young teacher unused to the demands upon my voice. There was something happening to me, and I wasn't sure what it was.

This was a second marriage for the bride and groom and they had chosen a hotel rather than a church. As we drove toward the reception area and parked the car, my heart had begun to palpitate at an alarming rate; a gerbil appeared to be trapped inside my rib cage. I smiled and tried to steady my breathing in a way I had been taught years ago when in labour. It didn't appear to be working. I widened my smile as I held the umbrella for my mother and aunt, and we crossed the pathway to the hotel entrance in the rain.

The service was modern but lovely, the bridesmaids utterly gorgeous, the bride elegant and composed, but I was not composed. I had expected to find it hard to listen to the vows they made while remembering our own wedding; I had believed that we would last for eternity, but there had been no warning about what would happen.

I hadn't expected that the right side of my face would start to twitch, collapsing as though I were about to have a stroke; that I could now look cross-eyed at the offending swollen nostril coated in glorious redness, brighter than lipstick.

During the service I put up a hand to steady my quivering cheek and Mum, who thought that I was crying, stretched out her hand to cover mine. I wasn't crying, but somewhere inside of me I was suffering a kind of breakdown which had affected my heart rate, my temperature, my outward appearance and I had no control over it.

I longed to lie down, to be free of the constriction of clothing and had begun to wonder whether I was about to have a heart attack. Please, not now, dear God, I prayed, not before the financial settlement.

I sat with close family and friends, doing my best to assume normality. By the end of the meal, my parents and aunt were having a wonderful time and were ready to hit the dance floor. They put me to shame, these older relatives in their eighties, with such energy and love of life while I wanted to collapse. And Mum, with cancer, had looked forward to this for so long.

In the bathroom at the hotel, I stared in horror at my red swollen nose and the blotchy rash which had appeared on my cheeks. Little wonder the cousin seated next to me at the table had stared, politely saying nothing but so obviously fascinated.

So, we left earlier than planned and it was my fault. I told Mum that I felt unwell and was concerned about driving us home, which was the truth. At this point, I felt so hot and so unwell I didn't think I could drive at all. She smiled and said that she understood, but she must have been so disappointed.

Returning to the dark house, I collapsed into the bed, fully clothed. I slept fitfully, sleeping and waking to the continued thumping of my heart, shivering through my sleep like somebody with a flu virus, and dreaming nightmarish dreams.

When I awoke early on that Sunday morning, I knew that I couldn't drive a car to buy medication. I called Marion, my sister.

"What's the matter?"

"I don't know for sure. I feel as though I have the flu, but it's worse than that. I need medicine, I think, but I can't drive," I said.

She knew then that it was serious. I drive everywhere; I'm a taxi service to my family. I drove after an operation on my uterus and I would probably drive with a broken leg, if I really had to.

She let herself in with the key that I had given her. I felt too ill and, by now, too frightened to move.

"What the heck happened to you?" was her cheerful greeting. "You look as though you've been punched on the nose."

She didn't drive to the chemists but called a doctor, and, because of my symptoms, the doctor called out the paramedics.

They were very kind, these paramedics – one younger and one about my age. They both wore beards and, if not for their uniform, they would have resembled members of an American Civil War society, which was somehow reassuring.

They told us that they had to come because the symptoms I'd explained could be the symptoms of a heart attack or of a stroke. They asked whether I had been under any stress or duress and I explained about the divorce and ways in which it had taken its toll. They listened sagely and asked me to take my outer garments off so that they could listen to my back and chest.

I sat up in bed then. Marion sat at the foot of the bed. Then I realised that I was still fully clothed in my wedding gear and that, because I was so cold when I arrived home, I was wearing a full body stocking which I couldn't remove unless I went beneath my skirt to undo the popper.

As I bent down to attend to this, the older paramedic remarked, "I don't think we are going to find your lungs down there, madam." He sounded like an actor in one of the Carry On films. Marion giggled.

After examining me, they said that I had to go to the hospital for further tests and asked whether I would like an ambulance, but I didn't want that, and anyway, Marion said that she would drive me there.

Simply the act of waiting at the hospital with my sister calmed me.

I had tests for my blood pressure and heart. Both were fine. The doctor sitting opposite me told me that I had not wasted her time. She said that I had been having a panic attack and that the symptoms caused by 'flight or fight' chemicals can be dangerous. It was right to go to the hospital.

Almost as soon as we left, the swelling in my nose subsided. Just like that, like magic. A panic attack, how ridiculous.

Marion took my arm and gave it a firm squeeze. "Carry a paper bag in your handbag and breathe into it," she told me. She knows about these things. She has a greater right than I do to have panic attacks.

I should simply have loved my husband. I should never have argued with him. Of course, I reason, it was necessary to argue with him. In the circumstances, Mother Theresa would have argued with him. Things changed.

Thoughts are spinning, going around and around in my head as Dad and I drive together to visit Mum at the care home.

"Tell me Chris, where is Mum?" A part of me wants to groan aloud, but I reach out my hand to cover his gnarled gardener's fingers before replying for the umpteenth time. He has fine fingers. They like to touch and stroke things: bedcovers, shelves, the cheeks of the people who love him.

"Put your hand on the wheel," he says, a little sharply. He always was a careful driver. He likes to tell visitors that he drives his own car. Out of love and respect, we don't contradict this. His driving licence wasn't renewed after the dementia diagnosis. He hasn't driven in ages.

We draw up to the gates of the care home in North Oxford and I key in the code. I take Dad's arm and he follows me, unsure of himself and where he is. A friend told me that as dementia worsens, the brain resembles a rotting cauliflower. We can read the effort in his face as he ploughs through the pictures of the people he knows or once knew. At times, recently, he has mistaken me for both Mum and his cousin. His brother, Don, who also had dementia, once mistook me for their mother, Louie.

The woman at reception greets us with a smile, recognising us. She leads us to the lift. Mum is on level one, in a little room that is strange and new to her. Everything has suddenly become threatening. She was convinced she would outlive our father, being younger by a few years. She was fearful for him, worried about how he would cope if she died first.

"Months, Cynthia, not years," was the doctor's brutally honest reply to her question.

There were tears in her eyes, then. All I could do was to clutch at her hand. But she would come away from the Churchill still determined to fight the tumour, and that spirit worked to extend her life, that bloody mindedness her children needed now.

We tried to bring things into her hospital room, her photos and treasures and knick-knacks, decorating the small spaces of the room to comfort her. The doctors and nurses tolerated large paintings of the sea, ornaments, photographs galore, but they had to say no to the seaweed from Polkerris beach.

When Dad and I enter the room, she is sleeping. I help Dad to take off his cap and coat and I watch Mum breathing peacefully. She has aged suddenly, over a period of three weeks. When I first took her to the hospital after the incident of the broken hip, she resembled a tiny ballerina with a scarf wound about her head to hide her lack of hair. She had always been beautiful and dressed with pride. Now, anaemia has turned the naturally olive brown skin she had since childhood to the colour of chalk.

She has her favourite blue bedjacket on. She sleeps with her mouth slightly open and her hands resting underneath the bedclothes; she never liked to have cold hands.

Dad moves the chair closer to the bed, dragging it noisily. In a voice too loud for the room, because he has poor hearing, he asks, "When do you think she'll be able to come home, Chris?"

"Sit down, Dad," I whisper, with the authority that Mum uses, and Mum opens her eyes. Her eyes, at least, remain sapphire blue.

"Oh, hello…" she says, so quietly that you can hardly hear her. "Howard was here; you've just missed him."

I kiss her very gently on the forehead. She used to love it when I hugged her, but because she is so frail and because her joints hurt so much after the chemo, I've not been able to hug her for over a year.

"Pass me a drink," she says, gesturing towards the bedside table.

I lift one of the small juice bottles – she no longer has the strength to lift them on her own – and squirt a little into a small plastic cup.

When she entered the hospital, she could hold a cup of tea. Then it became impossible for her and she had to have a cup with a straw; then, finally, she could only manage a baby cup with a teat.

Generally, if anyone, nurse or family, suggest holding it for her, she is irritable. She was an independent, dynamic woman in control of her life and the only autonomy left to her now is to push and rearrange things around her tray and to hold a baby's beaker.

"How are you feeling?" Dad asks as she drinks. The question is meant with love, but is so fatuous that she arches her eyebrows at me in a way that makes me smile, as if to say, "How exactly do you think I am feeling?"

"She doesn't feel good, Dad," I say gently, answering for her.

I walk to the foot of her bed to examine her swollen feet and legs and to peer beneath the under sheet. Things are becoming difficult, now. Of course, she wants to be kept clean, but changing the under sheet requires two or even three people and every small movement has started to hurt her. The nurses have increased her pain killers, now she takes morphine. We are careful as a family not to say 'morphine' because we know, and more importantly Mum knows, that it is the beginning of the end, so we call them painkillers.

Her feet were like a geisha's once, tiny in comparison to mine. Her legs were always slim, devoid of cellulite. Now her legs and feet are horribly swollen. The shiny skin over them is stretched too tight. In the hospital, we had to cut a slit in a pair of socks to place them over her toes. Her feet are always cold to the touch. A nurse told us that morphine does that. The days have become a series of minuscule actions which make all the difference to the quality of her life.

"Don't wrap them too tightly," she says, as I pull up the bedclothes.

I was afraid that the room would be cold for her when she came here. It is an old building, a private care home although Mum is an NHS patient. Howard found the place and we were pleased; but there are gaps between the window and the frame that let in the November draughts, so I covered the glass with cling film. The system of radiators is old, and being the first patient in the room for some time, it took a while for the heating to kick in.

A nurse enters the room, knocking first at the door which is propped open. She is called Miriam and she is from Senegal.

"Cynthia, will you have some soup?" she asks.

"No." It is barely audible and she hasn't the strength to shake her head.

"There's still some of the chicken broth I made; you liked that," I remind her.

"I drank nearly all of it; it was nice, but I don't want any now."

Mum was a good cook who loved watching cookery programmes. She was particular about food – is particular about food – I'm already using the past tense. Sometimes she would return restaurant meals if she felt that there was something amiss. Now, she eats so little. My instinct to feed her is strong. Food will keep her alive for longer, surely?

"Please, Mum, eat something." Inadvisably, I add, "You aren't a suffragette."

"I am a suffragette," she snaps back, with feeling, making Miriam smile.

I sigh and let it go. Dad has got up to kiss her. He is heavy handed, because he doesn't think about her fragility, and leans a hand upon the pillow. It causes her head to slide slightly to one side. The placement of her fine neck and aching back against the many pillows is crucial to combat the pain stemming from the tumour. Now her head has fallen at a comical angle. Except that it isn't funny at all. She withdraws her hand from Dad's and he looks dejected; I kiss him on the cheek and rearrange her pillows, holding her head still with my left hand.

She has had enough of the torture.

Beyond the window, the trees are almost bare. The last of the autumn leaves are blowing across the lawn.

"You are still so beautiful," I tell her, sitting on the chair beside her bed. "How come you got the Coppock good looks and not me?"

"You're a Coppock inside. You're like me…"

Dad is distractedly cleaning his fingernail; it's one of those times I'm happy that he isn't registering anything.

"I love you so much, Mum, more than anything or anyone," I whisper. I mean it, I do.

"Not more than him," she says knowingly, smiling at me. She means my ex-husband.

"Yes, more than him." I bite my lip. "I wish I had known it before, but I know it now. I love you far more than him."

"He came to see me again, you know." She smiled. She said it proudly, in the way that some little old ladies say, "I'm ninety-five."

He does that to people. He has charm and status. Once, he was everything to me. I feel myself bridle at her words. Did she not understand? I'm not ready to remember the good things that he did.

"Did he?" I ask. My tone is churlish.

"Don't be like that…" She frowns at me. She means it. I suppose that, particularly towards the end of your life, it is important to forgive. But I can't forget.

"It's Halloween tomorrow." I want to change the subject. "The staff are going to light fireworks just beneath your window."

She casts a wry smile and I feel helpless to improve her lot. At Halloween, Mum kept a basket filled to bursting with sweets for the neighbouring children and wore a green wig and a pointed black hat. It's already in the past. She will never do these things again.

The House in Headington Quarry

"Why have you stopped here?" my father asks suspiciously as I draw up outside the house in New Cross Road. Now, he seems permanently afraid that he might have to talk to someone. I have stopped here because my past is flying before my eyes, as though it is I who am dying, not Mum. I've stopped here on impulse as it's on the way home and because it matters.

"No reason," I say. "Do you remember this house, Dad?"

"Course I do, Mum lived here before we married."

It is nothing like the bright and beautiful house of my childhood. It reminds me of Hell Hall now, where the Dalmatian puppies were kept. It seems to cower in the dark shadows of overgrown conifer trees. There were no trees when I was a child; it had a proud face with large windows, a 1940s show home.

Nanny Edna was so proud of it. How lonely she must have felt when Gramps died. To pay the bills and fill the silence, she had to fill the place with strange young men: university students, just as I do now. After all of the laughter and joy and security provided by her own family, she lived with strangers.

I remember visiting her after Grampy Ron's death. I should have offered to stay overnight with her, but it didn't occur to me. I was a selfish teenager, then. I can remember her small figure seated in his armchair, swallowed up by the large living room. She had cared for our Gramps for so long that she became exhausted at first, then so lonely.

Christmases at New Cross Road were the best by far. There was room for everyone to stay, though I remember sleeping on the floor with Paula beside me on Christmas Eve and opening one of her presents while she slept, long after the adult laughter had died down and Father Christmas had come. It was a beautiful, home-made wooden wardrobe the size of a shoe box which Uncle Frank had made for her, while inside there were dolls dresses. Everyone encouraged Paula to play with dolls, but she was never interested, preferring pen knives and sports equipment. I can remember playing with the wardrobe in the middle of the night until I fell asleep again.

It's the love that Nan constantly directed towards us which keeps me strong. She cared so much; every child needs that at the start of their life.

When we were young children, in the bleakness of winter, she would be the first to get up in the cold and the dark to light a fire in the grate, then bring us downstairs to sit before it upon the rug. She made us sweet porridge and, instead of watching television, we watched the orange flames of the fire, seeing spirits writhing over the coals and logs. We would sit like this for ages.

"Chris, tell me, is Mum in the hospital or did she go somewhere else?" Dad's voice brings me back to the present.

"She's in the care home, Dad, in Summertown," I remind him.

We drive home. I make him a sandwich and a cup of tea and sit with him while he eats. As I struggle with the TV controls as I always do, yearning for the days where you only had to press a button, Dad says, "When do you think she'll be allowed to come home?"

There is stifling one's own grief and then there's the depression of having to answer that question again and again: calmly, gently. I hear the questions by day; Marion listens to them all evening.

I can't lie. We are too close to the end. I cross the floor on my knees and take his hand in mine.

"She can't come home, Dad. She's too ill, very ill. She might not live."

I have no idea about whether I should say this or not. I don't know enough about dementia.

"What? Are you serious? Don't tell me that... bugger me..."

He looks away from me. He doesn't cry. His eyes grow red but he doesn't cry. Perhaps it's a generational thing. His mother was very gentle; his father could be very fierce. It's a common enough story. Men weren't supposed to cry in his day. I can't take away his pain or hers and I feel so useless.

"We love you," I say. "We are going to take care of you. You are going to miss Mum, but you'll never have anything to worry about." I kiss his cheek.

His questions are too much to bear. Marion's daughter is a young woman, but we don't want to leave her alone with him because she will have to answer his questions again and again. I looked after my grandfather at the weekends sometimes, when I was fourteen, usually on a Saturday to give Nanny Edna a break from the care. But changing oxygen bottles and making Gramps tea and biscuits was straightforward in comparison to this.

"Why haven't you told me that before?" he asks me.

"I have Dad, but you forget. What channel do you want to watch?"

"I can't believe Mum is like this. She was one of the most helpful and intelligent people. I love her so much. She never did anybody any harm. Why did this happen? How did this happen?" His questions are so naïve, yet heartfelt.

"We'll go and see her again in the morning," I tell him.

He lost his father before he was thirty, and his mother from cancer not long after that. His wife took the place of his parents.

I leave a note for him, on a whiteboard, saying that I'm going to get my grandchildren from nursery and that Marion will be home from her school soon. I leave him with the sandwich and tea, to watch a quiz programme, and hope he will forget where we have been. I have to collect Dan from school.

Friends at the school gates ask after Mum. I stay with the children until Louise returns from work, then go home to cook the dinner and drive in the dark once more, back to her. I want to see her without Dad being present.

At the door to her room, I watch at a distance as she sleeps, as her emaciated body struggles for peace. Her thin shoulders rise and fall; her breasts are almost flat as her chest rises and falls beneath a delicate layer of fine, paper-thin skin. This isn't my mum.

A couple of evenings ago, I cried outside the front door of her house. She wasn't there of course. Marion had drawn the curtains against the winter night and it occurred to me that she didn't draw them in the same way as Mum, who used to leave a small gap where the light shone through, as though we were still welcome there. I stared at the curtains, imagining the time when I couldn't see her there, or talk to her, or kiss her. Like a small child, I wanted to hold her hand.

Now, Mum's mouth is open as she breathes. Her breathing is laboured as she struggles for air, her mouth is a small cave. She is still beautiful in this vulnerable state.

I cross the room to sit in the chair, trying not to wake her. Her tummy gurgles with the cancer. This year as we sat together to watch TV, her stomach would talk constantly, almost reassuringly. Now it is a worrying noise, the sound of water rushing through a broken pipe.

"Christine?" She is awake. Instantly she winces with pain. "I can't stand much more of this."

"Are you in very much pain?" I take her hand as lightly as I can because if I rest my hand upon her stomach, it will hurt her.

"Not much, not yet..." She sighs so softly. "No one could understand how debilitating, how humiliating this is."

She is very proud, so independent. She hates it when she has to be changed by nurses, hates it when a well-meaning nurse says, "Shall I feed you, dear?" She has made it clear that she would rather starve, and she will.

Once, when Mum first came here, a nurse said to me, "We need to change her; she is afraid that she smells!" She said it in a half whisper with a little laugh, as though she thought I might join in with the fun. Really, she meant no harm, but I knew Mum had heard it. I think some people don't realise that a decaying body can hold a keen brain that is functioning as well as ever.

Now, our eyes meet. I wait, watching her, holding in my breath.

"I can't bear this anymore; I want to go," she says, her voice hoarse.

"You mean, you want to get to the end of your life?" I say, falteringly. We haven't really spoken about death. She has tried to protect us, as we do her.

"You have no idea of the discomfort and frustration. I want you all to be able to get on with your lives, but you have to keep coming here."

That's when I cry. Until now, I haven't, for her sake; trying to be strong as I was when the doctor told her she would not have long to live. How can she possibly think we want to be anywhere else but here with her?

"Don't…" she says.

I grab a tissue from her box. "Sorry, Mamma. You've got it so wrong. I want to be here all of the time; we all do, all of us. We don't want to spend a moment away from you, even if we sit here while you sleep."

She nods. The frayed corners of her mouth attempt a smile.

"I had a lovely dream yesterday. I was standing outside an open gate in a wall, a bit like the gate at the Helligan Gardens, and I went through. There was the most beautiful garden on the other side." A wistful sigh, then, "I want to come home, I want to sit in the kitchen and drink coffee and watch the sunrise over the trees…"

Now is the time to talk about death. She wants to talk about death with someone, I think.

"You will go through a gate. There's no brochure, so I don't know what heaven is like, but you will go to God, and you'll see them all again: Nan and Gramps and Christine, all of the people you love, and it doesn't matter what you did or didn't do, who you liked or didn't like…"

My voice trails away; I am starting to sound like a vicar, but she smiles and gives a very small nod. I hope I have given her some hope and peace as she sleeps again.

The nursing home is very tolerant. We, her children, and Aunty Stephanie, her sister, are taking it in turns to sleep on her floor or in the armchair beside her bed. We don't want her to be alone; she is frightened in a way she never seemed to be in life. Perhaps she's afraid that she won't go to heaven, that there is no heaven.

"There is no such thing as hell, except on earth, Mum. We will all go to heaven, even murderers go to heaven and there we have to love everyone, even the people we disliked on earth."

How do I know this? I don't. I won't know until it's my time. I would say anything to comfort her and her faith in me is childlike.

She asked to see a priest from Holy Trinity Church, the church that her grandfather and great grandfather built. The congregation have been saying prayers for her there.

After an evening in November, when it was my turn to stay, I came home in the early morning having slept on the floor beside her bed. My brother and sister arrived to sit with her as I left the care home.

There is a mist rising from the river Cherwell as I drive toward home. I have been at home for an hour and a half when my phone rings.

"The nurse says she is dying. Hurry, come back," Marion entreats me.

I call James, our eldest son to come with me. He puts his arms around me, but I pull away impatiently because we have to go quickly, in a race against time. We drive to where she is and, as the roadworks prevent us from moving any faster, I cry quietly, in frustration and desperation.

I pull out of the traffic to drive the car into a one-way street, mercifully it's a short street. Since he left, I have been so cautious, neurotically clutching my handbag to me, locking doors repeatedly, that kind of thing; but not now. In the passenger seat beside me, James retracts his head like a tortoise disappearing into a shell and closes his eyes to it all.

Mum is everything and I couldn't see it. Now I want to be everything that she is. I want to be her, and to protect the people I love. I am crying without any restraint. James massages my shoulder as I pull into the road. He doesn't know what else to do. I chew against the inside of my mouth in an attempt to stop the choking noises escaping from me.

The phone nags me from my pocket. I take it out and lift it to my ear.

"She's gone."

No. It isn't true. I am one block away from the care home. I wanted to be there, I wanted it so much. We are too late; her last breath mattered so much to me. She had told me that, as a newborn baby in the 1950s, I had jaundice. I was taken from her for a week and for the first few days I was kept from her. That would not happen in this day and age. Perhaps, removed from my mother at such a young age, I have found distance from her hard. Now I will be distanced for ever.

Followed by James, I walk and then run through the corridor to the lift which stops outside of her room. We are watched by various sympathetic staff members. I don't stop, not wanting to talk to anyone. At the open door to her room, we both hesitate.

There is rigidity about her skeletal figure. The thin fingers which worked constantly against the coverlet are still. Her head rests against the pillows; her mouth is open.

Dad and Marion are seated on either side of her bed, and Ruby, Marion's daughter. Dad will call Ruby 'Little 'un' for eternity. Last January it was Ruby's eighteenth birthday and I danced with Mum and her friend, Aunty Dorothy.

I'm glad that we danced.

They are silent. All eyes are fixed upon our dead mother's face. Ruby, sitting next to Marion, is holding her hand very tightly.

It is too warm in the room. When Mum came here, I stuck cling film all around the sills where the wind blew inside, and complained that my mother's skin was icy cold. They said she didn't feel it because of the morphine.

I go to Marion's side of the bed, and she gets up to give me space. After that everything gives in to instinct. We haven't been able to sit upon her bed for fear of causing her pain. When they said she felt nothing and was completely unconscious, we had felt that it wasn't so; this was our mother and she had a lively mind. We felt that the twitching of her fingers was her attempt at communication. Their agitation meant that she needed her pads to be changed and once, when Marion took her hand and she was supposedly unconscious, she pushed and pushed at Marion's hand until it rested upon the tumour, as big as an elephant's ear.

I sit beside her and for the first time in forever I put my arms fully about her and draw her fragility against me, feeling the bones of her tiny figure, burying my face in her neck and smelling her. She loved to be hugged by us, and we couldn't do that all the while she was ill because it hurt her.

I cry loudly then, without dignity, without care. I must have squeezed her body too hard, and for a moment I pull my face back, shocked, half believing that she isn't dead after all, as the last warmth of her breath comes out of her lungs in a whisper against my cheek. A blessing, or the gift of love and strength. I shall never forget it.

A week or so before Mum's funeral, we meet with the vicar of Holy Trinity Church. I don't know whether it's a coincidence that he resembles Jesus, but it rather suits him.

He is a very spiritual man, but unlike some priests, you couldn't accuse him of being sanctimonious or giving advice based upon a sheltered life, or of being boring. His sermons include references to the works of Leonard Cohen and the questionable antics of Donald Trump.

To say that he is spiritual might also seem odd. After all, he is a vicar. It's simply that he doesn't pretend to have answers to everything; he doesn't produce any kind of brochure telling people what to expect when they go to heaven, whatever heaven may be. He has a faith in God without claiming to know all of the answers.

We meet at Dad's, which was recently Mum and Dad's house. Marion lives there with her daughter, now, to stay with Dad in the evenings, while I care for Dad in the day. Every day he wants to be taken to the hospital to see Mum. Despite holding her hand when she died, he still believes that she is alive.

Howard arrives for the meeting, with Michelle, who has made a delicious sponge cake. Marion makes the tea. The vicar arrives on his bike as vicars are wont to do. We introduce him to Dad, who shakes hands with him but frowns at him with suspicion. Perhaps because he doesn't want to or can't face that Mum has died and that the vicar may be party to the cremation. Dad glowers at the vicar as though it is all his fault before burying himself in the living room. At the time, none of us really considered how depressed our father might become. Dementia and depression, too much for the soul to bare, really.

We plan the order of service, which takes a long time and almost all of the cake. We decide upon 'All Things Bright and Beautiful', which everyone knows and because our nan used to sing it. Apparently as a child she used to think the words went 'All things bright and blue before.' The vicar reminds us about the politically incorrect verses endorsing people on welfare benefit to accept their lot and not be disgruntled about those in celebrity mansions, so we drop those verses.

But I am cross when the vicar mocks me gently, saying that I should write down what I want to say about Mum because he knows that I like to talk. I glare at him a bit.

"I think I can talk about Mum without needing notes," I coldly remark. "She was my mother and I was a teacher. I don't need notes."

"With all due respect, a cremation service has to be kept strictly to a timescale because one service follows another. I've done many such services before and it's far better to write down what you want to say beforehand, then practise it and time it," says the Jesus lookalike.

I'm annoyed then, because he is probably right. So, I don't agree anything right there and then, but a few days later, when I babysit for my daughter's children, I give in to this suggestion.

After reading to the youngest and playing Bananagrams with him, having got them supper and watched *Legally Blonde* with the girls, there is the usual weekend fight about whether anyone should ever go to bed at all. Eventually, safe in the knowledge that they are all asleep or drifting off, I sit down at the little table to write what I want to say at Mum's funeral.

There is so much to say about her love and enthusiasm and the brilliant colour of her life, it takes me a while to put pen to paper, until at last I decide to talk about three events in her life, in our lives, that show these things. I sit at the kitchen table, head bent over the paper until the light outside dims and I rise to turn on the lights in the kitchen. I am completely focused upon the task, unaware of the lateness of the hour in one of those rare moments, recently, of inner peace and quietude.

Our daughter's house is one that I know very well. She grew up there, along with her two brothers. I'm very fond of the old place. I know every corner, know the noise the pipes make when the heating winds down, know the creaking sound from the branches, blowing in the wind outside. I feel safe and warm there, as she and her children do.

I feel as though I have become my mother, as though she was inside me as I sit alone at the kitchen table writing her eulogy.

"I knew you'd come through," she had told me.

"I love you so much, Mum. I hope this is okay and I hope you approve," I say.

And in the total silence, the washing machine starts to whirr.

I look up from my writing, startled. No one has turned it on.

A little hesitantly and feeling slightly foolish, I walk into the kitchen in the manner of a woman waiting to be coshed at any moment, hearing the creak of the great fir trees that surround the house. I can see the branches, long, creepy fingers moving in the wind through the darkness of the garden.

Before I reach the machine, it stops as suddenly as it started. The red light is off. I'm being silly, must have imagined it. My heart beats rapidly as I make my way back to the table.

When I reach the chair, glancing down at the notes once more, I feel a sudden rush of happiness that I can't explain. I look upward, staring at nothing in particular, wondering about this odd feeling inside of me. And in this draught-free house with its closed doors, an icy breath reaches my cheek, in exactly the same place as the kiss after her death, the last sigh of carbon dioxide from her body as I held her in my arms.

Colder than cold, an icy draught directed at my right cheek, seemingly coming from nowhere. I press my fingers to the place and feel her arms about me.

7th January, 2020, almost four years later

It's Harry's birthday. According to the Greek and Russian church, it's the correct date for Jesus' birthday, too. Jesus was a Capricorn. Other than a tendency for compassion towards people with mental health problems, Harry is not like Jesus. He is a rapper who used to DJ for an Oxford based radio station. He's also a mental health worker, which was, at first, a trial by fire.

Christmas seems long ago. After Christmas, my entire family went to the Lake District. We stayed in a cosy house in Coniston with wonderful views of the mountains. It was ridiculously busy – so very packed with tourists that we had to walk some way to find any isolated spots. In the towns there were no spare parking places. We did a lot of dog walking and played games in the red-walled living room before the fire. This time, Dad didn't go with us.

Dad is almost ninety-two and has dementia. Last year, when we took him to Coniston, he kept getting out of bed at night to ask where the hotel receptionist was. At times, we could have believed we were on the set of *Fawlty Towers*. This year we decided the whole holiday experience was now disorientating for all of us, including Dad, so we left him with a carer from a care agency instead.

The carer was lovely, but there were some initial teething problems. She arrived from Hungary, a lady of about my age who looked rather careworn (resembling me a good deal). If carers are having to come from Hungary, this means there aren't enough carers in this country. Private care costs an arm and a leg, as we've discovered since Mum died and we began to look after Dad ourselves.

To settle the carer in, we had asked that she arrive the night before we left. This proved to be a very good idea. She told Marion and I about her Jewish background. Her mother was a survivor of the concentration camps. We ate a meal with her and listened to her family stories of courage and fortitude with respect and admiration.

She also lit nine candles to celebrate Hanukkah and left them to burn beneath Mum's chintzy curtains.

Marion, the sister who lives with Dad, had to tell her that potentially this might burn Dad's house down and that we couldn't go away if she was intending to do this for eight days. She agreed that it wasn't the best of ideas and admitted there is a great need for the fire brigade in Israel around the time of Hanukkah.

She certainly took good care of him; he was well fed and very calm when we returned. Also, there was a lot of chicken soup in the fridge but he couldn't remember her name half an hour after she had left us to return to Hungary.

No sooner had we arrived back from the Lake District, than it was Harry's birthday. Louise told me he wanted to go to a restaurant called Tycoon, at least that's what I thought she said, as that's what Harry would like to be; but in fact, it was called Thaikhun.

I've been a bit worried about money, having spent a lot on family at Christmas and in the Lake District. My pension adviser tells me I'll have nothing at all by the time I'm seventy, but a birthday is a birthday and you only live once, or so they say, although I'm not sure I agree. This time, we took Dad with us to the restaurant and Harry's best friend, George. George was sent from Cameroon as a child without choice in the matter; his parents wanted to protect him from something dreadful. He is waiting to see whether he can remain here and finally become British. He has waited a long time; it's a travesty.

The restaurant was loud for Dad, who is now extremely hard of hearing, but it's very popular with young people. He seemed happy enough, however, even though it must have been confusing for him as he often forgets who we all are. He had a good appetite and didn't appear to notice that we were squashed against one another on a boat-shaped table. He nodded and smiled a lot, a bit like me in France; but I'm not sure whether he heard a single thing we said.

Other than the fight in the car park – where Jess, who can be both kind and irritated with her brother in the space of seconds, slapped him across the back of the head for "kicking her in the butt" and threatened to leave our company when she was told off – all went well. Ned is a six-year-old risk taker. His action was unwise.

Louise has brought the children up as a single Mum; fortunately, she is far more effective a parent than I was as a young woman. Had it been Louise at fourteen, she would have kept to her word and I would have lost her in Oxford. I remember entering a well-known night club once, in slippers and a cardie, pushing my way past the security man to find her.

I had brought a cake with me so we sang 'Happy Birthday' to him. In previous years, Lucy and the two girls would have been there, but last year, Harry and she parted company. On this particular evening, the girls were with Lucy. He is nervously waiting to hear whether he has joint custody. I am trying to teach him to cook, something he has never shown the slightest interest in before, despite my encouragement. Both his older siblings can cook, I hasten to add.

Walking back to the car, Lou tells me that her father is unwell and off work. It's rare that he doesn't go into the office where they both work as lawyers. "He has sickness and diarrhoea, and a kind of brain virus," she adds, with the concern of a loving daughter. I'm very fond of my ex but was married to him for thirty years and let's face it, men get man flu while women get on with it. Brain virus seems a little extreme to me.

"Try not to worry," I say. "Tell him to sip water and take diarrhoea powders."

I slept in the cabin at the end of the evening, after the festivities. It's an occasional retreat and needs attention. Ironic that after the big house I shared with my ex, I now choose a cabin to sleep in. It isn't that I did badly in the divorce settlement, I did rather well thanks to my own input and some rather good lawyers; it's to give my family a home, homes costing as much as they do everywhere. Truthfully, the cabin is getting damper by the day with the rain we are having. Painting it with deck varnish isn't enough. I'm not afraid of spiders and insects, never was, and as a teacher, I often handled creepy crawlies, but I don't particularly want them as bed fellows. I don't want any species of bed fellow any more, other than old Jack, the faithful collie. When my uterus fell out recently, and was skilfully patched up with mesh, I asked the lovely Russian doctor whether she could sew up my vagina at the same time. She said emphatically that this couldn't and shouldn't be done.

So, after the meal I sit on the cabin doorstep with a glass of wine and a forbidden cigarette and feel glad that the rain has stopped at last. There are stars above. Jack investigates the large hedgehog I recently tripped over in the dark, almost falling into the pond. Then, I put on my dressing gown, pulling it over my clothes, and Jack and I settle down for the night, he on the rug and I on the small bed.

8th January

Rose, my cat loving neighbour, comes into the garden and Jack wakes me with his barking. I let him out and he goes to find her.

I have two cats who I neither love nor hate, but having taken them on five years ago, I am ultimately responsible for them and they are happy cats. They have returned to being companiable after shredding my arm to bits when I tried to separate them in a scrap. (Charlie picked a fight with Tiger a year ago.) I didn't think quickly enough to chuck a bucket of pond water over them, reacting by sticking my hand into the fray instead. Disloyally, both cats gripped my forearm with vicious claws. My skin burned red for two days and I had to have an injection. Both cats are now spayed, which serves them right, but it worked to calm them down.

Rose volunteered involvement because she could see that, struggling to cater for the needs of my family as I was, I hardly had any time for cats. Since Rose came along, Tiger and Charlie are loved as they should be, but in Tiger's case, a little overweight.

The vet tells me to, "advise Rose to cut down on the treats", as though he knows her well.

I chat with Rose for a bit, mostly about the cats, then excuse myself to pull on my coat to race to Louise's, and let myself in.

Firstly, I shoo away the crazily irritating, self-obsessed pug, Luna, into the garden for her business. I empty the inside bins into the outside bins and try to coax Jess out of bed. Being a teenager, she leaves this to the last moment and grabs a pain-au-chocolate to eat on the way, or, on a bad day, a packet of crisps. "No, no" and "Go away," are her usual greetings.

Lauren is up, applying make-up, which she assures me all of her friends do. She is twelve.

I then empty the dishwasher, stack plates away and do some general tidying up which includes tutting a lot in Lauren's room at the crisp packets and chocolate wrappers strewn across the floor, later banging on to her about mice and cockroaches, all the while knowing that it'll make no difference at all.

When Lou and the girls are gone, I go up to see Ned who has already had a bowl of porridge. I tell him to get dressed and he might get a second breakfast and then I often run a shallow bath and get into it. After he has had a second breakfast, I bribe him with biscuits to read to me, which he does as a rule. I write in the little reading record book which the LEA use (sometimes I think they use it to beat exhausted parents up) that Ned has read and what he read. On occasion, I just lie about it, as he is not always keen.

Sometimes we go to school with Ned riding his bike and sometimes he rides a scooter. This morning we catch up with Zohaib and his grandfather. On Friday of last week, Ned was playing a silly game with Kira and threw his water bottle on the playground like a Greek celebrating a wedding. He said it was an accident, but I'm not convinced. Zohaib often gives him a kind of wide-eyed, surprised look that I have empathy with. He is loving, clever, has a kind heart; but still tends to do surprising things.

After seeing him into his classroom, I walk briskly to Dad's house to arrive there before Donna, one of Dad's carers. He has to have a bath this morning. He only has two a month, otherwise we give him a body wash. As Mum used to say, "He has always hated water." Bath time is the only time Dad becomes obstreperous and argumentative.

When Mum died from cancer, Dad coped with depression as well as dementia. How hard it must have been for him that, although she died with him holding her frail fingers, on a daily basis he can't remember that she had gone. As Marion and I were only just getting used to his state of mind, we sometimes wondered whether he was in denial.

"Where's my lovely wife?" he would ask, scratching his head.

"She's in heaven, Dad," we would say, patiently, lovingly.

But once, a frustrated Ned, having heard this a million times, snapped, "She's dead, Grampy!"

He was only five, good with Dad, as a rule; his companion in the supermarket and the park while I had care of them both. Relatively uncomplaining when Dad gave him a cuff around the ear for doing next-to-nothing, or, once or twice, absolutely nothing at all. It's just that Dad was remembering what adults did to him as a boy. Maybe he feels that it's restorative justice.

I was taken aback and then rather impatient when I first tackled Dad about bathing. It was probably fuelled by my own frustration at Mum's horrible death, at my horrible divorce, at being a constant carer, then. Now, I have acclimatised to my care role, knowing that I am lucky to have this large family who loves me and for whom I have my uses. What I did to Dad was appalling, and it was only one month after Mum's funeral.

I went up to his bedroom and gently stroked his white hair and asked him if he would like a cup of tea as he lay beneath the duvet. Then I said he needed a bath. That was enough. He refused, point blank, gripping the duvet with root like fingers, opening one eye to glare fiercely at me.

"No. I had one yesterday."

"You didn't, Dad. You don't want to be smelly, do you? You have to take a bath sometimes."

"I'm not getting up."

I had to think on the spot; it was clear that he wouldn't release the duvet.

"Please, Dad. Don't make this harder than it needs to be…"

"I'm not having a bath. If you run one, I'll pull out the plug. I'll have one tomorrow."

I know that this means we will simply have the same argument tomorrow; anyway, we have an appointment with his doctor.

"I'll make it nice and warm," I coaxed. But things deteriorated, to me tugging at the duvet and his tugging back. His mind may be frail, but his body isn't. Then I used threats.

"Look Dad, you're not having any beer if you don't get up."

I had no right to say this. His doctor has said he can have two cans per day but no more. He was the landlord of a popular pub and beer is his lifeline. Telling him he can't have it is tantamount to depriving a vampire of blood. The threat does nothing to change his mind, beer time isn't until this evening. Too far away.

Never wind up an old man with dementia, the first rule of dementia care. A man who is generally kind and amenable, but that's what I did. I got the flannel, ran it beneath the warm tap and squeezed it over his forehead. The speed at which he rose was dangerous for his age. Then I grabbed the duvet so he couldn't get back into bed and threw it onto the landing.

He was extremely angry. He only ever hit me once, when I was six and I believed he was my best friend, so it was a bit of a shock when he put me over his knee and whacked me with a slipper.

"Bugger me..." he said. But sat up and started to unbutton his pyjamas.

9ᵗʰ January

At Louise's, I pick up a postcard from Cape Town to Lou and the children from my ex and his new partner.

"Having a lovely, relaxing time. We have hired a car and are following the coast, visiting the wine region…" etc, etc.

I grunt with irritation, saying, "Lucky old you…" aloud, before acknowledging to myself that if he had at least ten working breaks last year, I had three holidays with our family, so I am luckier than most. However, in the meanwhile, I nurse a toothache which will cost me dearly to fix, thanks to a dentist who did a bodge job in my mouth some years ago. Also, my car requires some serious attention.

I should really go back to teaching.

Today, Dad has a new carer I haven't met before. It happens. I don't suppose that Dad remembers. He has carers every day; they come for forty-five minutes, twice a day.

This young woman is Muslim. She has two children, she tells me, as I instruct her in the making of porridge. This should be a pretty basic instruction; but he won't eat it unless it's loaded with both sugar and jam. As carers are not allowed to insist that he eats, and porridge is a good way to start the day, it has to be made in a way that he can't resist.

As we chat in the kitchen, Brandy, the docile-with-humans but specifically not with poodles, shar pei, trots into the kitchen to smell the stranger. The new carer squeals at the dog and clings to my arm.

"It's okay. I promise you, Brandy is a gentle dog; she'll never hurt you. Didn't they tell you at the agency?"

"No." She releases my arm but still looks terrified.

"Really, I promise you, she just plods about the place until someone lets her out for a wee. She's just curious…"

I notice that Sana is wearing rubber gloves. This will certainly worry Dad.

"You don't need to wear those," I smile. "The house is very clean."

I remember my Muslim students and that it is Haram, forbidden by Allah, for Muslims to have contact with a dog's saliva. The carer appears a little downcast by the dog and my reference to the gloves.

"It's okay. I'll explain that you need them to do the washing up," I tell her; "not to give him a lobotomy."

She stares blankly at me, not getting the joke. "I have a severe eczema," she says.

"Ah, sorry," I say. I make her a coffee to make amends, telling her a little about Dad and the kind of conversation she could try out on him. Then I leave her to it, going to

Louise's to put some washing on and to Harry's house to take his dog for a walk with Jack.

In the Shotover woods, I call Teachers' Pensions and wait until the recorded message says that I'm number seventy-seven in the queue. I decide to call back later, on the basis that if life is too short to stuff a mushroom, it's certainly too short to wait that long.

"Where are we going?" Dad asks, as soon as I return. He asks this roughly every five minutes, even if he has just spent an hour in the supermarket, an hour having coffee with Aunty Dorothy and then an hour in the pub; because he forgets that we have been anywhere. When you remind him, he says "Did we? Have we? I don't remember."

This morning we are going to the dump. It's one of his favourite places, familiar, easy. He used to go there with Mum, and the blokes are always friendly towards him, offering to help him and trying to engage him in conversation. It makes him feel respected in a world where he can't remember. On occasion I've been annoyed with people who have known Dad for most of their life but cut him out of the conversation when we meet them in the street. They make him feel so stupid. I can sense it. I suppose that some people are self-conscious and unsure about the disease.

I never expect Dad to pick up heavy things, of course. But he carries the smaller things for me and I thank him profusely and sometimes take him to one of the pubs he knew when he was a driver for the Ministry of Agriculture during the war. The Seven Stars near Nuneham Courtenay, The Talkhouse at Stanton St John, the White Horse at

Forest Hill, where he talks about a landlord called Freddie Munday who he liked during the war; although he speaks of him as though he argued with him about the price of beer only yesterday. He talks about his brother, Uncle Don, as though he is still alive; although he is buried in Holy Trinity churchyard close to Mum's grave. Every time we pass his grave, I say "Morning, Uncle Don." Dad and I visited his brother often in the home; he had a very dry sense of humour and I was fond of him.

Before the dump, we pick up all of the things that Louise has thrown out. Then the stuff that has still not been removed from Harry's house since he moved from Kidlington to Sandhills. The car is filled with so much rubbish that I have difficulty shutting the boot.

"Where are we going?" Dad asks from the front passenger seat, bearing in mind that there are planks of wood hovering over his head and that his feet are wedged in by a paint pot and a cracked potty. He has been there a million times before but asks it repeatedly; he also asks whether I have enough petrol.

Driving towards the dump, inland seagulls swoop above us, escaping rough weather and to scavenge from the supermarket car park. I open the window to hear them and Dad tells me to shut it because it's cold.

"Can you hear that, Dad? Do you hear what they're saying? Maurice, come to Cornwall!"

He laughs at me and I sing the Cadgwith anthem. A mistake, because he asks, "Where's my lovely wife?" Mum and Dad would go to Cornwall as often as they could.

Later, after their school day, I take Jess and Lauren to the cinema to see the new *Little Women*, with Emma Watson. Jess tells me I mustn't talk through the film, not a word. She's read the book as I once did and is looking forward to it. The tickets are relatively cheap, the popcorn and fizz not so. At first, I dislike the flashbacks. After a while I approve of how they work without changing the story.

I cry when Beth dies. When we were younger, I imagined myself as Jo, while Paula, loving the piano, was Beth, and we labelled Marion as Amy. Really, I was crying about Paula, I suppose.

At least the girls appeared to enjoy it. When I last took them to the cinema to see Dunkirk, they spent most of the time in the toilet. Still, they were a bit younger then.

Friday 10th January

There are times when my garden cabin is very useful. There are not many instances when I can use it nowadays, but on the rare occasion when there's no family care, I can be entirely alone to sort out all kinds of things. At the moment, it's pretty damp; the front walls are inhabited by woodlice. I wake smiling at the thought that it would make a grand coffin one day, like the Neolithic tomb on a farmer's field in Orkney that I once lowered myself into on a skateboard. "Don't worry about a funeral, guys. Seal me up in the cabin and talk to me sometimes through the walls."

I pace myself today. I have a week of helping Harry with the girls and it's knackering.

I do the shopping for Harry at the co-op, Dad pushing the trolley until he gets tired; then he sits down by the tills. Somehow, he realises it's Friday because when we emerge, he asks, "Are we going to the pub?"

"It's ten o'clock, Dad. Too early; anyway, they won't be open."

I drop off the shopping, then collect Jack and Monty for a run on Shotover, once a royal hunting ground for boar and deer, now the closest thing we have locally to the Lake District and Cornish woodlands. Dad knows it well. Up to a year ago, he would agree to a short walk with us. Now he makes a fuss; he's getting older, so we buy the Daily Mail, which was Mum's choice, instructing him to stay put in the car, which he does. I don't think that Dad reads the paper any more. He flicks through it, but familiar things reassure him. He was a driver for years, firstly for the Ministry of Agriculture and then for the army in Egypt. He loves driving and it's sad that he can't do it now. He used to love reading books about military strategy, books about the wars, gardening books and especially books with maps in. He could memorise the route from one place to another in a country far away that he had never been to.

"Stay there, then…"

"I will. Don't be long." That's what he always tells us, but we are never long.

Monty and Jack race across the place known as 'the Plain', each holding the end of a stick. Jack is almost fourteen, slower but with strong jaws and determined not to let the younger dog win the prize. Dogs are idiotic, behaving like some men and children.

After a while, Monty grabs the stick and runs away; he is a springer spaniel who failed the gun dog test. His tail wags with a life of its own. Jack limps towards me for a fluff-covered treat from my pocket. He has arthritis, and so do I. That's when I hear the woman yelling from the woods. "Dana! Dana!" At first, I think she is calling a lost child.

No. It's a rather large black mongrel who, now, hurtles through the ferns and bracken towards Monty. I grab Jack by the collar, wondering what will happen next, restraining my old dog because he might seek to protect his friend. Swiftly, I clip on the lead, just as the black dog, Dana, pounces on Monty with full force. No bottom-sniffing or introductory pleasantries but, bang! Leaps on top of my dog and lays across him, growling and barking profusely.

Monty's yelps and cries echo around the woods, piteous appeals for help, the sound of a dog caught in a snare.

I don't know whether Monty has been bitten or not, hard to tell because he makes that same noise if you trip over him when he lies across your path.

Only Monty isn't my dog, and I'm worried. There was the sudden yelp as though he had been injured.

The woman who is walking him now races through the undergrowth. Red bobble hat over shoulder-length red hair, red puffer jacket, pale face. She hurtles past me, a distance of several metres, grabbing Dana by her collar and pulling her away from Monty, who then runs, limping, towards me.

Having tethered the dog, she walks away. Just like that. It is rude. No apology, no friendly enquiry. "Is your dog alright?" Nothing.

Monty is covered in red clay from the soil and the puddles he loves to frolic in. His white hair is earthy and mud spattered. I check him over, but it's hard to tell red mud from blood. I can't see any wounds but he may well have a cut or two. So, I call out to her. "Hello. Excuse me..."

The woman stops. Turns in surprise, mouth open. She is several metres away.

"Hi," I call. "Would you mind giving me your name and number? Just in case he needs the vet? He isn't my dog, you see."

There's a short pause. "Check him now. I'm not giving you my bloody number," the woman says.

I ignore her tone of voice and vocabulary and persist.

"I have tried, but it's hard to examine him properly while he is so dirty, so I'll have to do it at home. I'm sure he's fine, but just in case I need to make a claim..."

I am really not expecting her answer. "Check him now. Silly bitch." She isn't talking about the dog, that much I understand.

An innocent passer-by, happily dogless, comes into view.

"Get him to check your dog!"

I am not about to ask an innocent bystander to risk being licked to death and covered in mud by Monty. Dana, meanwhile, is lunging at the lead to be off.

"You don't need to be unpleasant. It's just that I may need your details for insurance purposes," I try to assure her.

"Bloody stupid old bitch," she spits, venomously, staring at me and not the dog. I give up then. Possibly she has severe mental health problems.

I don't want to push the point any further. I will just have to hope that Monty isn't injured. I certainly don't feel like walking any more. I latch Monty to his lead and start walking towards the car. But it doesn't end at that. She follows me across the Plain, calling me every name under the sun, generally finishing with the word 'bitch'.

In the end I retaliate, tired of her harsh, bitter voice. At the car, I lift my fingers over my head, my back to her, making a gesture like a duck's beak opening and shutting.

I can't wait to climb into the driver's seat.

"Is that a friend of yours?" Dad asks, waving to her in an amiable, greenhorn manner.

I can't be bothered to explain. I now need the pub as much as Dad does. So, we drive to the White Hart.

Sunday 19th January

I did something very silly, something that was a poignant reminder of another time. Today is the anniversary of my niece's death. Such a beautiful, vivacious girl. I try to imagine what this is like for Marion, one of the strongest women I know, what it would feel like to lose one of my children. I can't even bring myself to think about it.

Ruby is currently having a weekend in Amsterdam with some friends, and although Marion wants her to do these things, since her elder daughter's death, she is quietly terrified of losing Ruby; but she can't let this show because she doesn't want to hold her back.

Last night I stayed at Dad and Marion's house. After Dad went to bed, we watched TV and drank a couple of glasses of wine each. We talked about Mum. We speculated as to whether she was trying to tell us something, because it's rare for Mum's music box, bought long ago in San Francisco, to start to play. Very rare, as the mechanism has long since broken. Both Marion and I have heard it do that when it's very quiet in the house. Odd.

When Marion went to bed, I locked up and put the chain across the door, just as my parents used to. I slept on the settee with Jack and Monty lying on the carpet (Monty stays with me when Harry works nights).

At about one o'clock in the morning, when everyone was asleep, I heard Marion's ring tone through the ceiling.

Immediately I thought of Ruby. Dear God, please don't let anything have happened to Ruby, I thought. No doubt that was exactly what my sister thought when she woke. But when I heard Marion's voice it was steady, quite calm, so I knew it couldn't be anything really bad, and I settled back to sleep, only to hear Jan's voice, the student from Peru. How selfish to wake people at one in the morning, I thought. Selfish student.

It was only on the following morning I realised that he'd tried his key in the door, then discovered the chain was across! That was me, of course. I was the bloody idiot who had put the chain across and had caused the phone call.

Dad was like a racehorse raring to go this morning. None of us really got a lie in. Up at seven, he went around the house rattling the doors like Wee Willy Winkie in his search for family members, dead or alive. He came down fully dressed to find me on the settee. There was no surprise on his face. It was as though he believed I slept there every night of my life.

Later, Marion and I went to buy flowers to lay upon the graves. We also drove to the crash site, to place flowers in a jar there. We lit candles in closed lanterns. It looked very pretty. Since 2013 this place has meant so much to my sister. The police are very good; they have never told her to stop the practice.

28th January

So much has happened. I went to a sauna with Anna and Inna, where we had a brilliant time, swimming and in the sauna, eating and lolling about on water beds, talking about all kinds of things. Mostly taking the piss out of men, both Russian and English. It was good to have a day out with friends, special sorts of friends who wouldn't leave the car park at the start of our visit without opening a bottle of Prosecco and producing the Russian cigarettes.

I had two helpings of lunch. At least, since the divorce, I've stopped worrying about my weight.

On the days that I haven't had the girls, I've been coaxing Ned to ride his bike to school and at last he's cracked it. No more pushing him up the hill. He has been a very good boy recently. The last time he was naughty was in the park after school, where he embarrassed me in front of a number of parents by yelling at me to 'Shut my little face' when I requested that he come out. A term he had got from his teenage sisters, no doubt.

He has also stopped peeing out of the window because he can't be bothered to go upstairs to the toilet, stopped yelling at his mum, and stopped getting up at five thirty to use a play station (after Louise disembowelled it). He has also been polite to me and has been asking for things, rather than demanding. I think the rock climbing he has been doing at Brookes with his lovely PE teacher has been good for him. He didn't want to go at first, but he has embraced the satisfaction of climbing up and up and it's proven to be good for his confidence. Three-year-old Delia is much the same when I take her to Whizz kids. She climbs the steps to the top of the high slide, then waves and hurtles down, a huge grin on her face.

Lauren and Jess still maintain that Ned is a 'little brat'. I've advised them that they should stop giving him mummy cuddles when I tell him off and he runs to them for comfort; it's not helping and makes me out to be the baddy.

It's still very dark in the mornings, although I suppose not so dark as in areas like Iceland or Orkney, where one friend lives. She has horses and says that, in the winter, they can't be exercised first thing in the morning because you can't see anything.

I've got good friends, but I don't see them enough or call them enough. Another refers to me as 'My shit friend'. I must make some calls before the month is out. Children and Dad take up most of my time. I love to write but, admittedly, when I can. Philip Pullman says a writer must be like a caged tiger. Hence the cabin; here I am caged with a dog, two cats and the woodlice. It may have something to do with growing up in a busy pub; I can never be caged alone.

Rain has fallen for most of January, but I think it's warming up, ever so slightly. Things have been so difficult for people across the world. Vast forest fires, sweeping across Australia. Flooding in Worcester and across the North of England which has had devastating effects upon ordinary people and no doubt on farmers, too. Glaciers are shrinking. Children all over the world are starving. So much to feel depressed about. Once, I contemplated buying a barge as a home, so that my family might be safe when the floods worsen.

On TV a few nights ago, Boris Johnson vowed to prevent the annihilation, degradation and murder of peoples across the world. Let's hope that this is more than rhetoric on his part; even God has failed to do that, so far.

Later, I spend half an hour trying to find Freya's tooth, which fell out in the night and which became lost in the duvet. She was very worried that the tooth fairy wouldn't come. Then I spend fifteen minutes searching for a tiny fragment of gravel in the garden, which might resemble a tooth. Welcome to my world – a world filled with tiny but important things like your first teeth.

31st January

Brexit Day cometh. Most of the people I speak to have lost the plot with the Brexit business. Mr Patel, our local shop keeper, and his Ukrainian employee have had lots to say about it; one of the issues around the whole thing is that many of those who originally came from a different country feel unwelcome. Many, many parents at Sandhills school didn't want to leave the European Union. On the day of the voting in 2016, some of the mums wore the yellow stars of the EU flag stitched to their clothing. One little boy was very confused. Having studied the Second World War in school, he asked a friend of mine, "Are you Jewish?"

All I know is that I agree with John Donne, and that Dad's old friend, Bernard, the communist, used to say this a lot. "No man is an island entire of itself; every man is a piece of the continent, a part of the main."

1st February – almost spring, hoorah!

In the early morning, I have a short but such a lovely dream. I have had lots of dreams about my parents, in fact, my wider family, even though so many of them have now gone. I talk to my dead relatives often, the people who loved me and made me what I am.

I dreamed that I was sifting through a box of decorations as a younger woman, living with my family at the White Hart pub, and the next thing I know is that my mother and father are both hugging me. Often, now, it's the people who have gone that keep me strong, their love, their belief in me: my grandmothers, grandfathers, my sister and niece and even those people who I never met, like Christine, the aunt I was named after.

Dad may be gratuitously repetitive, but beneath it beats that loving heart which asks whether we are okay all the time and "Where's my lovely wife?" The people who love and loved you give you the strength to keep going.

In the day, I buy seeded potatoes, dig a vegetable patch, which is satisfying but makes my back ache, and finally, I plant them. This is something Dad used to do, and generations before him. I would like my children to do it but know that time is short in every way. I keep trying to encourage James, it's important. I have many memories of Dad in the long vegetable garden behind the White Hart.

Gardening makes me happy too, brings me closer to the birds and earthworms, I suppose, though I'm not sure I want to be closer to the earthworms.

In the evening, driving back from the supermarket, I am holding my mobile phone in my hand as I listen to radio four. My hand is firmly on the steering wheel; the garage said that it would cost a lot to fix my car radio, so I use the one on my phone.

On the motorway, a young man in a large white van deliberately zig zags the van ahead of me, then slows down so he is next to me and opens his window at the traffic lights to talk or, rather, to yell at me.

"Get off your phone!" he orders.

I wind down the electric window. "I'm not on my phone; I'm listening to the radio!" I yell back, adding, "You're the one who's driving like a lunatic!"

"Four-eyed slut!" The man yells back before tearing off as the lights change. People are getting more abusive than ever, I muse. Still, at my age, perhaps the term slut is a compliment.

6th February

Outside it is frosty. There was a thin mist floating at the foot of Shotover as I walked Ned to school. I am still trying to work a way to get first Ned's and then Harry's girls to school in two very different places, with daily traffic jams and without breaking the speed limits or using the bus lane. What am I, Hermione Granger?

In the end, I decide I will have to make the three children take turns to go to the breakfast clubs and after school clubs, so that I can make it fair on them. This is going to cost a lot, but Ned spent almost a year going to these things and Louise is right, it isn't fair just to expect him to do it.

Anyway, the girls are becoming far more confident about the separation of their parents and routine has helped a lot. I know the staff at both schools will be kind and respond to all their needs. The subject that is difficult to tackle is "who's going to pay for it?" My lawyers told me that my divorce settlement was meant for me alone, but it's hard to deny money when your family needs it. I know there are plenty of grandparents out there who have to dig deep.

I helped to start an after-school club at the school at which I worked for almost twenty years because I believe in them. I don't believe that women, principally, should have to carry the burden of both working and scrambling to get to their children on time, which is what I had to do. Proud to say that this particular after-school club feeds the needs of about three hundred children, now.

In the evening, I got very involved in some catch-up work for Lauren. Her teachers told Louise that they were very pleased with her work, but that she could do with some catch up in history, geography and work on her knowledge of cells for biology. I started with history, cos I personally liked all three of those subjects, but my favourite was history. So, I produced a chronology in different coloured felts which took ages. I have to admit that I became rather too hooked on Matilda, a plucky gal for her time. She was the granddaughter of William the Conqueror.

One snowy winter's night, having been lowered from the tower, she escaped from Oxford castle having contested the throne, to skate across the river Isis on a pair of Normanesque skates to freedom in Abingdon. (I had no idea that the Normans used skates, but I suppose they were invented some while ago.)

Actually, I know little about skates at all, having bought ice skates instead of figure skates for Jess at Christmas and then having to change them.

Sunday 9th February

We all went to Shotover for a walk together with the four dogs. This was instigated, as many things are by my own big Matilda, aka Louise. She could not be faulted for energy and enthusiasm. The car accident she had at seventeen turned her into a tough cookie. None would believe that she has had two operations on her spine.

The rain bucketed down for most of the night and the wind was so strong that even some of the heavy-duty plastic recycling bins in the street had been blown over. I suppose little wonder that Harry exclaimed as I came off the phone, "What? In this weather?"

Rain and storm still howled through the trees when we arrived at Shotover. No sooner had we tumbled out of the cars than the heavens opened again. The dogs and the children seemed to enjoy it as they leapt into muddy puddles. In the end, we went for a short walk until we became so drenched that we had to half close our eyes as water was streaming down our faces – walking turned into tripping over fallen logs of wood and the branches blown down by the wind.

"I know, let's all go swimming instead," Louise suggested.

Harry glared at her as though her enthusiasm for life was getting him down.

"Actually, it's not a bad idea, Harry," I pointed out. "What else are we going to do on such a rainy day? Freya was really starting to swim in Croatia, but she hasn't been swimming for ages."

He wasn't so much convinced, as outnumbered. All of the kids thought it a great idea.

So, we went to the Abingdon pool where the water was warm, at least, and everyone, including Harry, had a good time with a snack afterwards.

Afterwards, I went out to Summertown to collect Jess from her friend's house.

When I arrived back at Harry's, I was a little knackered and lay down on the settee while the girls watched *Paddington Bear* and used me alternately as a nurses' patient and make-up model.

Delia smeared my entire face in assorted lip glosses from the dressing-up box, while Freya attached my chin to my crown with hair bands, saying, "I'm just making sure your brains don't fall out…"

Very wise. Sometimes I worry that my brains will fall out.

Saturday 15th February

The months are rushing by too quickly. I can't seem to get enough done.

The girls came yesterday; Harry picked them up after school. We had fish fingers and Mac n cheese, which I cooked because, he may be a very good Dad, but I'm still trying to coax him to do some things he will have to do if anything happens to me.

Later, Harry read a story to them at bedtime. There was no difficulty in getting them to sleep this evening. The separation of their parents was hard for them both, once upon a time. They love me and trust me, I know that, but even though Harry and I don't talk about it, because it's painful for him, too, what they have wanted all along is their mother and father, together in the same house, as they once were. But it wasn't working. One day they will understand that a little better and they are certainly lucky girls and loved by everyone.

We jolly them, make them laugh, play with them and encourage them. They enjoy all of the things that children like: making cakes, dressing up as princesses, painting, going to the park, make-believe. Often, they remind me of Jess and Lauren when they were that age.

This morning, Harry and I took Freya to a drama group. Ned goes there and she's been saying that she wants to go for a long time.

I get the impression that the Freya we know at home isn't the little girl her teachers know at school. A short while ago we had a little Valentine's tea party for her friends and their parents at Harry's new home. She loved it, despite the fact that she was quite tongue tied and shy at times. Lucy came too, which was also good for her girls.

She pressed against her dad's legs at first, watching the other children with wide green eyes. But the staff were very good with her, coaxing her to join in with the songs and dances. When she came out, skipping towards us, she was very excited.

My car breaks are squeaking. I really must get them looked at. Should have the MOT done at the same time. It's an old car and I've thought about getting rid of it, but it's a good car; I wouldn't get much for it and it is very reliable. It was part of my divorce settlement and it's used to help everyone. I was so relieved when my lawyers said I could keep it after the divorce. It's been used to take children to school, for frequent visits to Kidlington to help Lucy, to ferry Dad about and currently, on the days when Harry has the girls but is working, I have to get Ned to school. After this I have to drive Harry's girls to school in Kidlington.

So, yes, I need my battered car.

Monday 17th February

This week is the children's half term, so I won't get anything much done, let alone diary writing. In previous years, we have been lucky enough to go to caravans and rented houses in Cornwall, where we have had a great time. If we haven't gone away, we have taken the kids to Warwick Castle or Blenheim Palace. But this year we are going to Sicily in August, and renting a villa along with the flights has proved rather expensive, so we will do things at home.

Doing things at home involves Louise's children having their friends over. The girls are staying with Lucy, probably just as well, as I might have gone quietly mad if I had to have five children with no help.

I have had to explain to Louise's children that there isn't room in the car for three children and their friends. So, I say, this will be your day, tomorrow your brother's day, etc. In the meanwhile, you all have to cooperate and do a lot of baking, which I am naff at, but fortunately Jess and Lauren are excellent cake makers.

Marion is home from school, so she will care for Dad.

I start the week feeling extremely tired, which isn't good. This week I have had to cover for Harry and Lou quite a lot, including physiotherapy sessions after her work, which Louise must have on her back. It has meant either having all five children together, children ranging from fourteen to two and a half, and cooking a meal for three children before racing to Harry's to cook for the other two when Louise gets back from work.

This is the first time I have actually looked forward to the week in the Easter holidays when my children and grandchildren go with my ex-husband and his partner to Barcelona. I might get time to do all of the things I've been waiting to do. I might get a lie in – there's a thought. It will be odd not to go with them, but I no longer feel as upset as I was the first few times they went out to dinner with him and without me. Thankfully, I have passed that milestone.

Delia has few summer clothes, so I've bought a few little items for when they go to Spain and have adapted some of Freya's old dresses (my nan taught me to sew when I was quite young). I've also bought some clothes for her from second-hand shops. I make two piles, ready for when the girls go to Barcelona, so that Harry has two outfits per day for them, one for the day and one for the evening.

22nd February

The week passed reasonably pleasantly and without the children killing each other, or indeed, me killing them. Ned and I argued a bit about the play station, but we found quite a few friends in the park, most days. I took Jess and Lauren to see *Emma* at the cinema, which Lauren enjoyed, even though she said she didn't want to see it and that Jane Austen is boring.

On Friday evening, James and I went to the Vicky Arms in Marston. James doesn't have children, which may be the reason he is one of the most peaceful people I know to spend time with. His job finished recently. He worked as a lawyer for his dad for a long time and he has started applying for other jobs, but not in the law. We had a good long chat, and he said he would like to go on a walking weekend with me to Cornwall, which I'm really looking forward to. We go out for a meal every now and then, or a drink. I really enjoy his company. The last time we went out was to the curry house in Wheatley.

On Saturday morning, Marion, Ruby, Dad, Louise, her children and I all drove to Wantage with the dogs. There was a reason for this: we hadn't done very much and I wanted to show the children and Ruby the place where we lived when Marion was a baby, the Post Office Vaults, Dad and Mum's first pub. The idea was to take the dogs for a run on the White Horse hills and then go for a sandwich in Wantage.

Don't know why, except that I get a bit anxious about money, so had it in my head that I would put off filling up with petrol. That proved to be unwise. I was also a little distracted. As soon as we reached the Berkshire Downs, miles away from a garage, my car began to run out of petrol.

I had to flag everyone down and Louise became more than a little irritated with me (not helped by the fight the kids were having in the back of the car). Anyway, I decided that prayer was the only option, that Louise had a bloody cheek as I said nothing when she ran out of petrol in the early hours of the morning after her friend's party and asked me for a lift, and that I'd just keep going until we reached the car park at the foot of the White Horse hills. Thankfully, I didn't run out.

It's a place I know well. When we were children living in Wantage, we didn't have a garden, so Dad would bring us here for a run around most days after school. Sometimes we would see the racehorses in the distance, hooves pounding across the hills. Sometimes Dad would make our poor old golden retriever, Brandy, race after the car because pub dogs can grow fat.

Often, I suspect, it was Dad's dreaming place. He wasn't made to spend his life in towns, missing the Bletchingdon fields and his pigs and chickens and geese.

As soon as we arrived there, Dad insisted that he had to pee and, of course, there isn't a toilet. So, I tried to lead him behind some bushes; but he wouldn't go, inhibited by the people in the busy car park. So, we decided that we wouldn't have to be very long and left him in the car with the newspaper. Fortunately, his bladder is generally good.

This is a place I have taken the children to over the years. As we crossed the car park, Jess and Lauren made it very clear that they didn't want to hear a word about the greatness of King Alfred, or about Vikings and that I should direct all conversation towards Ned, who was trying to operate his remote-controlled car, so wasn't interested either.

It was extremely cold and windy, but we managed to walk some way to the foot of the white horse, pushing against the wind which distorted our faces and bit into our clothes, before deciding to head off to Wantage.

The Post Office Vaults is called that because that's what it was originally. Mum and Dad ran the pub for about four years. Sir John Betjeman was a frequent customer and I have a vague image of him sitting at a table by a window and reading his paper. In the end, just as he saved many old buildings and monuments, so he saved the Post Office Vaults; at least he saved the exterior of the place, which is rather imposing. Inside it has been turned into shops, offices and residential flats.

We headed for the pub, which is now in the cellar and reached by a flight of stone steps. The place appeared to have shrunk; it was much smaller than I remembered it as a child. We crowded together at a table, just for a drink.

"Do you remember being the landlord here?" Marion asked Dad.

"I remember the pub," he replied, but he was frowning a little, always a sign that he's confused.

"Do you remember Sir John Betjeman, who used to drink here?"

Dad stared a little blankly into the distance. "Not really."

I don't think he knew what we were talking about. It is so sad. He was always a fan of Sir John Betjeman's poems about Cornwall; he used to be able to recite parts of the poetry. On many occasions we have walked to St Enodoc across the cliffs, the place where the poet is buried.

After our drink, we wandered through the rest of the building, trespassing. I tried to explain to the children which was the huge living room, which was our parents' bedroom, mine and Paula's room and the large kitchen. Now, inner walls have been knocked down, so it isn't quite the same. It was a wonderful building with large rooms, many stocked with Victorian treasures.

"It's huge!" Jess exclaimed, and I felt a rush of pleasure. It can be so hard to engage her interest nowadays, or to impress her.

I wanted to have lunch in another pub, but the kids wanted to go to Greggs, so that's what we did. Afterwards I stocked up on petrol. Dad seemed tired on the way home and kept fretting about whether I had enough; he frets about petrol constantly, but this time it's totally my fault.

23rd February

Harry's girls came yesterday evening. Freya gave me a big hug. At first, Delia wouldn't let go of Harry, but she came round when Freya and I started to play on the carpet; after that, all was well.

I made them pancakes with chocolate spread on. After this, they made little fairy cakes to take to Worcester. All of the family are going except me, because it's my ex-mother-in-law's birthday. It's okay now as it means some time to myself before they return. I hope there won't be any problems as Worcester is deep in water. Mercifully, I don't think her area has been affected; she is further back from the river.

Lauren asked me about the word pathos, asking me what it meant. I explained, then told her about the history essay I once handed in at school which stated that Sir Francis Drake had circumcised the globe in 1577.

Actually, Lauren's life has caused me several problems recently. Yet again, she has decided to revamp her bedroom. In the process, she has thrown her clothes all over the place so that nothing can be found. In the morning, I have to help her find her uniform and swimming costume. Then… there was the massive antique mahogany wardrobe she wanted out of the house.

"Could you help me move it?" Louise asked a few days ago as I stared at her in horror.

"Are you joking? What about your bad back? We can't move it on our own, Lou." She has shown herself capable of superhuman feats of strength at times, but no.

Fortunately, Lauren's room is downstairs. At least, I thought, I might be able to move it towards the door without help. But try as I might, I couldn't shift it; so, at last I stood on a chair and successfully pushed it over onto the bed, where it bounced and settled. I stared at it for a while and called Harry. He was once a wrestler and is very strong.

"I'll do my best, but I'm at work most of the week," he said. Others turned me down with various good reasons ranging from sciatica to "I've just had my nails done at the nail parlour."

Local charity shops also declined, so I called various removal firms at first, knowing they would hardly do it for free and dismayed at the price they charged for removal. I was getting nowhere.

With Lauren's help, we managed to shove it through the door and into the garden.

After a play date for Ned, when various boys (but principally Ned himself) tried to climb on it or inside it, I called the council who said they would collect it but that it would have to be moved outside the close. The wardrobe began to haunt my dreams. It wasn't only an obstacle, it was a very beautiful object made from beautiful rose-coloured wood, Mahogany, I think – a real Lion, Witch and Wardrobe, wardrobe. If I had my own place, I would have kept it, but it would certainly not fit into a cabin.

At last, I had a brainwave. I called the local fire brigade. They were so kind, saying that it sounded like a health and safety obstacle and they couldn't guarantee when they would come, but they would do so, in order to carry it from Lou's house across the close to the front.

They were clearly tied up with the more important task of fires and other more important things, and the wardrobe lay by the garden gate for several days until, one day, I opened the garden gate to find that someone, or rather Harry, had kick boxed it to death and it lay in pieces on the lawn. I rescued two rather lovely panels; at least my problem was solved. Only I forgot to call the fire brigade, who arrived in their fire engine as I was taking Dad for a slow walk around the estate. I was both apologetic and embarrassed, and will now make a donation to the Firemen's Benevolent Society.

24th February

I don't know what happened to me yesterday evening. I can only be glad that the girls slept and that I didn't have to get up to them. I have rarely felt so ill.

It started with a feeling of being cold earlier in the evening. Colder than usual, although I had several layers of clothing and a warm jumper on. At the start of February, both the older girls were off school at different times, so I wondered whether I could have picked something up from them. But their illness was some while ago.

I felt shivery and unwell, and, in the end, I went to bed early, lying beneath two duvets, too cold to remove my clothing.

I couldn't sleep because my heart started pumping as though it would pop, making me feel fully awake. In the end, I got up to find the thermometer that I had bought for the girls and stuck it under my arm. Thirty-three point seven, which I believe could be hypothermia!

This frightened me so much that I lay in bed, worrying more and more and thinking about death. I wondered if it was a panic attack, like the one I had at the wedding.

I couldn't be ill. I knew that. The children needed me; my grandchildren needed me. I had written only one novel and I had so many other books to write. I want to visit so many places that I've never seen. I couldn't die. Not now.

If I called a doctor, they would take me in and I wouldn't be there for the girls tomorrow. Still not knowing what the heck was wrong with me, I prayed, prayed hard, and eventually I fell asleep.

When the children woke me, I had a heavy cold and little pains on the right side of my head. I was sneezing a lot, but I felt better. I have never been so grateful for recovery.

26th February

James has been looking for work. While he is pouring over advertisements on the internet, I clear out the tiny cupboard beneath his staircase, reminding myself what lay inside the bags and boxes I had stuffed into the far corners. So many things. No room in this house, which is a quarter the size of the home we had lived in, much as it's cosy and I truly love it.

I find useful items: a toaster, a kettle, a sandwich maker, as well as photos and three landscape paintings of various places in Cornwall. Then I find the cutlery box which meant so much to me once upon a time. It hasn't been a cutlery box since we received it as a wedding present thirty-plus years ago; it contains other treasure.

It houses the love letters from him, written after I first met him at a party at Homerton College in Cambridge in 1981. I was a teacher at Newnham Croft School, my first job as a teacher, and he and Tim were visiting Anne. That's how we met. Love at first sight, sex not long after. The letters are all dated 1981 and 1982. Love, baby, marriage – all in the wrong order, depending upon what you feel about marriage; but we loved each other and that love lasted a long time and gave us strength to do all of the things we did in life.

So, I stop cleaning up and rubbing marks off the floor and sit against the radiator to read through some of them, in a world of my own, remembering my room in Cambridge, remembering what he was like then. I don't read all of the letters, because within the pile of musty papers there are about fifty love letters and notes, and assorted cards with romantic pictures of Victorian ladies. Sometimes, he would write every day from his room in Birmingham, where he attended the College of Law. I remembered how he looked while he wrote essays, his head bent over the desk. I remembered how handsome he was.

I think I came close to crying. Perhaps I still love him a little, but the situation has changed so much that my thinking head knows I can never go back; I realised in the end that, if we were still together, I would not have found myself again or been able to do the things I have to do.

First, the note, typed on an old typewriter in my room. I don't have it any more, but Grampy Ron had salvaged it for me from the offices at Oxford United. The paper is crumbling and torn. The message reads, "Gone to catch the train. Don't work too hard. I love you, you're beautiful."

I smile to myself, clamping my teeth onto my bottom lip, letting the note fall while I pick up the first letter.

Tuesday 9th February, 1981

141, Brookvale Rd, Witton, Birmingham

Dear Chris, how are you today? It was a close thing with that bus on Sunday, just as well Tim came up. I hope it was quicker than the last one you caught and that you managed to get a taxi home. Hope the landladies are behaving themselves.

I'm trying to write the last chapter of my dissertation today, just as my lecturer has disappeared with raging toothache. Marvellous!

I found your pens on my dressing table. I'll bring them with me on Friday.

Soon we'll be able to spend a whole two weeks together. I'm a bit broke, so I ought to get a job at the weekends. It'll all work out alright anyway. They've begun to sell tickets for the Legal Society Dinner, so any chance you could send me a cheque for ten pounds?

So, I'll see you on Friday though it's too far away for me to be happy about it. Take care, slow down and don't work too hard. I love you more than anything and care about you so much. You're beautiful. All my love forever XX

Well, not quite 'forever' as it turned out.

Friends tell me they worry that their husbands might leave them after our divorce. I say dismissively, "No, he loves you and he is so proud of your children..." But really, I don't know the answer to that. It was a big shock, a trauma, really; not even the possibility of an affair, but that he loved her more than me at the end, after all those years.

1st March (St David's Day)

Can't stop sneezing. I have the mother of all colds. When I was a young teacher, unused to talking to thirty different children for long periods at a time, holding individual conversations with several six-year-olds on innumerable subject matters, my teaching aunt suggested that I gargle with (though not swallow) a cap filled with whisky in the evening to protect my throat.

In 2010, helping to organise the library campaign against closure and inciting protest in deep snow, I discovered that I had bronchitis. Later, when I needed a chest X-ray, the doctor told me I had a small amount of fluid on my chest.

Nine years later, last November, I received a letter from my own doctor, saying that I had to rid myself of it with a strong course of antibiotics. The antibiotics got rid of it, but nine years is a long wait.

When reports began to talk about a virus in Wuhan, theories abounded on the internet, many from people who had long condemned the wet markets in China. I had condemned them too, for herding animals in cages before torturing them and boiling them alive on the basis that it makes the meat taste better. But I don't think there is any factual evidence as yet that it caused the virus.

Other Facebook theories stated that the virus had either deliberately, or accidentally been released from a laboratory in Wuhan. Hard to know what to believe.

Everyone who heard about it must have felt anger and sorrow for the brave doctor who tried to warn colleagues about the new threat he had not encountered before.

For me, my own illness and the death of this Chinese doctor started to awake the primeval fight or flight instinct. I am older, have lived through cancer deaths, the foot and mouth disease, the fear of Aids, Ebola etc. Yet, even at this point, I thought as others must have done, naively believing that the virus was far away in China.

So first, two people in the UK are identified as having the virus, and then others around the world. Ten cities are identified as danger spots in Italy and countries move to quarantine measures, stopping cruise ships from being able to dock, stopping passengers from arriving in their countries.

Italy, the focus of lovely holidays, the place where so many grandparents diligently care for their grandchildren, is left almost broken by the daily deaths and the burden on hospitals. Nineteen elderly people dying in one care home alone. Medical staff are filmed by TV crews, exhausted and broken. Hospitals are swamped, funerals banned, convoys of lorries taking the Covid dead far away from the places the deceased had lived, to burial grounds where there was some space for the corpses.

Maybe it was then that most of us started to wake up, as the virus crept closer – a jewel-coloured parasite. A daily symbol on the television. We watched, fascinated and horrified as the scientists explain how it latches onto a lung. The thought that it has a mind of its own is more terrifying than any horror film. A parasite, latching on, clinging to its host and impossible to remove. Integrating itself with the host, killing the host until it can find another human to destroy. Pure science fiction, except that it's real.

I have a cold. But a cold like no other, perhaps. My chest is sore, feels tinny, often in the evening, but in the morning, the feeling goes. Have I got it? My temperature is normal again. I don't call the doctor for many good reasons.

How will Harry see his children if, with a new mortgage, he has to work? I can't get ill.

Who will care for Dad?

What will happen if Louise has a problem with her back. Who will look after the kids?

I cannot be ill, no.

If it has reached the hospital – our local Oxford hospital – I'm not going there, no way. The last time I went to the hospital in 2016 it was because Mum, very ill with cancer, broke her hip. I took her there. We waited for five hours in accident and emergency until Mum could not sit with this painful hip for another second, and with anger bottled up inside me, I demanded a porter's trolley so that she could lie down. That was my clear memory, of a hospital in chaos.

My cold dissipates but I start to cough up sticky green mucus. From the day my cold began I wore a scarf wound about my mouth. Parents in the playground don't stare at me as though I might be ill, they stare at me as though I'm a peculiar breed of exhibitionist. No one else is wearing a scarf or mask about their mouth.

"I have a cold," I tell a parent who is also a childminder. She takes a step back and looks at me with the expression of the witchfinder general. So, we are all scared. It isn't just me.

2nd March

I have to go into Oxford to collect my reading glasses. I don't take Dad. I've started to worry a lot about Dad, who is almost ninety-two and who has emphysema.

Normally I might try to get a couple of other jobs done as I rarely go into Oxford. Soon it will be Jess' and then Ned's birthday and I have time to buy their presents, but fear has kicked in. I am not going to linger in the city.

As I walk briskly through Oxford town centre, I note that there are more people wearing masks, now. I am by no means the only one. I mull over the slightly racist comments made on Facebook, some months back, about women who wear the Burka. Now we are all wearing the Burka. My granddaughters' pretty smiles will be veiled, their expressions hidden from view. Jess has asthma. Where do you get masks from, anyway?

I note how many elderly people are in the city today, going about their business without any protective masks. Perhaps you reach an age where you believe you are invincible; perhaps you simply don't understand how dangerous this is. I decide to stop taking Dad into the supermarket with me. He will have to wait in the car.

Later in the day I watch a short film posted on the internet by a friend of two women fighting over toilet rolls in a supermarket. Is that really happening? I decide to try shredded newspaper as they did in the war. I'll get print on my bum, but I'm not going to fight over loo rolls.

Louise calls me from the supermarket, her voice is high pitched, panicked, uncomprehending, to say that shelves are stripped of pasta and rice.

I think she must be exaggerating until I go to do my weekly shop.

I don't stockpile; yet during the week I turn Harry's unused, unplugged freezer on, stocking it with food so that we won't starve. Besides, I can hardly take Dad into supermarkets at the moment, with COPD, he's certainly a candidate for illness, so I limit my journeys and buy enough to last a long time.

Going to the supermarket was a most unpleasant experience, although initially it resembled the day before Christmas Eve because the queues for the till were as long. Women looked anxious or preoccupied. Grumpy men bought full boxes of beer, just in case the store might run out. Only the noisy children behaved in the usual way.

There was no seasonal good will; there was no social distancing; no one apologised for ramming a trolley into my hip. People gasped or stared blankly at the empty shelves.

I take off my scarf when I reach home, dropping it into the wash basket.

Later, Dad, Marion and I watch the news together, Dad from his chair while we sit on the settee as we used to with Mum. We try to explain about the virus. "It's like the Spanish flu epidemic of 1918, or was it 1919?" I ask, not expecting a reply because of his memory loss. But to my surprise, I get one.

"Oh ar," says Dad, in his Oxfordshire twang. "Air Mum and Dad had to have an injection."

Marion and I stare at one another in surprise. He recalls things that happened long ago so clearly.

"Did you and Uncle Don have to have an injection against the virus when you were little?" Marion asks.

"No, don't think so." We feel sure that he would have recalled an injection, hating injections as he does. It's good that he remembered this event. But of course, he doesn't remember why we keep putting a mask on him when we go out and he wears it under his chin. Nothing is protected and we have to keep pulling the mask back into place.

A part of me feels as though I have spent a large part of my life waiting for this calamity. Perhaps I am a pessimist at heart. Perhaps, having spent so much time in my grandmother's company and having been born twelve years after the end of the Second World War, I have absorbed some family anxiety, some inner austerity. I remember when James was a toddler, thirty-seven years ago at the start of the Falklands war and my having grown up with talk of a possible nuclear war, reading the bittersweet cartoon story by Raymond Briggs, about an old couple storing tins of food and wearing their old wartime gas masks in the face of a nuclear explosion. I remember packing a case with baby clothes and tins of milk so that my little family could leave in an instant. When Mike came home from work, he laughed. But I had been deadly serious about all of it and very afraid.

Six hundred deaths in Italy quickly becomes 18,200 deaths. People become numbers, people whose lives meant something to others. Dead and forgotten except by their family.

New words enter our vocabulary: PPE, Covid 19, novel virus, social distancing, lockdown. I'm sixty-two and have never heard the term lockdown.

Louise says, with a sense of panic that panics me, "Mum. There's going to be a lockdown. You have to stay in your house; you won't be able to care for Ned or the girls, but Dad's going to let us work from home."

Her lecture makes me feel like an old fuddle-head. I'm not going to avoid my grandchildren, I determine.

"What if anything happens to your back?" I ask. Louise has a very bad back after a car accident when she was young. She has had two operations and has learned how to deal with incredible pain. Besides, she has a habit of lifting things that are far too heavy when I'm not around.

"It will have to be okay. Jess has asthma, you're sixty-two, people of your age are dying. I don't want any of us to die, so you will have to keep away," she says in her determined voice.

"We'll see," I mumble. "Well, I can't keep away from Harry and the girls. They need to see their father and he has to work…"

"Then you'll have to lock down with Harry."

Except on one occasion in my life, I've taken my freedom for granted. This is like a war, and perhaps we won't be free for a long time. Poor Jess and Lauren, who are at the age when you start dreaming of travel. As soon as I was eighteen, I began to travel. Travel was cheap then. I slept under bridges in Amsterdam and on beaches in France. Would they be able to enjoy that kind of freedom?

Now I pray with fervour. I pray every night for my children, grandchildren, father, sister, brother and his wife, and for their children. I pray for my ex and his partner. I pray for individual friends and their children, for people good and bad, for every nation, for people I don't know and will never meet.

My thoughts and dreams are crowded by guilt and fear for others. The refugees, the homeless, the families who can't afford food, families crowded into small flats and without gardens. The impossibility faced by children who are being abused in their own homes. Then the teenagers kicking off in lockdown, the elderly who aren't able to see their families and may die before they do. My son, caring for people without the correct PPE, some of whom are aggressive and have developed Covid.

Surely, statistically, one person in my family will become ill. It will be Dad, or me. Everything that has happened in my life is now reduced to this. I am nothing, a statistic only. My sense of self shrivels.

I take Dad to visit Aunty Dorothy in the care home where she is being nursed. We have been there often and have sometimes been able to take her out in her wheelchair for coffee and cake. I'm shocked, upset and offended when we are told that we can't come in. The care home has already gone into lockdown.

But I think, with a rush of pride, that her daughter will come up with something. Susan, who was awarded a medal for helping to find the cure for Ebola. I write a letter to Aunt Dorothy and draw a cartoon picture of Super-Susan in her superhero cape flying above the earth.

At the chemists, the anti-bac and Dettol shelves are already empty. I buy a tub of hand cream and some Dettol when I can find it, then mix the cream with the Dettol. I make my own pots of it. Jess and Lauren say that it stinks and refuse to use it.

We celebrate birthdays before we are told to stop. First Jess's, then Ned's birthdays. Jess has a sleepover and everyone is kept awake by excited shrieking from her bedroom.

Marion and I visit Aunty Steph, Mum's sister. She owns a family run pub, the Masons, in Headington Quarry. Her sons run the pub. She's in her late eighties and fully active, so there's hope for us all. She was once a teacher like me. She is also very involved with her grandchildren and she is never afraid to voice her feelings, especially upon the matter of local building and changes to the village that her ancestors helped to build.

The government are saying that the likelihood is that pubs will have to close. Steph's pub will have to close, and presumably, at her age, she will have to lock down in her flat which is next to the pub. Possibly, knowing her as we do, she might chain herself to the car park railings in protest...

We listen to the rules at the start of the new daily briefings in the late afternoon, deciding that as we can't attend the pub-restaurant we had booked for Mothering Sunday, we will have one last meal together before the lockdown. I buy the lamb while Marion buys the vegetables and with Louise, we cook together. Our brother doesn't come. He and Michelle have already 'locked down'.

Marion has been told that as the schools will close, save for a few pupils, she isn't presently needed. I'm so relieved; it means that she can care for Dad in the home where they live together. It also means that I will only be able to blow kisses at him through the window and leave little presents on the doorstep from time to time. We try to explain the situation to Dad, but really, he forgets why we wear masks or can't give him the cuddles he is used to, despite our frequent explanations. He thrives on hugs and kisses.

Marion digs out a box of face masks left over from the period when Mum had cancer and had to avoid infectious people. We share them out.

Louise will have to deal with a very stressful situation, working from home, jollying three children to do their homework, dealing with their emotional health while struggling with the pain from her own bad back.

James is in between jobs and his sciatica is causing a problem; if it is sciatica as doctors aren't examining patients and you have to describe symptoms over the phone. He is finding it hard to get up and down the stairs.

Harry's job, already demanding is about to get worse. Things like this worry me to sleep. When I wake, I push myself to positivity. When I'm not caring for the children, I volunteer to do the shopping or any tasks for my neighbour, a cancer turned Covid nurse. I volunteer to do shopping for two aged gentlemen close by, giving them my number and worrying afterwards that they might think I'm a flighty divorcee on the make.

Louise and Marion's students fret about when they will be able to return to Japan and Peru, respectively.

My friend's Mum dies amidst all of this. Only five people are allowed at her funeral. She had so many friends.

Her children determine to celebrate her life with a party as soon as this Apocalyptic mess is over.

What will my children do if I die? I rewrite my will and compose a practical list on the very day of the lockdown:

If you put long rubber gloves on and stick your arm down the loo, you don't need a plumber. Ninety-five per cent of the times you have called me out to unblock the toilet, all it needed was someone to manipulate the poo. We are a family with large feet and large poos. Put the gloves in a plastic bag, then a bucket and disinfect them.

Put one of those sink blockers over the kitchen sink plug hole, that way the pasta, rice etc won't block up the sink pipe.

Take your vitamins and omega oil capsules.

Blue berries and walnuts keep you calm.

Flies hate mint, keep a jam jar of mint in the kitchen.

Refuse men get very eggy if you don't put the right things in the right bins; never allow food to get into the large bins or in summer, you'll have to deal with the maggots!

Don't have pets unless you can afford them.

Don't buy that modern, screw together furniture that doesn't last a year and results in the drawers collapsing.

I run out of suggestions and imperatives. Anyway, this isn't the most important thing to hand on to them after I die. There is something else they should know before my mind deteriorates like Dad's. So many things to pass on.

Kenneth and Louise Jacobs

The little girl scowling on the right of the picture is our grandmother, Edna. She wanted to be a bridesmaid like her sister, but there weren't enough page boys!

A Bit of Family History

Most people would probably claim their hearts lie somewhere far away, Thailand perhaps, or somewhere that's beautiful and fashionable both, like Nice or Rome. While I like to travel and a part of my heart lies in Cornwall, mostly it lingers in the places that my parents came from, close to the city of Oxford. A small estate that was built at the start of World War Two which is flanked by fields on the one side and a motorway on the other. It leads to Oxford in one direction and to London in the opposite. It is called Sandhills. The other place of my heart is an upsy-downsy village with a past reputation for rogues and libertarians: this is called Headington Quarry and although nowadays it is connected with C.S. Lewis, who is buried in Holy Trinity churchyard, the village has a far more compound character, which is why it is quite unique.

Sandhills, the little estate where we live and where Grampy Maurice lived with his brother and parents as a boy, is very much the opposite of the Quarry. Looking at it now, through the window of Harry's living room, it is beautiful. The small and regular red bricked houses have hardly changed since they were built in the 1930s. Sure, there are small extensions, here and there, and perhaps the widening of frontages with garden walls knocked down to hold larger cars than the Morris Minors that were once the pride of the family. My children and grandchildren all reside in Sandhills. Harry is saving for his front wall to be knocked down, to be made flat for his large Ford Kruger, no gate posts required. He wants to be rid of the little garden with its pretty flowers planted so long ago by someone who loved their house and loved gardening.

It is the evening, presently. Through Harry's windows, the blue sky is mottled with plumy white and silver clouds and the windows reflect the gold tinted, dying sun; tree-lined avenues of ash and lime, planted when the houses were built. It is a quiet place where children have always been able to play football and tennis in the streets in summertime. The streets are always quiet, except for the distant rush of cars on the motorway beyond, as people make their way to work and back past this anonymous place. Currently the ambulances have started to increase as paramedics rush those with suspected Coronavirus to the hospital. Their sirens grip me with panic; my body tenses every time.

Sandhills estate was built in the early 1930s on land given to the people of Oxford by the Miller family of Shotover House. There was, then, a grave shortage of housing. At this time, there was no motorway, only a single road leading to London. Now, the motorway chops the estate away from the Shotover woods, and to reach the woods you have to descend the underpass.

The younger Major Miller was the Crown Equerry, ensuring that royal events passed without a hitch. When we were younger, Paula and I were allowed to ride horseback over the Shotover Estate, so long as we were accompanied by old Mrs Shepherd, our riding teacher. Giving the people of Oxford a portion of the land didn't stop some of them from poaching on it during the war, but there was a greater need then.

Before D-Day, on the site which is now the Thornhill Park and Ride, American soldiers were based upon the Miller's land, while British soldiers were preparing for D-Day on the other side of Shotover park. The local boys would run errands for both, which is why Uncle Don had a helmet as a trophy, although the soldier who gave his helmet away before such a mission can't have been very bright, unless he had two helmets, of course.

So, Dad and his big brother, Don, grew up at number 21 Delbush Avenue, Sandhills; one of the first smart and new houses to be built upon what had been Brigadier General Alfred Douglas Miller's land. How Grampy, Maurice's Dad, our great grandfather, Kenneth, earned the money to buy that house is a matter of true heroism. This is the story that my cousin William, Don's son, told me – but there were many details that were missing in the story, so I have made some presumptions.

I have a faded, black and white photograph of Grampy Ken, their father. A rather round-faced young man in a sailor's uniform, aged somewhere between seventeen and nineteen. He stares out from the photograph with a fixed and wide-eyed expression. He looks fearful, to be honest, little wonder faced with war at such a young age.

Grampy Ken Jacobs was a sailor, an ordinary seaman on the ship, *Iron Duke*, which was the dreadnought flagship and battleship of the Royal Navy. Grampy Ken lived with rheumatism all his life. There was no NHS until 1948 and only wealthy people could really employ the services of a doctor, although some doctors saw patients for free. So, Ken was frequently in pain.

Ken's surname was Jacobs. Many Jews and non-Jews are called Jacobs. There were those killed in the concentration camps called Jacobs. What I do feel, because of the things that my dad said to me, is that there were times during the war when they must have been fearful of being thought of as Jewish. When people became aware of Hitlers persecution of the Jews and of the very real threat that Germany might invade Britain, Grampy Ken was perhaps fearful that his family wouldn't stand a chance in German occupied Britain; they wouldn't even be asked whether they were Jewish – they would be destroyed.

Dad says that there were several times in his life when he was asked whether he was Jewish, including when he went into the army, and that his father always said, "Just tell them you are not." He also told me that Nanny Lou would attend Holy Trinity Church and that Grampy Ken often read the bible, so they were not practicing Jews.

But I know that many Jews came to Britain in the nineteenth century and as far back as the time of Oliver Cromwell, fleeing both economic hardship and persecution, and that many Jews from Spain and Portugal converted to Christianity, perhaps to integrate themselves better and perhaps because they did not have the rights of Christians. Many Jews settled in Oxford. It is therefore possible that Ken's very distant family were Jewish? I don't know.

Ken's boyhood was shortened by war, but before that, his childhood would have been spoiled by other things. He came from a relatively poor background. His father, Charles William Jacobs was a painter and decorator. His mother was called Frances Selina Young. They moved from 13

Windsor Street, in Marston, Oxford, to 62 Lime Walk in Headington. Kenneth had an older brother, William, and a younger brother, Herbert. Most boys look up to their older siblings and I am sure that Kenneth must have loved and revered his older brother.

Aged sixteen, when Ken was only thirteen and Herbert, ten, William was arrested in Headington for behaving badly with a group of lads. We don't know what he did – young people were sent away for crimes we would pity them for today. Perhaps he had stolen something, perhaps he had been rude to someone in authority or damaged something, maybe he didn't legit as fast as his friends, but ultimately, he was sent to a reform school for boys in Towcester. A harsh place where boys could be beaten and probably worse. It must have been a dreadful, heart-breaking experience for his family. No doubt Charles and Frances were very anxious that the same thing should not happen to Ken and Herbert.

William's childhood was finished at sixteen. I am not sure whether he became reunited with his family for long. When the First World War started in 1914, he signed up or was encouraged to sign up with the Oxford and Buckinghamshire light infantry and then became a 'Sapper' in the Royal Engineers.

Mid 1916 he was wounded in battle. He was patched up to fight again, then sent back to fight in a second battle in 1918, where he was very badly wounded. Finally, he was sent to a military hospital in Stockport, where he died on 30th December, 1918 after a short and very violent life.

In the end, though, his parents must have been so proud of him, the reform school forgotten, because having arranged for his body to be brought back to Oxford he is buried in Headington Cemetery in Dunstan Road. His grave says '311313 Sapper W.G. Jacobs, Royal Engineers, 30th December 1918, Age 24'. It is one of 40% of war graves which bears a personal message from his family, 'Angel voices ever singing round the throne of light.'

Possibly, these events – coupled with the fact that Ken worked as a security policeman at the Cowley plant during the threat of bombs falling from German planes – may have formed our father's character. Dad has always given the impression that he is a calm, kind and rational man. But Mum always said that he was anxious. I didn't get it then because I was younger. It wasn't until we started to look after him that we realised just how anxious he is. He has a very mild form of Tourette's syndrome; strangers and even close friends don't detect it, and before the dementia, as when he was in the army, he could keep it under wraps. But his dementia has brought the habit back.

I asked him once where he had got the habit from and he told me his father had had it. When he is most anxious and unsettled it manifests itself in soft little grunts or fish like, popping noises.

So, Ken and Louise, now married and living in the little house in Sandhills had three children, but the little girl didn't live. Nanny Lou had a miscarriage after the two boys had been born. First Donald Bernard in 1925, then Maurice Kenneth in 1929.

Both Dad and I have memories of the house and talk about it as we walk around the estate. He remembers that he shared a room with Don, who was older and handy with the whacks at times, as big brothers are; but they were close, too. Uncle Don was perhaps tougher and braver of the two. Dad adored him and talks about him to this day – believing he is still alive.

When she was young, Nanny Louise had been in service at Shotover House, working long hours with only a little time for herself on a Sunday. When her children were born, she became a stay-at-home Mum. Her best friend, her sister Clare, lived along the road with her children and they were often together. She cared for the children, cooked the vegetables that she and Ken grew in the garden, made jam, knitted clothes, all the things that a wartime Mum might do.

Dad went to Stanton St John school on the school bus. His best friend, Basil Keep, lived a few houses away. Like other boys, they met together after school and sometimes went down to the fields just below Sandhills to play army games. Once the farmer arrived and picked another friend up by the scruff of the neck, shaking him as a warning because the boys had been chasing and upsetting his cows.

There were three shops on Sandhills during the war, and a dairy. Dad remembers the milk from the dairy flowing down the street gutters. He loved cherry curd, which his mum made from wild cherries and cow's milk, I think he said it was called that because blood from the cow sometimes seeped into the milk. It doesn't seem to have put him off as it might the children of nowadays, more used to take-away food. He loved cherry curd. The other shops were a grocer's shop, a chemist's and a bakery. There is only one local shop, now, which is on the Risinghurst Estate opposite Sandhills.

I have always thought that Uncle Don resembled Ken, while Dad resembled Nanny Lou. She was very beautiful by all accounts, which is validated by photos of her. Tall, with very dark hair which was cut in a bob, Nanny Lou came from the Quarry. Her father was Braddy Webb, a large man who lived in a cottage at the centre of the village and who had a horse and cart. (At Uncle Don's funeral, my cousin showed me a very old, dog-eared photograph of Uncle Don as a toddler, seated on the back of Braddy's horse.)

Like most men in the Quarry, his work was had where he could get it. He had an allotment at Stanton St John where he grew vegetables; he kept birds like chickens and cockerels (cock fighting went on in the Quarry long after it was banned in England). These he sold, and sometimes he caught wild birds such as goldfinches, bullfinches and linnets which he would send for sale in London. He also worked at the brickyard on Shotover as a building labourer. Braddy could be intimidating or so they say.

His wife, Granny Webb, was kind and affectionate according to Dad's memories and was known locally as a healer of ailments – pretty important when you had no entitlement to a doctor. Dad said he remembers an old lady with long skirts and white hair, who always wore the same brooch at her neck.

I don't remember Grampy Ken, who died shortly after my birth, but I remember Nanny Lou and that both my grandmothers had me to stay with them. My memories of Lou are hazy, but I remember some things clearly. She had a corgi called Judy who once dragged me along the street in Bletchingdon when we lived there as I was afraid to let go of her lead.

She was kind and patient with me. I recall that after playing at Nanny Claire's house along the street with her granddaughter Jennie, we had an argument about something and, feeling cross, I ran back to Nanny Lou who listened to me patiently from the living room door as I played with something on the floor. I can still recall her tall, elegant shape as she stood inside the door. In old age, Dad is tall, thin and elegant, too.

In 1942 or 1943, Uncle Don, having served in the Home Guard as a young man (Dad said his new-found authority made him a bit cocky), was called up to fight in the war. He joined the Navy as his father had. Although in later years he loved the song Bali Hai and no doubt he saw some beautiful landscapes in the South Pacific, his experiences would have been terrifying at times.

Nowadays, people have been used to travelling the world at an early age. But even without the world wars, people didn't travel as they do today. No cheap flights. Prior to the Army and Navy, Don and Maurice would not even have had a holiday in England. Their experience of the sea was a day spent in Southsea or Portsmouth with their parents. Dad has fond memories of going to the seaside in a charabanc.

Joining the Royal Navy during a war was not a trip to the seaside in a charabanc. Ken would have known only too well what dangers his son would have to face in the South Pacific. Whether Don was assigned to the Indomitable, the Victorious, the Formidable or which ship he was employed on, I don't know, but he would have faced the threat of German Avenger planes, Kamikaze attacks, torpedoes, fire at sea, not to mention sharks if you ended up in the sea, and the skin cancer that he endured in later years from a climate that the vast majority of sailors were not used to.

What Ken and Nanny Lou would also have known is that many young men were not returning home and had been killed in action. I can't even comprehend the fear and sorrow that Don's parents would have felt when he left, but Dad remembers it and recalls missing his big brother.

The end of the war did not mean the end of army conscription, which didn't happen until the 1960s. It meant that Dad, aged nineteen, received his call-up papers for a stint in the Royal Engineers, with his army service training firstly in Hampshire.

He still remembers the day when he walked down the road to the house in Delbush Avenue, having returned from Egypt for good. As when Don returned, they had a little party at his home to celebrate. By this time, Uncle Don was walking out with a nurse called Dorothy, our Aunty Dorothy, while Dad met Mum at the Holyoake rooms in Headington, where he asked her to dance, then took her home on the back of his motorbike.

Headington Quarry has been tamed, very gradually, although there are still pockets of resistance. Now it appears unassuming, a picturesque residential village of expensive dwellings and comfortably well-off residents and with its own little weekend farmer's market.

So obscure is it on the world map, that I was amazed to hear a question built into the Mastermind quiz recently; actually, it was a question about the Christian writer C.S. Lewis, who is buried in Holy Trinity churchyard in 'the Quarry' as it is called locally, and who lived in the older part of Risinghurst, the estate opposite.

As a child, Headington Quarry was perhaps the most important place in the world to me. It's recreation park, the little alleyways, the bakery and the grocery at the end of New Cross Road and most of all, number 19 New Cross Road, the house built by my grandfather and his friends. Most weekends, my world centred around the Quarry.

Older than the Sandhills estate, it is much younger than most English villages and it started life as a squatter's settlement on waste land in the early 1800s. A neglected piece of land, where, under the noses of the respectable Victorians of Headington and Oxford who did their best to ignore it, the poorest of the poor snuck in to build their own flimsy houses and hovels. These were poorly constructed Quarrymen's shacks with a few thatched dwellings. Often there would be two rooms for eight or more children. Nanny Edna, our mother's mum told me this, and Harry Kimber, with whom I was friendly as a young woman.

These houses were built upon the sides of the stonepits as they were worked, or when the stone lode was overworked and the pit became redundant. It took a while for the Victorian middle- and upper classes to notice the development; by the time they did, they couldn't rid themselves of this blot on the landscape.

The stone from the quarries was moved by horse and cart. There were no railways close by and no proper roads except for a track that went along the Barracks Road between Quarry and Cowley. The horse and cart would have passed the gypsy camp and the marching soldiers from Cowley barracks. Water had to be drawn from an abandoned clay pit in the Quarry when the first houses were built and before the wells were dug. There was no piped water in the village until the First World War.

Mum's family name was Coppock. Coppocks were nonconformists. Many of them left England for the America's when Charles II came to the throne, refusing to accept the ways of the old church. Later, they became Methodists, following the teachings of John Wesley. In England they were builders and stonemasons and sometimes, for example in Great Yarmouth, sailmakers. In America they were abolitionists. Two brothers, Barclay and Edwin Coppock joined John Brown in the Harpers Ferry raid of 1859, which set the stage for the American Civil war. Edwin was hanged in Charlestown in West Virginia.

Nanny Edna told me that many of the children in the Quarry had to take it in turns to go to school because it was common for one large family to own only two or three pairs of shoes which they must share. The school and church were built by local men, including the Coppocks, with the support and donations from various benefactors who presumably saw the village as a lawless place where policemen were pulled from their horses and tossed into wells (a mid-nineteenth century election protest).

Nanny Edna was very proud to have married a Coppock, and who became successful in more ways than one. She didn't come from the Quarry, so I think it more likely that her stories about the place came from Grampy Ron and his siblings, or Aunty Gladys Coppock, the head teacher of Quarry school during the Second World War, or Aunty Stella, her sister-in-law, who was also a teacher and had taught at Quarry school.

I loved listening to the stories that she told and they stuck in my memory. She told me about the Quarry women who made some extra money by taking in washing from the local gentry and later from the Oxford colleges. About the explosions from Saccy's Pit when they first used gelignite to free the stone, having used picks and shovels before then.

She told me about the cockfights in the pits and the Quarry roast, when they roasted a pig and the whole village came together; about the dark, unlit lanes where young men might pounce out on you and the dogs that prevented outsiders from entering the village.

She told me about three of my grandfather's sisters, Miriam, Molly and Marjorie, who would draw a line with an eyebrow pencil or marker along the back of their legs so that it looked as though they were wearing nylons at local dances during the war. She told my sister Paula and I colourful stories about the Coppocks, the Kimbers, the Traffords and the Gurls, all Quarry names, as we walked through Coppock Alley and past Coppock Close to the bakery.

Like our grandfather, Ron Coppock, Nanny Edna was one of many children. She had grown up in the Cowley area, living there for most of her life. Her Maiden name was Cooke. Her father was called Earnest and her mother, before she married, was Florence Annie Mills. Nanny Edna had many siblings but I can only really remember Aunty Eunice, who ran a sweet shop in St Clements and gave Paula and me free sweets, and Aunty Jack, who was very kind and brought up their sister Bubs' daughter when Bubs tragically drowned herself in the river Cherwell after the death of her husband in the First World War... Oh, and Aunty Millie who had been paralysed since babyhood. Their mother, Florence, had left Aunty Jack, as the eldest, to care for her. This was something that often happened in those days. Millie slipped from the table she had been placed upon and never walked again. I only saw Milly twice, but despite having spent her life in a wheelchair, she seemed a very happy and positive person with a lovely smile. She and Aunty Jack were always very close; it was clear that Millie loved Jack very much.

Nan had a great sense of fun. She told us that her father was a jolly person who had his fingers in many pies. He ran the Star public house in June Street; from there he also ran a Bookies shop. He had a butcher's shop in Cowley Road. He raced greyhounds, which Nan and Eunice would dress in baby clothes and push around the streets in a baby's perambulator. He once owned a racehorse which broke loose and ran amok around the fountain on the Plain in Oxford, until it was caught at last by a bunch of students.

Florence, Nan's mother, so Nan told me, came from Windsor and had been brought up by a very authoritarian grandmother after her own mother became pregnant by a young Italian man. This grandmother was called Granny Burge.

A photograph of Florence with Nan's brother, Aubrey, at her knee, shows a clear likeness between Nanny Edna and her dark-haired mother. But Florence was made older by the many children she had: cheekbones taut, almost sunken, body thin in the long stiff dark brocade dress.

Florence was a hard worker. Tired one evening, she carried a candle to the attic of the Star pub to take down the many items of children's clothing from the beams where they hung to dry, not realising that the candle flame she held was systematically setting fire to the clothes. The fire spread quickly; Florence gradually woke from her tired wanderings, sniffing the smoke behind her and the horse-drawn fire engine was called to put out the fire.

Grampy Ron and Nanny Edna met when they were in their older teens, in the early 1920s, at St Giles Fair in Oxford, when there were merry-go-rounds and coconut shies, swing boats and stalls.

At the time, Nanny Edna was living with her older sister, Jaqueline. Aunty Jack was married to a man who managed accounts for the university, leaving the running of the boarding house where they lived in Beaumont Street (at a boarding house for the university students) to Aunty Jack. Nan's younger sister, Eunice, who was also her best friend, came to Aunty Jack's to meet Nan and they went off to the fair together to have some fun.

Not long after they had joined the throng of people, they were chatted up by two young men, one of whom was Gramps. They went on some rides together and Gramps seems to have stuck to Nan like a limpet. He also did something very silly and dangerous, according to Nan, and when a snooty lady in a wide-brimmed hat stared reprovingly at them, he lit a match and singed the hairs at the back of her neck. Had the four young people not run away through the crowd, he would certainly have been arrested. He did come from the Quarry, as I said, although clearly this isn't an excuse for setting fire to a lady's hair.

Ron was one of eight children; his father was Earnest Coppock. Both were handsome young men according to the dog-eared photographs. They look too delicate for the stone trade that they followed, the major source of income for Quarry men. I don't know where Earnest's father, Stephen, came from originally, but the Coppock name can be found in generations from the London borough of Southwark to Cheshire and frequently in America. Mum gave me a map, once, which was a reproduction of a medieval map of Cheshire. It had a village marked upon it, the village of Coppock, gone now. I've wondered whether it was one of the villages that became deserted after the plague.

Earnest and his father, Stephen, built Earnest's house in New Cross Road. It is one of the oldest houses in the Quarry. It wasn't simply their house, but was where their stone trade was operated from. So, in the beginning, the drive would have been covered in white stone dust, the limestone and Kimmeridge clay with which they worked.

I remember seeing Grampy Ron while he was a director of Axtell, Perry and Symm masonry in Oxford, covered in the same dust, but sitting at a drawing board and sketching out a building. In those days, a mask against the lung damaging stone dust wasn't considered essential as it is today, and in later years he suffered from the inhalation of stone dust.

It was the house that Paula and I used to run in and out of when we stayed with Nanny Edna, the house where Grampy Ron's older sister lived. A beautiful house, something like a farmhouse inside. I remember the dark, polished wood and rough stone walls.

Earnest met Amy Reading, his wife, when work dried up in the Quarry. While a young man, he walked all the way to Rugby. Perhaps he intended to walk to Birmingham following the old Banbury Road to find work there, but he ended up in Rugby. This is less than one and a half hours by car or train, but on foot, it must have been a considerably greater distance.

It seems remarkable, in this day and age, that he walked there, stopping at night in whatever shelter he could find against rain or frost – a vagrant, grateful for any food he could get.

One way or another, he arrived at a farm in Rugby and was given the work that he asked for. Amy was one of the farmer's children and it was Amy he married and took back to Headington with him when he returned home.

What I know about Amy from her Nanny Edna and Aunty Stella is that she liked to read more than anything else, that her daughters frequently saved the stews cooking on the stove because of her addiction to novels, and that either she declined to be a washerwoman or that Earnest didn't want her to do that work.

Grampy Ron and Nanny Edna lived in Kiln Lane, not far from C.S. Lewis and his brother, until he built his own home in the Quarry. Gramps was a stonemason who worked on the Oxford colleges, supervised repair work at Blenheim Palace and was asked to build individual monuments such as the monument in Bournemouth to the memory of Ian Fleming. He was consulted about his knowledge of stone working in Oxford by geologists and writers and he became the Managing Director of Axtell, Perry and Symm, the Oxford masons.

But what he really loved was football. Early photographs of him show a handsome young man sitting cross-legged with his team, Headington United, a broad grin on his face. He was an enthusiastic footballer who never missed a training session or a game, until the day came when, in digging the vegetable patch for his father, he put the garden fork through his foot. The damage wasn't permanent but it stopped him from playing football. Grampy Ron had to leave school at fourteen; in fact he was offered a scholarship at Oxford school, but by the time he left school, his father was invalided and he was needed to work in the stone yard.

Nanny Edna's one grumble as the years went on was that Gramps put all of his money into Oxford United. I'm sure that not all of his money went that way, as we had some pretty nice holidays in Wales, Bournemouth, Yarmouth and Cornwall when we were younger, and theirs was a modern, 1950s house with lovely furnishings of the time.

The house in New Cross Road had a huge apple and plum orchard beyond the garden. It has since been built upon, houses now, but I've dreamed of that colourful orchard where we would eat the sticky plums straight from the trees and munch the apples down to the core. From these, Nanny Edna would make plum and apple pie and then show Paula and me how to make pastry. It was a lovely long garden, with an old couple called the Perks on one side and the Wilsons on the other. The stone wall that Grampy built was low enough to talk to these neighbours.

Immediately beyond the house there was a rose garden. In the late summer, Nan would give us old bottles she had collected and we would strip the roses of their sweet-smelling petals to make our own perfume. The garden was divided by a small grey concrete pigsty, unused for some years. Paula and I used it as a den when we wanted to stay out in the rain. We learned a lot in that garden; every child should have a garden.

What I knew in the fourteen years before Gramps died, but didn't appreciate as a child growing up, principally because I didn't know the Aunt Christine I had been named after and who died before I was born – was the toll that her death had taken on him. There is a picture owned by the Oxford Mail of Grampy Ron reclining in a chair. It was taken in the 1950s. In the photograph, he is unsmiling and perhaps a little intimidating, not the grandfather that we knew at all. Nan told me that the photograph was taken just a few years after Christine died and that he and Christine were very close.

When I was young, and Nan used to lie on the bed with me to get me to sleep at night, she would peer through the gap in the curtains and say, "That bright star is Aunty Christine." She would talk about her, telling me how kind she had been and how good at sport she was. Sometimes when I was young, I would feel as though I was competing with that other Christine for Nan's affection.

29th March 2020

I am a little angry, a little afraid, probably impatient and sometimes fearful. Occasionally lonely in this lockdown. The loneliness doesn't come from being alone. I like being alone, I don't get much time to myself. It comes from losing my Mum, my sister, my niece. It comes from not being able to explain my feelings to my father, who gets nothing, now. It comes from having to make my own decisions because I am single but worry about my family. It's a deep well from within which I can't fill. How much worse must it be for Marion?

I'm very lucky, all things concerned. I talk to my sister often, my brother too. Old friends catch up with me and I call them. We send our love to each other and say, "Stay well."

When the children aren't here, I walk around the house with my phone pressed to my ear, listening to radio four, generally to the news, but to other programmes, even the ones that I might find irritating or boring. Once, I drop the phone into the washing up bowl and mercifully it survives. There is nowhere to get it repaired right now as all the shops are closed. If I like a programme, I listen avidly and it helps me to do chores. If I'm impatient and in a hurry, I'll berate the presenter as though it's all his or her fault, muttering things like, "Really, Melvyn, I don't have time for ancient Greek philosophers this morning!"

I know why Nan used to watch the TV, and why Dad sits before it, gazing at the screen, rarely making sense of anything. Just voices in the background, making you feel less lonely, that, in some way, you are still a part of the world you once knew. Nanny Edna became very lonely. She never recovered from losing Gramps. Once, visiting her as a teenager after his death, I had a dream in which she was a tiny woman sitting alone in a huge chair in a massive house, which was the reality for a long time. I don't have a massive house; I have a cabin and it is cosy. I can leave whenever I like and I've been so used up that I don't get enough time there.

I'm lucky in that my family are all close to me. I know grandmothers who hardly get to see their children and grandchildren because they live in another country: Inna's mum, for example, who lives in Ukraine.

Having got half custody of his girls, they live with Harry for half of the week. This week, their mum called me from Bicester because Delia had hurt her arm. I drove at night to pick them up and took them to the hospital. Delia was okay, her arm was just bruised. I took them home at midnight – for once we didn't have to wait for hours – but I'm getting too old for panics and late-night driving.

I do what I can for Louise and my other grandchildren with the Covid restrictions and without contact or, when I was called upon to unblock the loo, with a mask about my mouth.

I mow Louise's lawn, dig the flower bed for her, go to the chemists if she needs medicines and to the shops when the girls want to bake. I try to provide enrichment activities for Ned.

Really, I'm very proud of Lou. At the moment, in lockdown, she's doing her own work as a lawyer, sitting on the children to do their schoolwork, cooking the meals and looking after a student. Generally, I do housework for her, but not now, obviously. And although the girls are mostly responsible and helpful, they are young teenage girls and all young teenage girls can turn into the Salem witches on occasion. I fear that many women will be forced to take a retrograde step having fought hard to compete with men.

I think one of my real fears, Marion's too, is that Dad will become ill. That he would need the hospital. Made to die alone and confused amongst strangers, because no one is currently allowed to stay with a patient, or comfort them by holding their hand. I know Dad would need this, just as Mum did when she died from cancer.

A young boy aged thirteen died of corona virus a short while ago; no one was allowed to stay with him. I understand the fear of the virus and the reasoning behind it, but how terrible must that have been for the child and for his parents?

I'm glad there is no virus in Aunty Dorothy's care home and glad, too, that we made the decision to keep Dad in his own home. Care homes aren't being given the PPE, older people are dying, wiped out, their memories obliterated, as though their lives meant nothing. There is something terrible about that. People matter, they matter for ever; they carry on in the hearts of generations who loved them but they also influence the generations to come.

Next, we'll be painting red crosses on our doors but, rather more cheerfully, we are getting children to paint rainbows for the NHS.

News reports tell of the overcrowding in South Africa, Syria, the Yemen and of the problems that this overcrowding will create with the rapidly spreading virus. People all over the world, living in tiny, fragile tents and tumbledown shelters without proper sanitation. What can they do but use soap to wash their hands beneath pumps? No hospitals and limited provision.

Our schools close, our libraries and parks, the shops, some garages, leisure facilities, pubs, restaurants, cafés, hairdressers, book shops and, incredibly, churches, mosques, synagogues and anywhere where you want to pray collectively to God. Only food shops and chemists remain open, and the queues for both are unbelievably long.

The government spends millions on bailing businesses and individuals out. The outcome of everything is uncertain. I realise that behind the problems we all face, our country has always provided some security and freedom and choice; or has it? Perhaps only for the middle classes; maybe the less fortunate have had a great deal more to worry about. When bad things happen to you, it's easier to see another person's point of view.

I realise trivial but interesting things in the lulling periods of the lockdown. That Jack, the collie, looks left and right when he crosses the road and that Monty, the springer, pushes a toy into your leg to nag you into throwing it.

Perhaps, more importantly, when the girls come, I encourage Delia out of nappies, to use her knife and fork and discover that Freya has enough phonics from her teachers to pursue the magic 'e'... Oh yes, that she is learning to add and subtract.

Both girls express their imagination through dance, painting and play. Freya is not only expressive when she dances, but also rather graceful. She asks to play with her cousin and we have to tell her that she can't because of the virus.

I talk to Dad through his back door, a mask on my face, leaving newspapers and biscuits for him. I do little dances at the front of his house when he looks down from his bedroom window, all to make him smile. I blow kisses at him, shout that I love him and make my hands into the shape of a heart. I miss him and often leave the house tearfully.

At first, the Saturday morning cookery programmes are a novelty. When I was married, my ex used to like them. I've never really watched them since Rick Stein, who I used to enjoy because many of his programmes were filmed in Cornwall and, before him, Keith Floyd, who was genuinely entertaining; principally because he often appeared to be funny and unashamedly drunk.

The lockdown cookery programmes are a novelty for me. As I do a cleaning job on Harry's house when the girls aren't there, I contemplate making marmalade and dandelion wine, but I can't find time to pick the dandelions. It's not my life anymore; it's a fake life. I've enjoyed feeding my family as much as I've thought to myself, 'Bloody hell, what'll I cook for dinner?' But I'm really not keen enough to make marmalade.

One Sunday afternoon, I watch *South Pacific*, crying foolishly about Dad and Uncle Don. My mood is something to do with the lockdown. I must have been a child when I last saw it, a ridiculous Hollywood musical against beautiful sunsets and with fantastic songs. I find myself humming them for the rest of the day; the songs become an earworm that I can't get out of my head.

Standing in the car park at the supermarket on a chilly March morning, I queue at the obligatory two metres in front of a woman and behind a man as we crawl forward to do our shopping. I hear two seagulls close by, not flying, but raucously fighting over discarded litter. They lift my spirits as they swoop upward and into the wind. I smile behind my home-made face mask at their triumphant guttural squawking. For a moment, I can imagine cold sea water swooshing about my legs; I'm in the sea in Polzeath, and wearing my surf suit as I stare back at the beach.

My imagining comes to an end as the woman behind me, also in a mask, impatiently nods me forward; but I can't see whether she is smiling or frowning behind her mask. I can't tell if she is friend or foe. This is one of the most distressing things about being masked, you can't discern the feelings of other people.

As I move forward in the queue, I notice another line of people beside me, all of them older than me. At the end of the line is a sign saying that it's a queue for pensioners. Standing adjacent to me is a gentleman in his mid-eighties. He has a fine face and reminds me a little of Grampy Ron. My first impression is that his clothes are more outlandish than the suits and casual trousers that Gramps used to wear.

He wears black and white checked trousers in bold checks, and a blue, lightweight jacket over a white shirt. He looks cold, and better suited to the pier at Weston-super-Mare than the supermarket, but I like him for some unfathomable reason, and perhaps I simply admire him for doing his own shopping and feeling that old age doesn't mean that you have to be less vibrant.

I hear my father's voice, although he's not here, repeating the phrases he can recall, phrases that give him something to say.

"Big trolley or little one? Want me to push it?"

And I miss him. It's not safe to bring people in their nineties to the supermarket, although there are still many elderly people valiantly doing their own shopping.

Inside the shop, I forget to buy the oranges on my shopping list and walk neurotically backwards for half the length of the aisle so as not to break the follow the arrows signs on the floor. It's stupid; I am stupid; everything is stupid, now. As Marion put it, it's as though some celestial god is taking the piss out of us mortals.

Later in the day, a police car parks outside the old shop on Sandhills. It isn't a shop anymore, but people who once used it, myself included, still refer to it as Mrs Reed's. Mr Reed fought in the Spanish civil war, while Mrs Reed sometimes sold individual cigarettes to teenagers at a high price, which wasn't as admirable.

The one bad experience I had after shopping there one evening was that I bought four oranges which Mr Reed put into a previously used plastic bag. When I arrived home and tipped the oranges onto the kitchen table, a used condom fell out. I had to throw the oranges away and disinfect the table.

Harry, who lives opposite the old shop and was sitting on the garden bench at the time, struck up a conversation with one of the policemen.

They were in communication with a helicopter circling above. They told Harry that a person had been spotted climbing over a garden fence and into a second garden.

Here we go, I think. Poverty, or the need for drugs with no funds. One Christmas, a burglar broke into two houses on the estate and stole kiddies Christmas presents. I almost felt sorry for the burglar, knowing how children nag and how you feel at Christmas that you must fulfil the dreams of your children. It makes me want to change my religion.

They catch the man. He doesn't try to resist the arrest. We go inside as the police bundle him into the car. I stop pulling up the weeds in the garden and Harry follows me.

Thursday 2nd April
(Howard's birthday)

Drove to Wheatley, deeming it an essential journey as it was Howard's birthday. The older he grows, the more I can see both Dad and Mum in him. He is slight of build, like the Coppock men, but facially like Dad when he was younger. I am built like the Webb's, Nanny Lou's family, a bit like a pit pony, which is why, so far, my skeleton has sustained all of the heavy lifting.

Resentfully, I once asked Mum why Marion had all of the physical advantage. She is small, delicate, blue-eyed. Mum said that apart from my big bones and Webbed feet (a pun on a family name because my feet are large and flat like Frodo Baggins), I had the heart of a Coppock. Tactful.

My grandchildren are all thriving in this peculiar state of lockdown. It has been good for all to see Louise coping so well with her three, who are aged between seven and fifteen. Most of all, it's been good for her own children to see what a kind, clever and resourceful mum they have. Perhaps, at heart, I am disappointed that she appears to be doing so well. Maybe I won't be needed as much.

Ned is missing his school and friends most of all, even though he doesn't say that. He's a very sociable child. When the girls aren't with Harry, I've taken him for a walk or to the shop; it's all I can do at the moment, but it gives Lou some time out and it gives Ned a break from the house.

I try to catch up with things, sewing buttons onto school shirts and darning Dad's socks to save money. I've also started making PPE masks for the family and the paperboy, also, as he appears determined to catch the virus. Shops are selling masks in expensive little packages. Now we have to spend out on these as well as sanitary towels.

I derive huge pleasure is seeing Freya's rapid progress with the one to one she's been having in lockdown. Some of the things her teachers sent home were quite hard for her, so we have worked up to them gently, but she can see how much she is achieving and her confidence is growing fast. I'm sure that other people are having the same experience. I want to see children back into school for the good of those children who won't have spaces to work, or computers, and may have parents who are insecure about what to teach. Equally, it is a joy to be able to give a child one to one teaching, so long as you are confident about assessing their next need, which is basically what teachers do.

When I was a teacher, we did an interesting exercise in a staff meeting – around the time the government were bringing in the National Curriculum. We calculated that each child received about ten minutes of individual coaching per day within the class setting; this ten-minutes was to cover every subject in the curriculum. It was based upon thirty children covering English, maths, science, PE, art, music and the humanities. It didn't leave much time for design technology, which I believe is of great importance in teaching a child to solve problems.

Delia's speech has also come on in leaps and bounds: whole sentences, imaginative play, her confidence, too, although she still becomes hysterical if she sees an ant or a fly or any insect and I spent half an hour chasing a fly around their bedroom recently in order that she would sleep. Must do some stuff on friendly mini-beasts to encourage her.

Lauren once called me back from Oxford to remove a spider from her room. I never kill them because Nanny Edna used to say, "Let a spider run alive and all your life you'll live and thrive."

Harry and his colleagues must have been given protective clothing at last, because he's been bringing it home to wash. I had believed, wrongly, that he had it all along but was removing it at work.

On the first occasion he came home in it, the girls rushed to hug his knees and I had a pink fit about the danger involved, stuffing it into the washing machine to cook it at a high temperature.

I'm as scared and neurotic as everyone else, I suppose. This is a terrible period in history.

Friday 3rd April

(I woke up thinking it was Tuesday and I had better put the bins out. Totally disorientated – every day runs into another.)

Took half an hour to write the above sentence. Have been boiling eggs for the girl's breakfast as they watch a version of the Palm Sunday story on my laptop. Wonder, as many must have wondered before, whether the young think that the Jesus born at Christmas died at the hands of the Romans just a few months later.

I had two very strange dreams last night, possibly made more peculiar by a gin and tonic.

Delia has got boiled egg on my computer. Serves me right for not letting them watch Number Blocks today.

Sunday 5th April

During the day, I count nine ambulances screeching along the motorway behind Harry's house. For the first time I have the impulse to cover my ears with my hands. The sound of their sirens now fills me with dread. I might have thought once, "I hope it's nothing serious," but now I'm thinking, "Will my family be next?"

My neighbour, a nurse, rarely at home and for whom I have done shopping, has slept through the whole weekend. She is clearly exhausted.

The Queen gives a speech to the nation at eight p.m. Most of the nation are heartened by it, including Marion and Louise.

I see James in his garden while I'm watering the potatoes and carrots. His leg is really bothering him. The doctor says he has sciatica and the physiotherapist has given him a list of exercises over the phone, the most important of which is agony to do, apparently. What's the point, without the human contact and encouragement that people truly need?

James' hair has grown very long; the hairdressers are shut, of course. I fail to get his permission to cut it myself, even though I would wear a mask and gloves. Even I, his mother, will not be permitted to get that close.

Marion says that Dad's breathing is worse. Apparently, he said that his heart hurts. I'm going to call the doctor tomorrow for some advice.

Monday 6th April

Boris Johnson has the virus. He can't have the virus when we are in the midst of a catastrophe; how dare he?

Louise's back and neck have got worse because she is working from home. In the office, she has a special back chair. I get her another table to work from so she can sit up straighter and won't have to slouch.

In the evening, I walk the dogs and stand beneath a little tree to stare at a pearly white moon through the branches. At least nature hasn't changed: in fact it's thriving.

Monday 6th April

Something strange and awful is happening to me. I am becoming racist: not towards black, brown or Chinese or Asian people, not the LGBT community, not towards anyone except for, very specifically, dyed blonde-haired women with fake suntans and very long nails. I don't know why this is. I am trying to rationalise it. I think, somewhere in this lockdown, I lost a bit of my rationale. Maybe I'm aware of my own ugliness and I'm jealous. I know it's quite unreasonable. I think it's temporary, so hopefully not serious.

I am overtired and the stupid dreams are not helping. Last night I dreamed that I was banned from visiting Cornwall for life after walking across Cornish fields with an old friend I went to college with and who is married to a farmer. I actually got out of bed, went downstairs, sat on the front doorstep and smoked a cigarette.

This supressed irritability made me impatient with Woman's Hour on the radio. I used to like listening to the radio four programme when I could. But a few days ago, I decided that it was overly middle class and then I exploded over an item about a couple who had parted company but locked down together for the sake of the children. This is all well and good, but what about the ex-couples who had very difficult relationships which were unhealthy for the children? To exacerbate my feelings, the woman introducing the programme said, "What do parents who are co-parenting do, when the children have to stay in lockdown?"

The children don't have to stay in lockdown! And it's essential that the public know this, or some parents might abuse the law. The law society, family lawyers, judges all say that the children must travel between parents if they are well, and be locked down once more in the home of the parent they are going to. The reason that all must be aware of this is that the courts are very busy with cases where, mostly mothers, I suspect, are refusing to let go of their children; perhaps using the excuse that a child is showing symptoms of the virus.

I sent *Woman's Hour* an email to that effect, but haven't had an acknowledgement.

Also, why is it that all women are depicted by *Woman's Hour* as self-sacrificing angels? They are not. It's unreal. And why would I, at sixty-two, want to listen to endless stories about women having babies?

My fault. I will simply have to stop listening to it. Woman's hour, women with fake suntans – I used to use a fake suntan. Where is my impatience coming from; where did it take root?

10th April Good Friday

So tired. While Harry works, I have been in lockdown with the girls for almost two weeks. I just need one day without them. Having thought this, I realise that when they do go back, I will miss them so much. I also know that there are mothers and often single fathers, grandmothers, who are getting absolutely no time without their children and having to work from home on top of this.

I do what I can to support her. Sometimes I buy fruit for Lauren, tennis balls for Ned, exercise books for them to write in, felt pens, cookery ingredients for them to bake cakes, biscuits, crisps and lollies, trying to ensure they have fun things to do after their work. Louise is there around the clock and that must be harder, trying to do her job at home and caring for the children.

At bedtime, Freya asks for a hug and I don't hesitate, don't think about it; we are a demonstrative family. As I bend over her, she emits the most violent sneeze.

With no mask on, I fly backwards in shock, falling over a little chair in the middle of the room to collapse upon the floor. Both girls fall about laughing, choking into their pillows. I laugh too, when I have recovered myself from the floor. In normal circumstances, minus the virus, I wouldn't have reacted at all to a sneeze. After all, I was a teacher for twenty-five years or so, being coughed, sneezed and sicked upon was pretty routine, not to forget the small hands I held without thinking about the consequences of nose picking.

I try to explain about the danger once again, with an extra bedtime story. I remind the girls the story of the nursery rhyme, 'Ring a Ring o' Roses', and about the plague, and how children can carry things like a virus without getting ill, but that a sneeze can be very dangerous to an old granny like me. I explain that 'Atishoo, atishoo, we all fall down,' means in fact that a person can die from a virus, but there is a lack of focus. They are tired, already dismissing the information and thinking about what we will do in the morning.

This is the first time in my entire life that we haven't celebrated Easter together, that we won't be eating together. I'll have to leave the chocolate eggs on their doorsteps. In the past, we have followed Easter trails amidst boats in a Cornish harbour, in the pampas grass of a Northumbrian beach and amongst the rocks of a Welsh cove.

Thursday 16th April

A tiny, plump and helpless brown baby blackbird, cowering against the wall, beneath the garden table provided a diversion yesterday morning. Monty, Harry's springer spaniel, gun dog reject, found it there when I let him out for a wee.

I heard a lot of crashing about of wooden chairs and found Monty, who hasn't an aggressive bone in his body and is much kinder than the cats, excitedly bouncing upon the chick with his large, floppy forepaws, nudging it with his muzzle as though it was a new friend to talk to. I had to shoo Monty back indoors, then crouched over the baby bird who stared at me with tiny eyes and a large open orange beak. Its feathers were smeared with Monty drool.

From the small tree at the foot of the garden, the mother bird was screaming at her baby to hide or fly, or possibly she was screaming at me. I donned a pair of rubber gloves. Eventually, because the little bird was quite nippy and tried to hop away, I managed to pick it up, carrying it to a safer place at the end of the garden to hide it beneath its mother's tree.

The mother bird and another blackbird, I guess it's the father, have watched over it from the trees for all this time, while I try to keep Monty inside the house, which is not always possible. Every time I let Monty out, the mother bird goes crazy, screeching at the little bird to fly. She becomes hysterical and I feel so responsible.

Once, when I was about ten, I tried to protect a little bird from a cat in the same way. I was terrified that the white cat (Arthur was his name) would get it. I remember throwing the chick into the air from my palms, thinking that it would fly away. Dad caught me out. He said that the bird would die of a heart attack or that the mother would abandon it, so I hid it in the bushes.

I took Jack and Monty for a walk over the Risinghurst fields. When we returned, I searched in the bushes for the baby bird, but it appeared to have gone and its mother with it, so I guess it was okay.

Friday 17th April

Yesterday in the daily briefing they said that almost 14,000 people had died from COVID-19, a horrendous statistic, and that the lockdown will be for another three weeks. I have walked the dogs, cleaned the windows downstairs for Louise and planted more carrots.

Having been writing a kidnapping, set in Iceland, where I felt that I knew exactly where I was going, I have stopped seeing a clear path and, today, did practical things instead. Today my right arm aches; good job it isn't clap for the NHS night.

Louise called me today, and just about succeeded in concealing her panic. Apparently, she had three hundred wills to complete, so I'm not the only person anticipating death.

She was also very excited about the Red Kite bird which swooped down and landed in her garden! I've never known this to happen. I've seen plenty of Red Kites flying over Sandhills before now, but never seen them land in a garden. I told her it was an omen, or at least that the Romans would have thought it was a symbol of courage and victory. Probably it was simply because the wildlife is getting bolder since we became locked up in our homes. The courage and victory explanation is far more empowering, though.

Thursday 23rd April
St George's Day

The pavement outside Harry's house has become a calendar of events. On Easter Sunday, after we had hidden Easter eggs in the garden for the children to find (a beautiful garden, with a rhubarb patch and with the roses and flowers planted before the 1950s), I read the Easter story to the girls as they stuffed their mouths with chocolate.

After this, I took them outside to the front pavement with their big chalks and we drew three green hills with crosses upon them and the words, 'Happy Easter' beneath. After remembering, I also wrote the words 'and Happy Rama', although I'm not entirely sure whether it is Ramadan just yet, to be honest.

Then, today, St George's Day, I took the girls outside after telling them the story of St George. We also read *The Paper-bag Princess*, a story about an unorthodox princess who saves a prince. We decorated the pavement with a giant green dragon, complete with red eyes. I'm becoming a regular Bert (from the Mary Poppins story).

Wednesday 29th April

I've been very busy with children and one thing and another.

James' sciatica became really bad and, when I went into the house, I found that he has been experiencing so much pain going up and down stairs that he has been using a bucket as a piss pot so that he could avoid climbing them. He was lying on the floor, struggling to pull his leg into his jeans. The culmination of all of that is that he called the doctor, who prescribed painkillers, and at last he seems to be more comfortable and has returned to searching for a job. The pain must be bad, because James' favourite pastime is to climb mountains in Iceland and Scotland.

An incredible and terrible amount of people have died. Real people, full lives, whose stories need to be told. There are 26,000 people by now and still they don't have the statistics for care homes. Never would I have believed that something like this could happen in my lifetime.

Monday was the start of the fifth week of lockdown. On the television, those same families who had embraced the chance to be at home with each other are now asking repeatedly when the lockdown will be lifted. Marion and I take it in turns to visit Aunty Steph at the Masons and yell at her balcony from the car park. Her middle son, our cousin, Chris, has started a remote quiz night on a Saturday by using Facebook. The quiz has become really popular. People miss the pubs for all kinds of reasons, recognising that having a beer is only a small part of it. Apparently, the Mayor of Oxford is joining the quiz.

The pubs and restaurants must be suffering terribly, despite the vast amounts of money injected into businesses to keep them afloat. My heart goes out to them. I'm a landlord's daughter, and very glad my mum and dad didn't experience this, but sorry, too, for the worry that Steph and her family must be facing. I am from a family of teachers and publicans. Almost everyone is suffering, one way or another.

To give Harry a break from me (not many men of twenty-eight want to live with their mother, albeit every other week), I lock down in the cabin until the children return.

The outer wood of the cabin has become very damaged because of the rain and I will have to pay somebody to fix it. On the first evening I am in there, all of the electric lights blow. This doesn't simply mean they need changing, I reason. The fixtures in the ceiling must have become damp. I have had to call an electrician. Much as I don't mind spiders and woodlice, I don't particularly want to sleep with them in total darkness; it's a bit like being in a tomb. I borrow a lamp from James and use the torch that Marion bought me for Christmas.

The Lake District seems such a long time ago. James was musing that he expects it looks beautiful at the moment. I expect that it does, but none are allowed to go there. At least we have dreams and memories.

30Th April (Forever, Captain Tom's birthday)

It is impossible to escape from one's own emotions, I suppose. Angry, afraid, impatient, fearful but often peculiarly content. Up and down like a yo-yo. When the children are here, I wander about the house with radio four pressed to my ears. The only thing that causes irritation, beside *Woman's Hour*, is *The Archers*. I always enjoyed listening to it, even though a busy life meant that I would miss vast episodes of it. Now it bores the pants off me. Because of Covid, it's being recorded in the individual actor's homes, this entails meaningless monologue and no action. But I appreciate many of the radio four programmes, which keep me informed and make me laugh. I carry my phone about in my bra or tucked under my chin so I can use it as a radio.

Once, I dropped the phone in a washing bowl; fortunately, it fell into a frying pan. Another time, I dropped it into the toilet. It's only a cheap phone, but I need it and there are no mobile shops open right now because of the virus. Without a phone I can't reach the people I love.

James still hasn't got a job, although he has applied for many. Unsurprisingly, he's very nervous about going out into the world. His hair was growing really long so I put on a mask and cut it for him in the garden. Not a bad job, I don't think he's noticed that the fringe is a bit lopsided; hopefully it won't be noticed if he gets an interview.

Whoever could have imagined this world of science fiction where we can't see, touch, hug, kiss or meet the people we love in case we kill them?

Marion and I dread that our dad will have to go into hospital, because sometimes now his breathing is laboured. Only they don't allow family to accompany the elderly, or anyone in fact; and in Dad's case, he wouldn't have a clue what was going on. He would be so confused and lonely.

Louise's girls, teenagers, have been working well from home but are now starting to miss their friends. I buy the ingredients to make cakes, which always cheers them up. They make wonderful cakes, a skill gained from their mother. My cakes are hopeless, like crumbly biscuits.

The late news tells of overcrowding and the lack of resources in Syria, Yemen and South Africa. People are living in fragile tents and shelters with only one water pump to several hundred people. Our shops may be closed but what is a haircut compared with these situations?

I've offered the help I can to two old gentlemen who live locally and to my neighbour, an exhausted nurse. My neighbour on the other side of Rose, the cat lady, is elderly; he only recently recovered from cancer. When he gave me the good news that the cancer had retreated, calling me from his bedroom window, I was standing on the front drive with a basket of laundry. I threw it all into the air and did a little dance to celebrate, which made him laugh.

When the girls arrive, Freya actually asks me to do schoolwork with her. It's lovely to have grandchildren who generally want to learn. We cover the magic 'e' and simple subtraction. Ned has been a good boy in lockdown, but often requires a lot of encouragement. He's very clever, and learns quickly, although threats that he won't be able to use the PlayStation generally work to motivate him.

Suddenly the BBC are talking about how many Dyson ventilators can be produced and saying the government are buying PPE from the Turkish.

Standing in the car park at Tesco's on a chilly morning I stand at the obligatory two metre distance, slowly crawling my way with the other people towards the supermarket entrance. It's reminiscent of the dole queue in the 1980s, a people leveller. I watch the inland gulls fighting over scraps of food. I'm wearing a home-made face mask. I've made several. The teenies won't wear them, they're not cool enough.

The gulls remind me of Cornwall. Suddenly, in my imagination, I can feel the cold sea swashing about my legs as I stand in my surf suit in Polzeath, striding forward into the sea. How I wish I could do that right now. Unimaginable freedom.

Inside the supermarket I get confused by the arrows newly placed upon the floor. When I have to backtrack because I've forgotten oranges, unconsciously, I walk backwards as though that will mean I'm abiding by the rules and I get shouted at by a fellow shopper. People are tense and anxious, snappy, unfriendly. I don't like this new world at all.

But by the evening I feel differently, a little more mellow. At least we have supermarkets, whereas a Facebook friend who cares for his community and runs a school in Uganda uploads a photograph of several plump rats he has caught to feed a group of children.

And then we have the lovely Captain Tom, whose birthday is today, and who has raised so many millions for the NHS. What a fantastic person. Soon it'll be Dad's birthday. He's my Captain Tom. Wish I could organise an RAF flyover for him, but balloons and a banner will have to do.

1st May

This year I had told the children I was going to wake them all up at five in the morning to walk into Oxford for May Day morning. This is a chance to listen to the choir singing from the top of Magdalen tower in the clear, chilly air; to wear garlands in your hair if you are young, and watch the sillier students who break their bones leaping from the bridge into the River Cherwell or fight to get to the bar in one of the many pubs that are open. But hey, no, Nonny-Nonny No in fact, because the virus has robbed us of May Day. Not since Oliver Cromwell have such revered festivals been cancelled. No 'Summer is a comin' in, loudly sing cuckoo…' I'll have to sing it to myself.

I was rather tired, so maybe it was a lucky escape. Getting up at six is early enough. But next year I'm determined that I shall. Instead, I made garlands for Freya and Delia and stuck blossoms above the doors at their house – Louise's and James' houses, too.

Painting the pavement with chalk drawings and decorating houses with garlands of flowers are not things I would usually do, but I think I feel a kind of sadness for the children that this Covid year is a year out of their lives, a year that's been lost. In the afternoon, the two little girls dress up in ballet costumes and give me a performance of *Swan Lake* with Alexa providing the music. It's very good, actually. Perhaps post Covid, they can go to a real ballet school.

8th May VE Day

So, I've watched the film *Darkest Hour*, having meant to watch it long ago, and think it's brilliant. Then we wonder how we will do VE Day, what with the no large social gatherings business but with a large and very close-knit family.

Marion, Lou, Ruby and I decide to have tea and cake in the little close outside Louise's house, with social distancing, of course, placing the garden chairs at distanced intervals from each other. I don't have time to make the bunting that the local community is suggesting but, fortunately, other people have done so and it looks very jolly. I've been too busy making face masks when the children aren't with us.

Jess and Lauren made cakes; they were amazing to look at. I made cakes with the younger children. They believed they were amazing to look at, because they covered them in icing, but actually they were lopsided and had hardly risen at all.

We put the Alexa outside to play Glen Miller tunes, Chattanooga Choo Choo and In the Mood. I tried to get the family to dance but they were having none of it, except for Marion, who is usually game for a laugh. We drowned out the rap coming from next door. After a while, a fleet of 1940s vehicles including a jeep started circling the estate, which was fun. I don't know who had organised it. We could hear other wartime tunes being played in other gardens.

The only person missing was Dad. Because of his age and vulnerability, we had to leave him in the living room so we could pass tea and cake to him and wave and blow kisses. But not being able to bring him outside made me feel teary. Having cared for him since Mum died, I haven't been able to hug or kiss him since the start of lockdown. I've never been distanced from him like this.

I do respect everything we've been trying to do to stop him from getting the virus and I completely endorse it. Marion has been with him since lockdown and has kept him safe and I've thanked her often. Perhaps it's that we used to watch *Dad's Army* together, and that I've listened to and loved all of his wartime memories; certainly, it's because no matter how annoying his dementia is, I've really missed him.

Anyway, I think that Marion had a reaction to all of this vigilance and care of him, just as I had a reaction from being distanced from him. It must have made her uneasy, having to watch over him all of this time and with few breaks. So, a while after Dad had blown me a kiss and then retired to his chair in the living room, I felt really sad and had this knee jerk reaction when I saw the front door left open.

I ran inside the house, into the living room, and sat on the floor before his chair. I wanted to explain again about the virus and how I couldn't come and see him – not that he would remember – but I simply wanted to. As I sat on the floor in front of him, he held out his hand to touch my cheek and just as I took his hand in mine, Marion appeared behind me.

"Are you trying to kill him?" she asked, in a voice like Mrs Danvers saying "Jump, why don't you jump?" I jest, but certainly she was very serious. I felt all the joy leaving my body in a long hiss of pain.

I understand how important it is to follow these rules but, at the same time, I hate the sense of paranoia it brings about. It's a little bit the same with other people I love. I think, I can't stop doing things that matter just because I'm sixty-two and there's a virus and, to an extent, people have to keep calm and carry on. Anyway, I left the house after she said that, and she came after me and didn't give me a hug, because that would be too risky, but she said she was sorry and that she loved me and I said that I understood. We have a very strong relationship. I've said things I regret to her and she to me, but we know how much we love each other and what we mean to one another. No hurt lasts long.

She has had to keep him safe for too long.

11th May

I decided, after VE Day, life being short and unpredictable as it is, that I was going to break the rules and take Dad out. With a bit of sympathy for the way I felt, Marion didn't argue with me. I knew he wouldn't remember that we'd been out, he never does, but that wasn't the point somehow. I promised that he wouldn't get out of the car and that I would wear a mask for the whole time, and I kept to my promise.

I took a cold can of lager with us and a clean glass. We drove into the countryside and I talked to him again, about when he was a boy, about his parents and his brother, about the Ministry of Agriculture and the army in Egypt, about Mum and the White Hart. His memory for the long past is quite good. We drove to Elsfield, Forest Hill, Wheatley, Stanton St John, all those places he knew well. "I went to Noke and nobody spoke. I went to Brill and they were silent, still. I went to Beckley and they spoke direc'ly…"

When we reached Royal Oak Farm, the pretty farmhouse overlooking the fields, the place he had his first job aged fourteen, I parked the car and got out, then poured him his lager from a can, as carefully as I could, although I was never good at working behind the bar as my sisters were. I opened the car door while he sat there, drinking the cold lager, and we gazed at the fields opposite the farm which stretch past the woods and towards Barton.

Friday 15th May

Caught up with James this evening, haven't seen him for a while and he's such a good man. I'm very proud of him. I'm very proud of all three of our children, but James is always peaceful to be around. I suppose one of the big factors in this is that he doesn't have children. He's had several really lovely girlfriends, but his relationships haven't lasted for one reason or another. I remember asking him once why he'd split up with a girlfriend that he'd had for eighteen months. He said that he'd been looking at another girl's legs in a pub. Just like his father.

James trained as a lawyer and worked for his father's firm for seven years before he decided that he wanted to do something else, but since then, he has mostly held short-term posts.

I think we are quite alike in our interests and in other ways. We both have an interest in history and geography, in places and plants, and we never run out of conversation. We sometimes have marathon Bananagram games or Draughts contests or go out for a meal together. But our favourite thing to do is to have a bonfire in the autumn and to sit before it with a Peroni beer, a drink James introduced me to long ago. It's not autumn, but I had accumulated a lot of rubbish from both Louise's and Harry's houses, stuff that I couldn't recycle or take to the dump, so we had a bonfire this evening.

It took a while for the bonfire to catch, but when it did, it burned well, and we sat talking and drinking Peroni until late, while the flames kept us warm on a cool evening.

25th May, Dad's Birthday!

I hang a banner around the bushes that face Dad's living room window. It says 'Happy Birthday, Dad!' in large, colourful letters. Through the day, we take our presents to him and at teatime, a cake. Howard, Michelle, Joseph and Edward come and we all sing 'Happy Birthday' while he is allowed to sit on a chair outside the front door. He smiles and looks pleased with it all.

When he first had dementia, I used to tell him that he was eighty-six, because I knew he was afraid of dying. He believed me, but then the time came when we had to tell him his real age.

After a while, while we eat cake and chat, he starts to ask, "Where's my lovely wife?" Marion and I feel sure in our hearts that he knows, because after a while of thinking, he will say, "In heaven?"

Often, now, we have to remind him of her name and when we say it, he remembers. I know how much he misses her. Every time something important or difficult happens, I want to tell her about it and am overcome by this terrible feeling of emptiness that she isn't there to tell. I find myself thinking about her all that evening, and of the last time that she and I shared, in the hospital, and the touching faith she had in me that somehow-I could move mountains.

ONCE, in the depths of night , I heard him call out to Mum.

"Bags? Come on my love, get back into bed, it's cold," he said. Then he went back to sleep.

Love is just there, even when you can't recall the name of someone you haven't seen for a few years but shared a lifetime with. Love hangs on even when someone is six feet under.

Amy's dream
Rose Cottage, 1910

The night was warm, and the smell of honeysuckle from the garden stayed with her despite the dream. In her slumbers, Amy suddenly found herself surrounded by deep virgin snow. Half awake, half asleep, she wondered whether she had a fever.

A bad dream, exactly the same as before. She mumbled incoherently, gave a small cry for help and struggled through the heaviness of it all to wake herself up. She stared through the dark at familiar objects: the ceramic washing bowl and pitcher, Earnest's trousers lying over the wooden stand. In the faint light of the moon, the objects took on a ghostly life of their own.

Who was the girl, blue eyes widening in shock and terror as she stared back at Amy through the mirror of her dream as though she was imploring her to help, but help with what?

Earnest worked too hard for them. She didn't want to wake him again, though she knew he would be kind, and she longed to have him pull her against him and hold her to sleep as he had the last time. The dream left her with a feeling of dread, making her heart beat in panic beneath the bodice of her nightdress. She stared at her husband, asleep on his belly, the patterned coverlet pushed into a heap across his buttocks. Sweat trickled down his spine in a silvery stream. He was so tired that he didn't stir when she sat up in the bed. His snores reassured her until at last she relaxed.

To her relief, the baby had not stirred in her wooden cot. Earnest had made the cot and Stella was the second child to sleep there. Amy leaned out across the bed to look at the little girl lying with her fist pressed to her lips, dark lashes closed over her cheeks, deep in sleep and dreaming.

Amy pushed herself back against the bolster and inhaled the scent of honey suckle and jasmine mingling in the air through the open window. She sniffed the familiar smells of the chickens and the greedy sow with her contented litter in their pigsty at the bottom of the narrow walled garden.

Earnest slept on, his fair hair matted to his forehead with sweat, the small moustache rising and falling on his fine face as it turned towards her, deep in sleep and oblivious to the obtrusive and incomprehensible sounds and the strange lights of her dream. Innocent of the explosive shimmer of coloured lights which shattered the air about her and lit up the white snow of her nightmare, something that she had only ever witnessed when gelignite was used in the quarries to free the stone.

The children slept on, Stella in her little crib, snoring like her father, a pink fist tucked beneath a rosy cheek. Bernard lay upon his side in the same small bed in which Earnest had lain as a baby.

And remarkably, the unborn child slept through Amy's own, fearful dream, seeming calm. Amy had never experienced bad dreams as a child, never woken to call her mother and yet, since moving into the cottage, the dream had come to her. The blue-eyed girl in the narrow mirror resembled her sister. When she thought about her family as she did often, it was that sister she missed the most, so close to her in age.

She was happy in this place, she reflected, happy with Earnest and the children. His own family were very kind to her, treating her as a prize. Yet, since they had moved into the cottage, where she was very content alone and by day, the same dream often plagued her.

Always she saw the girl's face first. A small, elfin face, so much like Amy's own that it startled her. But her own face was a little fuller, her own cheekbones less defined. Amy's hair was straight and fair. In the daytime she wore it in a bun; whereas the girl in the dream had thick, honey-coloured hair with one wave at the shoulders. But her eyes were like Amy's. A light, attractive blue, almost the colour of a summer sky. And, in some indefinable way, the girl felt a part of Amy.

Always the eyes stared out at her as the dream began, eyebrows drawn together in a frown of concentration, framed by the strange shape of the little mirror – a narrow reflection. Then suddenly, just before the flashing colours came, the girls mouth seemed to open in shock and she shouted something, as though she wanted Amy's help. It was always then that she would wake from the nightmare, unable to reach the girl, never able to solve the mystery. The girl's panic became her own, but Amy woke before the dream could harm her. Behind the girl, outside the room in which she was imprisoned, hard white crystals of snow swirled about them both. Always she felt the cold outside, breathing cloudy, frozen plumes of air that misted the little mirror.

A squashed piglet squealed suddenly and indignantly from the brick-built pigsty, bringing her back to the present. The little child inside her woke, stretching its limbs, kicking uncomfortably against Amy's bladder. Amy tensed, waiting for Stella to wake, but the little girl slept on.

Earnest rolled onto his back and flung out his arm towards her, linking his fingers through hers. She felt their roughness, calloused by the stone with which he worked.

"Are you dreaming again?" he mumbled, half asleep still, but anxious for her.

"No," she lied. "I have to go to the toilet, that's all."

He opened one eye, twisting his head to look at her. She knew that he didn't believe her but she didn't want to tell him. Sarah, his mother, treated her as her own daughter but she had heard the words from Sarah, in her own house, when Earnest had told her that Amy didn't sleep well since the pregnancy.

"She's a little fiddle footed, our Amy. Came with a silver spoon…" Sarah had whispered when she thought Amy was in the garden. The woman hadn't meant unkindness; she, like Earnest, was proud of her new daughter-in-law, although, perhaps, concerned for her son. The last thing Amy wanted was for Sarah to think her mad; she wanted Sarah's approval but it was true, at home, on the farm, she had been allowed to read and dream; she had been spoiled, perhaps. She knew how to cook but had rarely been expected to do it. It wasn't so, now.

She clambered from the bed, bare feet crossing to the chamber pot in the corner of the room. It was almost full.

Her bladder contained enough liquid to fill one of the stone jars in which Grampy Stephen made dandelion wine. Amy wrinkled her nose at the pot, half turning to the bed to ask Earnest to empty it, but he had fallen into a deep sleep once more. He would do anything for her, but he'd worked all that day in his father's stone yard moving the heavy, yellowed stone that was needed for repair work at Magdalen College. After this he had dug the potatoes. He'd a right to sleep.

There was more to her than a silver spoon. She would empty the pot herself.

The tiny staircase which Earnest had built spiralled from the bedroom where the family slept, to the scullery below. Amy waddled uncomfortably, pigeon-toed, carrying the full pot before her while minding the hem of her nightgown. First a boy, second a girl. This one would be a boy too, she could feel it, same as her own mother had.

She set the pot down on the stone floor and drew back the bolt as softly as she could so that she didn't wake her family.

Meg lay in her kennel outside. She lifted her soft black head as Amy came out into the garden. Meg brushed her feathery tail against the dry ground.

Amy walked a little way down the garden, emptying the full pot beneath bushes. Dispensing with her ladylike reputation, she decided that her bladder ached so much, she couldn't make the long walk across the garden to the latrine beside the pigsty. She looked up at the latticed window of their bedroom and then, quickly and furtively, stared at the houses on either side, to be sure that no one was watching; she dodged behind the coal shed and the gooseberry bushes, lifting her nightclothes to relieve herself into the emptied pot.

Earnest said she was like no other woman he had ever known. This wasn't so, although she might have been brought up a little differently to the Quarry women he was used to. For the most part, they were a friendly lot and she didn't understand their reputation for bad behaviour; some of the young men, perhaps, could be a little on the wild side.

Her eyelashes closed as she relieved herself. When she opened them, Meg was standing opposite her, head cocked, wagging her tail. "Lie down then. Good dog," she whispered, fondling her ears, and the old dog smiled at her familiar voice.

She returned to the open door, resting for a few moments upon the stool outside, the place where Earnest liked to smoke his pipe. She lifted her chin to the stars, leaning the back of her head against the rough stone of the cottage wall. So many stars, shining in the velvety sky. What were stars? She tried to recall what her brother had told her about them. But her mind returned to the dream as it always did. There could be no ghosts, surely, as there were in some houses? The building was new, built by Earnest and his brothers.

"If you're not a ghost, who are you?" Amy asked the stars.

The girl had the expression that Amy had seen many times on the faces of the village washerwomen as they worked their cloth with soap to remove a stain – a look of intense concentration, a difficult job at hand. If they failed to get the things clean, they wouldn't be paid.

She didn't think ghosts were real. For all those years at the farm, they had lived with the ghost of an old lady who walked through the chimney breast, so they said. But no one had ever seen it. To make them laugh, her father had once donned Grandma's black hat and cloak from the basket in the attic, walking towards them with his hands held out. It had made her younger sister cry and cling to her skirt.

Yet the dream was real and, sometimes, her own body would jerk and fall; for all the world it was as though someone had tipped her out of the bed. Both she and the girl in the mirror would be sent spinning through the whirling snow, through the cold dark night, until her body refused to tolerate the dream, and she woke with a start, grateful to be released.

Amy shivered. Back to bed, beside Earnest's consoling snores. Mercifully, the dream of the girl in the mirror never came more than once in a night. She would sleep, now.

Far away, at the foot of the garden, there was the noise of a fox scrambling over the wall beside the chicken coop. It had been before, which was why Meg was untethered. The old bitch left her kennel instantly, growling and snapping her jaws at it and the fox fled towards Saccy's Pit.

*

In their Sunday best, Earnest stooping a little to clasp Bernard's chubby fingers, the family walked from the church to the big house that Stephen, Earnest's father had built. Here he lived with his remaining, unmarried children and his wife, Sarah. The Coppocks were Methodist, mostly, but not Earnest's parents. His father, Stephen, had helped to build the church with a team of masons. Holy Trinity Church lay beside the meadows below the forest of Shotover, to the edge of the village. The morning sermon had been about kind, beneficent and Godly actions towards our fellow men, but most people knew it was directed at William, the elder Trafford, whose sons had set their dogs upon two lads who had strayed into the village from Headington. Earnest wasn't a churchgoer, at least he hadn't been before he married Amy. But this morning, Amy had wanted them to go together, as a family.

Stella wriggled in her arms. She had been a good little girl through the whole service, chewing the end of her toy rattle with hard gums that had covered her dress in dribble. The old people were kind and tolerant about the small noises she made but Mrs Gurl, the widow, had stared at them most of the service as though she was cross. Amy ignored it, feeling secure next to her little family. She spoke to Earnest about it as they wandered slowly along the church lane.

"Don't have to mind her," he said serenely. "She's a poor old woman, really. She lost three babies when she was young. Ask our Mum about it. People say she's a bit touched."

Amy felt bad for her then and made up her mind to try to talk to her the next time she saw her.

During the service, she had felt the baby kicking inside her and the memory of the previous night came to her. Should she pray for the girl? She seemed to be in trouble. Or was the dream something bad, the girl herself something bad: ungodly? Amy decided to pray for her anyway, as though she were a real person as, indeed, she seemed, those times when she came to Amy. Did the Bible not say, "I have not come to call the righteous, but sinners?" She felt that the girl was not this, a sinner, simply someone who needed help. So, Amy had prayed, silently moving her lips through folded fingers.

The little girl cried out suddenly, wanting to get down on the mossy grass. She had just begun to walk, wobbling on plump, unsteady legs. Amy crooned to her. If she put her on the path, they would be late for Sarah's. Plenty of time to walk when they arrived. Amy wanted to help with the cooking, show Sarah that she was more than a 'silver spoon'. She bounced Stella upon her arm and she stopped crying and giggled. It was hot; both she and the baby sweated beneath their bonnets and Amy's extra load drooped beneath her dress.

"Let me carry her. I can take her on my shoulders," Earnest implored.

"I'm alright. Almost there," she replied, feeling uncomfortable but strong enough as the child sat across her pregnant belly.

Bernard ran ahead of them. He was sure of the lane and where he should stop. His brown hair was shiny as a conker in the sunshine. When they walked alone, without Earnest's company, Amy made him walk beside her, inventing stories about the fairies she had seen in Coppock's Quarry to keep him going. She spoke animatedly, giggling as she described them to him, and her imagination was so convincing that Bernard hung upon her every word. It was a way of gluing him to her side. She didn't like it when he ran off, feared some of the Quarry dogs more than anything; they were not like gentle, obedient old Meg.

They stopped very briefly at the edge of Coppock's Quarry to pick the wild flowers growing there: cow parsley, red campion and corn cockle. She wanted to take some for Sarah to put in a jar. She picked them thoughtfully, while Stella sat on the ground and plucked at the flowers enthusiastically, removing them from the stalks. The green banks of the pit were studded with summer light and shade and shadow beneath the trees.

"No, little Stell. Don't eat it!" She brushed a wet dandelion stalk from Stella's gums.

Bernard had been practising blowing a piece of grass to make a reedy whistle, while his father showed him how to place the blade between his thumbs.

"Mamma, is there wolves in the woods?" he asked, looking thoughtfully towards the Shotover ridge.

"No wolves," Amy replied.

"There's boar, so they say," Earnest told him.

"What's boar?" Bernard asked, his head on one side and his eye closed to the sun.

"Big, dangerous piggies, like you, except with tusks!" His father grinned. He lifted the little boy and turned him upside down in his strong arms to make him laugh before setting him on his feet again.

"Are there?" Amy asked excitedly.

"Used to be, but I don't think so, not now. Come on, little piggy, you must be hungry." He grinned.

Earnest's mother and father owned one of the largest houses in the village. It had been built by Stephen and Earnest with the help of their friends and the men who worked with them. It was a barn-shaped building with tiny windows and Sarah, plump and bustling, kept it spotless and clean for her family and the many visitors who dropped in to take tea and to see how old Grampy was fairing. It was more than their home, it was the stone yard for the pony to bring the cart, laden with heavy stone, which was emptied and stacked in the yard.

On any other day but Sunday, the village would echo with the noise of metal on soft yellow limestone. But it was a sleepy, sunny Sunday and no one had thoughts of work but the vicar.

When she and Earnest had first married, and Earnest returned to his home with a wife no one had expected, Sarah had clearly been hurt at her absence from the wedding. But with time, and Amy's respect, she put this behind her, seemed to have blamed Earnest for it, anyway. Sarah was generally a jolly, optimistic person. To her credit, she had always made Amy welcome and sought out her company when she had time. And it was Sarah, not her own mother, who had attended to both Bernard's and Stella's births.

She was a good grandmother. She loved her grandchildren and didn't hesitate if Amy asked her to mind them for a while, always saying yes.

Now, the little family turned the corner of the house, crossing the dusty yard where the large blocks of yellowed stone were stacked against the sheds. Amy set Stella down and smoothed the wrinkled material of her dress and her large bump with fluttering fingers. She turned to Earnest, then brushed away the marks left on his waistcoat by Bernard's small booted feet. He stood patiently while she did so, then she kissed her forehead before they went inside.

Bernard had already flung himself at his grandmother to be smothered in her large, aproned breast before wriggling free to skedaddle towards the house. Stella took his place, younger and more cautious, staring up at Sarah with large brown eyes.

"Hello, my duck. Coming to Nanna?" Sarah offered the little girl her fingers. Stella accepted them and followed her inside.

The inside of Stephen's house was dark and cool, the light from the windows criss-crossing the beams and heavy wooden furniture with dusty sunshine. From the skillet on the stove rose the heavenly smell of pork, apples and rosemary.

Sarah greeted her son and daughter-in-law with a kiss for both, smiling at the flowers Amy handed to her, turning to take a bowl with which to arrange them.

"I'm sorry we are late; I'd wanted to help you with the cooking..." Her voice trailed guiltily.

"It don't matter, chick. I've had a peaceful morning. Gramps has behaved himself for a change."

The old man made no comment. He appeared to be sleeping on his day bed, the long, white beard rising and falling upon his chest and his mouth, a gaping, toothless cavern that yawned wide as he slept. Sometimes a member of the family would gently prod him to discern as to whether he had died at last.

By 'behaving himself', Sarah meant that he hadn't been shouting at her or demanding things today. On their last visit, the old gentleman had wandered down the garden, leaning upon his walking stick, but had then fallen into the long ditch between the garden and the blackberry bushes which grew there. Not for a long time did they hear his wavering cries for help; they had all been so animated in conversation that they hardly realised he had risen from the couch. When they found him, his shirt and beard were caught up on the thorny brambles and he had to be cut free before they could lift him out of the ditch. He wasn't too injured, and they bathed his cuts and scratches with witch-hazel.

The house that Earnest and Stephen had built several years ago was a grand one. It had four bedrooms and had been built right next to the stone yard where Grampy Coppock had worked all of his life, before the rheumatism left him crippled and stooped. He was bedridden now, except for visits to the latrine and an occasional wander along the garden path to admire his large vegetable patch and his pigs. He supervised the pig's castration, and added mumbled, incoherent words of wisdom about their health. His bed, night and day, was the couch beneath the window in the large room adjoining the scullery. This was as much for Sarah's convenience as his continued integration within family life, as then she didn't have to respond to the bang, bang, bang of his stick upon the floor or follow him up to bed each evening on a narrow wooden staircase.

"Let me help you, Sarah," Amy pleaded. "There must be something I can do." She stared about the kitchen, wanting to help but dismayed because everything appeared to have been done already.

"Sit yourself down at that table while I get a drink for you. You look too hot; your cheeks are flushed; that's what you can do. We don't want that baby coming too quick. If you insist, you can make the crumble for the Goosegogs."

She bustled about, setting a bowl of flour before her daughter-in-law, looking distractedly towards the door through which Earnest had wandered after the children.

"Where is that husband of mine? He said he'd be a few minutes. He was going to visit William; heaven knows what for unless to borrow summat. Better not have strayed towards that ungodly Masons or I'll give 'im what for..."

It was as Amy busied herself with the flour that Stephen arrived, a little flushed from his brisk walk, but just as eager to see his grandchildren. He was familiar with his wife's unfettered threats, which were all huff and puff and could be quashed with a kiss, as a rule. He set Bernard down and took something wooden, like the top of a spade, from his trouser belt.

"Knew I'd given it to someone." He smiled, waving the dibble at them before patting Amy's arm.

"Good," Sarah remarked without looking. And how's William?"

"He has a guest."

"Oh?" Now Sarah turned about to stare at him with more interest. Who would be visiting William Kimber on a Sunday?

Stephen sat opposite his daughter-in-law, sweeping Stella off her feet to sit on his lap. The little girl's face puckered as though she was about to cry before he handed her the wooden dibble to play with.

"Do you recall the tall, well-to-do chap who watched the Morris dancers at Christmas?"

"Can't say that I do..." Sarah mumbled.

"I know who you're talking about. He watched them for a long time, took a great interest in William's concertina playing." Earnest's eyes narrowed in memory before he frowned at his father. "Dad, take that thing away from Stell', she's going t' get splinters in her mouth..."

"He's called Cecil, apparently, or Mr Sharp, but William called him Cecil," Stephen continued. "He came this morning. Sittin' on a stool while William sings old songs and plays the concertina and he writes the songs down. They were talking about pigs an all."

"That'll go straight to his head!" Earnest scoffed. "Visits from the gentry."

"Right," Sarah interrupted, her cooking done and not particularly interested in the subject at hand. "Earnest, see if old Grampy is still sleeping. I'll feed him when we've finished if so; otherwise, can you bring him to the table please?"

Grampy wasn't asleep. He lay very still, deafly listening to their conversation. When Stephen covered him with his shadow, the old man called out in a husky groan, "I'll have it here, Sarah."

"Well, if you're hungry now, you'd best come to the table or you'll be slopping food everywhere. I can't feed you and feed myself."

Her tone was stern, but then Grampy Coppock could be very argumentative and it was generally Sarah who cared for him, washing him and spoon feeding him with genuine patience and compassion if not always fondness. Over the years she had learned that better progress was made if she refused to be argued with.

She crossed the kitchen to join her son. "Earnest, you take his other arm."

Between them, they lifted the frail old man to his feet, leading him to a chair as his legs wobbled and his feet dragged drunkenly across the flagstones. At the table, Sarah covered his white beard with a cloth, tying it behind his neck, then lifted the heavy skillet to the table and started to serve the stew to her family.

When they were all intent upon eating, and after a little while of banter between them, Sarah levelled her gaze at Amy.

"What about you, love, morning sickness gone now?" She asked the question gently. Beneath the gentle tone, Amy heard both concern and a reluctance to probe too far.

Amy nodded. "Yes Sarah, thank you, all gone now." She knew in an instant that Earnest must have told his mother about the strange dreams which woke her. She couldn't blame him; he had been worried, but she did not wish to discuss them with Sarah who might believe her possessed with madness.

"But the dream keeps you awake," Earnest said quietly, bravely, reaching across the table to take her fingers.

She wouldn't talk about it. Not here. It was just a dream, that girl with the blue eyes, the girl she was unable to help. What was the point? She also felt a kind of strange loyalty to the girl, a connection with her that she couldn't explain to anyone but which made her feel defensive in the face of questions.

"Yes, they wake me sometimes, but they are only dreams after all. When the baby comes, I expect they will go."

Sarah nodded, smiling benignly.

"All you need know, Amy, is that if you are worrying about anything, anything at all, you can talk to me. I'm always happy to help. You know that. As you say, it's probably something to do with the pregnancy."

She pulled back in her chair and gently slapped the table.

"Let me have the children in the morning. Bring them to me when Earnest has gone to work. You can rest a bit longer in bed. Your cheeks are very pale and your eyes smudged beneath." Her eyes widened in thought. "Here's an idea! Let him bring them with him after breakfast; you can rest a while and come to collect them when I've given them their midday meal."

Amy looked from one to the other of the children, now munching on pieces of bread they had dipped in pork fat. She thought of the yawns she'd tried to suppress in the daytime. It wouldn't hurt to grab some rest.

"If you are sure, it would be helpful perhaps, just tomorrow, so I can get a little more sleep," she said gratefully.

After all, Sarah had looked after the children before and she was very good with them, Amy thought later as she picked the Buddleia that straddled the alleyway from a large garden. It was called Coppock's Alleyway: her own married name.

Earnest and the children helped her to carry the purple blooms home. The baby had kicked inside her on the walk, and although it made her tired, it made her feel contented too.

She arranged her flowers in two cracked jars and a vase, to stand in the kitchen window, and in their own bedroom. Then she dressed the children for bed, telling them two stories, one about an escaped cow of her childhood, the other Stella's favourite, *Little Red Riding Hood*.

Then she sang 'Come Little Leaves' and 'Naughty Jack', which always made them laugh. Stella happily clambered all over her brother, pulling at Amy's hair and kissing her. It was the routine which made them sleep more than anything else. The sound of their mother's voice, the songs they always asked for.

*

The perfume of the flowers helped her to sleep undisturbed by the dream until the cockerels began their bugle and the sun streamed through the gap in the curtains. Then she felt Bernard's small, plump fingers reaching out to her beneath the eiderdown, and she reached out and drew his plump little body into the bed beside her, kissing his cheek and smelling his hair.

She lay between Bernard and Earnest for about half an hour until Earnest woke. He stroked her arm and tickled her neck with his moustached kiss. He rose from the bed to dress for the day, while she listened to the familiar movements. He came to the place where Bernard was snuggled against her and picked him up.

"Come on, my boy. Don't wake Mummy. Let's get your sister up. Time for breakfast."

She drifted back into sleep, a lovely luxury. How long she slept for, she couldn't be sure. When she woke, there was only the sound of bird song and the distant pounding echo of picks against stone. There was silence downstairs. Earnest and the children had gone. It must have been Meg who woke her, barking at a cat for daring to enter her domain.

Her limbs felt heavy, still, but the fog of tiredness had subsided. She had to get up; there was a lot to do. The chickens would peck at their own eggs if she left them for too long. The white cotton lay upon the dresser with the needle and thread, waiting for her attention, too. The child inside her slept on.

Amy padded downstairs, barefooted, to the kitchen to pour the pan of water, which was still lukewarm, into a large white bowl. She carried it back upstairs to wash.

Through the bedroom window she saw the half-finished sundial that Earnest was making for the garden. He'd left his tools on the chopping block beside them. She must remember to remove the tools before Bernard could get hold of them.

When she closed the window, the sun had grown weaker. Clouds were scuttling across the sky. It would rain later.

After she had dressed in her everyday frock, she turned the small, round mirror that Earnest used to shave towards her to look at her own reflection.

The smudges beneath her eyes had gone. There was colour in her cheeks once again. She had slept peacefully for the first time in a long while, a deep, dreamless sleep.

In a moment, the girl's face stared back at her, every muscle tensed in a grimace framed by the mirror. Amy stiffened; it had to be a trick of the imagination, vanishing as quickly as it had appeared. She clutched her pregnant belly instinctively. Was she going mad? She had half feared that Earnest and his mother might think it.

Her breathing quickened. She had seen the girl as clearly as if she were before her now. Her long auburn hair, the small, upturned nose, the blue eyes wide with concentration, the movement of the stark trees behind and the flurry of snow. Why now, in the light of day? And the sharp tingling in her arms spread to her fingertips.

So real was it that she looked over her shoulder, as if she might see the girl there. Something was wrong.

She listened for a moment to the thud of her own heart as she tried to control the panic inside her. Then her fingers stumbled rapidly over the task of buttoning her blouse.

Ridiculously she ordered the child inside to answer her, stroking her own belly for reassurance, and after a few minutes she was comforted by a small kick.

Not the child.

Not this child. It repeated itself in her head, a malignant whisper.

Amy ran. Too fast. Descending the narrow staircase, leaving the chickens, the door to the cottage hanging open with Meg chasing after her as though it were a game. She ran through the garden gate, the child bouncing up and down inside of her.

Fat Mrs Hedges stopped to stare after her, a basket of onions on her arm.

"You alright, my duck? You're gunna have that baby early if you don't slow down."

Amy didn't stop, didn't answer, didn't wave. She ran on.

She began to sob, little gasps of panic and grief she could no longer stifle. There was something wrong. A sequence of small electric shocks pinched the skin of her arms and fingers as she ran toward the Beaumont Road, turning into the alleyway – her heart pounding with the fear that had overwhelmed her. She ran into the alleyway beside the Chequers pub where the Morris men met. Outside the pub, a row of old, toothless men called out to her in astonishment and amusement, amazed to see Earnest's gentle wife racing along the road in a blur of petticoats.

She took a shortcut through the nettles, heedless of their sharp barbs, running breathlessly, senselessly towards the New Cross Road. She passed the men working deep inside Coppock's Pit, following the very path she had taken the day before with her little family. She was running so blindly, she didn't see Mark Kerry walking towards her, or the set frown on his troubled face. She stopped, suddenly, seeing Stephen's friend before her. Panting, she dodged to sidestep him until he placed a hand on her arm.

"Mrs Coppock? I've been sent to fetch the doctor..."

He reached out to her, his cap screwed in his fist, his broad face afraid.

"I'm so sorry, little Bernard, he..."

But Amy didn't wait to hear more, pushing past him, uttering it aloud in a plea to God to be heard, "No!"

She had almost reached the house when the piercing whinny of a horse caught her heart like a spur, strangling her to stillness. At the corner, she fell against the wall, clutching her elbows across the pregnant belly. She stared at the men, kneeling as though in prayer, helpless and bare-headed, while dogs barked in the distance at the sudden, frightening noises.

The large bay horse lay helpless on its side, its hair gleaming with sweat, pinned to the floor by the harness. The cart had collapsed with the weight of the stone. Only the wheel spun on its broken axis, and the only human sound came from Sarah whose confidence and surety had been felled in one moment that would hurt and damage her for ever. Her cries, shuddered sobs so terrible to hear.

And Amy heard Earnest's voice. A loud wail of pain on one single note, an animal caught in a trap, and she looked for him.

He rose above the others, slowly, helplessly. Lifted something in his arms. A dog, perhaps, Amy told herself, hoping and praying, just a dog.

But when Earnest turned away from them to see her against the house, his face crumpled in anguish and despair.

A small, plump leg in its little man trousers fell limply from the jacket he had wrapped around the boy. Their boy.

The small arms were twisted backward, limp and swinging. The little head she had cradled that morning was now a pulpy, bloody mess. Thick red blood, dripping onto the yellow stone dust, as Earnest held the lifeless child to his chest.

*

Second row from the back – the fifth young woman
from the left is Stephanie, the eighth figure is Cynthia
and beside her is Christine

Christine 1943

Not once in all the years had Amy seen the girl or dreamed of her before last night.

She dreamed of Bernard often. In her dream, she could smell his little body, and feel his baby softness and sweetness. Those dreams were like being with him in heaven, always good, always with her arms about him, holding him safe against her heart.

They had buried him in the churchyard of Holy Trinity, a little grave for a little boy who had been the centre of their world, their pride and joy. Every day, for so many years, Amy had visited his grave to lay whatever flowers she could find upon it. No one prevented it. Everyone knew how sorrow had changed her, sorrow and anger.

As the other children were born, people suggested that it would ease her sadness. To an extent it did, but you never forget, never really recover and never lose your deep love for that, one, special child.

Earnest had made his gravestone. After several years, her anger seeped away, but not the feeling of loss and guilt.

She forgave them all, in the end. Certainly, at first, Amy had blamed everyone. She blamed poor Sarah; she blamed Earnest and his men; she blamed God but most of all she had blamed herself. She did not blame the girl. The girl hadn't caused it. She'd been trying to tell Amy what would happen, of that, Amy felt convinced. She told no one this, except her unmarried sister, who, to her joy in later years, came to live in Headington Quarry.

When she thought of Bernard, she imagined what he would have looked like if he had lived, her little friend who would have been such a good and loving son, and how she would have been so proud of him in adulthood.

When the next baby came, they called him Ronald; born into a bittersweet sadness, he had a solemn and serious expression which both parents did everything to change, and life went on. Amy bore four more girls and another little boy. They were happy children who loved life, playing together and quarrelling in equal measure.

It took many years for her to trust others with her children but, in the end, they grew older and she couldn't imprison them, had to let them roam the alleyways with other children and send them to the school beside the church where Stella became a young teacher. She had to release Sarah from her own grief as well as Bernard's father.

"Well," she thought, staring towards the new morning light through the curtains, "I'll see him soon, and Earnest, too." He had died several years ago from the stone upon his lungs. She didn't need anyone to tell her that this pain in her side meant that she was dying. Nothing could be done, although Doctor Richards came whenever Stella asked him to, injecting her with something to alleviate the pain. He was a good man and knew the family well.

She would be sixty-six this year, if she lived that long. It didn't matter. She was tired of being tired, of worrying about them. Stella and her young husband were very kind to her and now they lived in Stephen's house. Amy now spent her remaining days in the double bed once shared by Sarah and Stephen. There was only one thing that she wanted from the living. She wanted Dennis to come home. The letter that came from the Red Cross said he was in a prisoner of war camp. At least Dennis was alive, her youngest child. She wanted to see him, just once, before she died, to know that he was well.

She hadn't dreamed of the girl for all these years, until last night. The dream was still disturbing, the girl staring out at her through the little mirror as though something terrible was about to happen and she needed help to stop it; but Amy herself was helpless. Perhaps she had come to tell her about Amy's own imminent death; maybe she was an angel.

This time, Stella came to her having heard her mumbling in her sleep, believing that she was in pain.

"Just a dream," she said. "It's gone now." She hadn't wanted to worry her daughter, to disturb her sleep. Only Earnest had known what the dreams were about; she'd spoken to no one else.

"What are you trying to tell me, girlie?" She had whispered this aloud in the darkness.

Was it Miriam? So besotted with the American soldier, handsome and high ranking? Miry, so headstrong and independent. Ron wouldn't let his little sister go; she had heard him telling her so. But when the war came to an end, which, God help them, it must someday, would she still listen to her brother? She had an unyielding determination, soft and beautiful to look at but with a will of iron.

She loved them all, but it was Ron who reminded her of Earnest and that little boy who had gone to heaven so early in his life. Ron who had Earnest's looks and sense of humour.

The ache in Amy's side and her back was not unlike the ache in pregnancy, though far more painful. She tried to lift herself, to ease her position on the bed. Later, when she had finished her tasks, Stella would come upstairs to draw back the curtains, turning Amy onto her side and helping her to the toilet.

Amy had Grampy Coppock's stick with which to bang upon the bedroom floor if she needed anything, but she rarely used it. Stella had too much to do as it was.

Ron was away also, not fighting, but using his technical skills to repair damage to aeroplanes that had returned from bombing missions. He was allowed to return to his family for short spells only.

On his last return, he'd told them the tale of the headless airman, strapped into his seat, and of the bloody head in its helmet that he had found and retrieved. It had rolled to the back of the plane. He, too, had nightmares after it.

Earlier in the morning, there had been several explosions from the direction of Risinghurst. No longer gelignite for the nobblers to break open the stone, but the American soldiers who were based on the Miller's land at Shotover House, practising with firearms.

The pits had been overworked, becoming dangerous and exciting playgrounds for the children. They were beautiful and familiar pock marks on the village landscape, where the gnarled roots of trees and ivy smothered the crumbling stone banks. Ron and Dennis were fine stonemasons, Earnest had been their teacher and Amy had been proud of that – then the war took them away.

The latest tale from Miriam's young man was that the Americans had accidentally blown up an ancient wall on the estate, so that the Miller's private herd of muntjac deer had escaped to roam the surrounding countryside.

She had smiled at the story. Her girls – women now – would not be happy when the war ended. That wasn't true, of course. Everyone wanted the war to end and they wanted to have their brothers at home once more, only they were having such a good time dancing to Glen Miller and Victor Sylvester and doing something called the Jitterbug with young Yanks, that they would surely miss these things. There had been fights between the Americans and the British boys, so Miriam had said, as well as some threats from the white Yanks that they would beat up any black soldiers who came to the dances. It seemed ungracious when they were all fighting on the same side. The girls assured Amy that they were keeping well away from any fights. She wasn't sure whether she could believe them, all the same; especially Miry and Molly who seemed often telling her half-truths.

Amy slept until past ten o'clock, until she heard giggling in the kitchen below. The giggles came from her three granddaughters, Ron's children, a spirited trio. She heard Frank talking to them. Stella would be at school by now.

In a while, they would come upstairs to see her, having finished with school. Cynthia was a secretary at the dairy;

Stephanie was about to go to a teacher training college while young Christine was yet to get a job. Amy had been concerned about all of them. The girls idolised their three young aunts, but recently they had begged to be taken to one of the dances at the base. Really, they were a little young. Cynthia was eighteen, that wasn't so bad, Stephanie seventeen, but little Christine was only just sixteen.

The giggles were stifled as they reached the landing outside Amy's room, coming upstairs in their bare or stockinged feet, shoes removed. Amy smiled at the sounds and waited, her eyes wandering to the door. It was often deathly dull being an invalid. Their company lifted her spirits.

Cynthia pushed it, peering around the door, wide smile, dancing blue eyes. Her face was framed by short glossy dark hair which curled at the neck. Each of Ron's four children had their mother's dark hair, but they each had the blue eyes of the Coppocks. She stepped into the room, closely followed by her two sisters: Stephanie, considered the prettiest; and Christine, the youngest of the three girls. All blessed with pretty faces.

Stephanie held a cake on a plate before her, which she placed upon the bedside table. It was a small but grand cake, a work of art such as Amy had never seen before. A fairy cake topped with pink icing and butterfly wings. Whether her stomach would allow her to digest it was another matter.

"Goodness me. Where did you get that?" In this strange and terrible return of war, Stella had returned from Mr Deard's grocery shop a few days before with her ration coupons spent, saying, "Still no sugar. We'll have to ask Mr Berry for some of his honey."

"From the party!" Stephanie said, unable to stifle her excitement.

"What party was that?" Amy smiled, readily guessing the answer.

"At the base, at the Churchill, the American base there. Milton asked us."

Amy fought with the urge to raise a disapproving eyebrow. Milton might be her son-in-law, one day soon. You were only young once, she told herself.

"So, did you go, Christine?" She levelled her gaze at the youngest with an innocent smile.

The girl nodded. Quieter than the older two, sweet natured and generous with her time, she visited Amy more often. Amy patted the bed beside her and took Christine's small hand in hers. The child sat down on the quilt, mindful of the swelling and the pain in her grandmother's side. She was the prettiest of the three in Amy's book, although she considered herself to be plainer. She didn't yet wear make-up, and she always wore her hair down and, as yet, without styling it. Chestnut brown hair, with a permanent natural kink at the shoulder.

She couldn't blame Edna. It would have been hard to stop Christine from going when her older sisters had been invited. She knew that from her own experiences with teenage girls. But Ron wouldn't like it. Christine was his special girl, the one who always ran errands for him, the sporty child. He wanted her to go to teacher training college like Steph.

"Did you dance?" Amy asked her.

Christine smiled, a wry dimpling of the corner of her mouth. "A bit, but I'm not very good. I only danced with Steph."

"Steph's not so good; she fell over!" Cynthia giggled, while Stephanie glared at her.

"I was alright. I slid in my heels, quite a few people came to rescue me, including Liam…"

Amy didn't ask who Liam was. Stephanie had blushed at her sister's teasing.

There was a whiff of nicotine on Cynthia's summer frock. Well, she was an adult now, working in Oxford as a secretary. Amy supposed she might be able to afford cigarettes.

She patted Christine's hand. She had always been a skinny little girl who wore her older sister's dresses, but she always looked nice. All the girls did; their mother wouldn't have had it any other way. Edna was handy with a needle. When Cynthia and Stephanie were infants, they had worn tiny woollen coats. Marjorie, amused, said that they looked like the princesses Elizabeth and Margaret.

As Amy smiled at Christine, she realised for the first time that the girl was skinny no longer, but developing a fuller figure. It startled her. She hadn't seen the girl for a few weeks; the pale cheeks were familiar, but the roundness in her breasts was something new. Amy sucked at her bottom lip, grabbed suddenly by unwanted concern.

"I would really like to see your mum for a chat," she said. "Do you know whether she might be coming here this week?"

Cynthia shrugged. "Don't know, Nanna, shall I ask her?"

Amy nodded and feigned a smile.

The girls stayed for twenty minutes or so after that, bringing a little of the outside world into Amy's life. It occurred to her that, as they were there to help, she would like to see the bird that sung on her windowsill in the morning, perhaps glimpse the people passing in the street, be part of the world once more, at least for as long as she could. She asked them to call up Frank and between them, little by little, they moved her heavy bed towards the window so that she could part the curtains herself.

When they left, soft hair tickling her cheek as they kissed her goodbye, she was tired once more. She reached out for the cake, touching the icing with her fingertip and putting it to her lips. That was enough. She stared through the window for a while, seeing a car and a young woman with a black perambulator. The sun streamed through the gap in the curtains.

She thought back to another hot summer and to the girl, wondering why she had come after all this time until sleep overtook her.

*

When the girls skidded breathlessly into the kitchen, arguing about who had taken the Pond's cream from the dressing table, their mother was on her knees in the pantry as she mopped the floor with a soapy rag. Her small, bony bottom wriggled from left to right as though she were dancing. There were ants again. Edna hated them, squashed them with her thumb without compassion.

The pantry shelves were less full, these days, but neatly stacked with the jams that Stella gave her and other precious foods in tightly screwed jars. The pantry was painted white, the coolest place to be on a hot day.

Her house was her pride and joy. Ron and his brother had built it, just as Earnest and Stephen had built theirs. A modern house with five bedrooms and a large living room, it had a sitting room and a large kitchen, and it was the thing that Edna loved best, after Ron and the children. All life in the house, all events, all ordinary, daily activities happened in the kitchen and sitting room, while the large living room was a show room, kept for Christmases, special occasions and guests to the house. Ron had built a beautiful fireplace made from real Italian marble.

Edna stood now, wiping her brow with a handkerchief drawn from her bra.

She was not beautiful as her children, exactly, but there was a mischievous side to her, a wonderful spark of fun in the dark eyes. Her children had not known their maternal grandmother, but according to Edna, her own mother, Florence had been an illegitimate baby, had grown up in Windsor, where she met an Italian who didn't hang around for too long. Her own mother had known disgrace. Edna lived in fear of disgrace.

Her hair had grown back now, at long last. For a while, after Ron had left for the Ministry of War, she had been anxious about most things, from paying bills to feeding the children. She developed alopecia, which she had gradually recovered from. Dr Richards said this was caused by stress. Her hair had fallen out in great clumps, so she was forced to wear a hat to leave the house.

"What on earth's the matter now?" she asked the three girls, a little irritably.

"I bought the cream in Oxford with my money. Give it back!" Cynthia shrieked, indignantly, fists clenched in angry balls.

"I told you, I haven't got it!" Stephanie replied with equal force. As usual, Christine stood back from the terror of a real cat scrap between her older sisters, loitering outside the kitchen in the sunshine and shadows of the garden.

"Give it a rest, both of you. I don't want the Wilson's hearing you! You left the cream in the loo, Cynthia. No one took it."

"Oh." She stared with narrowed eyes at her sister. "Well, I didn't, so she must have put it there. Nanny Amy wants to see you," she added, taking a slightly green, slightly sour apple from the fruit bowl and munching on it happily. "Well, she didn't exactly put it like that. She asked if you would be popping over at any time this week."

Their mother collapsed into a chair, tired from the cleaning, tired of worrying. She stared up at them with a puzzled frown.

"Oh? Why would she say that, I wonder?"

Edna often popped over to see Stella, and always made a point of seeing Amy, but it was rare that Amy would make a point of asking for her to visit. The old lady was very ill. Perhaps, she mused, it had something to do with Ron.

Geoffrey, her youngest child, a skinny, gap-toothed comic of eight years, alternately spoiled and shouted at by his older sisters, ran into the kitchen clenching his favourite toy of the moment, an iron aeroplane. He emitted the sound of a bomber, plunging it into the fruit bowl. Stephanie lightly slapped the back of his head with her hand as he passed. He dodged her to run out into the garden, passing Christine, the one he always sought out in any upset.

Still musing upon Amy's request, Edna carried the bowl of dirty water outside to the front of the house, slopping it over the roses planted by Ron. There, she nodded briefly at Mr Webb from the house opposite across the grey stone wall and looked up at a pale sky, smudged and scorched by the sun. It had been so dry; the grass was parched corn colour. It would rain before long. She blew out her cheeks in a sigh and stepped back into the kitchen.

"I'd better go then; Dad would be upset if I didn't. Besides, she never usually sends for me," she said aloud. But the girls had retreated to their rooms. She was left, lips parted, hanging upon the last word.

She went into the hallway, gazing at her reflection in the mirror, patting her short, dark, bobbed hair into shape. She wished her nose were less snubbed. Dr Richards said that she was too skinny, that she should stop giving her rations to the children. At least her hair was growing back; she would no longer need to wear a scarf over her head when she went out.

Edna caught Christine's reflection in the mirror as the girl paused at the foot of the stairs on her way to the loo. The summer frock seemed tight on her all of a sudden. She turned, resting a hand upon her daughter's shoulder, examining the front of the dress with a critical eye.

"Have you lost a button? There are some in the needle box. Go and match it up and stitch it back on please, or change the dress. It's too tight, Christine, why don't you put on another frock?"

The other girls might have argued, but Chris did not. She peered over her chin at the place, then lifted her head and nodded in agreement.

In a reaction that was swift and tender as it was rough, Edna pulled the girl towards her and kissed her cheek. She wasn't given to sudden demonstrations of love, but it was good not to be argued with when life was often so difficult. Christine smiled, placing her arms around her mother's neck for a moment. "I'm growing, aren't I?"

Edna smiled. "Too fast."

"When I've done that, do you mind if I go over to Joan's house for a couple of hours?"

Her mother bit her bottom lip in thought. "I suppose not, as long as you're back for dinner."

Edna thought about her mother-in-law again. She would go, for sure, but the air was so heavy just now and, even at weekends, Geoffrey woke her at such an early hour. A morning lie in would be nice. She gazed longingly at the sofa. A nap first, before getting the dinner. Then she would walk to Stella's house.

She was asleep with one arm flung over her forehead when the thunder rolled. A distant hammer of drums towards Littlemore that darkened the Headington sky. Edna slept against the cushions, lips parted, a blessed escape from a mountain of worries.

She didn't hear the giggling from the bedroom above, or see Christine creep downstairs to retrieve her Mac from the hall stand, then hastily cross to the front door of 19 New Cross Road before her mother woke.

But from her invalid bed, Amy had watched as large, bulbous raindrops started to burst against the windowpane. She had seen the young man in the long grey Macintosh, who waited beneath an umbrella which dwarfed him, waiting on the corner for Christine.

*

Edna walked briskly along the New Cross Road, dodging the trees that were still wet with rain. She recited the chant "Margarine, bread, milk..." skirting Mr Perks' large white amicable goat, who had escaped into the road yet again. Sometimes the children helped Mr Perks to get the beast back into the garden. It never seemed to get into too much trouble, although it had once eaten a tea towel hanging on the line.

She wasn't going to the shop, but felt nervous, reciting her shopping needs always calmed her. She supposed she was worrying about what Amy had to say. It wasn't like her mother-in-law to summon her to the house, as a rule.

The house that Stephen had built was no longer a stone yard. A fine garden covered the place where the cart had fallen, crushing the little boy. Edna glanced up at Stella through the kitchen window; she was peeling potatoes at the sink.

It was a beautiful house, little changed from the time that Sarah and Stephen lived in it. Edna had envied Stella the house for a while, with its beautifully polished dresser adorned with old-fashioned lamps and floral teacups. But Ron had built her a house to be proud of, a modern house, and the envy dissipated with time.

She enjoyed Stella's company and her sister Doris' company, too. They were both teachers. Edna was a little in awe of them; she didn't believe herself to be very clever.

Now, Stella twisted around to smile at Edna, standing inside the open doorway. "Hello, come for a cup of tea?" she asked.

"Don't worry if you're busy," she said apologetically.

"Just getting dinner. Plenty of time. I was about to make a pot. Sit yourself down. Richard, move those cars for Aunty Edna."

Richard was about the same age as Geoffrey, a plump little boy, the spitting image of Amy rather than Stella with his soft fair hair. He crossed the room on his knees to drag the small tin cars into a box.

"Is Geoffrey coming?" he asked.

The two cousins were good friends, only the last time they were all here, the boys had fallen out and had fisticuffs in the yard. This time, Edna had decided to leave Geoffrey with his older sisters.

"Amy told the girls earlier that she hadn't seen me in a while. That's why I popped in, really. Is she sleeping. I don't want to disturb her?"

"No. She was awake when I went up there a few minutes ago. That's why I was making the tea."

Edna nodded her head, watching her as Stella tipped the potatoes into a pan. She was like her mother in so many ways, but earthier, a stronger build. "Don't think she'll live to see another Christmas." Stella sighed. "I'm going to miss her so much."

There was a small catch in her voice. Edna thought of her own mother, of her death, and was sorry.

She poured the tea through the strainer into two China teacups and handed one to Edna; then the two women sat together in the kitchen and talked about their boys for a while.

"She didn't say why she might want to see me just now?" Edna asked, a little nervously.

"No. She hasn't mentioned anything to me." Stella shrugged. "Maybe she missed you these past couple of weeks, missed Ron. Or, perhaps she has something particular that she wants to give you, something not in the will," Stella suggested hesitantly.

Edna nodded and smiled. A little while later, she took the cup of tea upstairs to Amy's room, carrying it with concentration as the pretty cup rattled on the saucer.

Amy was propped up against the pillows, her fingers rearranging a hot water bottle beneath the duvet. She threw Edna a smile.

"Hello, love. It's so nice to see you. Pull that chair across, come and sit down."

Edna set the teacup upon the table, kissed her mother-in-law's papery cheek and dragged the armchair closer to the bed.

"Would you like me to hold the cup for you?" Edna asked.

Amy shook her head, gesturing for the tea to be handed to her. The cup rattled against the saucer again. "Don't scald yourself," Edna said, reaching out to help, but Amy waved her away.

"It won't be hot. Stell' always brings it with plenty of milk."

"You've changed the room around," Edna said, waiting as Amy drank. "How are you?" It sounded silly to her own ears. She added, "Is Doctor Richards coming regularly?"

Amy smiled. "Oh yes. He comes quickly when I need him, on his bicycle. He's a good man." She took a small sip of the tea and looked up at Edna. "The girls are growing fast, so grown up now," she began.

"Yes. I think they miss their father, though. Perhaps Geoffrey misses him more," Edna mused. "Still, at least he's safe, here."

"When is Ron due for leave?"

"Towards the end of the month. They write to him, of course." She stared at the glorious colours of the beech tree across the road. The rain had stopped at last. Puffy white clouds hurtled in the wind across a bright blue sky.

Amy's small fingers reached for Edna's hand, startling her. Her thoughts had so easily drifted to Ron.

She frowned a little as Amy chewed her lip, as though wanting to speak, but thinking carefully on the words.

At last, Amy said, "I have a feeling about Christine."

Edna gazed blankly at her. "A feeling, about what?"

What on earth could the woman mean?

"I've been thinking about her, a lot. Her body has changed shape; she has changed, Edna…"

"What are you saying?" Edna's voice was fractured. "I think I know my own daughter, Amy." It sounded a little snappy, irritable, as she said it. "What do you mean?" she asked again, frustrated but softening her tone.

"She has a boyfriend." Amy squeezed Edna's fingers tightly. "I suspected it, but this afternoon I saw him waiting on the corner of the road under a brolly, and she met him there." Her voice was laden with apology.

Edna shook her head. "No. This afternoon she asked my permission to see her friend for a couple of hours. It can't have been her; you must be mistaken."

Not Christine. Christine never lied to her. On the rare occasions she had, she gave herself away by turning red as a beetroot. Why was she saying these things? Amy had never been unkind to her, not ever. Why now, when she was dying? And what was she implying? Changes, indeed!

Amy's brow creased in anguish. She fell silent for a while, wishing that she hadn't said anything at all. "Perhaps it wasn't Christine I saw, maybe another girl. But talk to her about it, Edna. I know how busy you've been, and how worried about things. I'm telling you because I think it's important. Maybe talk to her at the very least..."

She winced, then. Clutching at her side. Edna rose from her chair to help her.

"Are you all right? Do you want me to call Stella?"

"No. It'll be fine. I'm sorry, I didn't want to upset you. You know I'm very fond of you both."

Edna nodded, her voice softening. "Stop worrying, it won't make you feel any better." She pushed the chair away from the bed. "I will talk to her. I'll come next week and send Steph with some of my chamomile tea for you. I've worn you out. Get some rest, now."

Amy nodded and smiled, watching her, glad not to have lost a friend. But her eyes were closed to the window now, so she didn't see the small, proud, angry woman leaving the house, marching along the street with hurt and anxiety etched upon her face.

*

The front door slammed shut, only in part, the blustery wind.

She sat upon the staircase, forehead in her hands. Anger had given her a headache. Anger with Amy; irrational anger with Christine because she didn't know... she didn't know.

When she entered the house, the girl's laughter had ceased abruptly with the slammed door. Their mother didn't slam doors as a rule. The two young women peered over the banister rail. Geoffrey trailed down the staircase. She wasn't aware of him until he sat on the step behind her.

"Can I go and meet the others? We're only going to the field behind the vicarage..." He had reverted to a wheedling, infant's voice to persuade her. He put a hand upon her shoulder. She was about to say no, too close to teatime but stopped herself. He had met a small group of school friends before, all his age. The attraction was the thick rope tied to a sturdy branch of a tree. Getting him out of the house for a while would mean she could talk to the girls, talk to Chris. She nodded, her back to him, speaking through the folded fingers upon which rested her chin. "Wear your jacket, and only until the church bell rings, or I'll come and get you."

He had leapt past her before the end of the sentence. She wanted her own childhood back in an instant.

She looked up at Cynthia and Stephanie, still gazing at her over the white banister, then turned to tread the staircase. On impulse, she stood at the open door to Steph and Christine's room. Two, single beds, coverlets rumpled where they had lain during the day. Her eyes fell upon the childhood things that Christine refused to throw away: Molly, the blonde doll with one eye, the brown bear with bald patches in his honey-coloured fur. In the window, a collapsed pile of books that included two by Enid Blyton. Children's things. Edna's eyes brimmed with tears. She turned away quickly, as though she had seen something terrible there.

"Come down. I need to ask you something," she said to the other girls who watched her, in no doubt that something was wrong.

They followed one another to the kitchen. Cynthia made tea in silence. Stephanie swilled a couple of cups beneath the tap, nervously chewing her top lip. Even the bluebottle buzzing in the window seemed defeated by the atmosphere, collapsing onto the window ledge. Edna sank onto a kitchen chair and looked from one to the other.

"Is Christine seeing someone, dating them, I mean?"

Behind her back, the girls glanced at one another. There was no escape from the question.

"Yes," Cynthia admitted, hope in her voice as she added, "he's very nice."

"Who is he?"

"A boy called Drew. Well, Andrew really, but that's what they call him at the base."

"American? Oh, God. Your Dad will be furious. Why didn't you tell me?"

"She didn't want us to..." Stephanie said, quietly.

"You have a responsibility to tell me; you're her big sisters!" Her voice was indignant, angry. She was about to say, "Even your grandma knows," but stifled the comment.

"When did she meet him, and where?"

"You know the Friday night dance at the Hollybush, when you said she could go for an hour? A few months ago?"

"When Maurice brought her home?"

Christine placed the tea before her mother. "Yes," she said.

It was almost the truth. Maurice, Cynthia's friend, had not brought her home. Andrew had brought her home.

"Months ago," Edna repeated in despair. "She asked me whether she could go to the Tyrrell's house. Is that where she is now, with Joan?" The shrillness in her voice panicked them.

"Well, probably, yes, if that's what she said." Cynthia frowned. "Mum, you're making too big a thing of this. It isn't serious, just her first proper boyfriend, that's all."

Edna blew softly through her cheeks. They were so naïve. She had been naïve, too. She was shocked that Chris would lie to her. She would have to put a stop to it. She would be calm. There would probably have been kissing. Christine would cry, of course, try to persuade her to let it continue.

The key turned in the latch and the front door opened, Christine's familiar light step on the front doormat. Edna lost her resolve in an instant, flying from the kitchen sink to face her youngest daughter.

"Where have you been, Chris? Please don't tell me lies."

The girl's face crumpled in shock, tears coming quickly into her eyes, her mouth opening and closing again as though words had clamoured like food and would choke her. She looked down at her shoes, her hair swinging down to hide her face when she saw her sisters' pity. The gawkiness of a teenager unused to being rebuked. She blew through her fringe and turned away from them all.

Edna watched as she removed her coat. Her skinny little girl had a fuller figure; Amy was right about that.

When the coat had been hung up, Edna snatched impatiently at her arm. Shocked at the sudden movement, the girl made to pull away.

"Upstairs. Now. I want to talk to you in private…"

She slouched behind her mother, slowly mounting the stairs to her bedroom. Once there she collapsed onto the bed. Edna sat beside her.

"You lied to me."

She began to cry, stretching her body to reach beneath her pillow for a handkerchief, then staring into her lap. Wiping her eyes with the hem of her skirt, hiding her face from her mother before saying, "I'm sorry Mum, but I love him."

Edna heard it, the pleading note in her voice, but couldn't soften towards her. Their little girl, one moment playing with dolls and now this.

"He's American. You can hardly know him – you're little more than a child, Christine – Dad will never allow it!" She fought to overcome the tremble in her voice and lost the fight. It would bring disgrace to them all.

"You haven't done anything wrong, have you?" She wanted to shake her daughter for the first time in her life. "Christine, you haven't… slept with him?"

There was no answer. Christine flopped sideways onto the bed, buried her face in the eiderdown while Edna rose agitatedly to pace before the window, staring down blindly at the sunny late afternoon shadowing in the garden and the drooping roses.

At last, she turned back to the girl as she lay upon the bed, quietly crying.

"You have, haven't you?" she asked in a half whisper, while Edna worried at her silence and took it as an admission, fighting with her own ignorance. She had never even spoken to the girl about sex.

Christine didn't reply, couldn't bring herself to answer and Edna wondered at it. It seemed so impossible. Not Christine, so naïve about everything.

"When did you last have your period?" She ought to have known, perhaps, but with three girls, someone was always having a period.

The girl twisted her face upward. The skin of her eyes was white, blotched pink like the delicate petals of a flower. There were tears at the corners of her mouth. Edna drew the handkerchief from her sleeve and handed it to her.

"He loves me. He wants to marry me," Christine sniffed eventually.

"When did you last have a period?" Edna repeated.

Christine started to cry again, quietly, this time, until Edna sat beside her upon the bed, her anger replaced by sorrow. How could she, as a mother, not have known? How could she have let this happen? She lifted a shaking hand to stroke the hair from her daughter's face.

"I'm late."

"How late?"

"Almost two months," she said.

*

Dr Richards examined Christine with kindness. Others would be judgemental, Edna thought bitterly, imagining the wagging tongues, but the doctor knew the family well. Yes, he believed that Christine was pregnant, at least three months gone. He took a sample of her urine. He answered questions patiently and told them that Christine would be entitled to extra rations to buy orange juice, cod liver oil, vitamin tablets, milk and extra meat rations.

Edna determined to keep the girl at home for as long as she could to spite the wagging tongues. As they left the surgery, she decided that she would send a telegram to Ron, as well as a letter. She rehearsed the letter as she walked, hardly listening to what Christine was saying to her. They would have to grant him leave. The telegram would tell him how urgent it was. She had never considered sending a telegram before. Thank God she would get extra rations. Her thoughts were chaotic. Sleep would be impossible.

She would talk to the children, tell them to keep their mouths shut about it, not tell Geoffrey until the baby couldn't be concealed any longer. What would Ron say?

She wrote to him by hand on the same day that she sent the telegram, feeling alternately very small and very important as she dictated the telegram to the postmaster.

"You must come home," was all she said in the telegram message.

The district nurse came, bossy and bustling, worrying Edna, scarcely reassuring.

Then Christine, pale and apologetic, asked if Drew could come to the house. Stephanie had smuggled two letters from him into her hands.

Edna had wanted to pretend that he didn't exist, but he did. Edna said yes, but it would have to be soon as their father had been given permission to come home.

Edna was nervous as she flitted about the house the day that Drew came. Bashing and plumping the cushions, dusting the windowsills with frenetic energy. All these weeks, she had kept Christine to the house, watching her drift listlessly about the garden, belly fast growing. She was locked into a world of her own imagination and her own making, where she was his wife and they lived in West Virginia, which, Christine had told her, was where he came from.

Edna felt excluded from these dreams which she could never share, but not distanced from her daughter, now. That at least had changed. A fierce and formidable love snapped the visiting nurse into silence when she asked Christine if she knew the father. She was suddenly given to wrapping her eaglet in her ferocious talons. Edna didn't want to lose her to America.

Perhaps, this morning, she should feel hostility to this young man who had caused them such pain but it wasn't in her nature, not really. She could never turn the gypsies or the tramps away from the door without offering them something. She remembered the poorhouse that had stood on the London Road, where couples who had been married for years were suddenly ripped apart from one another. Edna's sympathy and compassion for other people often kept her awake.

No. It wasn't in her nature to be unkind. But the fact remained that Christine was only seventeen and this boy, Drew, twenty-two. He should have been far more responsible. Not good enough to say that they were in love, or that he was lonely, so far away from his home.

When she saw the movement at the front gate, the alien uniform of an American private, his jacket draped across his arm, her heart leapt in nervous anticipation. It beat so fast that she had to take several deep breaths to steady herself. As he glanced up at the house, she stared into the kitchen sink as though she hadn't yet seen him. He was not tall, only an inch or so taller than Christine; not handsome, which surprised her, but pleasant looking. As he snatched off his cap, she glimpsed the short fair hair and wondered whether the baby might be blonde.

Edna closed her eyes, briefly imagining the baby lying in her arms just as Christine arrived at her elbow, a little pensive, biting her lip, a smudge of colour applied to her cheeks from the rouge in her sister's special box. She pecked her mother's cheek and went swiftly to open the door.

Edna listened in the long silence as they embraced one another, finally emerging into the hallway.

She took a deep and unconscious breath, accepting the hand he offered her.

"Do I call you Andrew or Drew?" Her smile was slight, but not withheld from him.

"Whichever you prefer, ma'am. Most people call me Drew."

His own smile was a little lopsided, but there was something strongly likeable about it. She could tell that he was also nervous and felt herself foolish for being so.

"Shall we go and sit in the living room?" she suggested, leading him towards the large room kept for best. She had polished everything, rising very early in the morning. She left them talking for a while, and went to the kitchen to put together a tray of tea and biscuits that the girls had made the previous day. She listened. Drew's voice was low; Christine's was a mere whisper.

When she returned to them, Drew was holding a picture of the girls when they were younger, dressed as bridesmaids in winter velvet dresses for a wedding.

She asked him where his home was, and about his family. He came from Jefferson County in West Virginia, he said. He was honest enough, Edna thought, otherwise he wouldn't have told her that he came from a large mining family, and that they lived together, except for an older brother who was married. He and his two brothers and a sister, with their mother and father, lived at home. His father could no longer work in the mine because of an injury.

But when he asked her whether Ron might agree to them getting married here, after which they would move to West Virginia, Edna thought of the hillbillies that Milton had joked about. Her scalp tingled as though in panic, a hard knot formed in her chest, but she forced a smile as she imagined her youngest daughter in a worn-out dress, with several children clinging to her skirts, several thousand miles away from her own mother. She said that she didn't know. That they would have to wait and see after the baby was born.

*

Stella's Frank picked Ron up from Oxford station in his Morris Minor.

The girls had been encouraged not to go out too often after Christine's news. Edna was afraid of the gossip that might be spread if they ventured out too often. Although, to her relief, local people were mostly kind. Mrs Wilson used her old patterns to knit baby clothes; other people brought items for use after the birth. Edna herself didn't venture too far from home. So, they were all very excited about Ron's return.

He called in to see Amy, first, staying with his mother for a long while. Edna was glad; she seemed to have calmed him. So, when he arrived, his face a little gaunt from tiredness, carrying his small suitcase, the girls and Geoffrey dropped their various tasks and rushed from the corners of the house to meet him.

As a rule, Christine might have been the first to wrap her arms about his neck, but now she came slowly, almost reluctantly, hands steadying the tight, protruding belly.

Only Geoffrey, who Ron handed a bag of toffee to, was unaware of the small differences. The slight sadness in his eyes was brought about by concern for his youngest daughter, and that his mother held back as though she had done something wrong.

But when Christine reached him, he smiled, and all he said was "Well, this is a turn up for the books."

"Hello, Dad." They watched as father held daughter in a hug before entering the house. Geoffrey leapt from foot to foot, tearing at the packet of sweets.

"How far gone are you now?" Ron held her away from him, noticing the pale cheeks, the dark smudges beneath her eyes. Worrying.

"Almost three months."

He nodded. "Do you feel well?" She didn't look well, he thought. "Are you eating plenty, getting sleep?"

As they talked, Edna said briskly, "Cynthia, make your Dad some tea and a sandwich. There's cold bacon in the pantry, and eggs." Her voice held the high-pitched note of the nervous. The unspoken hung over them all, a charcoal-grey thunderous cloud, Drew.

"I don't want food," he stated wearily, shaking his head. "Not yet, I'm not hungry. Tea'll be fine."

They went into the living room: Edna, Ron and Christine. He closed the door behind them with a click and fell into one of the armchairs, reclining, gazing from his wife to his daughter.

"Have you met him yet?" he said with a sigh, staring at Edna.

"Yes. Once. He seems like a nice lad."

Ron emitted a low, bitter laugh. "Nice? Was it nice to cause all of this hurt, to do as he pleased without thought for anyone? I've a good mind to go to the base and have it out with his commanding officer."

"Please, Dad, no." The appeal from Christine was quiet but determined. "Please don't do anything like that."

Perhaps she didn't believe that he would, but she came to him, kneeling on the carpet before him as though she were begging for his life.

Edna waited on tenterhooks for more of the lecture, but it didn't come.

"So, what do you expect will happen next? Is he staying here, marrying you, bringing up your baby or what?"

Christine bit her lip. "He has to go back. His father is ill, but he says he will marry me here and take me with him when the war ends…"

"At seventeen? And who knows when the war will end? You don't really know him; you'll be thousands of miles away and without your own family to help." He shook his head. "No. You'll have to stay here. I'll meet with him and tell him that if he wants to marry you, he can do it in a year or so. He'll have to stay in this country and get a job here."

He got up from the chair, looked down at her, his lips screwing into determination, then walked towards the French windows. He stood with his back to them, looking towards the long garden, waving at his son who waited for him to emerge.

Christine had begun to cry. Perhaps it was the culmination of tension, or possibly relief.

"Stop that. Go and fetch that tea for me, then leave me to talk to Mum for a while."

She climbed to her feet, crossed the room to her father, put her arms about him, wetting his shirt with her tears.

When she left, the silence in the room felt so strained that Edna had to talk. "So far as I can tell he has a good heart. He's very popular with some of the local lads, and in his unit."

Ron stood back, turning to anger and frustration for the first time. "She's seventeen Edna, she can't travel halfway around the world with a stranger!"

"Miriam is going to New York with her fiancée," she said.

"Not if I have my way!" He glared at her. "Miriam is older and could take care of herself better. No. Frankly, at the moment, I don't want to lay eyes on the bastard. He can bugger off to West Virginia. I don't see how I'm ever going to like him."

She waited, drawing in her breath, holding it there. The white handkerchief in her hands fluttered to the floor. As she stooped to pick it up, she felt giddy, leaning on the mantlepiece for support.

In a desperate attempt to change the subject, she asked, "How was Amy?"

He sighed. "I'm glad I came back. She won't live long, now. She didn't respond to me a great deal and I didn't want to disturb her. I spoke to her as she slept and once, when I held her hand, her fingers pressed on mine. I think she knew I was there. I wish Dennis could come home; I wish she could see him before... I'll go back tomorrow," he finished.

She nodded slowly. Taking his hand in hers, she kissed the back of it, wishing that he didn't have to go away again, missing his authority and the confidence he gave her.

*

Summer passed. Edna snapped the heads off the roses, while kindly Frank and Cynthia's young man took care of Ron's pigs.

Edna kept any leftover scraps in a tin bucket outside, not that there were many scraps, but she encouraged the children to toss fallen apples and snails into the bucket. The ferocious pigs ate everything. Both Ron and Frank were members of the Small Pig Keepers Council. When it came for a pig to be slaughtered, a half of every pig must be handed to the Ministry of Food while the rest was offered to local elderly people and eaten by the family.

Drew came to visit as often as he could, until he and Edna found conversation easier. Edna grew more hopeful. There was always hope. Drew hadn't yet met with Ron and hadn't spoken again about his plans for the future. Neither he nor Edna wanted to cause Christine upset. Everything, every tiny conversation would be postponed, for now.

After little or no morning sickness, later in her pregnancy, she had begun to develop a few problems. The nurse who came to visit said they were not serious and were related to the pregnancy. She advised a hot water bottle for the pain in her back and declared that the tiredness, the shortness of breath and swollen feet should be resolved with more rest.

September was glorious, glowing with golden sunshine.

Christine and Drew sat in the orchard at the foot of the garden beneath the apple and plum trees. But she could never be coaxed into revealing what they had talked about. The couple lived in their own dream world.

Amy died peacefully, with her own dreams and in her bed with the curtains pulled against the bright sunshine so that she might rest. Ron returned once again, too late to say goodbye; he kissed her cold forehead three days later, as she lay in her coffin. He kept a long vigil with her, asking her to stay with him as he needed her spirit. The funeral was at the church in the Quarry, where she was buried close to Earnest and Bernard, as she had wanted.

Late in October, while Ron was away again, Christine rose from the bed early one morning, woken by the ache in her back and a stomach cramp. She rose from the bed to find blood on her nightdress and swayed, giddily clutching the blackout curtain beside her.

Stephanie woke, sat up in the bed opposite and shouted for Edna. They watched as Edna cradled the girl in her arms. Christine's face was waxen, white, glossy with sweat as she cried out with the pain and begged her mother for help.

"Cynthia, fetch Frank. We need to take her to the hospital. Pull your dressing gown on and run!" Edna cried, trying to feel in command when all she felt was panic.

She sent Stephanie for her handbag. There was a number there which Ron had given her on a scrap of paper when he returned for Amy. An official, someone with whom he worked. She had never used the brand new, expensive telephone that Ron had bought. She was stupidly afraid of it, of the strange noise it made when she lifted the handle. Besides, she couldn't leave Christine. There was no time to be afraid.

She rooted around in the little bag searching for the note and handed it to Stephanie. "Call this telephone number, ask to speak to Mr James, his name is by the number. Tell him that your sister has gone into labour; then stay here, please, and get breakfast for your brother."

As they eased her into the back of Frank's Morris Minor, Christine whispered, "Will you ask Drew to come? Stephanie knows where to get hold of him."

Edna nodded, trying to do everything to reassure her.

"Is the baby going to be alright?" she asked then, as though Edna was a doctor, as though she could give answers.

"Everything will be alright," she replied with a bright, forced smile as she kissed Christine's fingers and climbed into the car beside her.

Frank drove fast but smoothly, into Oxford, parking right in front of the hospital. He ran, with some agility for a large man, to get help. Moments later, two hospital porters came with a wheelchair and accompanied by a nurse.

"We will come and talk to you in a while. Could you wait in the waiting room?" The nurse with the white cap over her fair hair was pleasant, a kind smile with a voice of authority. Even so, when Christine looked up at her mother in an appeal, Edna begged, "Please. Can't I go with her?"

"I'm afraid not. We will take good care of her." It was kind but brusque. "Now, let's find out what's happening, shall we?"

She knew she would never forget it, that moment when her daughter was wheeled away from her. Remembered thinking that this was the longest, loneliest time in her life.

Everything would be well, Edna told herself; at least she was close to full term.

Frank had to go but he assured her with a hug that he would be back. She could do nothing but wait and pray, sometimes looking about her at the other people filling the waiting room, or drifting to the window to stare out at the rain and the new autumn leaves blowing down from the trees.

Four hours passed before the same nurse stood before her. Edna picked up her handbag in haste, believing that she was going to be allowed to see Christine. But the nurse put a staying hand upon her arm.

"Mrs Coppock, would you follow me to somewhere a little quieter so we can speak?" she asked.

She was led to a small white-walled room.

"Are they all right?" Edna asked in a tremulous voice, sitting herself opposite the nurse.

"I'm terribly sorry, Mrs Coppock. The child was stillborn."

Stillborn. Christine's baby. Stillborn after everything.

Edna froze, unable to process the terrible, unbelievable, shocking words. She clamped her teeth onto her lip so that tears wouldn't come. When she spoke, it was in a voice alien to her, rigid, unforgiving, but desperate too.

"You must let me see my daughter. I have to go to her. She will be in a terrible state."

The nurse dipped her head, a woman in her forties, someone used to the delivery of bad news. Not unkind but practiced, diplomatic.

"You can't, not presently. But she isn't in a state, as you put it. We have had to sedate her so she's very peaceful at present. The doctor has to examine her, Mrs Coppock. She appears to be unwell and we don't yet know what is happening to her."

"Unwell? What do you mean?" Her voice broke with a squeal of impatience. Christine, so good at sports, at running, so healthy?

"Perhaps it would help if you could tell me about her childhood illnesses."

Edna thought frantically, desperate to help Christine. "Scarlet fever, that's the only thing I can think of. Both Christine and my eldest daughter had it."

The woman nodded, saying nothing, but gazing at her thoughtfully for a moment.

She rose slowly from her chair. Interview over. "I'm very sorry; you can't see her yet but, as I say, the doctors are doing all that they can to find out what has happened to her. Doctor Cranston is an excellent doctor; she's in good hands. No doubt he will wish to speak to you before too long. Is there someone who could stay with you while you wait?"

"My husband is coming here, but he won't be able to get here until the evening. He's travelling a long distance by train."

It was as the nurse walked away that Edna remembered, asking with a catch in her throat, "Could you tell me the sex of the baby?"

She half turned, not meeting Edna's eyes. "A boy," she said. "I'm sorry."

In the waiting room, the girls had arrived and were waiting for her. They looked beautiful in the winter coats that Ron had bought them, but Christine wasn't with them.

Edna hadn't wanted to, but started to cry, twisting her face away, trying to hide beneath her fingers.

The two girls stood, placing comforting arms about their mother. Then, their little group went outside for some privacy, despite the rain falling fast now. Stephanie held the umbrella up to shield them. Ordinary people walked back and forth along the road, stared at them: students on their way to college, tradesmen to work.

She told them what the nurse had said. She would always remember that moment of grief. Stephanie incredulous, so young herself.

"The baby is dead?"

The deep sadness of it took hold of her, a dry well in her stomach. For months they had collected and stored the baby paraphernalia: small cardigans, knitted by both Edna and Stella; little gowns, tiny mittens, lovingly folded on a shelf in the airing cupboard. Edna had cleaned the old pram, ready for walks.

"And Christine is very ill, the nurse said, but they don't know what's wrong with her."

"Can't we see her?"

Edna shook her head.

"Is Dad coming?" she asked them, unable to carry the burden alone for a minute longer.

"Yes, he'll be on his way. Drew's coming too..."

Edna nodded but hoped he would come before Ron's arrival. She knew that Ron wouldn't want him there, especially now.

"Come back into the waiting room. You won't have eaten all day; you look so tired, Mum. We've brought some tea in the flask and a sandwich," Stephanie said.

She was glad of the tea but didn't think she would ever eat again.

They sat like wooden dolls, hardly speaking until Drew arrived. Nothing had prepared them for this numbness inside.

Ron arrived late in the evening. Edna kept Drew from him with a strong instinct that now was not the time. There had never been a good time. Their children left, eventually, with Drew, to find some sleep after they had been allowed to sit with their sister for a short while. They had watched her sleep, a dark-haired angel, still beneath the white cotton sheets. Each of them telling her what they needed to and hoping that, through her sleep, she would hear them.

The doctor spoke to them on the second day. No one had realised she had only one kidney, the other damaged in childhood by scarlet fever. Acute renal failure. She would live for less than a week, the doctor explained. Kind words that could do nothing to change the fact. Christine was going to die, going to die. It tolled, over and over again, in Edna's head as she prayed that there had been a mistake.

They sat about her bed, projecting their love to keep her alive. Ron seemed to be unable to speak and for the first time in his life allowed tears to roll down his cheeks unchecked when he wasn't with her. He held her hand while his heart told her that she was his most loving daughter and that he would never love anyone as much as he loved her.

"Am I going to die?" she whispered to her parents in a waking moment. A child's small voice, confused, afraid.

Mouths fell open as they acted incredulity, while wanting to hold her forever, needing to shake with their tears.

"No, silly. What a silly thought! We're going to the seaside next month, remember? With Aunty Stell and Uncle Frank?"

Geoffrey, the little brother with whom she had played and lavished her attention, took her old toys from the bedroom and held them every night, and his mother returned to lying upon the bed with him while they stared through a gap in the curtains at the biggest star: Christine's soul...

Paula 1992

Cynthia thought about her sister and her father often. Now, at almost eleven o'clock in the evening, after a long and busy day, all she wanted was her bed, but she thought of her father. They were lucky, having taken the White Hart on with no experience of running a pub, they had made it work for them. Doctors and nurses from the new hospital, students from the polytechnic and Ruskin College were all daily visitors. Right now, she wanted them all to go. Making her point as subtly as possible, she flicked off the lights in the now empty snug, moving about the tables with speed to gather empty glasses.

At the bar, she caught her husband's eye and mouthed the words "Jukebox." Maurice nodded, setting down the pint glass he had been drying with a tea towel to turn off the music.

A group of doctors and nurses wandered to the bar in helpful amnesty of their wine glasses. They called goodnight to the landlord and landlady, chatting to each other as they wandered through the door, stepping onto the cobbles of the autumnal street.

Marion had been helping behind the bar this evening. But Amy, her little girl had woken and wandered from her bedroom, calling her mother from the top of the spiral staircase. Since Marion's separation from her husband, the child was understandably anxious about the new world without him.

Cynthia yawned behind her painted fingernails. Briefly standing at the open front door to the street, she breathed in the chill air. At this time of night, smoke hung across the bar ceilings, a translucent, dirty cloud. It felt good to breathe something better.

Across the street, behind the high yellow stone wall, the powerful Norman church that dominated the village was shrouded in darkness and a healthier grey autumn mist. Momentarily she thought about the students they had served earlier in the evening. She had asked them to stop singing. Though the walls of the old pub were thick, she didn't wish to upset the doctor and the young family who lived next door.

She was about to go inside when she was startled by the slightly plump, middle-aged man standing behind her. All evening he had been holding court with a group of younger students. His smile was benign as he gazed at her over the top of his glasses.

Cynthia groaned inwardly. He was about to ask for a drink after time, perhaps. But in the distance, his young friends appeared to be preparing to leave.

"I'm terribly sorry," he started. "You are going to think me crazy, but I really need to tell you something…"

What then? A complaint? Or had he drunk too much? There had been few complaints across the years, unless someone had already had too much to drink and Maurice refused to serve them. Very possibly he was about to flirt with her. She simply wanted him to leave, now, so she could fall into bed.

But there was something earnest about him; he seemed neither drunk or a flirt as he gazed at her over the top of his spectacles with an air of apology. She didn't do earnest at this time of night.

"You go on; I'll catch you up," he told the group of students as they approached the door. They smiled at her as they passed. One of the women called goodnight to her and she waved a hand.

The man gazed at Cynthia, hesitated, smiled apologetically, then moved his glasses to the top of his head.

"Look, you don't know how reluctant I am to tell you this, but they've been bothering me all evening and they won't leave me alone…"

"Who won't leave you alone?" she asked, perplexed. Years of being a landlady had taught her the importance of being polite and patient, but he was becoming annoying now. "Are you talking about another customer?"

There were only two customers remaining, and they were nurses, friends of her daughter. He couldn't mean them.

"No. Not customers."

He had an accent that she couldn't identify. Northern, but northern from where?

He took the glasses from the top of his head, cleaning them on his sweater before meeting her eyes.

"Two spirits. Ghosts, if you like."

She recoiled, then smiled at him. Now he had caught her by surprise. "Ghosts?"

"Yes. Really. Spirits connected to you. Everywhere you go, they are following you this evening. I've been watching them all night."

From behind the bar, Maurice made a circling motion with his finger beside his own head. The man is crazy, a charlatan.

But Cynthia waited, held by the words.

"What do they look like, these ghosts?"

"Well… the man is slight of build, quite handsome, wearing a suit," he said without hesitation. "He has grey hair. He's older than you. He's standing behind you right now."

She turned, slowly, looking over her shoulder but saw nothing apart from the dying embers of the fire in the old fireplace. When she turned back, he told her, "I think it may be your father."

She took a sharp breath. That's who she had wanted it to be. Her lips twisted with a new thought. Although not well known, Ron had been frequently photographed by the local paper. But she had never met this man before and he seemed genuine. What did he have to gain from telling her this?

Thoughts of her father held her captive.

"And the other ghost?" she asked.

Her long, painted fingernails picked at the fabric on the back of a nearby chair. Nervously hopeful. Let it be Christine.

He nodded, still smiling at her, understanding her need. His words came slowly, as though he didn't wish to upset her.

"A girl, a young woman. Long dark hair. She's wearing a denim jacket, with jeans and heavy boots. But..." He paused as though he was reluctant to tell her. "She's crawling across the floor. It's as though she can't see. She is unhappy, distressed."

She shook her head, disliking the image in an instant, trying to visualise it then dismissing it.

"I don't know who that is. Not a relative or friend. I don't know. Why would she be crawling? I thought perhaps you were talking about my sister. She died when she was seventeen, you see. But she wasn't blind, and it sounds as though you're describing a blind person. I don't know..."

She stared towards the hearth again, blinking, as though she might see something there.

"Not Christine, anyway. She wouldn't have worn jeans or denim jackets, not then, it was the war..."

The man nodded.

"I'm sorry. I just want you to know that I'm telling you the truth. I have nothing to gain from this. I'm not a fake, I assure you. I'm a medium. I don't use my talent for profit. I'm a lowly lecturer from York. Before tonight I knew nothing about you, or the White Hart. I'm on a course at Ruskin College with some of my students. I just feel these spirits have some connection with you; they wouldn't be pursuing you unless they did, not in my experience."

There was a short cough from the direction of the bar. "We have enough spirits," Maurice joked.

The man nodded in fake appreciation of the tired joke.

"Well, I'd better catch up with the others. I've outstayed my welcome."

He held out his hand to her. "Thanks for putting up with me, and for a nice evening. Name's Peter. I'm back to York tomorrow but I hope to come down this way again."

She nodded thoughtfully. He hadn't come over as a crank. Maybe the girl was a past customer whose name she didn't know. Why would she be crawling? She would call Stephanie tomorrow to tell her all about it, she mused, as she dragged the heavy bolts across the door behind him.

*

Cynthia wasn't really a worrier, unlike her husband but one issue had bothered her since Paula, her second child, aged only three, had rejected the girl's clothes that her older sister loved. Paula was quite simply, different.

She was a rarity. She had friends and seemed well liked, certainly no enemies. But she had always felt uncomfortable in her own body. She had been the maverick in the family, tearing off bridesmaid dresses in exasperation, hating dresses, in fact. Always loving the things that seemed the prerogative of her younger brother. Playing a male role in imaginary games, climbing trees, carving things with a pen knife, fishing, football, bows and arrows, skill in sport; always that skinny little girl in shorts with short hair and round glasses, who everyone assumed was a boy.

The more that Maurice wanted her to dress like a girl, the more Paula wanted to be his son. That was Cynthia's concern. Members of the family had gazed askance at Paula on many occasions, remarking, "She doesn't like dolls, does she?" or "Aren't you going to put her in a dress?"

If you insisted upon dresses, the child would yell and scream until they were removed. Cynthia gradually gave up the fight while wondering whether they had wanted a boy so much that they had turned her into one.

As a young child, she had failed to have that one special friend. Girls rejected her because she wasn't interested in the games they played; boys rejected her because she wasn't a boy. So, Cynthia implored Christine to take her with her when she went to meet friends. In fact, the two sisters were very good friends, more so in the outdoors, riding bikes or horses at the stables where they volunteered their help, rescuing seagulls who'd swallowed fishing hooks or moles that Maurice had turned out of his vegetable gardens.

Perhaps it was the day a friend of Christine's had assumed she was a boy, asking her for a date, that Chris stopped going out with her unless they were alone. Paula's older sister lived in a world of her own making it seemed, a fictional life built upon novels like *Little Women* and *Little House on the Prairie*.

Cynthia was the first to realise what Paula was and what she wasn't. It frightened her, at first, because of the hatred in the world, but she was the one to take her side in her teenage years, when her husband and older sister attempted to persuade her into skirts and dresses that never suited her. Cynthia's heart broke when Paula told her, as an older teenager, that dresses and skirts made her feel like a man in drag, a freak.

There was no denying that the girl had tried, so hard, to please her father, even accepting dates from men. But it was clear that she was never happy, never enthusiastic about any relationship with a man. It was a terrible ritual she believed she had to go through to please other people.

And then, one day, her life changed. It changed when the group of nurses, close friends, regular visitors to the pub, befriended her. She grew happier in her skin at last.

She began a degree course at Brookes; moved out of the pub into a flat. It was then that she spoke to her mother, for the first time, about her true feelings. Suddenly she found herself amongst young women who were the same as her.

When Edna had been told, she said with a chuckle, "A lesbian? Don't you think we had those in my day?"

So, it was alright. Except that Maurice, from a very traditional background, found it impossible to accept and Christine – part conformist, in part fearful – also rejected it, saying it was a phase. It was the time of Aids, of hate crimes and discrimination. There was talk of Sodom and Gomorrah and divine retribution.

Christianity could be dangerous, Cynthia decided.

"I don't care what sex she is, so long as she is loved," Cynthia said, while her elder daughter raised her eyebrows at her mother's naivety.

It was really Greta who changed everything. A young nurse, Welsh accent, softly spoken, who Cynthia and Maurice liked very much. Maurice didn't realise that her friendship with Paula was so much more than that.

For the first time, Paula went on holiday with someone else other than her family, or alone, which was what usually happened. She went to Tunisia with Greta. They walked on soft, sandy beaches and swam in the warm cornflower-blue sea. They told Cynthia about the colourful streets and marketplaces. They rode on a camel. She and Maurice didn't talk about it, but it was clear to Cynthia that Paula and Greta were in love.

She was happier than Cynthia had ever known her. In the kitchen of the White Hart, she told her mother about their love for one another and Cynthia hugged her and congratulated her. It wasn't as important who you loved, she said, only to love and be loved; and she was glad Paula loved Greta.

Together, the girls moved into Rose Cottage, the house built by Earnest, which had eventually been left to Cynthia's cousin. They rented it, while Greta carried on with her nursing career at the new hospital, and Paula continued with her publishing course and worked at the pub and at a local farm shop in the small spare time she had.

She was no longer lonely. She had decided many years ago, as she walked home from the library at the age of eleven, her nose firmly planted in a copy of *The Ancient Greeks,* peering at the text through a pair of round national health glasses – there would be someone for her one day.

For the last two days, about the time the spiritualist had spoken to her mother, Paula had spent her time moving her possessions out of the flat and into Rose Cottage.

The tiny cottage had changed little throughout the century, except for the building of a modern spiral staircase and the addition of a small veranda which overlooked the long garden. In summer, hollyhocks and peonies, lilacs and daisies rubbed shoulders with the aristocratic roses. Now the lawn was strewn with fallen autumn leaves.

She walked the length of the garden path on her return. Her springer spaniel, Pippa, leapt from the ground like a springbok to greet her, plastering her clothes in mud. Through the back door, the Bangles sang from a boombox, while on the garden table, the remnants of yesterday's housewarming for friends who had helped them to move in. The shrunken candles, a wine bottle, an ashtray, brought the memory of the event back to her. It had been fun, although she had drunk more than usual, perhaps.

The kitchen door stood open, shining clean. A mop and bucket stood in the corner of the room. Piles of books and other possessions still littered the table. Neither she nor Greta had found time to put these things away as yet. There was no hurry to do anything.

Greta was sleeping on the old settee, her hair wet from the shower. Paula grabbed the dog by her collar and rolled her to the ground in a towel before the tiles were marked with mud. The dog flopped onto the rug beside Greta, panting as she grinned up at her mistress.

Greta looked so contented. Strands of her wet, brown hair had stuck to her cheeks, and a small trickle of saliva ran in a thin stream from the full lips. Paula wanted to kiss her but did not want to wake her. As she smiled at her, she felt the tenderness of a mother towards her child; she thought about the complicated nature of relationships, one person could symbolise so many roles.

She trundled to the fridge to examine it for any food she might cook them. There were the leftovers from yesterday and a salami sausage, a housewarming present. Greta wouldn't eat it; she was vegetarian. Eating meat was the only thing they disagreed about. She had tried, for Greta's sake, but wasn't a true convert.

She reached up to the cupboard for pasta and a tub of parmesan cheese, starting the tea.

Greta's passion for animal welfare was the second cause of underhand sarcasm between Paula and her sister.

The day Greta had persuaded Paula to accompany her to Beckley to sabotage the hunt, to confuse the beagle hounds, she and Christine had a ferocious argument.

"You're actually disregarding the savagery of hounds attacking a fox because it's tradition?" Paula had yelled incredulously, changed in her views, the hood pulled from her eyes.

Once they had stood side by side as young teenagers, gazing at saddlery in a shop window as another child might stare at sweets or toys. They didn't own their own horses, instead they earned their riding lessons by mucking out the stables. Their greatest horsy influence was joint master of the South Oxfordshire hunt.

"Paula?" The greeting was half glee, half yawn, bringing her back to the present as she rummaged through the cupboards for dinner.

"Shall I stick on the kettle?" she called back through the open door.

She watched Greta stretch her arms above her head, flexing her back beneath the dressing gown. "Could you chuck over the apple juice? Really dry mouth, drank too much last night... no time for tea all day," she groaned.

She put the pan on the hob to boil water, then clicked on the unreliable kettle and carried the apple juice to the settee, clambering over the dog to sit at the foot of the sofa beside Greta's small, slender feet.

Greta lifted her head, yawned and stretched languidly to take the apple juice while Paula watched her drink it from the carton and longed to kiss the line of her throat. She thought about the body beneath the gown, thought how lucky she was. Their eyes locked together in a smile and in two small, slow movements, Greta sat up, pulling her legs from beneath her, kneeling to place her hands upon Paula's thin shoulders as she stretched forward to plant a single, languid kiss upon Paula's lower lip. A rush of happiness flooded through her.

Later, as they ate dinner, she asked, "Would it be alright if I asked the family over one afternoon? Just sandwiches and cake. I'll sort it out."

Greta smiled at her across the table, an attractive crease at the corner of her mouth, but there was a barely noticeable frown between her eyes.

Paula waited. "Too early?" she asked.

"No." Greta hesitated. "Not at all, it'd be lovely. I'm sorry, love. I wish Christine liked me a bit more. Sometimes it feels pretty much as though she's ignoring me."

Paula bit her lip. "Ah, that's it... I see. She's not a bad sort, really. I promise. She's always had control issues; I think many big sisters do. I expect she would rather be the influence over me than you!" She smiled, trying to make light of it, desperately wanting the two people she loved most in the world to reconcile.

"Okay, well, whatever; but she hardly speaks to me and when she does, she can't look at me comfortably. I'm not imagining it; you know I'm not."

Paula placed her fingers over Greta's, squeezing them lightly.

"Greta, there's nothing about you that anyone could dislike. It isn't that..." She hesitated, searching for the right explanation. "There are two things. She's a conformist, I suppose, a bit of a control freak. She hates situations that are out of her control. Basically, she doesn't want me to be a lesbian; she wants me to be in a straight relationship as she is, with two children and what she sees as a normal life. She's finding this hard to accept, our relationship, despite everything I feel about you, that I never want to be without you..."

Greta nodded. "She really thinks that this is just a life choice, that you can be happy when you totally disregard your feelings?" she said softly. Then, a little more impatiently, "Good God! But all your family accept it! Marion, Howard, Michele, they couldn't be nicer; and even Nanny Edna said, "Don't you think we had those in my day?" and posted her housewarming card through the door! If she can accept it at her age, surely Christine can."

Paula chuckled at her grandmother's words, then twisted her mouth into solemnity, thinking.

"My father finds it hard to accept and she's influenced by him. She always has been," she said.

Greta sighed impatiently. "That's different. My father doesn't accept it either. I can deal with that and still love him, too; but Christine should see things differently, she's from another generation."

Paula gazed at her, thinking how, over the years, she had felt she had to prove to Maurice that she could do anything that Howard could by lifting heavy objects, running faster, climbing higher; and then about that time she had put herself through abject misery when she had twisted herself into girlie clothes and dated men, just to please him. Had Greta done that for her father, she wondered?

"It's complicated, more than that," she said. "Christine and I were close, despite everything. She loves me, really, and I love her. We have a lot in common; we were best friends. Now, you are my best friend. Could be, she's just jealous of you, and jealous that I no longer feel I must make decisions based upon what others think."

"What on earth did you ever have in common with her? You are so different," Greta asked, mystified.

"Shared family, shared upbringing, shared memories. We love similar things, the outdoors, reading, writing, painting, music; there was a lot to bring us together. She can't dictate things now. In a way, I feel sorry for her. But she really doesn't dislike you. I think you are so serene, so sure of what you are that you make her nervous. Anyway…" She reached across the table to squeeze Greta's fingers. "She has to accept it eventually, and she will, I promise."

Greta smiled. "Okay, let's drop it. I want her to like me. I'm fine with your family coming and I'll try to ignore the looks she sends in my direction. You know what she called our friends recently?" Greta added.

Paula shook her head. "What?"

"The lost girls, like in *Peter Pan*."

They grinned at one another.

*

Amy, Paula's niece and God-daughter – she with the expressive face and chubby, baby cheeks – sat cross-legged on a cushion before the television at the pub. She was suddenly distracted from the screen by a ladybird caught on a cobweb. Rising from the cushion, she tottered across the room to watch it as it struggled like a sailor on a boat, tethered to the cobwebby sail in a draught from the warped window frame.

She was confused, perhaps sad, but too young to express it. Daddy had gone away and she didn't know where he was. Mummy said they would see him soon. She knew she wanted to cuddle him; she wanted to rub her face against his cheek and have him lie down on the bed with her and tell her his stories.

But Mummy said she could stay with Aunty Paula, which was exciting. She had on the new dress with the little flowers that Mummy had bought in the shop and she was waiting for her aunt to collect her.

Paula and Greta had kept the little spare room as Amy's room so that the child could stay overnight. They filled it with second-hand toys and a little dolls house with a red roof from Paula's own childhood. They hung a painting from the 1930s upon the wall, an elephant at London Zoo carrying half a dozen children in a carriage upon its back. The same picture had hung upon the wall of the bedroom that she had once shared with Christine.

Amy stayed with them quite frequently. They took her to the local parks, kicking dusty clouds of autumn leaves in their wellington boots. They took her to the Cowley carnival and the fireworks at South Park.

The little girl was spontaneously affectionate towards everyone, unexpectedly throwing herself upon family and friends with her tight, sticky hugs and kisses. Paula had once dreamed of having her own children but wasn't sure that this would happen. The love that Amy showered upon them would make their own childlessness bearable.

They collected her at midday, took her to the park, ate pizza and watched a Disney film with her. When bedtime came,

Paula read stories to her and tucked her in. She went straight to sleep, happy and tired after so much activity, with a teddy tucked beneath her arm.

Paula had been sitting with her arm about Greta for some while, when the sound of Amy's voice reached them from the top of the wooden staircase.

"Aunty Paula…"

She turned, looking over her shoulder; she wriggled away from Greta to smile at Amy, a cute apparition in her pink nightdress with teddy clutched to her chest.

"Hello. What is it? Couldn't you sleep? Do you want a glass of milk?"

The little girl nodded.

Paula mounted the staircase, lifting her into her arms, smelling the baby sweetness that still lingered on her body. She carried her down to the kitchen and sat her on a stool, then took the milk from the fridge.

"Are you feeling okay, not poorly?" she asked, resting a hand on her forehead. "Want a wee?"

"No."

The little girl smiled up at her aunt, a smear of milk about her lips.

"The lady woked me up," she said. "She was looking at me."

Paula smiled, amused. "What lady? There's only me and Greta here, no one else, I promise."

How to explain to someone so young what a dream was?

Amy stared at her with big blue eyes, swinging her legs against the stool. Paula stroked her hair, planting a kiss upon her cheek.

"I think you were dreaming," she said. "Sometimes you think things – your brain thinks things when you are asleep, that's all." She tapped Amy's head lightly. "Your brain is in your head; it has lots of good ideas. Shall I lie on the bed with you for a while?"

Amy nodded.

She glanced through the kitchen door to smile at Greta, who had got up to join them, a query on her face, brows dipped. The cousin from whom they had rented the house had said it was haunted by a friendly ghost. But neither of them believed in ghosts.

*

The ache in Paula's lower back began a few weeks after this. She didn't think too much of it at first.

She remembered that she was semi-conscious of the ache while picking the bulbous green pears from the overgrown tree in the garden. Without a ladder, she had leapt from the ground to grab and shake the branches. A rotten pear fell past her shoulder and two drunken, angry bees managed to sting her shoulder beneath the tee shirt as they fell. Greta had laughed as Paula tore off her tee shirt to free them, then hurtled to the medicine cupboard in her bra to find the antiseptic cream.

For a long time after this, she was aware of the ache to the lower left of her back and believed she had pulled a muscle. But tiredness set in, starting with a cold she thought she'd inherited from little Amy. It caused fever sweats at night. Paula dismissed it all. It wasn't usual for her to be unwell, but it was as though she was constantly tired. Greta made her go to her doctor.

She had blood tests and waited for the results.

It wasn't until Christine asked her to come riding at a local stable that she had to admit something was wrong. As young women, they had ridden bikes through the countryside each weekend to muck out and groom horses, just so they might earn themselves a ride every now and then. Now, Paula had looked forward to an afternoon of riding as much as to her sister's company. It would be like the old days.

But as they cantered across the Botley fields beside the river, a gentle canter, nothing too demanding, the pain in her back became so intense that she had to stop.

"What's the problem? Are you okay?" Christine asked, reining in her horse and turning to look at her. Her face was white, the skin glossy with sweat.

"I don't know. I've been unable to hold food down for a while, or digest it. My back hurts. Don't always feel well," she admitted, panting to get her breath. "I'll be okay."

"You don't look okay." Christine frowned.

They dismounted to lead the horses the rest of the way, walking side by side until, gradually, the pain in her back subsided a little.

"There's clearly something wrong. You've definitely lost a lot of weight. Mum told me she was worried. You have to make an appointment with your doctor. Have you told Greta, or Mum?"

"Yes. They've said the same thing as you. I've had blood tests. Okay, I will. I'll do it when I get back, but it's probably just some nasty bug." She smiled, knowing in her heart she hadn't wanted to think about anything that might spoil the life she now loved, wanting to push away anything that got in her way.

*

Dr Chadwick was about Paula's age, pleasant, friendly. Paula had never met her before. She prescribed some tablets and referred her for an X-ray at the Churchill Hospital.

Greta took time from work to go with her, a different hospital to the one in which she worked. The car parks were packed; a line of cars wound their way towards the entrance as they fought to park their car.

"So many people with cancer," Paula murmured.

"You don't have cancer," Greta said, squeezing her hand.

They sat together in the crowded waiting room, holding hands, saying little. She lifted a glossy magazine from the coffee table but couldn't concentrate on anything but the pictures.

As she lay upon her back for the young male radiographer, turning her body as instructed, she begged God not to spoil her new life. Afterwards, she followed the young man, pattering across the cold laboratory floor in the loose green hospital gown which covered her thin body to peer over his shoulder at the X-ray on the console, narrowing her eyes to discern any shadows or dark matter. "Can you see anything?" she asked anxiously.

He had been frowning, she felt sure. But now he turned to her reassuringly, the frown gone.

"Not really," he said, with a shake of his head. "Make an appointment with your doctor again. The results will go to your GP in a couple of days."

She tried to put it out of her mind in the following days. Greta suggested they visit her parents in Wales before Christmas came. They walked by the sea in Aberporth and were happy, but the pain in her back would not go away, no matter what she did, although she tried to conceal it. The pain in her back grew worse.

When they returned to Oxford, a letter from her doctor asked her to come to the surgery.

This time, Cynthia insisted upon going with her. The strain and worry were beginning to show on her mother's face and in the fluttering movements of her hand and the frequent kisses she gave.

"It won't be anything serious, Mum. I'm going to be okay. Just some kind of long-term bug that won't go away; the doctor suggested it might be something to do with unwashed olives I ate in Tunisia."

She said it lightly. It was true; the doctor had said that.

Her mother smiled and nodded but gripped her arm tightly as they walked together into the surgery.

This time, she saw Doctor McIntyre, the head of the practice; a wise old owl, due for retirement but still holding the fort with her capable hands.

"Your blood test indicates that there's a problem with your white blood cells," she explained. "We need to arrange an appointment with a cancer specialist immediately..."

That was the first time she had heard the 'c' word in connection with herself. She felt her mother's hand reaching for hers, experiencing a numbness of spirit which rendered her inert for several seconds. It couldn't be so. She was young, had too much still to do, too many places to visit with Greta. The numbness left her and panic set in, a fear that spread through her thin body like frostbite. She filled her lungs with air to steady herself.

"Cancer?" How many people had asked that one-worded question before her?

"You may have Hodgkin's disease, a lymphoma located in your lower back, which is why you have been experiencing pain there. You need a CT scan at the Churchill to tell us more." The doctor gazed at them without any trace of emotion in her face, only her eyes betrayed kindness.

"It will tell us what we need to know and how to treat it."

I don't want to die, Paula thought. I don't want to die and leave this all behind.

Her mother's fingers closed like a trap over her own, but she couldn't look at her; instead, she fixed her gaze upon the trees beyond the surgery window, their branches moving in a gentle wind. She clamped her teeth upon her bottom lip to supress tears.

It would be Christmas soon. She tried to focus upon that, on the usual excitement and panic of food and present buying. They had little money between them, so she used her skill at woodwork to make three puppets for Amy and Christine's children, yellow ostriches with comical heads that bobbed on their rope necks as they walked. She felt pleased with them. It was so important to keep herself busy; if she didn't, the thoughts crowded her mind, and a kind of loneliness, a separation from those people she loved. What she was afraid of was depression; she consumed hope like medication.

Friends sent Christmas cards, unaware of her sickness.

She and Greta picked holly in the woods and decorated the house. She told Greta about a time when they had been young – she and Howard and Marion and Christine, bumping over Monty Soanes frosty fields in a jeep to reach the far woodland where the holly lay, how they had decorated the pub with it.

The fatigue continued. Her weight grew even less as she lost food to sickness and stomach cramps.

When the day came for the appointment, her mother accompanied her once more. He was so nice, the specialist, so damned nice. But hope changed nothing.

The cancer had advanced quickly, an army of white cells overcoming the red, located in her back and still spreading. There was nothing that could be done. No effective treatment to stop it. She felt her mother's fingers once more, claw-like, clutching at her own, never daring to look at her in case she broke down.

"How long then, how long do I have?" she asked, bravely.

"A matter of months, but less than a year, I think."

The fingernails of Cynthia's hand squeezed her skin.

"Will I have to remain in hospital?"

"Oh no. You can remain in your own home. With time, we will supply nurses to care for you there."

Hard to digest everything he said, the shock of it turned to anger and disbelief. With time...

In the car park, Cynthia stared at her through shrunken, red-rimmed eyes, looking directly at her for the first time.

"We'll get some more advice. A second opinion," she said, trying to push the inevitable away, her voice choking with grief as she spoke.

At home, Greta wrapped her arms about Paula.

"What about the hospice in Wales? They've had some really good results."

"But do they actually stop people from dying?" she dismissed, mocking her rudely for the first time in their relationship.

"Sorry…" she said afterwards. She hadn't meant to be rude. She didn't want Greta to stop loving her, couldn't bear to think of Greta loving someone else.

"If I don't have much time, I want to be with you and with my family."

She pretended calm, while her emotions became tumultuous, invisible waves, crashing against rocks in a distant land that only she had visited. Nanny Edna behaved all Christmas as though she was sorry for being there, sorry to be so old, sorry for being alive and not to be the one with the cancer.

Greta found Paula staring through the kitchen window into the dark cottage garden one evening. She put her arms about the skinny body, pressing her face against her back and Paula began to cry for the first time. She cried at the unfairness of it all, for the life they would no longer have, the cities they would never have the time to visit, the publishing course she would never complete and the child they had talked about adopting. She cried because they would lose one another and Greta would find someone else. She cried quietly for a million reasons.

"I don't want to leave," she said, her voice choking with emotion. "I don't want to leave anything. Not kicking through the autumn leaves with Amy, the way they rustle on the ground, or the sunshine in the morning; but mostly, I don't want to leave the people. I don't want to leave you, you're the person who made me happy and I can't bear to leave you…"

The spring came. Christine's idea was that they would all go to France together, to the Camargue at the start of June; term times didn't matter anymore, nothing much mattered anymore. They would all go, and for a while the meticulous planning put death away from them.

They drove by convoy, crossing the channel by ferry to drive across France to the south, four cars between them. Cynthia and Maurice; Marion and Amy; Christine and Mike and their children. Howard and Michelle brought Cynthia's sister Stephanie and Nanny Edna; and Paula and Greta with Greta doing the driving.

They stayed overnight in two hotels, the first in Fontainebleau near Paris.

In the early morning mist, Howard and Paula sat peacefully, side by side, to sketch the ornate, Cinderella stone steps which curved to the palace entrance while the children played around the gentle fountains; and time stood still, which is what they each wanted.

They drove onward until they reached another hotel in Sommier, wandering along the riverbank where the water smelled of silt and earth on an early warm summer evening.

They ate at a restaurant where the food was good, but tried not to watch Paula, who found she could manage a pear only, and had to peel it with a sharp knife. Her thinness was an obvious thing, now. Sometimes people would stare. Her family would stare back, protecting her from the gaze of strangers.

At last, they reached the ancient yellowed towers and city walls of Aigues-Mortes in the midst of the salt marshes and canals. The smells of seawater, of salt and lavender and the sunshine removed death from their minds. The people who loved her would have stayed like this forever and ever.

By the sea, beside the pools, tactfully as they could, they tried to photograph her – they would imprison her spirit and never lose her this way. She was aware of it, and once, sunbathing beside Greta while the children splashed in the pool beside them, she opened a sleepy eye and caught Christine taking a photograph. She beckoned to her sister, who sat on the stone floor between the two women, holding Paula's hand and blinking back tears.

A few days after their arrival, Paula woke in the early morning sunshine that streamed through the white curtains. "I'm going to go windsurfing," she said, while Greta said nothing but wondered how she would have the strength to do it.

She loved the sport, which she had learned by practising on a lake in Cornwall.

They came to watch from the shore, Cynthia with them, fearing that she would never have the strength to keep the mast afloat. None wanted to stop her from doing this thing. Paula's determination was not to be argued with, not now.

Together they carried the equipment down to the water's edge. There was a good wind, not too strong, and the white foamy sea horses swam against it and dispersed on the shore. The rest of the family sat upon the sandy beach, watching.

With Maurice and Greta's help, Paula pushed the surfer out into the shallows, then climbed aboard to pull the heavy mast out of the water. It was obvious to all the effort this took her, the strain upon her body showed in her face as she lifted the mast to the wind. But she smiled, even when the sail fell from her hands again and again and her frail body started to shiver with cold. In the end, she managed only a few metres, less than fifteen, before she was forced to release the weight of the boom and she and the windsurfing sail collapsed into the water. If she felt foolish, she didn't let it show.

"Shall we try a gentle swim, instead?" she called out to them.

Every morning of that holiday they tried to push away the thought of going home, of not being together, of the terrible, unbelievable truth that would happen.

It was during the October of that year that Paula stopped being able to work or to attend college. She began to face incredible pain, to the point where she could no longer walk up and down the wooden staircase, or hold a cup of tea without a trembling hand that threatened to spill it. Her great pain could not be managed at home any longer. The nurse who visited each week suggested she be admitted to Sobell House for palliative care.

She didn't want to go there, knowing it would be the end, but she didn't want to be a nuisance, either. She was afraid of dying alone, but told no one; she was afraid that this would be the last place she would ever see, that she could never come home.

She was never alone. Either Greta, or their friends, or a family member would stay with her, sitting beside her bed and sometimes sleeping next to her through the night.

She tried to stave off the powerful medication.

"I want to talk to you, and I can't if I'm asleep," she would say. So, her siblings would play silly word games with her and, together, they would forget she was dying of cancer for a short while, and they would laugh together, sitting around her bed in the hospital. No one spoke about death, but her parents remembered what grief was once again. Grief became part of daily life for all of them.

It was a few weeks after that visit, in November, that Paula started to decline. Their cheerful games had to stop. They sat beside her sleeping form, not wishing to wake her, silently crying. The doctor told them that to wake her from her gentle dreams would be akin to pushing her off a cliff because the morphine had delivered her to serenity. To wake her would be a shock that her heart wouldn't withstand.

So, they kept a vigil by day and by night, taking it in turns to watch over her.

They were with her on the morning that she died. Maurice was the last person to stay with her, at his own request, talking softly through her sleep. He told her how much he loved her, that he was sorry he had found it hard to accept who she really was and that he was so proud of her. He told her that there wouldn't be one day in his life that he wouldn't think about her.

*

Miss Independent 2013

Amy, aged twenty-three, loved her new job and generally found it easy to rise in the mornings, even in the darkness of winter with large water bombs hurling themselves at the windowpane. Perhaps, this morning, despite the sunshine streaming through the branches and the sight of the distant elm trees pointing at the blue sky, she was a little tired, a little jaded. To earn extra money, she occasionally worked for her great-aunt Stephanie, Nan's sister, behind the bar of the Masons public house. "Don't forget the fifty I owe Nan," she muttered aloud to herself as she pulled on her jeans.

Working clothes were usually casual in the rehab clinic. This morning some of the residents were playing a game of football. She smiled at the dusty photograph of her aunt Paula which stood in the windowsill: Paula with the three-year-old Amy, plump and smooth skinned, happy in her swimming costume. The photograph was taken in France. She was seated upon Aunty Paula's lap beside a swimming pool. The baby Amy was brown-skinned and rosy-cheeked in contrast with Paula, whose face was angular and sallow, and so very thin.

She thought of Paula frequently. The memories were hazy, but the love remained. Looking at the picture brought her luck, that's what she believed.

They lived in Rose Cottage, where Paula had lived. She, Marion and her younger sister, Ruby. Almost thirteen now and not so little, but often the focus of teenage arguments which generally ended with Ruby slamming her bedroom door in disgust and frustration with the world. Part of Amy's need to earn more money was to help her mum, who struggled with the mortgage and bills, having bought the cottage – which in all ways suited their needs.

Greta had moved to Bournemouth eventually, to live with someone else, in another relationship which started several years after Paula died. When she could, she visited them all. On Amy's birthday, she sent a present or money and sometimes she wrote to her. Amy kept all of her letters and sometimes wrote back to her, calling her "My dear, fabulous aunt…"

Beside the photograph of Paula was the one of Amy and Ali, taken on a beach in Turkey. They had talked a little about moving in with one another, and of marriage. They both knew that this was a distant dream. Ali was Muslim and his parents wanted him to marry into that faith. Amy, at least, wasn't sure that she had a specific faith. She was a fan of Stephen Hawking and didn't believe in the existence of a God, but she did believe that there was another world, somewhere.

In the room next to her, Ruby slept on. Unlike her big sister, who had to leave at six to be at work on time, Ruby had an hour and a half before her alarm told her to join her friends and get the bus to school.

Nan had helped Amy to pay for her pride and joy, the silver car she needed to drive through the traffic and arrive on time at the rehab centre. Sometimes, in the car, she would listen to the radio. More often, her own lyrics haunted her with worm holes drifting through the recesses of her mind during the day as she tried to perfect her songs. She had many followers, had been writing and performing her own music since she was sixteen at RAP venues. She had bought her own recording equipment over a long period of time and now her friend Amancia, a vocalist, was about to introduce her to the new recording studio in the Cowley Road.

The journey to work should only have taken a short while, but the village where the rehab centre stood was on the way to Witney and the traffic queues from Oxford to Witney were notoriously slow. But that morning, crawling through traffic through the early morning sunshine, she felt a buzz of excitement as she rhymed two lines about unrequited love, singing them to herself repeatedly to get them right, then grinning cheerfully at the young man in the car beside her.

Reaching the centre's office, she handed the receptionist her telephone and gulped down a cup of coffee, ready to collect her two football teams – a mismatched crew who would play six-a-side. She knew little about football, other than the few rules her cousins had explained to her, but her enthusiasm was great and she was rarely phased by new experiences.

In the September sunshine, she faced her two teams with the dedication of Alex Ferguson. She had managed to balance them carefully – this assorted group with serious addiction problems – some of them overweight, while some scarcely appeared to have the strength to kick a ball.

Twelve people, between the ages of twenty-two and fifty-six, male and female. Only five of them knew very much about the rules. It didn't matter, this was their fourth game, and they seemed to enjoy the exercise and the camaraderie. At least they smiled at her, now; and smiling was a formidable task when in the case of most of them, they were suffering from their detoxification. Low energy, low blood sugar, aching muscles, fatigue, dizziness… just a few of the symptoms standing in their way.

Three of the patients would be leaving soon. Sam, who was her own age, had been acutely irritable when he first came, swearing at her and, on one occasion, trashing his room in frustration. He had been on methadone for a long time. After a long while, he started to talk to her about his parents, ordinary people from the sound of things. People who loved him and didn't understand why he had done what he had.

There was Leslie, too, who had two children under the age of seven and had left them with her mother while she drank and drank, anything she could get hold of. A woman with such low self-esteem that she had slept behind the dustbins by the supermarket and had casual sex for money. Amy was most worried about her, but at least her parents wanted her to be reunited with her children, to come home. They, hardly wealthy people, had spent all of their savings to pay for her rehabilitation.

Then there was Roger, a chaotic depressive in his forties who had lost his job. His wife had ordered him to leave and he hadn't seen his children for six months. Amy had persuaded him to get a lawyer and not assume that he could never see his children again. Even now, his holdall at the edge of the pitch held the brown paper bags to breathe away his panic attacks.

Most of the people here had a family in the background somewhere, or supportive parents who could pay for their child's rehabilitation and who loved them, no matter what distance drug abuse had put between them. This was what aided recovery. Amy had overcome so much to forge a close bond with the patients with whom she worked. She would miss these three especially, she thought, as the Sweats and Fire-starters lined up to face her. The two teams had chosen their own names. Fire-starters was Sam's own private joke, the team had adopted it with dark humour.

"Geoff, you were great as defender last match, could you do that again? Leslie and Sharon, you take the midfield, okay? And Sam and Darsh, you work well together as strikers. Everyone okay with that?" She stared from one to the other of them, having already given the Sweats their positions, and they nodded at her. Each wore a red shirt, bought at great expense by the finance department, while the Sweats wore a yellow bib. In the case of Sharon, her red shirt was rather tight across her phenomenal breasts and some of the guys were trying not to stare.

Roger, large, ungainly, but very strong asked, "Shall I be goalie again?"

"Would you Roger? You are the best goalie we have. Are you okay with that?"

He half turned to check his holdall for the supply of brown paper bags, then smiled at her and nodded.

"My kids are coming to visit later on this afternoon. I'm hoping you'll be around so that you can meet them," he said shyly.

"Sure, I'd love to. I'm here all day." She smiled back. Then she called, "Try not to knock the nets down this time," as the teams scuttled off for the start of the match.

They were plastic nets. Really, what the centre needed was a proper football pitch with fixed posts, not the large piece of scrubland next to the centre. She wondered whether she could find time to do some money-raising activity, then strode, business-like, towards the centre forwards.

*

When she went to the office to retrieve her phone later in the day, there were two messages, one good, one bad. The first was from Amancia.

"Amy, Tariq wants to meet you. Can you get to the recording studio for six on Thursday?"

Tariq was the spoiled boy from Saudi with loads of money who owned the studio and managed the clients. No hesitation, other than her heart skipping a beat as her fingers texted back.

"Yes, sure, thanks."

The second message was from her mother.

"At the hospital. Ruby may have broken her arm. Very tired. Would you put the fish cakes and chips in the oven for dinner? There's a salad already made up in the fridge."

"No problem," she replied.

Then she called her father to say she couldn't come after all, but would be there tomorrow, instead.

Graham's house lay on the Witney outskirts, a little further on from the rehab centre. Unsuspecting visitors were surprised by the mess inside because the outside of the house was orderly and really quite pretty. Graham knew where everything was, which was what counted. A skilled carpenter and avid reader, his books stood in carefully balanced piles rather than in a bookcase, alongside his carpentry tools: wooden boxes containing chisels and claw hammers, saws and nails.

When he wasn't laying down tiles in someone's house or fixing broken doors, he relaxed by reading everything from Deighton to Dostoevsky and making wooden toys for Amy's five-year-old half-brother, Will: his son from a second relationship. He had a small TV, but rarely watched it.

Amy was proud of her father, an intelligent, peaceable man who had defeated his own demons. He was generally unshaven and cared little for appearances except when he had to do so. Amy didn't believe it was possible to love anyone as much as she loved her parents, though they were like chalk and cheese.

She just about remembered a time, long ago, when they had first parted. There were no big rows, there was no other woman – her father simply moved out of the pub. But she remembered the sadness inside and the scab she could never physically pick at, recalled the loneliness of missing him. Her mother had bought a kitten to distract her, which worked to an extent. The kitten was allowed to sleep on her bed. For a long time she had kept the dream alive in her heart that her parents would live together with her once more.

Now, Amy parked the car on the road outside his house and let herself inside with her own key. The house was quiet and, for a second or two, Amy held her breath, recalling a time when she and Marion had come to check on him having not heard from him for several days. A time when they might find the sink piled up with crockery, with empty cans and bottles attracting flies. She turned nervously to the kitchen but it was clean and tidy by her father's standards, only the recently used plates and pans still littered the sink.

She saw them in the living room and smiled with relief.

Graham was sitting cross-legged on the floor, opposite his son, Will. They were silent in concentration, making origami flowers with white paper, just as he had used to with her.

Will looked up at her and called her name in surprise while she met her father's eyes, blue as her own. The child threw down his paper efforts and ran to greet her, hugging her knees, almost knocking her from her feet.

"Hello. Cup of tea?" Graham asked.

"I'll make it," she said with good humour, "if I can get into the sink to fill the kettle."

She took off her jacket then rolled up her sleeves to root around in cold greasy water for the scouring pad. She replaced the cold with hot water and squirted everything liberally with washing up liquid.

"How's things? How's Ali?" Her father called through to the kitchen.

"Good. We're getting the Bond film to watch at the weekend; you know, *Skyfall*? Haven't seen it yet, though Amancia already told me that Judy Dench dies."

"Does she? I like Judy Dench. She's a good actress."

He ordered a Chinese meal for the three of them. Afterwards they played junior scrabble with Will and Amy took him up to the little room that Graham kept for him. It was littered with Lego and children's books. Some of them used to be Amy's. Her childish scribbles had marked them. She read two stories to Will, then left him to play with his Star Wars figures, creeping downstairs.

"How's the job going?" Graham asked as they sipped tea.

"Good. Guess what though?" She told him about the coming meeting with Tariq, finishing, "He's the son of a prince, apparently. He's got a flat in Summertown and pots of money so they say."

Graham chuckled. She loved to hear him laugh; his laughter was rare, his humour dark and often peppered with cynicism.

"Don't be fooled, don't get ripped off; stay true to your music and read the contracts, if there are contracts..." he growled, more than a hint of suspicion in his voice.

She stayed for a long while and it was late when she arrived home to park the newish car next to her mother's. Muppet, who was the fattest cat in the world, was prowling in the bushes and came out to greet her, meowing loudly and rubbing her soft black body around Amy's legs. She lifted him up in her arms, rubbing her face against the cat's whiskers before following the little path to the door and ducking her head beneath the bushes.

As she reached the door, her mother's raised voice grated on the other side of it. She rarely raised her voice. Amy knew it would be something to do with Ruby. The three of them got on very well but, recently, Ruby had been pushing her luck, as Nan would say. She clamped her lips together in a distorted grimace, took a deep breath, then put her key in the lock.

"That's enough, now. It's late. Turn off the light and go to sleep!" Marion called up the spiralling staircase.

She turned to Amy, her face angry, stressed. Amy saw the dark smudges beneath her eyes.

"I'm sorry love. I didn't mean to snap. Ruby is driving me mad. How's Dad?"

"He's good. Will was there. Why's she driving you mad?"

"She promised to be home on time to revise for her Spanish test; then at four thirty I got a text to say she'd just popped into McDonald's. Where did she get the money from, for a start?"

Amy shrugged and dropped into a kitchen chair.

"Skipped lunch, then used her lunch money? That's what I used to do," she suggested, following it with a small grin which was part apology, part empathy with her sister.

"Did you?" Marion asked in surprise. "Well, she shouldn't skip lunch, although at least that explains the money. I suppose it's what her friends all do."

"Do you want me to talk to her this time?"

Marion hesitated for a moment.

"Would you?" she asked. "Do you mind? She always listens to you; she yells at me."

Amy nodded and Marion's shoulders slumped in relief. "I wish she'd be a bit more diligent about her homework, wish she'd study like you did…"

She snorted with amusement. "Mum! Ruby is thirteen, whereas I am twenty-four. There's a bit of a difference you know. Don't you remember how Louise and I behaved at fifteen? Trying to get into night clubs, with you hot on our trail! I didn't actually give a monkey's cuss about exam results, then. I would have done a lot better at school if I had."

Marion put her arms about her daughter in a sudden rush of love and gratitude.

"I suppose that's right."

She thought, not for the first time, that her eldest child had a gift for putting everything into perspective.

She would have a chat with Ruby after school, Amy assured her mother. She made a cup of tea to take with her to her room, lifting Muppet's silky, floppy body under her arm so he could lie upon her bed.

She climbed the staircase, weary of body, light of heart. For a while, she read messages on social media. Her cousin had posted a picture of all of the cousins from last Christmas wearing silly hats.

She finished the tea and pulled the duvet over her, then slept, fully clothed.

*

On Wednesday evening, Ali strolled down the hill to Quarry Hollow to meet Amy at the Masons pub. In a few minutes, she would finish her work for the night. His tall figure was hunched against the wind that had started earlier in the day, his dark hair lapped the upturned collar of his coat, his bare hands were shoved into his pockets.

When he entered the little pub, most of the customers were leaving and Stephanie was in conversation with a small group of regulars.

"Hello, my duck," she called, as the open door brought in the wind and the autumn leaves. She had a lovely warmth in her greeting, always. Ali smiled at the way her eyes lit up as though in genuine pleasure at seeing him.

She broke away from the group to kiss his cheek. Behind the bar, Amy was drying glasses and stacking them on the counter. She stopped to fill a glass with apple juice. Ali neither smoked nor drank. It was something she admired in him, his self-control about all things. It wasn't because he was Muslim; several of their Muslim friends enjoyed smoking and drinking. It was his way, it was just Ali.

He stood for a while at the bar, waiting for her to finish her tasks, then pulled himself onto one of the bar stools. She reached across the bar to kiss him.

"Are you staying tonight, or do you have to get back?" he asked.

"Staying, if that's alright. Have to leave early though."

He nodded, understanding.

It was better for both of them, his moving into the flat on the other side of the Quarry. When he'd lived with his mum, they were forced to sneak about. She was never hostile or unkind, but not really warm towards her either; Amy knew she wasn't her choice for a daughter-in-law.

"You go, Amy." Stephanie smiled. "Thanks for doing those. Go and get some rest."

Together, her arm through his, they walked up the hill and past the park. Ali told her about a promotion in the bank where he worked. Their jobs, their lives were so different, Amy reflected. There was something safe about Ali that she admired and loved. He didn't flip in anger as Amy could from time to time. He rarely lost his temper, or that hold on his emotions, as she could. Yet beneath the surface he was passionate; he loved her and loved being with her, she could sense that without being told repeatedly.

Later, after making love, they lay side by side beneath the duvet on Ali's bed. Amy leaned upon her elbow, her auburn hair loose, tickling his cheek. She watched the rise and fall of his smooth brown chest as she lay in the crook of his arm, circling his skin with her forefinger.

"One day, I want to have at least two children," she said softly.

He put out a hand to stroke her hair and smiled as their eyes locked together. He said nothing, understanding the need for her to say it.

Neither of them really wanted to have children just yet. When they first met, three years ago, there was only mild attraction. The love came later. When they brought up the subject of children, it was a fairy tale. They encouraged the fairy tale while knowing, deep down, the unlikeliness of it.

Ali's mother wanted him to marry a Muslim girl. She accepted Amy as Ali's friend, but there would always be the unspoken condition on his mother's part that she parted from Ali... eventually. Once upon a time, the situation had seemed tragic and romantic. They were Tony and Maria from her favourite film.

Idly, she let her fingers wander to his belly button, until he doubled up with laughter, drawing his knees to his belly and grabbing her hand.

"Where shall we go on holiday next year, back to Turkey?" he asked, kissing her shoulder. "Shall we pretend to be married again?"

*

She was a little nervous as she applied make-up to her face in the ladies' loo at work. No need to be nervous, she told herself. Either he would like her songs and her voice, or not. Simple as that.

She hummed a few bars from her new and currently favourite track. It was called, 'I don't owe you,' written in memory of the boyfriend before Ali, a song about a control freak. The ex-boyfriend understood as soon as he heard it, although she made no obvious reference to him; he sent her a text ordering her to take it off, threatening to take her to court.

Empty threats. No one knew it was inspired by him. So, Amy refused. He'd made the tag cos there was a tag after all. Songs and paintings were like newborn babies, she thought. You couldn't simply rid yourself of them.

Martha, a co-worker, passed her in the corridor as she sped from the loo with her handbag gripped to her side.

"Going somewhere nice?" she asked cheerfully, noting the change of clothing and new boots.

"Sort of." She smiled without further explanation, except to say, "In a bit of a rush…"

The Cowley Road was always hell to park in, and she was running late. The left boot felt a little tight, but she ran, hobbling across the gravel to her car.

Amy had recorded in two studios before, both in, or close to the Cowley Road. They were lively but shabby places, filled with husky laughter as the musicians and technicians smoked inside and left their cans of drink littered upon the tables.

Tariq's studio was nothing like this. For a start, it had a real reception area, the walls of which were dazzlingly clean and white. There were expensive potted plants and a genuine receptionist. A very beautiful and skinny one, Amy noted, just before her friend Amancia bounced into the room to grab her arm, greeting her with a kiss on the cheek – her giggles stifled.

"Sorry. I'm a bit late, aren't I? Work, then couldn't park…"

"No problem. They're all in there; it's very relaxed and, anyway, you're not many minutes late. Come on, I'll take you through."

She followed Amancia, her flamboyant, voluptuous friend who always dressed so beautifully, along a white corridor decorated with modern paintings and impressive music awards, until Amancia pushed at the heavy door to a large recording studio to nudge her inside.

There were three men in the room, but she relaxed as she saw George who she had worked with before. In fact, he'd introduced her to the community of musicians and rappers in Oxford. He was a popular rapper in his own right, originally from Cameroon, who she had supported with vocals. Seeing him now was a boon and a gigantic bit of luck.

He greeted her with a warm smile and a discreet nod of the head, but didn't come across the room to hug her as he had before. His normally ebullient behaviour was a little reserved today, she noticed.

Then there was a second guy – who she didn't know.

Small, a shadow of a beard, a little edgy; a worrier, she thought. He was in conversation with the tall man in a leather coat. When Amy entered, they both looked up.

The tall man she took to be Tariq.

She gazed around the Aladdin's cave of mixing boards and expensive equipment, until he of the expensive leather coat and jeans called out.

"Ah, Amy? Here you are. Welcome."

He crossed the room, thrusting his right hand towards her. White shirt, confident smile. He appeared incongruous in the room, more businessman than musician.

"Hello… Tariq?" she asked. "Sorry I'm a bit late."

"Not at all, your timing is perfect. We've just been testing some new equipment; you'll be the first to benefit from it. Would you like a drink before we begin?" He turned to Amancia. "Would you fetch a jug of water, please?"

Whether he was aware of her friendship with George wasn't clear. But it was a bonus for her. Having poured herself a glass of water, she fumbled inside her bag for the lyrics she had brought with her. She knew them by heart. She had chosen 'The Real You' and 'I don't owe you'. George was familiar with 'The Real You'. He smiled, nodded at her to join him.

They ran through the volume setting and the beat, chatting with ease until, at last, they were ready. Her nervousness had passed; it always did when the work began and she was consumed by that interest. She trusted George and worked easily with him.

Tariq watched her all the while and to his credit, he gave them the space she needed.

He had a habit, she noticed, of tapping his thin lips with the side of his thumb as though deep in thought.

When they were ready, she leaned into the microphone, breathing the song into it as though it was a friend.

*

Less than a week later, Tariq called her. She hadn't recognised the number but knew the accented voice immediately.

"I was really impressed, especially with 'The Real You'. It's bittersweet, a little cynical, but never detracts from the love theme. Look, I have some ideas I'd like to discuss with you; can I meet you for dinner one evening?"

Amy agreed, pleased with his analysis and just a little excited.

Restaurants, in Amy's family, were for special occasions like birthdays. As a rule, she and Ali treated themselves to a Chinese or a curry when they were feeling flushed after a payday.

She had heard of the expensive restaurant where he had arranged to meet her of course and prayed that he would be paying for dinner.

It was in the Banbury Road: all glass and fairy lights and waiters calling her madam. He was sitting on a bar stool when she arrived. Again, jacket, jeans, but a tee shirt on this occasion. She felt stupidly guilty about Ali but knew she would tell him. A date was the last thing it was and Ali would get it; she wanted to progress with her music, that was all there was to it.

"Is it a date?" her mother had asked before she left the house.

"Absolutely not," she said, glowering at Marion. "I love Ali, I told you. I just want to promote my music. He's fairly good-looking, but I'm not in the least bit attracted to him."

She greeted Tariq with a brief half smile as she made her way around the bar towards him, catching a whiff of expensive aftershave, of sandalwood and patchouli. A waiter approached to take her coat.

"Hey. You look nice," he greeted her.

"Thanks. I've got a bit of a cold, nothing too much."

"Has it affected your incredible voice?"

She pulled herself onto a bar stool beside him and decided to order a Margarita.

"Noo, don't think so. It's only mild, nothing that gargling with lemon and honey won't cure."

He smiled. "My mother used to give me tea and make me gargle with salt."

"Sounds like a very sensible cure. Where does your mother live?"

"She lived in Jeddah, but she died a few years ago. My father's still alive."

"And you're a prince, is that right?" she asked, trying to sound interested but unimpressed, as though she had asked whether he worked in a supermarket.

Tariq laughed, his head held back, eyes creased at the corners; it was the first time she had seen him laugh and she smiled with him.

"No, it isn't right. I'm the second son of my father's third marriage and he's wealthy. But I'm not a prince. I went to university here, in Oxford and stayed on because I like the city. It became a home to me." He broke off rather abruptly. "Enough about me. You work with down-and-outs, don't you?"

She widened her eyes at him indignantly, her sense of loyalty offended.

"I wouldn't call them down-and-outs. Some are from very wealthy backgrounds. There's a fair smattering of the middle classes as well as those from disadvantaged backgrounds. They've got alcohol or drug dependency problems, which unites rich and poor, I think you'll find."

"No-hopers, then?" he asked.

Was he trying to goad her? Winding her up, testing how far she might go to kiss his feet for this opportunity?

"If they were no-hopers, as you put it, we wouldn't have such a high success rate. Perhaps you haven't had any difficulty in your life; maybe you've had an easy ride." Damn him, the spoiled rich kid whose life was perfect, with no idea of the kind of difficulties and traumas that other people had to face.

He gave a dry laugh. "Oh no, I wouldn't say that. I suffered horribly as a child when my parents parted. You have no idea, and I'm not going to explain."

She stared at him candidly. He stared back, thrusting his jaw defiantly towards her. Suddenly he laughed, resting a hand upon her arm.

"Don't take offence. It was something George said about where you work."

"George wouldn't have said those things," she murmured, coming to her friend's defence. "There are quite a lot of musicians who have suffered from alcohol or drug abuse. He doesn't judge other people."

"Okay. I stand corrected and I'm sorry." Finally, he held the palms of his hands towards her.

She nodded, signalling a truce.

She chose a Portuguese fish dish from the menu. They sat opposite one another at the table by a far window. Tariq ordered wine. Amy had one glass from the expensive bottle and then sipped water, determined not to give too much of herself away on this second meeting. She noticed that beneath the lights above their table, his hair was black like Ali's.

He spoke about his family and she listened, enthralled by tales of hunting with falcons, appalled by the stories of bully boys at his school. By the time they had ordered their desert, she liked him a little better.

"You have a boyfriend, right?" he asked her. She didn't want to talk about Ali, didn't think Ali would want to be talked about, either.

"You said you had some ideas you wanted to discuss with me – when you called me?"

Her sudden change of subject must have made him nervous. An imperceptible twitch of his lips, as though he was amused or startled or both.

The waiter brought their deserts. He leaned back in his chair, staring down at the delicious chocolate concoction placed before him.

"Of course." He nodded. "Two venues for your performance, in different places. The second depends upon the third. One in January, in Birmingham; the other in London, at the Consulate events room in February. But here's the thing; the first is a competition. Two winners will be chosen by celebrity rappers to perform at the venue in London. You have to win; so far as I'm concerned, you will win. You are talented, ambitious, determined. If you agree, George will assist you. You'll have to rehearse with him, often. You rehearse in the studio. You don't get a penny until you win the first competition, but after that you sign a contract and I become your agent..."

She breathed in hard, through her nostrils, listening to him, still watching his face while trying to digest it all.

"You really have that much confidence in me?"

Tariq nodded his head. "Of course. Wouldn't be here if I didn't."

"Then, yes… thanks. You're on."

"Good. I'll get the bill. Would you like to come back to my flat for a drink?"

He reached across the table suddenly, putting his hand over hers.

She hesitated, feeling a compulsion to do everything he suggested now, but wanting to say no. She withdrew her fingers slowly, smiling across the table.

"Thanks. I've really enjoyed this evening and I'm excited about the plan, but it's getting late. I have work tomorrow, remember?"

If he was offended, he didn't show it.

She drove home, thinking about Tariq, wanting to tell her mother and Ali, too. She parked her car beside her mother's and leaned against the driver's door for a moment, taking a cigarette from her handbag. She gazed up at the forest, a part of her trying to calm down, so many thoughts running through her head. Shotover had disappeared in a milky veil of mist. A small dog-like creature crossed the empty road before her. Foxes are lucky, so Nanny Edna used to say.

*

Amy worked hard, but never as hard as she did that autumn. After her day job, she alternated nights working at the Masons with nights at the recording studio. The same songs, over and over again, practising and practising towards perfection; she grew tired but never dispirited.

That George was working with her kept the atmosphere light, happy, always with the energy they were accustomed to feeling together.

Tariq stayed in the studio for most of the time, arms folded, sometimes that gesture as though he was deep in thought; the edge of his thumb tapping his lip, always watching them, seldom commenting. When he offered a comment, it was helpful and to the point. But they were always conscious of him being there. It didn't really bother them; he was the boss after all, but it seemed unnecessary much of the time. It was George's experience and collaboration that Amy needed.

Twice, Ali accompanied her to the studio, but he didn't feel comfortable with Tariq there. He knew George well and when she had finished, the three of them went to the pub, but Tariq didn't come.

"Do you like him?" Ali asked her after the second evening.

"Who, Tariq? I don't really know him well enough. I don't dislike him; I suppose I just need him to help me with my music."

"You were doing fine with your music," he said, putting his arms about her.

"Don't you like him?"

"I think he's another control freak. I think he fancies you…"

She twisted her head to one side, wondering. "You're not jealous, are you?"

"I'm the best-looking man in your life. Nothing to feel jealous about," he said, rocking her in his arms.

That autumn, she rarely saw her mother or Ruby, her father even less so. Then, in mid-November, Tariq told them he was going away, going home to visit his family. The rehearsal could stop, for a while. Her mother was the most relieved of all. It was commonplace for her to say, "You have dark smudges beneath your eyes, you're overtired. Get some rest."

Tariq's going away was a break for her, allowing her to relax a little before Christmas. She went to the new shopping centre with Ruby to buy presents. She enjoyed the annual family pantomime visit, organised by Nanny Cynthia. She sat with Louise's youngest daughter upon her lap, booing the evil villain and giggling at the risqué jokes. She visited her father with Ali, and they all went out with her aunts for an early Christmas meal.

After Christmas and the New Year festivities, her father sat in their cottage eating cheese and crackers and the remnants of Christmas cake in front of the log fire. A rare moment, her mother and father together and happy; drinking tea, eating cake, old friends who knew each other well.

He handed her a Christmas present, a cheque for one hundred pounds. She leapt up from the stool beside him, throwing her arms about his neck until he pushed her off.

"I got a bit more than I thought I would for decorating that house in Burford," he told her modestly. He had bought Marion a present too, a crocus in a pot.

"Your aunt wants to know if you and Ali would like to have a holiday with her in Dubai this year; all you have to do is find the plane tickets and your spending money."

His older sister, of course, a nurse who held a senior position in a large hospital in Dubai.

"Bloody hell, I'd love it!" she enthused. "Ali too, I'll tell him tomorrow. Are you coming to Harry's twenty-first birthday party? It's fancy dress."

He grunted. "Only if I can go as myself."

"You can go as who you like. Ali is going as 'The Cat in the Hat', me and Ru are going as Thing One and Thing Two."

He laughed. "Maybe."

Beyond the house, the garden was swathed in a blanket of powdery snow, covered in a smooth, sparkling veneer. Small spears of ice framed the window, too cold to melt as yet. It had been snowing on and off for days, snow on snow, just like the carol.

Tomorrow, Amy would help Louise to take the two girls sledging on Shotover.

As she plopped into the armchair vacated by her mother, her phone buzzed with a message.

Her eyes widened in surprise. It was Tariq. She was suddenly irritated, wanting to hold onto the feeling of contentment inside for a while longer.

"I'm back, very bored. Fancy a meal somewhere? Meet me halfway, or I can come and get you if you want."

"Ali?" Marion asked, returning to the sitting room.

"Nope. Tariq. Says he's back from London, asked me out for a meal."

She didn't want to leave; she was warm and comfortable where she was. But this was Tariq. Perhaps she ought to jump to it. She felt a pang of guilt. He was lonely when she was not.

"If I left now, I could give Dad a lift to the bus stop in Oxford so he can get home."

Marion stared at her in horror. "Not driving, Amy? Please don't tell me you intend to drive in this snow? The buses have only just started running again." She peered through the window into the darkening garden, at the deep pillows of snow and the sparkling, crystalline ice.

"It's a crazy idea." She turned to her ex-husband, waiting for him to object, a look upon her face which said, "Say something."

He stopped stoking the fire to look at them both. "Mum's right, Amy," he said after a pause. "You don't want to get the car out in this weather. It's likely to snow again and, besides, I don't need a lift, I can get a bus from Headington."

"Can't you just meet him another time?" Marion pleaded, knowing she had already lost the battle. If Amy had decided upon a course of action, she was unstoppable. Just like her grandmother.

"I'm not going to have time when work starts again, am I?" she pointed out. "Besides, I think I should go. It'll be fine. I'm a good driver and I'll be careful. Promise not to be too late back, honestly."

The snow creaked beneath the wheels, causing her to slide as she pulled away from the parking space with her father, once her driving instructor. Slowly, cautiously, she drove the car onto the main road. Thick snow lay at its verges; compacted snow covered the road.

She dropped Graham close to the bus station in Oxford, promised to be careful once more and hugged him, thanking him for her Christmas present.

As she sat in the car, waving goodbye to him, her phone pinged with another message and an address.

"Come to my flat," Tariq suggested.

It was in the Woodstock Road. An old house, Edwardian or Victorian, she thought, now divided into flats. A pathway had been cut through the snow to the flight of steps leading to the main entrance.

She pressed the buzzer. A few seconds later he appeared at the door, staring down at her. He wore a long black overcoat, both formal and casual; it looked as if it had been tailor made for him. He smiled, and yet there was an intensity in the bright, dark eyes which she didn't understand. He handed her his arm and she slipped hers through it, smiling uncertainly.

"We wouldn't want you slipping over in the snow," he said.

They walked to another restaurant, just a few metres away, one that Amy had only passed by before. Now, in the dark, with the yellow lighting reflecting on the snow, she realised how beautiful it was. She had not been to Paris yet, but perhaps this was the kind of restaurant you might find there, she thought.

As they sat at a table overlooking the street it started to snow again. Large, white crystals floated across the air, becoming denser as the evening went on. This should have been fun, she supposed, but, as yet, he had hardly spoken to her and his replies had been short. Tariq appeared tense, almost nervous.

This time, she accepted a glass of wine.

"How did it go, seeing your family?" she asked, trying to penetrate whatever emotion lying beneath the mask.

He thrust his lips forward, shrugging. "It was alright, I guess. I saw the relatives I needed to see. My father is no happier, although he has everything he wants: a young wife, a good position in the government, grandchildren. He had little to say to me, but that's normal. He isn't exactly the most affectionate parent. He thinks that I'm wasting my life."

"I'm sorry," she said, trying to understand, thinking how lucky she was to have approval from her own family, no matter what.

They talked about the music; about the competition to come. He said that she should return to rehearsals as soon as possible. It felt safer to her to stick to that subject; it was easier to talk about that. And suddenly he dabbed the corner of his mouth with a napkin, then stared at her with an intensity which made her heart gallop. Briefly, she imagined herself astride a horse, in danger, wheeling the reins to ride away from a sudden enemy.

"Do you like me?"

The question made her start, made her more nervous, still.

"Of course. Yes, I like you. I wouldn't have accepted your invitation this evening if I didn't," she said. But she frowned, couldn't help herself, at the swift turn in conversation which made her squirm with discomfort.

Slowly he nodded.

"It's difficult to gauge whether people like you sometimes. Being in charge makes a person insecure, perhaps…"

He smiled at her.

She felt sorry for him. She started to talk about her family and their failings, which were many. Talking too fast, laughing too much, trying so hard to make him feel better. She sensed that he was angry, had been angry all evening; she didn't know what else to do but this.

When she stopped talking and he was smiling again, which had been her objective, he asked, "Coming back to the flat for a nightcap?"

She grimaced apologetically.

"Not sure it's a good idea. It's starting to snow again and I promised Mum..."

It sounded lame. Why had she mentioned her mother, for Pete's sake?

He nodded without protest but looked so crestfallen that she relented.

"Oh, alright. Thanks," she added. "But no more wine; I'll have coffee, and I really can't stay very long."

It was a large flat, very modern and beautiful, meticulously clean and tidy. An art gallery rather than a home, she thought as she drifted through it. The walls were decorated with expensive Egyptian artwork, with paintings and bright tapestries adorning the wide, high walls. She grinned at the comparison with her own home, where socks were dried before the fire, crockery of all shapes and sizes lined the shelves in the kitchen and a cat curled up on the constant pile of washing on the ironing board.

While Tariq made the coffee for her in the shiny, chrome kitchen, she took off her jacket and sent a text to her mother to avoid a lecture later. She had already received two messages telling her to come home before more snow settled. After that, she wandered about the living room, examining the paintings and photographs of his family, a family from a very different world than her own.

As she stood before a painting of dazzling white mountains and a wide, lemon-yellow beach which stretched before a violet sea, Tariq came to stand behind her, silent as a cat. She started as he touched her arm lightly.

"Do you like that one? It's a print, of course. The artist is called Mahmoud Said. I think the original hangs in an art gallery in Cairo."

"I love it; it reminds me a little of the place I went to with Ali, in Turkey."

She turned around to face him. He was too close for comfort. She could feel his breath on her cheek so took a step back, then seeing the little white cups set upon a tray in the centre of the room, took it as an excuse to move away. She remained standing as she took one. The coffee was sweet, mocha coloured and with the vague taste of alcohol.

Tariq sat beside her, taking a heavy and expensive looking book from the coffee table, searching for a particular page.

"My mother was a photographer, quite a well-known artist. These are some of her photographs."

She had to sit, then. Not to do so would be impolite.

He moved a little closer to her, showing her a scene of children playing in the street with water, a jet of water escaping from a broken pump. It was a joyful photograph. Amy took the book from him and for a while, she immersed herself in the images. The photographs were good, of street scenes and children, deserts and animal life.

His fingers met with her hair and she dropped the book, shocked and repulsed by the intrusion. She bobbed her head away, stretching her neck away from his touch, not able to believe it had happened.

"No thanks, Tariq." Her voice sounded angry to her own ears. She hadn't thought she could speak to anyone like that, but this was not what she wanted, not this.

She made to stand, but as she did so, his left hand came across her, staying her with the strength of a seat belt. Swiftly, his lips rested upon her neck as he pressed her back against the cushions. His breath was warm, his mouth kissing her skin, hunting for more.

"No. It's not what I want. Tariq, get off, please..."

She pushed back hard, taking his fingers and struggling with his hand, forcing his fingers away with the strength of her anger. She fought to stand up, trembling, her legs shaking, stumbling on her feet. He grabbed her knee as she fought to steady herself, pausing to stare at him for a moment in horror.

"What are you doing, what the hell are you doing?" she panted in fury; then, "This has nothing to do with our arrangement, Tariq!"

His eyes were heavy as though drugged, a lock of dark hair had fallen across his forehead. Still, he reached up to pull her back to him, seeming deaf to the angry words, grabbing at her forearm. She twisted it out of his reach. Raising her hand, she pushed at his face with all of her strength, hating it, the feeling of being trapped, of being tricked.

Dishevelled, filled with panic and loathing, Amy hurled herself across the room, searching for the place where he had put her jacket, fumbling and stumbling across the thick carpet. Everything was wrong, he was wrong. She felt claustrophobic, wanted to get out of this place. What a fool she was.

As she reached the door, he was standing before her. "You said you liked me…"

His voice wheedled into nothingness. For a moment only, she hesitated. Could he really be confused?

But there were no words, nothing to say. She never wanted to see him again; what was she doing in this place? Angry with herself she shrieked, "Fuck off!" Then she pushed past him, fingers fighting with the door catch so that she tore her nail savagely. She didn't know where he was, didn't look back, just wanted to get away from him.

Outside, breathing in the cold, clean air as she ran, descending the iron steps towards the snow, she let out a gasp, a sob of relief.

Only once did she look back, lifting her face to the snowflakes to make sure that he hadn't come after her. The door stood wide open as she had left it. Tariq was nowhere to be seen. She muttered angrily to herself, searching in her bag for her car keys with ice cold fingers. Finding them, she leapt inside the car and locked the door.

Ali. Call Ali.

She breathed slowly and deliberately as she pulled her phone from the coat pocket to call his number. She wanted to talk, wanted Ali.

But there was no reply.

The anger began to subside, relief at her escape took hold of her now. She started the engine, pulling the car forward across the white ground, heedless of the wheels spinning in deep snow she forced the car forward onto the near deserted road.

She couldn't go home. Her mother would be upset. She didn't want to tell her what had happened, didn't want to talk about it. Neither could she call Ali, she reasoned; he might want to punch Tariq, and then Ali would be in trouble.

She decided to drive to the pub, to Chris, her cousin. He would still be awake and he would let her borrow the spare bed for the night, let her recover before she returned home. The pub would have closed only a short while ago. She would send a text to her mother, reassure her before going home that she was okay.

There would be no music career, at least not one that Tariq would help her to achieve. It was over. It stung her for the first time. Had he believed in her, or had that been his objective all along? She shuddered, repulsed and ashamed, aiming the disgust and guilt at herself.

The windscreen quickly became covered in snow crystals as snow started to fall again, boundless white swathes from a purple black sky. She turned on the wipers and the car heater, shivered against the bitter cold, following the line of the road. It was almost impossible to see the edge of the pavement as she drove along the deserted road.

The car lifted, tyres crunching over the compacted snow, sliding a little as it met the roundabout. Her arms and fingers were stiff with effort and tension. Once, she screamed aloud, shuddering with the memory that repeated itself inside her head.

She sucked the bleeding finger she had scraped on the door lock, holding the wheel tightly with her left hand as she did so, pulling into the almost empty motorway from her exit.

"You stupid, bloody idiot!" she cried, glimpsing her reflection in the driver's mirror as she started to cry tears of anger and self-loathing.

Amy leaned forward, the better to see through the windscreen. The wipers were battling to rid themselves of the snow which was falling fast. All she wanted to do was to go home; but right now, in the state she was in, she would upset her mother. A friend was the next best thing. Chris. Somewhere she could sleep and feel peaceful again. Tomorrow would be a new day; she would go sledging with the girls, forget this, forget it...

She drove to the second roundabout. There was one car ahead of her, going slowly, oh so slowly and carefully on the compressed ice.

"Breathe," she told herself, but the anger took hold of her, feeding her with impatient energy.

"Get a move on!" she shouted impatiently at the driver in front of her, as though she was shouting at Tariq. Needing home, needing to talk to someone.

She indicated, overtaking the car on the road that would take her back, then accelerating, biting into her lower lip with intense concentration, half blinded by the snowflakes that pirouetted before her.

Through the windscreen, she could just make out the white silver glow of the moon.

The scene would not leave her; it repeated itself once more. Tariq, kissing her, grabbing her.

Her fingers squeezed more tightly upon the steering wheel.

She pulled in front of the other car. She felt the thump of the kerb beneath snow, the impact forcing her upward in the driver's seat. Her eyes widened in shock and surprise, framed in the narrow driver's mirror. Her body stiffened as the steering wheel escaped her hands, spinning out of control.

Frantically, she tried to brake and take the wheel back. The car lifted and shook her from side to side until her head jerked back as her hands loosened their grip upon the steering wheel once again.

The car turned over once, twice. Windscreen glass cracked like solid ice beneath the weight of branches growing at the edge of the field; it turned at the command of the snow, sliding into the ditch. Into the cradle of black branches beneath the night sky and the pearly white moon.

She knew nothing of the two strangers in the car that she had overtaken, who raced across the snow in an effort to pull her out.

She knew nothing.

Marion sat before the dying embers of the fire, delaying her sleep to send two more texts, imploring her daughter to come home before the weather worsened, never knowing that evening of the time that would collapse into a long tunnel of pain and grief and longing, where little mattered any more. The world had ended. There could be no progress, no future for a very long time and even then – the world would never be the same.

27th May 2020

Marion is not the same. In the end it was Ruby, her younger daughter, who kept her alive. She didn't take any medication. She survived between the death and the funeral, because she could see Amy, first in the morgue and then the funeral parlour; still as stone and cold, with a scarf across the bandages which held her little head together. But at least she could touch and kiss her daughter.

When the police arrived, she told them angrily there had been a terrible mistake. Asked them how they could want to hurt her in that way. Then she drove around and around the sight where Amy had been killed, unable to find access because, of course, the road had been closed in order for the silver car to be removed from the ditch. The snow fell still, covering the car tracks. Beautiful, drifting snow which covered all ugliness. Marion would never see snow in the same way again. She would always be fearful as Ruby became a driver, years later, always say, "Please be careful," and fret until the driver returned. She learned to hate the snow.

There were hundreds of people of all ages at her funeral: family, friends, work colleagues, neighbours – those who were shocked at the tragedy and who cared about the people left behind. They filled the church, stood without elbow space in the gallery, sat cross-legged in the aisle and crowded the gardens outside when finding more room wasn't possible, listening to a transmission of the service. When Amy's coffin was brought inside and laid upon the catafalque, it was carried by her father, her lover and her four male cousins.

But it was after the funeral, when Marion could no longer touch her daughter, that the long years of grief took their hold upon mother, father and sister. They survived in the end through their own strength and by loving others. That is how we all survive.

28th May

The love Dad projects towards us is so strong; dementia hasn't diminished that at least. Sometimes it's suffocating, like having a small child with great emotional need. He wants to be hugged and kissed and needs constant reassurance. But the reality of that love will be gone when he dies; the hole will be so deep, I'm really worried about what I will feel and do in its absence.

"Where's my wife?"

"Who do I live with?"

"Where do I live?" The same repeated questions all day.

"If you go out, take me with you…" His needs can never be fulfilled.

Even when he has been out with us for the entire morning, as soon as his coat is removed, he will forget and ask, "Where are we going? Are we going out?" He is happiest when we drive around and around, just talking to him about the past. Gradually his sentences grow shorter. His struggle to find the language he needs is written upon his face in a wrinkled grimace, as though he has a headache. Marion and I try to help him, and sometimes that is impossible and we find ourselves saying, "Really, I see…" or pretending that we have understood in some way.

In the house, he follows us around almost constantly, wanting us to sit with him. If you don't rise in the morning when he does, he knocks and rattles upon the doors, perpetually restless.

Marion and I are drinking more frequently in the evenings. She, wine, while I, little cans of gin and tonic. For me, this is whether the children are safely in bed at last or after a day with Dad.

Michelle, our sister-in-law, would advocate yoga, but it doesn't have the same appeal, I'm afraid. Nothing beats a gin and tonic when the sun is well over the yard arm.

In lockdown, I joined the children, banging pans with a vengeance for the NHS who were broke and broken long before the virus.

I have my own experience of it. Until my mother died, I thought highly of the NHS and through the virus I suppose my faith is restored. But I've had a few disagreements with doctors both in and out of hospitals over the years. Very recently I tripped over a pile of laundry sheets and couldn't get rid of the pain in my leg afterwards. It really pissed me off to have a female doctor, who looked slightly older than my teenage grandchildren ask me if I drank before she asked anything else. Of course, I drink every now and then, is the Pope a Catholic?

But this was a sunny morning when I felt good, and I had the energy to attempt a lot of must-do chores before eleven. I actually couldn't see where I was going, the pile of sheets being enormous, and I tripped over a child's scooter that lay in front of the garage.

Anyway, as it turned out, it was sciatica and a problem with the non-existent arches of my flat feet.

Everything remains stacked against women, even more so after the virus. They cook, clean, nurse, teach, empty the rubbish, clean the grill pans, then work from home or get pushed out of their jobs. After this virus, they'll have a harder job clawing their way back to the top again, I suppose, unless they kick back loudly.

The night that I took Mum into the hospital, and she never came home again, that was the night I lost my faith in the NHS.

Long ago, in October 2016, when she had suffered from pancreatic cancer for longer than eighteen months. She resembled a small, frail ballerina and weighed less than seven stone. Her arms were so thin that the nurses at the Churchill hospital were forced to stab at her arms repeatedly, punching her with a needle until they found an area with just enough fat to attach the PICC line for her cancer treatment to work, while she smiled with great patience and only winced occasionally. Long ago when she would come out of that treatment and still have the will and determination to do her own shopping with Dad as support. (We offered to do it for her, frequently, but that's how it was, she wanted to do it herself; even though she was generally reduced to drinking slimy protein drinks, as she called them.) Long ago in 2016, she tripped over a bag in the kitchen and broke her hip.

For three days, she wouldn't admit to any serious injury, saying she had only bruised it. But I felt inside, knowing a little bit about bones (because Harry was once a wrestler) that her bone density must have been severely reduced because of her weight and her cancer treatment, that this was much more than a bruise. So, after helping with my granddaughter's birthday party, a party which, normally speaking, she would have liked to have been present, I went to their house to see her.

As soon as I walked through the door, I could hear her calling out from her bedroom, while Dad, who is partially deaf, could hear nothing in front of the television. When I reached her bedroom, she was lying, half on, half off the bed and crying in pain and frustration. She had found herself in such a position that she couldn't sit up and had been forced to pull herself to the edge of the bed.

I called Marion to come and be with Dad and half lifted, half supported her down the staircase to the car, then drove her to hospital.

It must have been about six thirty in the evening when we arrived. At the start of the evening, there were vacant chairs in the waiting area. We sat together, me holding her hand. Perhaps, like me, she was thinking about all the other times we had cause to be there, joyful births of her grandchildren, mostly. Thinking about the hospital she had seen built from scratch when she and Dad became landlords of the White Hart, thinking about the hospital staff who once lunched at the White Hart, seated in the once lovely garden with its Victorian plants.

Her hip must have caused her so much pain. I put a coat beneath her as a cushion but sitting on a broken hip can't have been easy. She smiled at me a lot, trusting me. It's a memory I will never forget.

Gradually the hospital filled with casualties, so many injuries and illnesses on a Sunday evening until by nine o'clock it resembled a ward in the Crimean war, but with crying babies and small children added to the mix. The doctors and nurses seemed unable to cope as they rushed from one patient to another, adding notes and updates to a screen in between. Many of the ward staff were both irritable and, sometimes, downright impatient with the suffering of others.

I remember how upset she was, not for herself, but for the old man with indefinable mental health problems who sat in the chair beside us when it was vacated by another. He had been patient for a long time, talking to himself, leaning against the wall while consuming a packet of cooked cocktail sausages. As he sat in the chair, he handed a sausage to Mum. He told her that she was a beautiful lady (she was always that, even in her eighties and with cancer).

As he rambled on about the sausages which he had very possibly obtained illegally from the hospital shop, two security guards dressed in black uniforms appeared. They gave no warning of what they were about to do, but grabbed him roughly, pushing him sideways, which upset Mum, spilling his sausages all over the floor. We both felt angry then. The old man was taken away while I picked up the sausages and sped after him, compelled to hand them back, furious at the way they were treating him. Surely not in this country, I thought.

So, I chased after the security men.

"That's not the way to do things," I called, in frustration, to the security man who appeared to be in charge. He stopped, stared at me as though I, too, were mad. It isn't the way that Harry has been taught to handle mental health patients, anyway.

"What on earth did he do?" I cried out in accusation.

"He was behaving threateningly to one of the doctors," the man replied, annoyed by me and now gripping the poor old guy by the arms as though he was resisting arrest, which he wasn't. He was meek as a lamb. His old, unhealthy, bearded face twisted towards me in an appeal.

"But he didn't resist you, did he? You didn't need to do that; you don't need to push him," I said.

They shrugged, walking away with the old guy held between them.

When I got back to Mum, she kissed my cheek and put her head upon my shoulder.

At this point we had waited for four hours for her examination.

At about half past ten, she groaned, gripping her hip. "I can't sit like this any longer," she said.

I nodded, feeling equally grim about her long wait. I got up and began to scout the corridors for a doctor or nurse. They were all in conversation, or busily examining charts. At last, I spotted an empty porter's trolley in the corridor. I took it without asking and wheeled it towards her until a nurse stopped me, her eyebrows arched indignantly. She asked me where I was going with the trolley. Irritably, I told her about our long wait and rather meekly now, she followed me. Together, we lifted Mum as gently as we could so she could lie down. At long last, she relaxed; she even closed her eyes.

Half an hour later, a senior doctor approached to wheel her behind a curtain. He apologised for the five-hour wait and examined her. He, too, believed her hip was broken and that she would need an operation.

I kissed her goodbye at about half past eleven that night. She wasn't worried about going off alone; she just wanted help and rest, poor love.

Since then, I've known without doubt that the NHS was in trouble. Before that night, the hospital had a reputation as one of the best in the country. No wonder the government were forced to focus upon hospitals at long last in the midst of a virus.

2nd June

We gathered outside James' house with birthday presents, balloons and cake while he stood at the front door, grinning at us. He is almost forty, I can't believe that, but I must.

Really, I have had no time to write. Every day is a winding road, as Alanis Morissette sang.

For some reason, I've had a phenomenal amount of early morning texts, from "Can you get me some tampons?" to "Can you keep the children until eight tonight?"

I've accepted these busy days; it is pointless to protest. So many family members have to work or have individual needs, but I could do with a break sometimes. At least my brain is moderately intact. So many people I know are experiencing mental health problems, even within my own family where OCD is a big problem. It rears its ugly, irrational head in so many contexts, from intrusive, unwanted thoughts, which I know are so hard to get rid of, to triple checking things to the point of total madness! How many times do you have to open and close a fridge door before bedtime? Or stand before a tap for several minutes until you are positive that it's off? Everything has been made worse by isolation.

We worked so hard to keep Dad safe, to make sure that he didn't get ill. Every day there are further reports of elderly people dying in care homes. I'm glad and grateful that we've been able to care for him at home, even if his constantly repeated questions make us think that we're stuck inside a Morecambe and Wise sketch for eternity. For a ninety-two-year-old ex-smoker, whose job as a landlord through the sixties to the nineties subjected him to thick palls of yellow smoke every night, thankfully, his emphysema is mild.

Rather, thanks to his genes and love of gardening, I suspect. Thus far, he is remarkably healthy.

Which is why it was alarming to arrive at his house and find him panting and shaking in his chair, seemingly unable to draw breath. Marion had taken him shopping, or at least, he had stayed in the car while she ran into the shop, and they had just arrived back. She was in the kitchen, hunting for the thermometer when I arrived.

"Dad, what's wrong?" I asked as she shoved the thing beneath his armpit. But he could hardly find the breath to speak.

"It's normal," she said, staring at the thermometer.

"I think we should call 101," I said. "If not an ambulance."

101 told us to call an ambulance, which we did. During that time when the NHS was suffering so badly, Jo had appendicitis; she was only about ten at the time. It took two hours for an ambulance to arrive on a very wet and windy night although they repeatedly called me to check that she was lying still on the settee, and whether the pain had worsened.

But this ambulance came almost instantly.

Two paramedics, both male. They took his oxygen levels and his temperature, which had risen to 39.2 degrees, and quickly making the decision to take him in an ambulance, began trying to lift him from the chair. By now his legs and arms were shaking and he couldn't speak at all. I wanted to cry, did cry, as I chased the ambulance in my car. His eyes had been wide with alarm as he was examined; he looked so confused and frightened. Now, he wouldn't know where he was or who those caring for him were.

What if this was coronavirus? I couldn't bear the thought that we wouldn't be allowed to stay with him, hold his hand and comfort him.

In the end, we weren't allowed to see him for two days, but the relief at being told that he had been tested and it wasn't the virus was humungous. The staff also told us that he was a lovely gentleman and very polite – without any mention of how annoying he is. We had taken in some photographs of Mum and of us, to help him remember, but he still asked repeatedly where his lovely wife was, apparently.

Then, on the third day, we were told that one of us could visit him. I had gone to the hospital on the day he went in, waiting to find out whether he was going to be alright, so Marion said that she would go to visit first and then Howard; but we had to give up after Marion's visit. He caused such a scene, trying to follow her along the corridor and threatening to drag the drip from his arm, yelling, "Take me home!" that we realised we were making it too difficult for the staff, who, before Marion's visit had thought Dad to be a gentle, quiet old gentleman.

Fortunately, they let him out the next day, so we didn't have to put him through that again. He was alright, which is the main thing, although they have decided to do some tests on his heart. They told us that he didn't sleep very much at night, which is why he slept like a log on his return, I suppose.

14th June

Dad asked where Mum was so many times today that, in the end, Ned lost patience for the second time.

"She's dead, Grampy!" he yelled, more than a little irritably.

Last year, sitting in the rear of my car, he asked, "Nan, are you going to die?" He asked so sweetly that I assumed he was worrying.

"Well, yes, one day, but not for a long, long time…" I answered, patting his knee gently.

"Only, I was wondering, can I have your car when you die?"

Such a healthy, opportunist attitude.

"By the time I die, my car will be a bit of a rusty wreck," I said, with more than a bit of rust in my own voice.

16th June

To be honest, I've forgotten where 'home' is. Home is with whichever family need help today. But I love my cabin in the garden, which I share with Jack the dog. This is where I store all of my worldly goods. The only problem is that in the summer it's so hot and in the winter, very cold; but I weigh myself down with duvets against the snow and often in summer, wake to take a turn about the dark garden with the dog. Once I was visited by the planning people after a helicopter took a heat reading and they thought I was an illegal immigrant or that I was renting the place out to refugees at a price.

The fact of the matter is that the house currently belongs to me, but I'm trying to give James some space. I love my cabin; it feels like home and, as I live in my head a good deal when I'm away from my family, I can be anywhere I choose, from Cornwall to Nice. It's a better home than many of the tumbledown shacks I saw in Cape Town.

18th June

Everyone says that Louise is just like me. Despite having had a broken back and often, tremendous pain with it, she is a lawyer, the mother of three children and works very hard, so I take that as a compliment.

If it weren't for her, I wouldn't have done so many of the things I've loved doing. Louise is always motivated and enthusiastic. She is also impetuous and often unstoppable and if something needs doing, she has to do it NOW. This side of her personality can be a little frustrating, because she always believes that I can do anything she puts her mind too.

I'd done quite a heavy load of jobs today. Up at six thirty a.m. when Delia woke, then took Ned to school and put the washing in, made Dad his breakfast, looked after the girls, took them back to their Mum in Bicester, took Dad out for a drive, fetched Ned from his other Nan's, did some paperwork for my pension company, and then Louise asked me to wait in for a parcel delivery; but with all of this, I forgot.

So, she called me to remind me and berated me just as I turned into the Islip Road. "I'll call Ruby," she said, a little impatiently, which is what she can be like towards me when she's working, and I get that. I reminded her that I'd been twice to the post office sorting place this week to collect parcels for her family but all she said was, "This one can't be collected."

When I arrived at her house, which is two doors down from Dad's, it was pouring with rain and a man was delivering a massive parcel, large enough to contain a baby elephant and delivered upon a trolley while Ruby stood in the doorway.

"I should cover it if I were you," the delivery bloke suggested with no further interest in the affair. So, I ran to pull the tarpaulin off the barbeque and did a pretty good job of tethering it to the box with cord. I knew with sinking heart that she would demand that it should be moved into her house and imagined her recruiting fifteen-year-old Jess to help her while trying to overcome the pain in her own back yet again. Louise always has to do it now, if you know what I mean.

Anyway, she called Harry and Ned's father in the end, and they moved it pretty quickly between them. It's a fireplace; apparently, she's having the kitchen and the living room 'done'. She might have told me when she suggested there was a parcel coming. I had imagined something small.

19th June

My telephone is blocked solid with requests from Jess and Lauren. Mostly texts asking if they can borrow Harry's house when the little girls aren't there and he's at work for a sleepover with friends. He is very tolerant about this, but I'd better check with Louise.

Lauren called me to ask whether there is a legal age to bleach your hair. Nooo! I told her that it was a terrible and dangerous idea, would require a qualified hairdresser and that she would regret it.

20th June

I cancelled our holiday to Sicily, which we were all very much looking forward to. They wanted me to pay the remainder of the booking fee, but as it isn't yet clear which countries the government is going to impose a return quarantine upon, after a family meeting, we decided to re-book for next year. We were all a bit fed up about it. Jess and Lauren were hooked on the idea, but mostly because Sicily is the home of the Mafia.

So, I've booked a week in Dorset in caravans instead. Not quite the same thing, but the kids will love it and we always have fun. Marion and Ruby aren't coming but Dad is meant to be staying at a home for respite care, so they'll get a break from living with him, which they really need. I also booked a night in a hotel in Ludlow for James and I. We both have a passion for history and I really want to show him Ludlow castle.

22nd June

Marion's birthday. I bought her a top and perfume. We took our presents round in the evening and had tea and cake.

Dad is recovered and back to his old self. I took him out earlier in the day. We took Lauren's bike for repair in the Cowley Road bike shop, then went to the White Hart for a drink so that I could recover from the Cowley Road experience. Dad can be hard work.

Because of his age and the social distancing, I left him in the passenger seat in the front of the car, which is usually okay. Only when I was in the bike shop the car alarm started to go off. I sped from the shop to find a small crowd gathered around him, trying to help him out. For some reason he had eased himself out of the passenger seat and into the driver's seat, tangling himself in the seatbelt in the process, so he was firmly tethered to the car. Good job I don't leave the keys in the ignition.

Poor Dad. Apparently, he needed to pee.

Peeing has started to be a problem when we're out. I've visited the bank with him on several occasions, in masks of course, now the lockdown is over. He seems to relate banks to the toilet. We are the only customers who shout. He shouts to me from the other side of the customer rail, "Where's the toilet in this place?" and I shout the reply, because he is quite deaf. "There isn't one, Dad, you'll have to wait!" Still, he shouts the question repeatedly as his memory grows worse and shorter than ever. The masks don't work in his case, either, as he pulls his mask down and wears it under his chin. He has COPD so is probably exempt from masks.

Marion, Ru and Gramps have spent all lockdown with a student from Peru. Despite being twice her age, he is besotted with the very beautiful Ruby and made himself quite a nuisance by mooning over her and following her about the house like a lovesick puppy. She was very kind to him as he was a guest, but she made it clear that she wasn't interested. It's all a bit embarrassing for Ru and her mum.

On one occasion, when she and Marion were taking part in the Masons lockdown, online pub quiz, and just as it was getting exciting and a little overheated, their student burst into the living room wearing a poncho, insisting upon serenading them with Peruvian love songs on his guitar. Marion came close to snatching the guitar and hitting him over the head with it a la John Belushi in *National Lampoon's Animal House*. Other than that, she says the poor shmuck is quite nice, really.

Anyway, he's going home next week, having had to wait for some time for entry to his own country because of the dreaded virus.

I have re-booked our summer holiday in Sicily for next summer and have managed to book a week's stay for the family in Dorset. At least, Louise and the children are coming for the first half of the week while Harry and the girls with his girlfriend and her children are coming for the second part of the week.

Also booked James and I into a hotel in Ludlow for one night with an evening meal and breakfast, so I can show him Ludlow Castle.

This means Dad going into respite care for one week; he hasn't been away from his family since his two years in Egypt, aged nineteen. He will hate it, but Marion and I need the break if we're going to carry on caring for him at home.

Monday 13th July

On 25th May, Dad's birthday, a man was killed in America and his death has done more, perhaps, to bring attention to the treatment of black people and people of colour than Martin Luther King or Malcolm X might have achieved.

George Floyd was killed while he was under arrest. He was a black man. He died, manacled, with a policeman's knee on his neck. The arrest was filmed as George Floyd pleaded with the policeman to take the pressure from his neck because he couldn't breathe. That was how he died, not being able to breathe.

This one death has made all nations sit up and take notice. What it has done is to make people think about how they relate to one another, what the problems are in society and, essentially, whether we are consciously or unconsciously racist; and although there will be some people, still, who will not connect with this or not care, I think they are now in the minority.

So, this one death has brought about an organisation called 'Black Lives Matter', which is a good name, because it says everything.

Then, in Bristol, the statue of a slave trader which stood in the city was pulled down and pushed into the River Avon. Other statues followed, while in Oxford, students, protesters and BLM supporters called for the statue of Cecil Rhodes to be removed from Oriel College in the high street, just as his statue had been removed in Cape Town because Rhodes was a British Imperialist who led British colonisation in South Africa.

So much of the anger must be about identity. Knowing who you are, who your ancestors were, where you came from, gives you pride and status and confidence. Being robbed of the family who came before you is an emotionally crippling injustice.

20th July

Louise has had so much treatment due to the terrible car accident that she had when she was only seventeen. Two or three operations, a total of fifteen hours beneath the scalpel while the doctors reconstructed her spine. Frightening, terrifying, life changing. It made her emotionally and physically strong but for a while afterwards, it almost broke her. We were told that should the operation not be successful, she would spend her life in a wheelchair.

Nothing else can be done to improve her skeleton now that she is in her thirties, nothing that won't endanger her life, this the surgeons have told her. So, she has learned to manage the incredible pain that she still suffers from, as best she can, although the strain has affected her internal organs so, now, she must have a colonoscopy.

The accident was before Amy's. Like Amy's, it happened in deep snow. She was travelling as a passenger with a boyfriend who picked her up after school. He drove them into the countryside, close to Brill, and the car wheels caught against a bank of snow, throwing the vehicle into the air, turning it over twice. Louise was thrown out of the window and ended up in a ditch, a ditch that saved her life, because without it the car would have crushed her to death.

Her memories of lying in that ice cold coffin – she remembers nothing between the time she was thrown from the car and then waking up in the ditch – gave her nightmares every night for many months afterwards. I remember her crying out in pain, the painkilling drugs she had to take and how helpless we felt to comfort her.

When she woke in that wet, muddy ditch, she tried to crawl out of the icy cold, dark space that she was in. She crawled with a broken back. Crying, moaning, as the boy who survived the crash unhurt tried to coax her towards him. An old couple who lived in a cottage close by ran to help her, covering her with their blankets and calling the ambulance that took her to the Stoke Mandeville hospital for her operation.

"Stay there, keep still, you mustn't move," they told her, as they crouched by the car to talk to her, but she didn't want to be there, beneath the creaking car in that cold and dark place, so she crawled her way out with a broken spine.

She crawled across the ground, this dark-haired girl, just like the girl who the medium talked to Mum about in the pub. "She's crawling on the ground," the man had said, "a girl with long, dark hair."

That fits the description of Louise. But when he told our mother about these ghosts, both Louise and Amy were little girls – which makes it a premonition.

Friday 14th August

Today, we took Dad to the care home for a week. Had we been going on our planned trip to Sicily, it would be two weeks. For his sake, I'm glad he's only going away for a week. I dreaded taking him there for good reason. Originally, he was supposed to have an experimental week at Easter, but due to the virus, we cancelled that. Care homes were very unsafe places at the time, with the elderly dying in their droves.

Marion packed a little case with enough changes of clothes, extra pants and his medication, with biscuits, photographs, pyjamas, etc for the week's stay, but it was just as well that we visited the place the day before.

Despite the social services saying that they had a place at the home for him, and having been let down already by another home, the matron told us they weren't expecting a Maurice Jacobs and couldn't take him! I felt sure that Marion might have a breakdown it we couldn't get the week's respite we were expecting. As for me, I certainly intended to go to Dorset. So, I had the breakdown instead.

We refused to leave the home. There was a mistake, we assured them. We had been told that he could stay there. The matron in charge stared at us coldly while one of the carers tried to hose us down with a bottle of strong-smelling hand gel.

We sat in the waiting room amidst the plants with our masks on, talking to one another in hushed voices. I swore a lot beneath mine. We tried to call the social services from mobile phones, calling their emergency number, but couldn't get through to anyone.

Eventually, after almost an hour, the matron and her colleague returned to us.

They apologised. There had been an email, they said, but it had gone to a staff member who was absent at the moment. Huge relief. I recanted at last, taking a tin of chocs from a plastic bag to thank them.

In the back of my mind, I wondered whether we had been blacklisted because of dear old Uncle Don.

Dad is very sweet-natured and a bit of a home boy, not at all rebellious (except at bath times) but his big brother, Don, had spent some time in this very home and, being a lot more adventurous and determined, had twice escaped from it during the night, finding an unguarded escape route through the kitchen. He had walked under the subway, long past midnight, and then into the Quarry, to be found by a neighbour, attempting to unlock the front door of his empty house with a bunch of redundant keys. It had occurred to me that the home had recognised Dad's surname and decided to blacklist him as one of the 'Jacobs brothers'.

Don had always liked the film *The Great Escape*, according to his children.

I was justified in my anxiety about taking Dad to the home. When the time came, we thought we would be allowed to go inside with him, maybe have a cup of coffee.

I suppose this was a bit fanciful in a pandemic.

"Where are we; what is this place?" he asked, repeatedly and suspiciously, as we stood at the door having our temperature checked and sanitising our hands once again.

We looked at one another, Marion and I. Should we have told him? No.

If you tell someone with dementia of any plans in advance, they will keep fretting about it, getting increasingly anxious, or they will forget. So, it's best to leave things to the last. Except that this was the last minute and his body language was that of a condemned man. How were we going to get him through the front door?

"Dad, it's a clinic," I lied. "The nurses are going to check you over and make sure that everything is okay. I'm sure it is; you're very healthy. But we can't come in, so we will wait for you." The last bit was kind of true, except for the part where we wouldn't be picking him up until a week later.

It wasn't at all funny at the time. It was heart breaking. He went inside with the carers, a little reluctantly, and they led him up the staircase to his room. We were still talking to the Matron when he reached the second landing and looked down for us through a window.

We watched his mouth moving as he spoke to us through the glass, his hands fluttering at the window like a bird against the pane, calling us back, while the trapped bird in my heart panicked with a real pain, hating to leave him there, even for a week.

We left the place for the short journey home and my memories of Dad flicked through my imagination like a slide show. Walking through Wantage, holding his hand as a little girl. Running across the Berkshire Downs with my siblings as a child. Crying on his shoulder in the car as a teenager when our old dog had to be put down. He is so irritating sometimes, but he is my best love and I can't bear to lose him. When I turn to Marion, we both have stupid tears in our eyes.

"It's like the first time you go back to work after having a baby," she says, and it is.

We had done what we could, a dated postcard each day to reassure him that we loved him and that we were coming back soon. A large tin of biscuits because, although he has a good appetite, without us his memory tells him that he hasn't eaten, so he will ask, "When is dinner?" five minutes after a large bowl of shepherd's pie. We had given careful instruction about his medication.

We worried about him until, after a day, we realised our freedom and what a strain it is upon us to feel so responsible. It is like having a baby, except that his poos are much larger and now he behaves in a way that he would never have done before dementia, spitting a tablet across the room if he can't swallow it so that we have to play hunt the tablet.

16th August

So, James and I went to Ludlow, on the edge of the Welsh Marches. It took us ages, neither of us have a sat nav.

In the end, he bought a map at a garage and we did rather better after that thanks to his map reading skills. He is probably my favourite travelling companion. He is calm but enthusiastic about things that I love, the countryside, history, music (although he went through a drum and base phase which I didn't share his enthusiasm for, as I recall). When James was young, he was an avid reader of books by Henry Treece, Geoffrey Trease and Rosemary Sutcliffe... oh, and Leon Garfield, too – all the good writers of historical fiction, in fact.

We had almost two days with an overnight stay at the Charlton Arms, but we made full use of it.

Ludlow is a very pretty little town, skirted by the river Teme, and is probably best known for its majestic and beautifully preserved castle. I suppose it was the Norman castle I wanted him to see. We have decided to do a full castle tour for a week in Wales, next year. I might rent a touring van.

When we arrived, we checked in and threw our few items into comfortable little rooms overlooking the river and the town. Then, as it was mid-afternoon already, we had a drink at the bar and wandered up the steep incline towards the castle and attractive houses. The town is a colourful timeline of the Tudor, the Stuart and the Georgian era. On one corner, an ancient Norman chapel has been turned into a summer house.

We bought sandwiches, a coffee and a milkshake and sat on the green before Ludlow Castle to eat before entering what must be one of the finest examples of Norman architecture anywhere in the world. Incredible that the original iron hinges remain upon the wooden doors, that the tower is so well preserved. Perhaps the weather is more clement in this part of the world although, today, the tower is closed because of a high wind. So, we wander happily with other tourists, trying to work out what purpose each part of the castle served.

Perhaps it is best known as the place where King Arthur had his honeymoon after his marriage to Katherine of Aragon. The beautiful stone features a delicate medieval carving of the lady in the wimple, which is high up in the little chapel, making me think of Katherine. At least, I suppose, she died with her head intact even if she, too, lost her husband.

In the evening, James and I went on a walk in the direction of the castle again, but this time we followed a very different route along the wide brown river which skirted the town.

It began with flat grey stone steps beside the pub, which we had scarcely noticed before a barmaid pointed the route out to us. This led us to a long, curving path overlooked by immense trees and bushes. The path must have existed for as long as the castle, we thought.

A summer's evening, warm with golden, late afternoon sunshine, busy with dragonflies and fishermen at the river's edge, I imagined the townspeople and riders using it to reach the castle in centuries gone by.

And rising above the river and the town houses which rose higgledy-piggledy towards it stood the majestic castle. The view which could scarcely have changed since Tudor times.

We were able to relax, taking our time, because I had booked our evening meal for eight. When we had crossed another bridge, reaching the castle walls, it was possible to enter the outer walls, the bailey, so we flopped down on the grass and chattered about this and that until our stomachs rumbled for dinner.

30th August

We had a nice time in Dorset and everyone appeared to enjoy the holiday: especially Harry. The kids loved it and said they didn't want to go home, which was nice to hear because Jess and Lauren are older now, and consequently harder to please.

In the second half of the week, it rained so hard that rain beat upon the caravan walls morning, noon and night and no matter how I tried to keep the caravan clean, the children brought mud in on their shoes constantly, mud and pine needles knocked from the surrounding trees, but they didn't care about the rain, except when I told them I wasn't going to swim in an outdoor pool in this weather. I would do anything for love, but I won't do that. No.

Louise had been away for a week in Nice, where her father and I had two apartments, one large and grand and a smaller flat. They belong to him now, although my settlement was a fair one. The large one overlooks the Promenade des Anglais; that's where Louise took her children.

Anyway, back to Dorset. Louise returned from her week in Nice, having changed her plane tickets to get home before the British government imposed a lockdown for travellers from France, and came to join me for a few days. Then Harry, with Sian and his and her children came for the second part of the week. I would normally have booked somewhere near Looe or Polzeath, one the south coast and one the north of Cornwall. Places I know and love very well. But at the time of booking, Dorset seemed a safer option with the virus and various Coronavirus rules in place.

I think Louise had the best of the weather, which I was relieved about because it would be hard to replace one word with another with the weather in Nice. Also, teenage girls are highly judgemental, in my experience, and I wanted them to have a great time.

I had to leave both dogs, Jack and Harry's dog, Monty, at the kennels as the caravan rules dictated no dogs. This was a pity; they love coming, love the sea and Jack always tries to surf with me. When we approach Polzeath I have to open a window for him because he makes endearing but annoying little whining noises, knowing exactly where we are (a bit like Dad, really).

Despite the rules (although maybe I forgot to point them out), Lou brought Luna, the incredibly annoying black pug who is well suited to her name. She's like an attention seeking child, barking to be played with, barking at the baddies on the television, which shows intelligence, I guess. Jack loathes her and tries to scramble out of any room when she enters it. He won't even share the garden with her. Her shrill barks puncture the ear drums.

Anyway, it was a large caravan, so everyone slept quite comfortably. Louise and I walked the kids and Luna over the cliffs to Lulworth Cove, very beautiful in a totally different way to the Cornish cliffs. Then we ate at a little pub in Lulworth village, where Luna disgraced herself by barking at everything whether it had four legs or not;

afterwards, we walked down to the tiny, busy harbour and bought an ice cream which we ate sitting upon an upturned boat, then paddled in the chilly sea.

We packed a lot into it. Lou seemed very happy, linking her arm through mine. Once she said to me, "I'd rather have a week in a caravan with you in Cornwall than two weeks in Abu Dhabi." That was very sweet of her, although absolutely untrue. She loves to travel.

I kept Ned with me when she and the girls returned to Oxford, knowing that if Louise had to work, even from home, she would be hard put to entertain him and that he'd probably use the play station rather too much. I'm glad I did. He was a good boy, and played equally with Freya and Robin, Sian's little boy.

We had two days of sunshine with some wind. On the first day, we went for a rather long and wild walk, unintentionally, after a bus driver pointed us in the best direction from the car park to get to Corfe Castle, or as Freya calls it, 'Bad King John's castle.' I told them that I thought the bus driver must have been the wicked Sheriff of Nottingham, because we were in the wrong car park and a bus driver pointed us in the direction of a long and tortuous walk with two under-three-year-olds in two pushchairs. It led us through dense woodland, across open fields shrouded by mist and even across a railway track before we could even begin to mount the hill to the castle.

We were exhausted by the time we arrived, and once there, the recent rainfall meant that the castle was closed to the public! The ancient walls aren't nearly so well preserved as the walls of Ludlow – bits of the castle are threatening to subside.

Undeterred, I bought five plastic swords at a shop and the children all attacked Harry on the drawbridge, which they thought was tremendous fun. After that, we went to a model village depicting Corfe, so they were very happy.

We had a good time in Swanage, paddling in the sea again (actually, Ned and I swam for a bit, though not for long) and eating overpriced Rick Stein fish and chips on the beach. Harry and Sian seem very cuddly. The relationship may be more serious than I had predicted but it's too early to say as yet. Her little boys seem nice, although God knows how two adults and four children will fit into Harry's house, if that ever happens.

September 6th, FINALLY, back to school!!!

Yes, I got very impatient. Not just for my own grandchildren, who have laptops and other resources, but on behalf of all of those children I used to teach who didn't have parents who were confident about assisting them, who didn't have computers; and who had difficulties at home or not enough food. David Blunkett is correct; without the schools being open, we are giving some children a disproportionate advantage over others.

I understand that teachers should not be exposed to the virus. I don't want to be exposed to the virus, but the world will suffer, everything will suffer if we aren't prepared to get children back to school. Inequality will be even more, the strain upon mental health even more, domestic violence more, poverty more.

In the meanwhile, the poor people on respirators with Covid look as though they are being eaten alive by aliens. It's horrible, heart-breaking. I get why people should be frightened and regret expressing my feelings to the head teacher at Ned's school. It isn't her fault. But we can't opt out of life.

Things are so strange on the first day back, after so long. Staggered queues, entrances and exits kept separate. No friendly parent familiarity with the teacher, little time to communicate with other parents, either. Most parents wear masks. I'm getting used to it. I do so in shops but sometimes it feels so unfriendly to do so. I hate that we can't read faces any more.

Five-year-old children, just starting school, who have to say goodbye to their parents as they stand in a line, waiting to go into class. So different to my teacher training and the school ethos we've been used to, where parents are welcomed in to settle and support younger children, and even at later stages are invited to read with their children in school before the day begins.

Reading books cannot come home. Too complicated, as everything has to be sanitised. I've never known a time when children couldn't take books in or bring things from home to show their classmates. What kind of strange, sad world are we in, now? No performances, no Christmas performances or end of school discos or parties or fundraising fetes.

On top of this, for me, getting children to school on time is more impossible than ever as classroom arrivals are staggered. For the first two weeks of term, there are mornings where I have to get four children to three different schools – on Sandhills, in Headington and to Kidlington. In the end I decide to be a 'bad granny' if that's what people want to think of me. I'm not going to risk accidents, speeding points and the police any more by driving rapidly in the bus lane. No. I'm going to chill. Defensively, I say to myself that the teachers haven't even been there for a term and a half so they will have to be patient with me.

I don't need to be defensive, because the teachers are very patient with my late arrivals and early pick-ups.

Then, there's this constant nagging list in my head again, which kills any other more creative thoughts. It goes like this, "Dad: porridge, jam, tablets from the chemist. Kids: packed lunches, water bottles, P.E. clothes. Ned, school uniform; Lauren, dentist. Dry the washing..."

I change my mind in an instant. Ban schools after all, at least there were times when things were peaceful, I think, as I almost knock my front teeth out on the car's electric window while reversing rapidly into a parking space outside the girls' school.

Then, at bedtime, I accidentally squirt verruca ointment into my eye because I'm totally knackered and the tube resembles my eye ointment. Ow! I've never known anything to hurt that much; it burns like billyo. I scream with pain instantly, threatening to wake Dad with whom I am staying. I rush to the bathroom just as Marion comes upstairs.

"Oh my God, what's happened to your eye?" she shrieks. "It's bright red!"

I try to explain as the tears gush like a burst pipe from my eyeballs. Then I try to wash it out with cold water for several minutes, but the pain won't go away.

"Try a bit of salt in the water," says the sister I trust implicitly. The pain is so terrible that I accept a bowl of water laced with salt and start to bathe it. But things go from bad to worse. The pain becomes intolerable, the salt having made things worse and tears gush from my rapidly blinking eyes.

"I have to drive to the hospital," I assure Marion. "You can't take me; you need to stay with Dad."

"Drive?" she shrieks, incredulous. "You can hardly see!"

But I drive, blinking, one-eyed, crying and moaning to the hospital everyone has avoided because of Covid.

"You should never have bathed it with salt," the triage nurse says, shocked by my idiocy. "The verruca ointment contains acid. By putting salt in your eye, you have added one burn to another." She puts antibiotic drops into my eye and the pain goes instantly. I love her. I want to marry her. I am so grateful. They check my eye for ulceration and say I must go to the eye clinic when I feel better.

Sometimes I drive with the Stealers Wheel song on a loop in my head, 'Stuck in the Middle with You'. Things are especially busy again. This is not my life, and yet it is. On Tuesday morning there were four hours where I couldn't stop to pee and almost wet myself; actually, the embarrassing truth is that I did wet myself.

"Are we going somewhere?" Dad asked, blocking the door as I arrived at the house for the second time.

"Please, Dad, just wait till I've used the loo!" I plead breathlessly as I squeeze past him to mount the stairs.

To add to the demented atmosphere, Dad's questions are growing more and more nonsensical.

"Where are you going?"

"Nowhere."

"Can I come with you?"

"We've been out. We're staying here, Dad. Drink your tea."

"But can I come with you?"

Plus, his hearing aid has gone missing.

"Where are we going?"

"To get a key cut Dad…"

"To get a teacup?"

But he still has a sense of humour.

"Where are we going, remind me again?"

This, after I've told him a dozen times that we're going to the shop.

"To the moon," I reply in frustration.

"Oh ar, that's a long way then."

I shall go quietly mad. My family say I've been mad for years, I just don't acknowledge it.

14th September

Apparently, we are now 'On the edge of losing control of the Covid virus'. Great. No hope for mankind, then.

Aunty Steph called me. We chatted for over an hour about the family and the difficulty of running a pub when you can only allow so many people inside and have to change all of the seating arrangements. I know that Chris and Mathew are working so hard to get things right. I feel so sorry for publicans. The local pub is a particularly British asset.

Pubs and churches are for the lonely and go hand in hand, somehow. I suppose that's why they are often opposite one another in an English village. One of the things I love to do most is to sing hymns at full voice; you can't even do that, now. (The other is to drink gin and tonic or a glass of wine in a pub.)

16th September

Unemployment has reached 4.5 per cent, with redundancy at its highest level. There have been several local house break-ins. I can't help thinking that robbery will be on the increase at any moment now. I feel slightly nervous alone in the dark in my cabin; fortunately, I have Jack. On the downside, he tends to fart a lot in the middle of the night and his farts really stink.

James has applied for so many jobs and has been rejected. Rejection is hard. But he is very sensible; he keeps a routine, cleaning the house, working out, going for a run, all things that help a person's mental health.

Currently, James looks a bit like Sir Lancelot of the Lake when he lost himself in the woods. I can't remember whether Lancelot went mad because he couldn't find the Holy Grail, or was on a vigil of some kind, or was doing some kind of penance because he'd been tricked into making love to someone other than Guinevere – who was doing the same thing to someone other than Arthur – but he was definitely in a wood at the time. Handsome, with a beard and tousled hair, which is very like James, who can't see the point in shaving any more.

The older girls and younger children are doing well at school, so far. So that's good.

Lauren introduced me first to the book *Stranger Things* and then to the Netflix series. I absolutely love it. While babysitting for Ned, Lauren suggested I watched the first episode. I quickly became hooked, watching four episodes in one evening while Ned put himself to bed, complaining about what a terrible babysitter I am.

Took Dad to the bank and for a coffee yesterday. Almost all of our local banks are now closed in Headington, which makes me cross. We are still very protective towards Dad and don't want him to catch the virus, but if we didn't take him out at least once a day, his dementia problems would get worse. All he wants to do is to come with Marion or Howard or I when we go out; he doesn't care where he goes but still asks to go to the pub and forgets that they are all closed.

He hates staying at home alone and becomes very befuddled if we leave him, even for short periods.

I have to go to a bank in either Kidlington or Cowley because of the current economy biased decision by bankers that older people with no access to the internet must be forced to travel by bus to remote areas as they are shutting down the local branch. Rather selfish of them if you ask me.

So, as soon as we get into the bank, Dad starts demanding the loo. Of course, there isn't one, only he can never digest this and starts by asking quietly, then ends by yelling, "Is there a toilet here?" Finishing with, "I'm going to wet myself" and then on one occasion, "I'm going to shit myself."

He isn't! He has very good bladder control, so far, but they don't know that. On the plus side it helps to be seen more quickly.

18th September

I walked the dogs late in the evening with James. We crossed the muddy fields and looked for fossils in the crumbly stones.

Some while ago, I believe it was last November 2019, many of the Sandhills residents met together in the school hall on a very cold and dark evening. There were between fifty and a hundred of us. The meeting was organised by a local man. I don't know him very well but, whereas the virus has engrossed the rest of us, the subject matter of the meeting must have taken over his life. We should be grateful for that.

The meeting was about our local environment, stretching from Barton and Sandhills and for many miles, which is currently under attack from the local planning authority, who are no doubt under pressure from the government to build houses. Not necessarily affordable houses for the young if the new Barton Park is anything to go by.

It was a well-attended meeting. The elderly, a few of them almost as old as Dad: men and women who had walked and played in the woods as children and who had used the fields to get to Beckley school, refused to allow a raging blizzard to stand in their way. In the open doorway, my old friend Ron arrived with icicles clinging to his coat to glare, narrow-eyed, at the assembled councillors at the front of the school hall.

Everyone is aware what new buildings will entail. Several people gave impassioned speeches about local roads and thoroughfares and vastly increased traffic and the likelihood of pollution affecting lungs. Others about the deer and wildlife being driven out; the Red Kite birds that have recently made a comeback; about the beauty before us which would be replaced by modern brick buildings; about the impact that those buildings would have upon the mental health of local residents who frequently walk across the fields to Stanton St John village.

Over the course of a century and before that, the families who have lived here for generations have used the fields to walk in to calm themselves through the wars. Nanny Lou used to walk in the woods when her sons were sent away to the navy and the army; Marion did so when Amy was killed. I did when I believed that Louise might have to use a wheelchair, and through my marriage breakdown and our mother dying.

We have walked all of the children here, throwing Pooh sticks into the stream in summer, sledging in winter.

I have known red deer to leap out in front of me, have disturbed muntjac deer, watched the Red Kites and listened to the cuckoo and to owls in the evening. It can't be underestimated how important local walks are or the impact of building new houses upon the fields. The landscape removes you from daily worries to realise there is something beyond and better than those worries.

There have been many such meetings in Oxfordshire. One of the institutions the local people have been fairly rattled by is the university, who own much of the landscape and are now willing to sell it to developers. How would the colleges react if buildings were erected on Christchurch meadow I wonder?

So, following that meeting, many of us have written to the planning authority. James says he will accompany me to take photographs as evidence. He takes fantastic photographs. We are going in the early morning, as early as possible.

In the meanwhile, banners and posters have been produced to put up all over Sandhills and the local papers are now involved.

People have to have somewhere to live but, in Oxfordshire, houses haven't been built for affordability, they are built for the wealthy. Anyway, I thought we were supposed to be protecting the environment?

The Boy Who Wasn't Jewish

He crouched next to the narrow, muddy stream to peer through the wet foliage into the depths of an ancient wood. Water had escaped through the holes in his boots, though he hardly noticed it. Time seemed to stand still as he held his breath, the hand grenade in his right hand. Only it wasn't a hand grenade, it was a pinecone, and the enemy wasn't a soldier, but just his older brother Don and Don's friend from nearby Risinghurst.

Alan was a tall, gangly lad with a large mouth and bad sinuses which made him talk through a permanently blocked nose, whatever the season.

Maurice was trapped in this place, unable to move in case they heard him, trying to avoid the stinging nettles and brambles of his hiding place.

Two older boys against one. Don and Alan were thirteen and he was ten, so he had to be the German, of course. But he was quicker on his feet. His reactions were faster after the years of dodging older boys. He rarely considered the unfairness of this. His friend, Basil, wasn't allowed out today so he was happy to be included in Don's game.

He prepared to run again as he heard their panting breaths and grunts of satisfaction as they leapt over the stream, crashing down on the bracken of the muddy bank on the other side. He thought fleetingly of what Louie, their mother, would say when they came home plastered in mud, but the moment was too real for prolonged thought on the matter. Besides, Louie was soft compared with their father.

Neither parent would be happy that the boys were messing about in the woods, especially during the pheasant shooting season, but as Louie had said on several occasions, "What the eye doesn't see, the heart won't grieve over." There was no reason their parents would discover the risk they took. He didn't want to make his mother unhappy; she had wanted the little girl so much.

He held his breath, almost laughed aloud with glee when he heard them so close and with no idea where he was. He wondered where Sandy had disappeared to, their small fearsome sandy-haired terrier. No doubt he'd chased after a rabbit or a pheasant. He would come when they called him.

A small holly bush met with the white skin beneath his shorts. Trying to move away, he toppled into the mud beside the stream, yelping at the cold mud sucking his backside.

"There he is, the little German bastard – get him!" Alan yelled in triumph, and the two boys fell upon him, roughly grabbing his sweater and arms, then grappling him into an armlock which would have made any Hitler Youth leader's chest swell with pride. Alan, always the commanding officer, took charge, giving Maurice a half-hearted punch in the stomach.

He managed to stifle a cry of pain. He wasn't going to yell, to show them he was hurt. He had only yelled a couple of times in his life, most recently when Ken had taken off his belt and given both Don and Maurice a hefty whack across the backside after they had woken him in the early morning. It had been a Sunday, the morning of the toffees that they had fought over, and of Maurice's birthday too. As Louie had pointed out later, dark eyes flaring with electrical anger, it was a fine tenth birthday present for him.

Maurice twisted about, stretching his neck towards his assailants. "Piss off!" he grunted, earning himself a kick in the leg as Don lifted him over the ground by the back of his jumper. He watched Alan's fists curl into vicious balls but saw something else.

Legs in green, tweed trousers. A man clambering down the side of the mossy, tree-lined banks ahead of them. He was descending into the woods with a steady lope, carrying a rifle for shooting pheasants, or maybe boys; his red face was sweaty with vengeful purpose.

"Get up, Maurice!"

Don's pleasant face had turned puce in his panic; suddenly he was intent upon saving his brother. They all knew the man; he was one of the gamekeepers. Louie knew him. She had once worked up at the big house on Shotover and she'd warned them about him before. He had the red face and hot temper of a drinker and had once shaken one of the stable boys until his nose bled.

"Oy!" the man now bellowed after them.

"Quick, quick Maurice, get up and run," Don hissed in panic. "He'll skin us alive!"

The red-faced man was bellowing at them now, his voice rousing the birds from the trees.

"You been told, time and time again, to keep out of these woods, you pesky buggers. Either you'll get shot or ruin the shoot!"

They started running, the smell of the damp, rotting wood filling their nostrils. Their chests heaved as they thrashed through the tangle of branches, snagging their trousers and grazing skin as they mounted the high banks by clasping at tree roots. No longer two nations at war but now with one common enemy, no one looked back.

Heaving themselves over the barbed wire fence by the ancient, rusting plough blades, they paused, bent over, clutching their knees as they tried to steady their breathing.

"It's all right." Alan wheezed a laugh as Don glanced back towards the woods at last. "We've left him behind; he's too fat and slow."

They began to canter away at a steady pace, using the path which followed the wheat field to Barton Farm and towards the dairy. Then Maurice remembered, his mouth falling open, and he stopped.

"Sandy. We've left Sandy behind!"

He stared at them, panic-ridden, glancing at the woods; would Sandy be shot if he was found? His eyes scanned the woods and fields for the sturdy ginger body on four short legs. But even when he called Sandy's name, the dog didn't come.

"Ent goin' back there." Alan shrugged, shaking his head.

Maurice twisted around to look at the two of them, hands clasping his knees as he bent over.

"I'm not going without Sandy…" he rasped.

"Don't be an idiot. Anyway, he came home once before, didn't he, when he couldn't find us? That's probably what he's done; he's gone back home. We have to get back soon. Dad'll go mad."

Maurice shook his head. "I'm not going home without Sandy. Gamekeeper shot that dog before, remember? He's allowed to, ent he? Something might have happened to him."

He thought of Louie, who had only recently begun to smile again after the death of the baby girl. "Mum would be upset if we lost him."

He started walking away from them, breath blowing clouds in the air before him. It would begin to get dark soon. He might lose his nerve if that happened.

"If Sandy has come home, Don, yell for me at the foot of the fields, 'cos I'll hear you," he called to them as they watched him walk away.

Alone at the edge of the woods there was an eerie silence about the place once more. Heart hammering, he looked about for the gamekeeper, peering through the trees and down the bank to the stream. Softly he called Sandy to him.

He waited for a few moments, hearing the squawk and peep of a pheasant, glimpsing its orange feathers flapping from the undergrowth.

He didn't much like being there alone, didn't much fancy meeting with the dead Roman centurion who a succession of boys, and his own grandfather, had claimed to have seen walking along the pathway from the Bayard that had stood on the hill when the Romans were here. In the twilight, the woods were ancient looking, dark and mysterious.

He stepped carefully over the broken part of the barbed wire fence at the point where it had been trodden down.

The gnarled shapes of the trees criss-crossed to a canopy of orange and brown. Soon the foxes and owls would begin their nightly murder of rabbit, duck and vole, and pheasant of course. Maurice made his way, once again, to the bottom of the valley where they had been mucking about since school ended.

"Sandy, where are you boy?" he whispered into the woods.

But there was no answering bark or whine, no rustle of the undergrowth.

He thought back, remembering the fox hole they'd passed, how he had grabbed the little dog by the scruff of the neck. He should have slipped the string in his pocket through the collar, not let Sandy loose to wander; but then they couldn't play at war.

He followed the stream to the end of the wooded thicket, moving stealthily towards the fox hole until he had to stoop beneath the low branches which caught upon his clothes and dirtied his shirt. Dodging the branches was so difficult that it seemed to go on for ever – until, at last, he could stand up straight in the small clearing.

There, sitting bolt upright, like an Egyptian dog at the tomb of the pharaoh, was Sandy.

Only the dog's eyes moved; for the rest, Sandy seemed to be turned to a stuffed animal you might see in a museum.

He stared at his dog in confusion. He had never seen Sandy inactive. Even when the dog was sleeping, the short hair seemed to bristle while his legs thrashed as though he were chasing a rabbit.

He had never witnessed the dog sitting bolt upright like that, in a trance, except that his dark eyes moved restlessly. Upon seeing Maurice, the haunches moved, as though he were trying to wag the stump where his tail would have been if he had one.

That was when Maurice realised Sandy couldn't move, he was tethered by the neck.

He crept forwards gently, not wishing the dog to strain against the wire, until he reached the lethal collar tethering him to the tree. It had cut cruelly into the dog's ginger ruff; blood spattered his fur above the collar.

Sandy stared at him helplessly and whined very softly. Maurice stared back, knowing that every movement would hurt his dog.

He felt in his pockets for something sharp; there was nothing to cut the wire with.

He tried working his forefingers into the ruff beneath the snare, but it wouldn't budge. Any slight pressure only making the snare tighter.

It would be dark soon.

"Stay," he told the dog, who couldn't do anything else. "I've got to get a knife."

He ran again, his breath coming in pants and grunts of effort, feet pounding on the wet grass. Across the fields, back past the school, along the avenues and almost to his own front door. He ran blindly until he almost knocked down his own mother who had come to find him.

She was without her headscarf, her belted coat worn over her apron. Donald followed her.

"Why didn't you keep him on his lead?" she grumbled. "Dad'll be home soon and wanting his dinner. You didn't find him, then?"

"Yes. He's in a trap thing. He's got wire round his neck – we need a knife."

He didn't mind that she was angry, not then. He was afraid the dog would choke.

"We need pliers. A knife won't do it," Louie answered. "Don, run back to the shed…"

She blew out her cheeks in frustration, changing her mind suddenly. "Never mind, I'll get them. I know where they are, stay here."

But they followed her, watched while she yanked the shed door open and rooted around for the pliers in Ken's toolbox, leaving the door open to run back along the street towards the fields. They followed her without speaking, sensing her

353

panic and irritation. She wasn't scary like Ken could be, but she could be just as stormy at times and she loved the dog.

He led them back to the woods, to the trembling terrier surrounded by bushes. It was Louie who cut the wire while Don wriggled his fingers beneath the snare and Maurice who stroked the little dog to calm him; they worked together until he was free at last.

Maurice carried Sandy home in his arms while the dog licked his face and Lou ranted without pausing for breath.

"I've told you before to keep him on the lead, and you, Don, shouldn't have left your brother. Maurice, you're filthy. You look like you've been dragged through a hedge backwards. Get upstairs before Dad sees you; put your other shorts on and give me those, you've torn them. Wash your face and hands…"

They didn't argue with her, didn't say anything. Ken wasn't back. They'd had a lucky escape.

When Ken did return, having left home at five in the morning, he stared at them blankly across the dining room table, his eyes reddened by tiredness. He hadn't noticed that Sandy's ruff was smeared orange with blood. He hardly seemed to see them at all, telling Louie that there was a problem at the factory. Despite their rubber gloves and overalls, one of the girls had a burn mark on her neck which had come up in the day. Fluid had splashed from the jug she was using to fill a canister. They'd had to let her go home. Dangerous places, munitions factories.

They let him eat in peace.

*

Louie was thin as a reed and attractive. She had dark hair and dark eyes. She was, so they said hereabouts, a little like the American woman that the Duke of Windsor had fallen in love with, Mrs Wallis Simpson. Her dark bob framed a fine face. She dressed well as she could and repaired her own clothes with a Singer sewing machine.

Since she was fourteen, she had worked as one of the many maids at Shotover House. This was before she had married Ken. Then she had worked there every day from the very early morning to late at night with only a few hours off on a Sunday.

Sometimes, Louie dressed up in her Sunday best and went to take tea with friends. Often, she went on her own, but she always took Maurice with her when she went to visit the Rosenburg's on a Saturday morning.

To be accurate, Mrs Aida Rosenburg. Lou seemed particularly keen that Maurice was friendly with Joshua, the only son. He was Maurice's age, but apart from that, they had little in common. Maurice had plenty of friends at school and he didn't really care for Joshua, who was a bit of a show off. But he did like Joshua's toys.

Josh Rosenburg had more toys than any boy Maurice knew. The small cars that could be wheeled in and out of a wooden garage fascinated Maurice most of all. The garage itself was just like the garage that Mr Rosenburg owned according to Josh. He also had a toy train set, even had a large metal racing car that could be pushed around their large garden in Risinghurst. But the things Maurice admired the most, and would really have liked to possess, were the painted toy soldiers.

Josh had a whole box of them. Metal soldiers, a little taller than his smallest finger. British, mostly, in olive-green uniforms, but also American. They had tiny rifles and helmets, but quite a few of them carried instruments: a bugle, symbols, even bagpipes. The American toy soldiers were made from plastic and, despite their tanks, would fall down if you blew at them. The metal ones were far tougher.

Josh even owned a Royal Artillery Unit. He was so lucky, Maurice thought resentfully, dreaming of owning the soldiers himself. In fact, once or twice, Maurice had thought about hiding a couple of soldiers in his pocket. So far, he had resisted temptation. God saw everything, his mother once told him; but even more than this, Ken would probably give him the back of his hand.

In the absence of German soldiers, they used his brightly painted Scott's guard on horseback. They had belonged to Josh's grandfather, so Mrs Rosenburg said.

The Rosenburg's had the largest, grandest house in Risinghurst. They were the wealthiest family around – at least, the wealthiest family that Louie knew. They lived in Kiln Lane, and there was nothing posher than Kiln Lane.

When they reached the house that morning, Louie took off her coat and went into the kitchen with Mrs Rosenburg, telling Maurice to "Mind his manners," as she usually did. It was their first visit after the loss of the baby girl. Louie hadn't wanted to go anywhere for a long time afterwards.

The two boys stared at one another and Maurice remembered why he had felt cross at their last visit. Patched knees, that was what it had been about. That's why he had turned red with embarrassment, wanting to punch Josh. But of course, he couldn't. Through the open kitchen doorway, while Maurice played with the soldiers, he had heard Josh's voice, hushed, but inquisitive, asking his own mother the question as she spoke to Louie.

"Why has he got patches on his knees?"

He heard Lou's flustered reply, an apology to a ten-year-old. He remembered feeling embarrassed for his mother.

"Oh, well… Maurice fell over in the school playground last week. They're second-best trousers, you see."

Until he could fit into Don's, this was true enough.

Now, his stomach felt angry again as the words came back to him but silently he knelt upon the floor beside Josh to set their armies up.

In the kitchen, the two women were talking about the shortage of food.

Though the two boys were not paying any attention to their conversation, sometimes a phrase or two would float through to them. It was Mrs Rosenburg doing most of the talking; she had relatives in Germany who she had not seen since she was a child. She told Louie how worried she was about them.

Josh was on his second biscuit and his first cake when they started to share out the soldiers. Again, Maurice was 'the Germans', while Josh took the part of the British. Maurice didn't mind this, except that the German soldiers had come off the worst for attack in the past. Some of them had lost their guns and helmets, and in two cases, their heads, though it didn't stop them from fighting.

They spent some time setting up strategic positions amidst the cushions from Mrs Rosenburg's sofa, which were the hills and valleys and fields. They spoke little. Hesitantly, Maurice took a cake from the nearby plate and took a bite. It was delicious.

From the kitchen, the women's voices continued to drift towards them. They seemed to have stopped their conversation about Hitler and turned to the lives of their children.

"Are you going to get him done?" Mrs Rosenburg's voice seemed to have dropped to a whisper, as though she were afraid of being heard or had used a swear word.

"Oh no, not now, I don't think Ken is really interested," Louie replied.

Maurice lifted his head away from what he was doing to gaze through to the kitchen where his mother's frail form was perched on a wooden chair. She turned, as though she had felt his eyes upon her, and smiled reassuringly. He lost interest, returning to the game. The women were discussing Lou's baby girl, now.

The British Army had advanced in the interim while Maurice devoured the cake. Hastily he knelt amidst the cushions, planning his counterattack. The two armies faced one another. There were no particular rules, although it was understood that the British Army was acting in the best interest of mankind while Hitler's troops were not.

Mrs Rosenburg peered through the open kitchen hatch. "Can you boys be careful not to get crumbs on the carpet?" she called.

Amidst this distraction, Josh had brushed a hand towards Maurice's main infantry, and had swept them all over in one foul scoop.

"Oy! You can't do that; we hadn't even started yet!" Maurice objected.

Josh shrugged, grabbing his ill-gotten gains before Maurice could stop him.

He didn't want to argue. It might upset Louie. He puffed out his cheeks and started regrouping what remained of his army.

Mrs Rosenburg brought forth another plate of home-made biscuits.

"Can you eat them at the table, boys? I don't want crumbs all over the carpet," she said, wheeling about on small brown heels to leave them.

Maurice really wanted a biscuit but wasn't going to risk losing the remainder of his soldiers.

"Hey, where's the field marshall gone to?" Josh's eyes turned upon Maurice suddenly in accusation.

"Dunno," he shrugged. "He was on top of the hill."

The hill was a green silk cushion. Maurice stared at it. The soldier had gone. He lifted it cautiously, then went down upon his elbows to peer beneath the velvet-covered armchair.

"Empty your pockets," Josh demanded, eyes narrowed in mistrust.

"I ent got it!"

Resentfully he turned out his pockets. A handkerchief and a fossil from the fields fell onto the carpet. He glowered at Josh, who was greedy and didn't play fair. All of a sudden, his resentment became a top-heavy load he could no longer bear. He shoved a hand against the boy's chest, pushing him against the armchair so that he gave a loud "oof!" of surprise.

He wasn't hurt, Maurice figured, he hadn't been shoved hard. But the crying and wailing was loud. Now he'd be for it. Only, along with that thought was a kind of satisfaction, like when you scored a goal in the playground.

That satisfaction didn't last long. All of a sudden Josh gave a blood-curdling howl, throwing himself upon Maurice, pushing him backwards. Before the women could reach them, the two of them started fighting, crunching the metal soldiers beneath them as they rolled across the soft carpets in a bundle of flailing legs, arms and fists.

Mrs Rosenburg reached them first, all tuts and lavender. She stood over them, pleading with them to stop. But it was

Louie who pinched Maurice's ear so that he reeled in pain and let go of Josh's jumper.

"Maurice Jacobs! What on earth has got into you?" she hissed at him, giving him a small shake of the arm.

He stood up, breathing heavily, staring down at Josh who was clutching his chest and crying.

He hadn't hurt him. He knew that he hadn't.

Mrs Rosenburg smiled frostily at Maurice as he stood meekly before the two women for the lecture. She told him that the reason Josh liked him so much was that he wasn't the kind of boy who liked fighting, not as a rule. Perhaps he was feeling a bit off today.

But mother and son left soon after the incident. Maurice refused to play any longer, while Josh carried on crying and reassembling his troops.

In the kitchen, Louie listened for a while to Mrs Rosenburg with a strained smile that was not quite hers, somehow. She ignored Josh's whimpering's when normally she might have asked whether he was alright.

Annoyed, she ignored Maurice, too.

After a little while, Louie told Mrs Rosenburg that they had some tasks to do and excused herself.

As they walked away from the house along the front path, she clutched his hand firmly as though she thought he might try to throw another punch. But there was some other thought that his mother had locked inside. He felt sorry for her again; after the little girl, she had cried a lot.

Safely away from the house, he looked up at her, pausing in the street. She returned his gaze with solemnity.

"I didn't take his stupid soldier," he said. Then, cautiously, "I don't want to go there anymore."

To his surprise, she gave his hand a little squeeze. "Me either," she said. "We'll go and visit Granny Webb instead, shall we?"

*

Granny Webb was very old when Maurice was born. Being considerably older than Maurice, Donald had more memories of her. How she spoiled them with apples and biscuits, for example. Don remembered the old carthorse that Grampy Webb, known locally in the Quarry as Braddy, had let him sit astride. Leading him around the yard behind the house when he was a very small boy.

Granny Webb had many friends in the Quarry, who over the years had visited her for advice about various ailments and family problems. In her eighties, now, she rarely went out and wore the same black dress every day with the twisted silver brooch that Braddy had bought her on the little white collar at her neck.

Braddy was one of the largest and strongest men in the Quarry. Ruddy of face and in good health, still, he took his geese and chickens to the market in Oxford and knew all of the farmers hereabouts. He kept and sold caged birds. He had a large allotment close to Beckley and most days he rode a bicycle all the way there, up the hilly Roman road from the Quarry.

In his time, he had worked at the brick kilns and quarried the stone. He was a Jack of all trades with a lively sense of humour, but it was unwise to get on the wrong side of him.

Don was close to leaving Beckley school when the new teacher, Mr Bickerton came. He was an ex-soldier, so they said, and his long cane helped to support a gammy leg. He was a tall man, gangly and with a large Adam's apple. Sometimes he had a blinking fit in class and would stare at them, saying nothing, doing nothing for several seconds, until he had overcome the blinking. God help anyone who sniggered when this happened.

When Maurice was ten, he was taught by Mr Bickerton. In the main, he taught history and geography, which both Don and Maurice were good at. Both boys had escaped corporal punishment over the years, although they had both suffered a slap around the back of the head on occasion. Liking these subjects and not wanting to seek trouble, the boys rarely risked unwarranted attention.

Not long before their Christmas holiday, in his last year at school, Don and his friend Alan were sitting beside one another at their desks in Mr Bickerton's class. Neither boy was stupid enough to take risks in school, though both had been known to do so outside the classroom.

Don's dark head and Alan's ginger were twisted down towards their books. All heads were lowered, as Mr Bickerton paced up and down before them, his walking stick resounding upon the wooden floor with military precision. He had set the older pupils to write an essay on the subject of William the Conqueror's defence of Britain after the invasion, so the class worked in silence.

Mr Bickerton had been a soldier in that earlier war. This was the reason for his damaged leg and the walking stick, or so he said. Perhaps there was less obvious damage to his psyche resulting in the blinking fits. The class had quickly learned to ignore them, or at least, not to register surprise anymore; not since Harry Walker had received three of the best for staring.

Just as Don was searching his memory for William's many fortresses, a loud thump came from the windowpane behind them. The class turned as one toward the tall, arched window, high up in the wall, as a woodpigeon flapped at the pane with its one working wing, before sliding down, a tiny eye pressed against the glass.

There was something darkly funny about the crooning, stifled sympathy of the girls and the way the bird's beak and bright tiny eye stared at them through the window, smearing it with goo as it sank down, still clinging to the glass with an injured wing as it fell toward the bushes. At least, Alan found it so, and he could no longer supress the snort of laughter, while Donald turned to him, grinning.

Neither of them noticed that Mr Bickerton's eyes had begun to twitch, his lashes to blink furiously against the taut skin of his face while the Adam's apple moved up and down as though he were attempting to swallow a bone.

When he thumped his cane upon the floor, every heart beat faster in that room. Every child turned suddenly to stone as though Mr Bickerton's eyes, rigid pinpoints of fire, had magicked them so.

"You think something is funny, boy? You think something as mundane as a pigeon hitting a window is funny. Or are you laughing at something else?"

No one failed to miss the danger in his voice, few dared to look at Alan who sucked in his cheeks, straight faced at last.

"No, sir," he answered, without a hint of bravado.

"And you, Donald Jacobs? You find humour in this? You think your friend is funny?"

Don shook his head. "No, sir. I wasn't laughing," he muttered.

But Mr Bickerton had already turned to his desk and was hastily writing a note. He ripped the page from an exercise book and turned back to them.

"Take this note to the headmaster. See that it's delivered. You take it, Jacobs."

They abandoned their work, rising slowly, walking quietly away from the desks.

Alan's mouth worked anxiously as he followed Don to the door, closing it behind them.

In the passage outside, Don hissed, "I told you, don't smile. He don't like it when you smile."

"What do the note say?"

They were five paces from the headmaster's office.

"I'm not going to read it – he might come out. Anyway, you know what it's going to say."

The waiting would be worse. They might as well get it over with.

Outside the room, they hesitated, listening to silence. Don lifted his knuckles to rap on the door.

He was a small, thin man who had been headmaster for eternity. Now, through round-framed glasses, he smiled from one to the other of them as though they had come for tea, then took the note from Don without a word, to read it. Finally, he nodded.

"Come inside, then. Donald, wait here, please."

There was something that could be mistaken for kindness in the benign expression. Something which gave a moment of hope that they might get away with a lecture.

Don leaned against the wall, his head back, eyes closed, chewing the inside of his mouth. Listening to the sound of the headmaster's voice as a chair was moved aside, but these innocuous sounds told him little.

He had never been caned in all of his thirteen years. He thought the headmaster liked him.

But there was no mistaking the swish that broke through the air. Not once, not twice but three times. No mistaking the stifled cry from his friend at the third swish. The sound made him want to wee. It must have taken less than two minutes though it seemed a lifetime to Don.

When Alan emerged from the room with watering eyes, he looked straight past and headed for the toilets.

"Come in, Jacobs."

The door closed behind him as he shuffled forwards. All thoughts seemed to have left his brain while he felt the dull beating of his heart quicken its pace in anticipation, telling him in those few seconds to run, though he knew he could not. He avoided looking at the teacher, staring beyond his window at the rooks foraging on the field beyond.

"Take hold of the seat, lad. Grab the seat, a hand on each side…" His explanation was impatient, as though he had forgotten that Don had never been in this situation before.

"Keep your legs straight and your head down." Don did this. Waited, his eyes shut to the world.

He felt two small taps on his lower bottom and thought, that can't be it. Perhaps he's going to let me off.

And just as he thought this the air seemed to move in a mighty draught, a distant roar of wind. The stick landed upon the material of his trousers and just as the searing pain reached his bum, a second swish followed it in quick succession, making him want to yelp, to grab the place where it burned the most.

Tears sprang into his eyes, impossible to stench the flow.

The air parted with a third vicious swish and this time his knees buckled and his hands shook, but the last thing he could do was to sit or to relax. His ears rang with the pain, the sound, the memory. He would have to return to class.

"Stand up, lad," the headmaster growled as though from another room.

"Keep out of trouble. Next time, it'll be six of the best. I don't want to see you here again."

Don tried to straighten, reached into his pocket for a handkerchief. He gulped in as much air as his lungs would take, hating all teachers. He would never look at the headmaster again.

"Hope the bastard slips up in pigeon shit..." he muttered when he stepped out into the corridor again.

Alan laughed, clutching at his bottom.

"I'm going to get Bickerton. One way or the other," he said.

On her next visit to Granny Webb, Louie told her parents all about it, that she had insisted upon examining the red wheals that stretched across the top of his buttocks and had given him a little bit of margarine to rub on the wound. The anger had eaten at her for over a week.

Braddy listened, nodded, and kept his fury to himself all the while, except to pat Louie on the shoulder. He loved his daughter and grandchildren, but as the eldest grandchild, Don was rather special to him. Some might say the apple of his eye. A good lad who had helped him on the allotment many times, and with heavy lifting, too. Don was clever and made Braddy laugh; they shared a dry sense of humour.

He rode his bicycle with some speed that day for such a large man.

In his later years, he was more than a little overweight. But now he rode as a younger Braddy with a clear purpose, as though the German's had invaded, in fact. A solitary figure, puffing a little as he mounted the hill beneath the November sky. He was followed by a flock of crows overhead. The patches of golden light that peeked from the grey and blue clouds of late afternoon shone down at him with a biblical vengeance. It would be dark soon; the schoolchildren would be home by now. The allotment was not his destination, this time.

By the time he reached the school lane, Braddy was breathing heavily. He wondered for a moment whether the teachers would have departed. The little school stood at the end of the quiet lane, the tall, leafless trees that fronted the fields standing stark against a landscape that he knew well.

But there were a couple of lights on in the school.

He rested his bicycle against the wall, slowly savouring the earthy smells through a large handsome nose. He rested his hands upon his hips and flexed his aching back, then cleared his throat – thought about spitting phlegm into the bushes but didn't, just in case anyone saw him. He climbed the few stone steps to push open the arched door.

His heavy footsteps creaked upon the wooden floor.

There were male voices coming from a room ahead of him. Braddy peered through the open door of the first classroom and saw only the empty desks in tidy rows. In the next classroom was a woman, a young teacher, sitting at her desk and munching on an apple. She was marking exercise books, her curly brown hair moving left to right, in rhythm with her reading. When she heard Braddy's footfall, she looked up very quickly and frowned.

"Hello. Can I help you?" she asked, alarmed by his sudden appearance.

"I've come to see the headmaster, or Mr Bickerton, or both…"

His tone surprised the teacher. Not apologetic, he hadn't even taken his cap off. But then, perhaps, it crossed her mind that he had come to repair the broken window.

"If you would wait here for a moment."

She crossed the floor on small hard heels that echoed in the cold, empty classroom.

"I'll follow you," he said. "Wouldn't want to put you out."

In the last room in the corridor, two men were seated at a desk facing one another. A cigarette burned in an ashtray on the desk between them. The lady teacher knocked at the partially open door and the head teacher looked up in surprise, too late to mask a frown.

His companion twisted around in his chair.

"This gentleman wanted to see you, Headmaster. It appears to be a matter of urgency."

"Thank you, Miss Cabot."

Braddy's eyes locked with those of the man in the chair. From the description Louie had given him, the seated man must be Mr Bickerton.

"I'm sorry, Mr...?"

He looked from one teacher to the other. "I'm a grandparent, Donald Jacobs' grandfather."

Then he glimpsed it, leaning against the wall beneath the window, the cane used to give the boys a beating.

"My name's Mr Webb. That's what I've come about, that thing, there..." He nodded his head towards the cane.

The head teacher seemed to wake up, realising that the interview wouldn't go smoothly; his tone became conciliatory. "Mr Webb. You must understand that Donald and his friend were..."

Braddy leaned forward, brushing against Bickerton's shoulder to slam his fist upon the table. The fist landed with a dull thud, jolting the lighted cigarette from the ash tray.

"I won't beat about the bush. Donald is a good lad and a good scholar, according to past teachers, he always has been. Never needed a beating before, Alan neither. They've been mates since they first came to the school as littlun's..."

"Ah. If I could make a point, Mr Webb, the boys are growing a little older, perhaps a little bolder. Mr Bickerton and I were just speaking on that very subject. Alan is possibly at the root of this..."

But Braddy wasn't about to give room for discussion, or to shift blame.

"They were smiling at something what occurred to them as funny," he said, his voice now low and dangerous. "Neither deserved to be beaten for that."

Mr Bickerton, who had held his silence thus far, shook his head.

"Your grandson and his friend were threatening to disrupt the class!"

His indignance broke in a shower of spit. Braddy stared at Mr Bickerton without compassion.

"You beat the lads to humiliate them," he said in a voice loaded with disgust, turning slowly from one to the other. Then, after a few seconds of silence. "Right. I shall keep this to the point, which is – if you or anyone in this school ever strike my grandson, or his friend again, if you hurt a hair on their heads, I'll do the same to you. Teacher, headmaster, whoever you are. I'll knock your bloody block off. Ask anyone around here and they'll advise you to take me seriously."

There were no more words. He wheeled about then, strode to the school entrance, his heavy footsteps echoing on the wooden floor while the school cowered in shock.

He took his bicycle from the wall and started the long ride home in the dark.

*

Once a week, Louie would find the time to visit Ken's father, Charles.

Since his wife had died, he had lived alone in the modest house in Headington. His living quarters were confined to two rooms, the front living room where he also slept and the kitchen which overlooked the garden. He rarely went upstairs, using a chamber pot and occasionally the old toilet in its garden shed.

Neither of the boys were keen to visit him. This was in part because the rooms smelled of cabbage, or so they said, but also because they were both expected to 'help out' with chores the old man couldn't manage alone, but they would never have argued with either parent about it, knowing how much it meant to Ken.

They usually travelled on the bus with Louie, sitting either side of her. Don with the punctured football held between his knees in case of a chance to kick the ball about in the street outside.

Old Grampy Charles met them at the front door of the house in Lime Walk in Headington, his shrunken figure dwarfed by the door frame. The house always seemed dark inside, despite the fire in the grate in wintertime.

With white hair and pale skin, he appeared to them like old father time, older than anyone alive.

His memory wasn't so good, now, which was why Louie visited him so often.

When they arrived at the front door, he would frown at them uncertainly, as though they were strangers. Sometimes,

Louie feared that he hadn't eaten since her last visit, he was so thin. She always brought food with her and sat with him to see that he ate. Sometimes she gave him a wash and a shave. When his hair got too long, she cut it herself.

A spine twisted by old age made it necessary for him to force his face up to look at them, an action which, though uncomfortable, he had perfected over the years.

"My chamber pot is broken," he said, greeting them on the front doorstep. "I've a second one in the attic. The boys could go up and get it for me."

Louie nodded. "Let me get these things through to the kitchen first, Grampy; the basket's heavy."

She coaxed him back into the house, hanging up her coat in the hallway and checking her appearance briefly in the yellowed, tarnished hallway mirror. The boys watched as she took out the bread and milk and the things that she'd brought for him to eat.

"Where's… my son… Ken?" Grampy called through to her, remembering his name at last.

"He's well but working, Grampy. Sends his love. He's going to come and see you on Sunday."

She began making the tea, wrinkling her face at the unwashed teapot with its ancient stains and the cups standing in the sink. Grampy stared towards the boys.

"There's a ladder under the stairs. I think there might be mice up there. I heard scratching earlier in the week… don't think its rats. You could take up my thing and leave it there..."

"Take up what thing?" Don asked.

His thoughts and voice were becoming slower, Louie thought, more confused.

"Gramps means the wooden mousetrap. Here, stick some crumbs in it and set it up there." She tore off a tiny piece from the loaf, rubbing it to crumbles in her hand and took down the trap from its shelf.

"I'll ask Don to bring over some poison to put up there, Grampy!" she shouted, in an effort to overcome his deafness.

The boys stared at one another, interested now. Much as they didn't want to meet rodents of any kind, they had spoken together about what they might find in Grampy's attic, especially since the conversation between their parents. Ken had said that Gramps was a hoarder who hid his money. Together, they unlocked the back door and went to the tumbledown shed to forage for the ladder, carrying it between them back into the house.

The old man must have read their thoughts. "Oy," he began, in the surly they were used to and never questioned. "Only m' second chamber pot, mind. Don't go touching anything that ain't your business."

Don nodded, more interested than ever, and they carried the wooden ladder – once used for painting and decorating which had been the old man's trade – up to the landing above.

The upstairs landing smelled of dust and damp rot with a whiff of urine. Maurice looked at Don and held his nose, pulling a face, while Don took a quick peek into both of the empty bedrooms, their beds piled high with possessions that were fifty years old or more. The curtains smelled of damp and there was dark, dank mould upon areas of the wallpaper.

They began the business of manoeuvring the ladder into place for the climb.

"You go up. I'll hold it," Don directed. "I'm stronger than you."

"If you're holding it, hold it tight and don't let me fall," Maurice replied doubtfully, frowning at his brother in suspicion, the lazy brown eye closed in a habit formed when he was very young.

Maurice didn't much like the idea of the dark, musty corners, of mice and giant spiders, but there was an overwhelming curiosity within him about what he might find and, anyway, he wasn't going to show Don he was scared. Don believed there was money lying about, a small fortune maybe, a treasure trove of coins and notes from the time that Grampy had worked as a painter and decorator many years ago.

"Hold it hard Don..." he called back, more than a little nervous as the wooden steps beneath him wobbled. He heard a laugh from his brother, who had shaken the thing quite deliberately to unnerve him.

Louie came up the staircase, then, carrying a lighted candle in its brass candlestick.

"No fooling about. Both of you, watch what you're doing. Open the latch, Maur, and push the door back, then take this carefully – we don't want the place to burn down."

The ceiling door gave a soft click and fell towards his waiting hand. He let it go, placing his fingers upon the dusty opening to pull himself up and into the dark cavern until his knees rested uncomfortably upon the attic floor.

Louie climbed the first few rungs of the ladder to pass the candle to him.

"Be careful with Grampy's things…" she called up to them as she returned to the kitchen, leaving them to it.

He gazed at the various shapes looming out of the dark, the boxes and piles of rubbish made eerie by the candles light.

What were they looking for? He reminded himself, oh yes, a chamber pot.

He rested the lighted candle upon a beam, dangerously close to the spider's webs. Edging forward, he listened all the while for the squeaking of mice. He set the trap on a flat space, ready primed with the cage door set open ready on its spring. Very quickly he became disillusioned about the prospect of a treasure hoard as his fingers met with piles of old papers, magazines, boxes of unused household utensils. The tin pot that Grampy needed so desperately was easy to find; it stood apart from anything else on a wooden beam.

He lifted it to his chest and had begun the difficult crawl back to the attic door when the thing caught his eye.

It shone through the dark as though it were made from solid silver, jutting from the packing case like the Queen of spiders herself.

Cautiously, Maurice lifted it from the soft, dusty material wrapped around it. The knobbly metal was decorated, although he couldn't make out the motifs in the dark. It had seven prongs sticking from it: a candlestick, surely, but a very ornate one.

Why would Grampy have such a thing?

Avidly listening to his progress, Don had heard the rustling noises and the pause in his brother's progress. Suspiciously, he called, "What have y' found?"

"Not sure…" Maurice's voice drifted back, "a box, with a sort of candle thing in it, might be worth something, though."

He groped about in the box once more. His fingers met with a rough, leathery binding. He ran the edge of his right thumb down the many fragile pages. "And a book, a fat book," he mumbled. But the book didn't interest him so much and he let it fall back into the box.

He crawled backwards from the packing case, struggling to crawl while holding both the chamber pot and the candelabra.

"I'm bringing it down," he called excitedly, momentarily wondering if he had indeed found gold and whether they could be as rich as the Rosenburg's.

As he reached the attic door, he snuffed the candle flame with finger and thumb as Ken had taught him.

Don's mouth hung open as he peered up at the dark square from which his brother was emerging. He stretched out his hand to take the candle first, setting it dismissively upon a chest of drawers and let the tin potty drop to the floor. As Maurice reached the bottom rungs, he gazed at the ornate candlestick, his fingers stroking the smooth, embossed characters in wonder.

"It's silver," he breathed. "Got to be worth something."

It was as Maurice landed beside him that Louie's voice coming from the top of the staircase made them jump.

"Grampy told you not to touch anything," she grumbled; then stopped mid stride, her eyebrows dipping in a kind of fear, her fingers covering her mouth.

"Give that to me."

Her fingers fluttered towards Maurice. Taking the candelabra from him, she stared at it in wonder at first, turning it slowly in her hands to gaze at the ornate decorations and the nine branches curved upward like a peculiar, static tree. Lifting the hem of her skirt, she rubbed at something that had caught her attention.

Maybe, Maurice considered, the thing was like Aladdin's lamp and rubbing it would grant his mother's wish to have the baby back.

The look of wonder on her face changed suddenly to fear.

"What is it?" he asked.

"Just a candlestick, nothing more, not worth anything."

"But it's silver, real silver," Don objected.

Louie handed it back to Maurice. "Go and put it back where you found it, please."

Maurice opened his mouth to object, but his mother's expression was too solemn, too grave to argue with her. He glanced towards Don for support, but Don's face was expressionless, now.

"No, give it back to me," she said, suddenly. We have to throw it away, get rid of it. It's dangerous. It's Jewish."

Maurice frowned. "We could sell it; it looks like silver," he tried, in a small, hopeful voice.

They watched her movements as she flitted into the smallest bedroom, tugging a pillowcase off one of the pillows so that yellow feathers flew about the room. Turning the candlestick upside down, she dropped it into the open case as though it were a dangerous weapon.

"I'll get rid of it," she mumbled, more to herself than to them. "It's not something he should have in the house. He probably got it in payment for work. Not something to have here, in case..."

But she didn't finish the sentence and Maurice was left to wonder. "In case of what?"

Don answered for him. "In case the Germans invade," he said solemnly, his shoulders falling with disappointment at the thought of wasted treasure.

*

A couple of weeks before Christmas, Maurice woke early on a Sunday morning to the sound of scuffling noises in Don's room. Now that the homesick evacuee boy had decided to make his way back to his mother in London – stealing the grocery bike to do it and cycling all that way – he had a room to himself once more. Maurice missed the lad; he was good to have around, being closer in age, but at least he had the room to himself once more. The two boys had got on very well, but it had been a bit of a squash.

He sat up in bed to listen at the wall dividing his room from Don's. It was icy cold. A long time ago, he had broken the catch on the window so that it didn't close properly. On cold winter days, his breath made plumes of cloud in the air.

Don was dressing. It was too early. Now that he'd joined the Local Defence Volunteers with Alan, as well as the job Ken had secured for him at the factory, he liked to lie in on a Sunday; so, what was this all about?

He crawled to the end of the bed and flicked at the blackout curtain. It was dark outside. The street dense with smoky white fog. He dropped the curtain once more and listened again. No sound from their parents' room. They were having a lie-in; none dared disturb Ken from a lie-in. He thought about the leather belt. Only twice in his life had he been whacked with it, both times when Ken had lost his temper, but not since he and Louie had argued about it. He wasn't about to risk Ken's anger for anything, so he climbed out of bed to click open the door softly as he could.

After a few seconds, he heard Don's footsteps moving to the door of his room. He closed his own with a gentle click.

The footsteps moved softly down the staircase and towards the front door. Maurice crossed to the window.

Of late, Don had been a bit cocky. That Ken and Louie were so proud of him was making him worse, Maurice mused. Louie had hugged him when he first came back in his army issue battle dress. He had a real rifle, too. He'd told Ken that some of the men in their unit had to move the rifles from Headington library to an unused chimney breast in Quarry school. When he told them this, Louie covered her mouth in shock, thinking of all those schoolchildren. But Don said the guns were pushed well along the chimney breast in the teachers' room where they'd never be found. Then threatened to beat up his brother if he told anyone.

Maurice told his friends at school about Don's new venture. He was impressed that Don now had the power to tell people not to have bonfires and to draw their blackout curtains across so you couldn't see chinks of light.

He didn't want to play army in the woods anymore, though. It didn't bother Maurice; he went with Basil, who lived in a house in the next street.

He lifted a corner of the curtain and watched his brother leave. He wasn't going anywhere posh, or to meet a girl, because he wasn't wearing the new woollen blazer that he'd bought with his first pay packet from the factory. His shoulders were hunched against the cold in their father's ancient tweed jacket. As Maurice watched, Don leaned against the house to pull Dad's wellies on, then trudged past Ken's little Morris Minor.

He closed the gate quietly; then and, glimpsing Maurice at the window, put his fingers to his lips before making the victory sign to him with a cheerful grin.

He watched Don descend the road towards the fields, half remembering the conversation at the dinner table a couple of nights ago. Grandad Braddy was providing the chicken for Christmas dinner, but Ken had remarked that he hadn't eaten rabbit pie for a long time.

Poaching. But Don hadn't a gun with him for his walk. Anyway, even Maurice knew you had to be careful on college land and he was headed for the woods, so perhaps not.

Thoughts about Don occupied him all through the morning, until he found distraction in the objects wrapped in brown paper and string with crayoned tags, made by his mother, hidden in the airing cupboard that smelled of mothballs.

Braddy had made presents for all of them, he knew that; but there were other things. Mum had said that people weren't supposed to waste money on presents but should contribute to the war effort instead. Seemed a bit mean to him, but the parcels restored his faith in Father Christmas.

The soft things were the sweaters she had been knitting, for Louie knitted sweaters every Christmas. He always thanked her, but he wasn't so much bothered about these as the hard metal shape in the package with his name on it and the parcels which crinkled like sweet wrappers.

He got dressed eventually and went downstairs. He read a comic then played with Sandy, who licked his face appreciatively and made several runs around the room, threatening to knock the small Christmas tree down. Braddy had dug it out of the Bernwood forest earth. A nice little tree; Maurice had made the paper chains and Louie lacquered the pine cones. For the rest, they were decorations cut from old Christmas cards.

Louie sang as she came downstairs, "Run rabbit, run rabbit, run, run, run…"

She seemed happier than usual for a Sunday morning, but then, it was almost Christmas he supposed.

She went into the kitchen to make porridge. Half milk, half water, with any luck a dollop of the blackberry and apple jam she made pots of in the late summer, storing them in the pantry. He followed the dog into the kitchen.

"Don went out this morning," he said.

"Did he? I expect he's gone to see a friend." There was no surprise in her voice.

"Can I go down to the fields with Basil?"

She placed the porridge before him, slapping the back of his hand for attempting to help himself to more of the jam than the dollop she had given him.

"Will Mrs Keen mind if you go round there?"

"No. She likes me…"

"Well… leave it until ten, you don't want to disturb them too early."

She moved the jam pot away from him. There had to be enough until next September and both boys preferred the blackberry to the rhubarb.

Maurice and Basil had been friends since starting at Beckley school. Being a Sunday, the streets were quiet as they wandered towards the bridleway beside the fields. The fog had lifted a little but at the field's edge, the tree branches projected stiffly through a milky white mist. In early summer, they picked the hawthorn leaves on the way to school, chewing them in imitation of the American soldiers chewing gum.

They broke branches from the trees to whack each other with as they walked, pretending they were swords. Through the rising bushes they glimpsed the American training camp. Its Nissen huts and barrack housing had stood there for less than a year but, to the local children, it felt as though the Americans had been there for ever.

The American base was on the Miller's land. Once, when the Yanks had only been here for a short while, they accidentally blew up an old wall within Shotover park during military training; the private herd of deer escaped into the surrounding woods.

"So, why did he go, then?" Basil asked, continuing their conversation about Ed, the evacuee boy.

Maurice shrugged. "Dad said he missed his mum and his dad – but his dad is fighting the war, so he can't see him. He's a flight engineer on a bomber…"

Basil widened his eyes, impressed. "He never told me that. Pity he left, he was alright, was Ed."

Maurice agreed. When they first picked him up from the school, he'd thought he wouldn't like him. They were the same age, but there was something posh about him. From the first day at school, he worried he would have to look out for Ed – smaller than him, likely to get a walloping. But it wasn't like that. Ed knew how to stand up for himself. He was funny, too, doing imitations of Hitler and some of the teachers.

When they reached the little wooden bridge over the stream, they heaved some of the heavier stones, slamming them into the water to create a dam.

"Bad really, weren't he, to steal Mr Reed's bicycle and ride to London?" Basil chuckled. "He didn't get it back yet, did he?"

"His mum sent money for the bike and Dad gave it to Mrs Reed. Wanna have a look at the base? We could walk round the back of that hut again."

They started towards the army camp, all the while dreaming of snow that might come so they could sledge. "It's cold enough," Ken had said, knowledgeably.

The high wire fence around the camp was extensive, stretching from the estate and out towards Wheatley village.

What the boys had found on their previous visit with Edward was that there was an area behind one of the huts that didn't seem to be guarded by sentries. This is where they headed for. Here, it was possible to peer through the wire fence and glimpse the soldiers in the distance. There were fewer of them, now. Some of those they had got used to seeing had gone away to war and not returned.

They stood side by side, their cold fingers woven into the hard wire, breathing misty condensation into the air, until a voice called out to them, so close that it made them jump.

"Lads. You ain't supposed to be this close to the base..."

The man was leaning out of an open window, smoking a cigarette. They'd started to walk away when he called again.

"Wait. Hang on a minute."

A yank, a soldier, and, as Mrs Hill, their next-door neighbour had once said, "Black as the ace of spades."

He threw the cigarette onto the wet grass and his khaki shoulders disappeared back into the interior of the hut.

The boys waited. Seconds later, he reappeared. Tall and elegant in his olive-green uniform, and broad of shoulder, giving the boys the impression of high rank, though in truth, neither of them knew a private from a general. He loped across the grass towards them.

"You like chocolate?"

They nodded open mouthed, unable to believe their luck. Chocolate was a thing Maurice had dreamed about for a long while, imagining the sweet taste in his mouth. This was an early Christmas present.

The soldier drew two things from his pocket, the chocolate in its beige wrapper declaring 'Hershey's sweet chocolate' and a note which had been folded several times.

"You from the estate?"

At first, they didn't know what he meant.

"Sandhills is where we're from," Basil declared.

"Right. That's what I meant. Could you do a small task for me, and deliver this note to number forty, Burdell Avenue? I need it to go as soon as possible."

He smiled at them, handing out the note and the chocolate. It was swiftly taken by Maurice, who nodded, expressionless. Then the boys walked back in the direction from which they had come across the field, tearing off the wrapper and watching one another avidly for fairness, giving no thought to the note – only to the taste of chocolate, but a deal was a deal.

It didn't take them long to find the address. The house stood in the road behind Maurice's own. They opened the metal gate nervously, glad there were no dogs, and shoved the note through the letter box.

When Maurice arrived home, the kitchen smelled of the wet fields. Louie stood over the chopping board, her apron covering her dress, sleeves rolled to the elbow. She was too busy to notice the muddy shoes he was pulling off at the door. Her face was contorted as she cut the fresh meat from the rabbit's bones.

He started telling her about the American soldier and the chocolate and the young woman at number forty who answered the door. But she didn't seem as impressed as he had hoped, turning to him once with a slight frown, saying "Number forty, eh?"

Don had gone back to bed after his exercise. From the living room came the smell of his father's piped tobacco and the sound of the wireless. He left the kitchen, putting his head around the living room door. The dog alone registered his appearance, wagging the stump of a tail from his cosy basket.

"Look here," Ken greeted him after a while, without looking up from the newspaper that covered his face. He was cheery voiced at the prospect of rabbit stew.

"At what?"

"The paper, Maurice." He folded back the pages as Maurice leaned in to look, scanning the small print for the article he was meant to be looking at.

"The young men serving on the *USS Reid* will never be forgotten in the battle to free the world from the scourge of Hitlerism and Japanese militarism..." Ken traced the words with his finger as he read.

"What does USS mean?" Maurice asked tentatively, fearing that he should know.

Patiently, pleased with the question, Ken rested the paper on his knees and reached out to the wireless to extinguish Sunday half hour.

"USS means United States Ship. It's about a ship that sank after a Kamikaze pilot hit it while it was in the sea close to the Philippines. You're good at geography, so you know where that is?"

Maurice nodded, though he wasn't so sure. He knew what a Kamikaze pilot was, though; they had incorporated them into their games on the field.

Don chewed his pipe thoughtfully, resembling the pictures Maurice had seen of Churchill. Though Ken wasn't fat.

He liked being this close to his father. There were times he didn't feel so relaxed in Ken's company, although he couldn't put this into words. Just now he felt warmed by the fire, more confident after successfully delivering the message from the Yank. If he asked the question, he knew he could keep his father there, even though he had heard the answer many times before. Yet there were times when he spoiled life with the question and Ken would say "Not now..."

The story of how Ken, the deck boy, jumped from his ship to escape fire, straight into the icy waters of the North Sea.

"What happened when you had to jump into the sea?" Maurice asked.

"It was cold, icy cold. Colder than that bomb shelter in the garden..."

Ken fixed his gaze upon the wall before him as though he saw something else there.

"Before I joined the navy, I'd never been nowhere, except for Aylesbury a few times, and once to London. But I was fit and strong and I was a good swimmer, learned to swim in the Cherwell with the other lads."

Maurice knew the photograph upon the mantelpiece well. The picture of Ken in uniform as a young man. Solemn faced, a little lost, lips parted as though in surprise that he should be going to war at all.

"The sea waves smack you in the face, the salt blinds you and your clothes drag you down so you can hardly swim. Icy cold water, black water that burns your skin like fire."

Ken laid down his paper and stared at the clock on the mantlepiece. He had gone back to that time in the navy, a time when so many friends hadn't returned to Headington.

"So, what did you used to do on the ship?"

"It's a hard life for sure," Ken mused, chewing at the end of the pipe. "You don't get to sleep for long and when you're awake the tasks are endless. Your officer keeps you on your toes at all times: cleaning, keeping the ship tidy, painting… you don't get an idle moment. You boys don't know the half of it."

"What happened when your ship got hit?"

"A grand ship… the best. We didn't know what we were going to face, only that it was going to be hard. Anyone who said they weren't scared would be lying. We had more ships than the Germans but still we were scared. Mostly kept it to ourselves, too afraid to talk about it."

He puffed on his pipe, staring into the fire, as though he could see the ship there and the other sailors, too.

"When did it start, the battle?"

"On an afternoon in May, in 1916, while many of the men were still asleep in their hammocks and I was on the afterdeck. There was an explosion which was so loud it hurt your ears; directly after that the ship rocked like a toy boat in the bathtub, and we opened fire on the German ships. We were in deep anchorage and a Jerry ship was spotted on the horizon; it was clear, several of us saw it."

Maurice wriggled onto the edge of his father's chair, pressing closer.

"I was manning one of the smaller, exterior guns on the port side of the boat, checking the ammunition. Anyway, then we heard the alarm and we was all scared to a man, even the older men. So, we'd been waiting, feeling threatened all the time, and it hadn't made for good sleep; even when you was allowed it. But we were ready. The waiting had been worse."

The Lea helmsman had been keeping watch: a big, powerfully built man, he was. We'd been keeping watch all night, under the stars, wondering if one of the German ships would come up at any time.

The sea was calm, shining dark grey like a saucepan, and the sky was still showing light. There were silver pock marks like white stars bouncing off the surface, but it was smooth and still."

Ken tapped his pipe out into the ashtray as Maurice waited. He packed it with tobacco once more and relit it. Then he stared at a place above the fire at the picture of the hay wain, as though he were not seeing that, but as though the room had been replaced by the ship and the sea.

Maurice tried to imagine the ship as his father had seen it, cutting through the wide expanse of water, thundering with the strength of a plough, leaving white foam in its wake.

"Our ship was no mean target; she was the flagship from which everyone else took their command. My eyesight was strong. I saw the German ship, then, some thirteen miles towards the horizon. Others around me saw her too and the orders were given to take up the anchor and give chase…"

Ken shook his head slowly.

"We was scared, like I said, but that's good, cos you're tense, ready for anything, and when the engines start up, they rumble and shake like a mighty giant, the loudest sound you can imagine. It goes right through you, see? And pretty soon, there are men running all about the boat, each with his own task that he's practised time and time again, so it's not chaos. There's order to it all, and we started giving chase, chasing that great German ship out of the English waters and away…"

Sam Greenaway was nineteen too, he was a mate, and the two of us went about our duties on deck. My heart was hammering, expect his was, but there was a sort of excitement that we was going to do what we'd been trained to do all along. Then out of the blue, there was a massive explosion which took us off our feet and sent us sprawling across the deck in opposite directions. But we weren't hurt then.

I looked across at Sam, and his eyes were staring at me in panic. Cos now there was a great, leaping wall of fire, taller than us both, licking around the deck. It was pressing towards us, spread by a great gust of wind, cutting us off from everything, so we couldn't escape. You could feel it, hotter than the sun, scalding your skin from a distance, and he knew – like I did. We was trapped and we could only do one thing. There was only one way out before we was burned to a crisp, but it was him who moved first, Sam who gave me the courage to do it. He climbed up onto the rail around the *Duke* and looked down at the water for one brief moment; then he lifted his leg over and balanced for a split second there, like a kite bird before take-off...

I didn't wait a moment longer, the fire scared me far more than the sea, so I followed him. I kept my arms straight at my side, like a pencil, and I jumped. I jumped feet first towards the great waves beneath.

When I hit the water, it was like not being able to breathe, and a pounding in your ears all the while you're falling, but it's quick. I went down like a spear shaft. It takes all your breath away from your lungs, and your eyes are shut, screwed up tight as you plunge under and go down. I remember wondering if I was going to die.

Then you bob up, like a piece of wood, breathless, and the ship is pushing you away from her in the wake of the waves...but she can't stop, see, not in a battle."

Maurice nodded, trying to imagine it: the loneliness of his father, bobbing there in the vast sea as his ship sped on. The *Iron Duke*, the ship was called, his father remembered it with pride – an important ship, the flagship for the navy. Somewhere in the house there was a yellowed postcard of the *Iron Duke*.

"Did you see Sam in the water?" he asked, hoping his father shouldn't bob there alone.

"Didn't see nothing just then, just great grey-blue waves, bigger than I'd ever seen before, slamming towards me and drowning me as I tread water," he said quietly. "I saw the ship when the waves she'd made subsided. I watched her go about her business, the bows moving away from me as she plunged through the sea at speed.

"Then, when the waves calmed, I started to get really cold. My teeth were chattering and there was the shock of hitting the water, too. But I could swim away, at least, now that the sea was calmer and the ship had gone a pace. I could swim, I knew I had to move, had to swim, couldn't just stay there, hoping to be picked up. An ice had started in my belly.

"I looked for Sam then, tried to shout his name; the waves were smaller but it was all I could do in the cold to swim through them. I've never felt lonely as that."

Father and son looked at one another. Ken's reddened eyes fixed upon his son's young face as though seeing him for the first time that morning.

"My arms and legs ached after only a short while from trying to keep afloat. My clothes weighed me down. There was such a powerful smell from the sea, of oil from the boat and salt mixed. But I knew I had to keep going, keep swimming towards the nearest stretch of land. If I didn't keep moving, my body would freeze completely. Only the land seemed so far away...

"I thought about our mum and dad, how they would miss me; how much I wanted to see them again, and that kept me going. Sometimes, I tried to turn my head in the sea and I could just about see our ship still chasing the German ship and hear the explosions coming from both of them. I could feel the vibrations beneath the water. I thought our ship would chase it right over the edge of the earth.

"Well, then at last my arm struck against something hard – it was an old piece of driftwood from a fishing boat. So, I grabbed it like it was a life jacket and held on, then at least my arms could rest for a while and I only had to use my legs to kick through the water."

"How long was you in there for?"

Ken shook his head.

"Don't know for sure, maybe an hour? Trouble was, the driftwood might have been the cause of my death, cos I was so exhausted I almost lost consciousness, almost fell asleep with my arms wrapped round it; my fingers and arms were rigid. I was exhausted and didn't seem to be getting any closer to the shore, so I suppose at one point, I nearly gave up."

He shook his head, a grim smile upon his face.

"When I first saw the sea, at Weston-super-Mare, I must have been your age, and I loved it. When I was a young sailor and I looked down at the sea over the bows, I thought how beautiful the white foam was as it spread about her, fanning out like lace. It fascinated me, how the sea could turn from grey to green to blue so quickly.

But I saw enough of the sea that day to last me a lifetime; all I wanted was to see the fields around my home, to have my feet on firm ground. Didn't think I ever wanted to see the sea again…"

He looked down at his hands, resting upon his knees, and gently brushed the cloth of his trousers.

"I was picked up in the end by one of our ships. I was young, so I suppose I had a strong constitution. Any older or weaker and I might have died there, in the sea, as Sam did, 'cos they never found him. They fished me out of the water. I was so stiff with the cold I couldn't help myself any longer. I was grateful, I'd prayed until I couldn't think any more. It took me days to stop shivering and be free of the fever. But I was so lucky, 'cos thousands of men were lost in that battle and never came home.

"They dragged me up into their boat and wrapped me in whatever they could find to warm me. They said my skin was blue with cold. I couldn't speak; my teeth and jaw were set like stone by that time…

"When I came home, after some long time, I went to find Sam's family in Banbury and told them what had happened. Sam's mum knew; she didn't say how she knew; maybe they'd already contacted her. She was grateful though, that I'd jumped with him, and glad he hadn't been killed by fire. She thanked me for coming all that way and gave me a hug. She showed me a photo of Sam in his uniform, like the one of me on the mantelpiece. You couldn't see from his photo that he had freckles…"

Maurice stared at him. He had the urge to hug his father; he wouldn't hesitate to hug Louie. Perhaps he didn't need to as their eyes, so similar in colour, locked together.

"Go and ask your mother to make me a cup of tea…" Ken said finally, putting his memories behind him, turning the radio on once more.

He did, then mounted the carpet stairs to his room, all the while thinking about his father in the cold waves. When he reached the landing, Don's door stood open like an invitation. Knowing how angry Don could get if you went into his room when he wasn't there, Maurice cautiously pushed against the door.

Don was lying upon his scarlet bed quilt, shoeless feet crossed over one another. He was awake and staring at the ceiling. Maurice waited for the "Get out!" to come. When it didn't, he grew bolder.

"You went shooting this morning…"

"Well done, Mr Brains," Don muttered.

"Take me with you, next time?"

"Maybe."

Maurice glanced around the room, envying the fact that Don's was larger. He looked from the drab brown curtains, now parted to let in the winter sunshine, to the bedside table. A fat, paperback book lay upside down on its surface along with an unopened letter and a tin of tobacco, the face of King George embossed upon the lid. It was an orderly room; their parents wouldn't have it any other way.

"Dad's been telling me about when he was on the ship," he said, in a voice that wanted to score points.

Don gazed at him, now, with one eye closed.

"Which version?" he asked with humour.

"What you on about?" Suspicion sharpened his voice.

Don stared at him, expressionless now. He drew his knees up, resting against the wall behind him.

"Hand me that tin," he said, without explaining.

Maurice reached for the tobacco and papers, handing them to Don before sitting, unasked, at the foot of his bed.

"It's time someone told you the truth." Deftly, he opened the tin, taking a pinch of tobacco to roll.

"The truth? You mean Dad's made it up?" Maurice's eyes widened in shocked disbelief.

"Not exactly, some of what he told you is true. He was on a ship that caught fire, but that wasn't when he ended up in the sea, that was later in the war."

Maurice's mouth fell open as though to expel the hurt and anger at a lie, and Don softened.

"He was a hero, but he lost a lot of friends. It's summat he don't want to talk about but I know cos others know the truth. It's why he gets in funny moods sometimes, goes off for a walk without telling Mum. But you keep askin' him about that time, so he tells you another story. It ent exactly a lie."

His voice softened to sympathy, hushed now. One eye closed as he stared at his younger brother.

"It's probably cos you're just a kid and you might get upset or go telling everybody." He paused. "And because they had to swear to a captain and an admiral that they wouldn't blab; it was a secret mission under Churchill and the government, then; they had to swear under the Official Secrets Act. Ask our mum, even Lord Nuffield knows about Dad; that's why he gave the security job to him." He hesitated." But Mum thinks he feels guilty, as if he didn' do enough to save them..."

Maurice nodded, his faith returning. "Save who?"

Swiftly and without warning, Don leaned forward, grabbing his right arm beneath the elbow.

"I'll tell you, but if you go blabbing to any of your mates, 'specially not Basil, I'll give you a good hiding."

He kept hold of Maurice's arm, eyeballing him into submission.

"I promise. I won't tell no one," Maurice winced, trying to pull his arm away.

Don let go at last, leaning back against the wall as though nothing had happened between them, then licking the paper to wrap his cigarette.

"He was on a ship bound for Russia with his squadron, a place called Archangel. Churchill sent them to fight with the

White Army against the Red Army, the Bolsheviks they were called and Churchill must've thought them a threat."

Maurice frowned. "I thought we fought with the Russians; like now, against Germany?"

"We did, it's complicated – shut up and listen, I want a rollie before dinner. So, the Allies, that's us, were on the side of the White Army against the Red. Only when the Bolshies started to win, a lot of the White Army joined them and turned traitor on us."

He thought of a game of chess, but a game of chess had rules; these war rules seemed unclear.

"The thing was a shambles and the British lost thousands of men. People wanted the men to come home cos millions had died.

Then, at one point, some men from the Oxford and Bucks Light Infantry were stranded in Norway and needed to be brought home. That's where Dad's story begins. The ship's commanding officer asked for volunteers to take a craft from the ship and sail it to the coast of Norway to pick these men up; only it weren't just about volunteering. They were told that anyone who went would be paid well for the job cos it was dangerous – not just the sea, but the mines that were under the sea – the HMS *Hampshire* had been sunk by a mine just a short time before this…"

Maurice plucked at the bedspread, guessing. "So, Dad volunteered?"

Don nodded, deep in thought for a moment.

"The volunteers were told they mustn't talk about it to anyone when they got back. That it was a secret mission. Anyway, they took the landing craft from ship to shore and rescued the soldiers waiting there... only it went wrong. The weather weren't bad when they picked the men up but it got worse as they travelled back to the ship, the sea got rougher – Dad said it changed from blue to the colour of slate. Then, the bow ramp started to swamp with choppy waves that got bigger and the men on the boat got panicky, cos they were army, not marines, and a lot of them couldn't swim, Dad said."

He paused again, watching Maurice, mollified by his rapt attention.

"When the landing boat got close to the mother ship there was a sudden surge in the tide and the boat tipped right up on its side and threw all the men inside it into the sea. Freezing cold sea. Dad said he thought he was going to die then. Most men wouldn't last a few minutes; well, they didn't...

"Some died from drowning. He said you could hear the shouting for help through the wind and the mist and spray.

"Others were killed after a few minutes just from the shock of hitting the water. It was still winter, so they died from hypothermia. He heard their shouts for help and he couldn't reach them as the bodies drifted further away in the wake of the boat. Says he could hardly help himself. Even Sam and the volunteers who'd come with him drowned; until Dad thought he was all alone there and going to die or turn to ice.

"They didn't know how he survived. They said he was strong. He must have been bloody strong. He kept moving, says he held on to some driftwood broken off the craft. Mum says it was his own will that kept him alive.

"But there were only three survivors when they were rescued after a good fifty minutes: Dad, Old Jack and young Jack. Just those three. The others were all killed."

Maurice gazed at him. He wanted to pull their father out of the water there and then. He imagined it.

"That's why he has rheumatism every winter. It's why he goes off on his own sometimes, too. He's remembering all those men."

Don got up from the bed, stretching his arms above his head. The smell of dinner being cooked drifted up the staircase making them both feel hungry, but the story held them there.

"He got the job as a security policemen cos Lord Nuffield heard what he done and what he bin through, but our Dad didn't tell him."

"Who did?" Maurice asked.

"They think it was young Jack," Don said. "You have to shut up about it now, all right?"

He nodded.

Once downstairs, Maurice peered at his father through the crack in the living room door. He seemed to be hiding behind his paper again. Quietly, he crept away.

*

"You've only five weeks till you finish school," Louie pointed out towards the end of the summer term, a short while after his birthday. She stared at him as she sat at the kitchen table with concern upon her face, a small tremor in her voice, because he needed a job and because she could scarcely believe that his school life was over.

She'd been very quiet since Don went into the navy, sometimes hardly speaking, which wasn't like her.

Proud of him, but too terrified to imagine what he might face now that he was with the British Pacific Fleet in Australia, they told Maurice little, although he gleaned much from their conversation. They had sent Don with money, more than the boys had ever seen before.

It was strange to cycle out to the local villages with his parents but without his brother. They took bike rides into the countryside, stopping for a drink at the Fisherman or the White Horse to chat with the landlord, Freddie. It helped to ease the separation.

"Grandad says that Monty Soanes, the farmer at Stanton St John, is looking for a farm labourer."

He looked up at his mother, one eye closed, a habit since he was very young. Doubt was written across his face.

"I don't know anything about farming…"

"Course not, but you've helped Dad with the vegetable plot and you're good with animals," she said with a broad smile. "You'll learn."

So, a few days later they rode their bicycles to the fields above Stanton St John, to the place where the Royal Oak farm stood, on the edge of the Brasenose woods.

The rambling old farmhouse, a rather beautiful building, stood before the tall trees at the edge of the wood, facing the fields which sloped toward Barton.

Hot and tired, they propped their bicycles against the stone wall and looked about them for the farmer. Louie pointed out the turkey behind a fence while Maurice followed her nervously towards the farmhouse. In the fields opposite, the harvesting was underway. A solitary man guided a large bay horse across the wide yellow field.

An old man, his brown jacket tied by string, appeared from behind the large barn while a flurry of red and white feathered chickens clucked at his heels. He doffed his flat cap at Louie and smiled a toothless smile.

"Can I help you, Missus?" he asked Louie, smiling at her, glancing briefly at Maurice.

Louie explained the reason for their visit and the old man nodded.

"Monty, Mr Soanes, is down at the bottom fields, close to the brook. He won't mind if you disturb him; you could cycle along the track." He stabbed a dirty finger at the long hedge to indicate the pathway.

They thanked him and set off again, towards the group of men in the far distance. As they approached, they noticed the boiler suits with yellow circles stitched on them, guessing the man at the centre, his shirt sleeves rolled to the elbow, must be Mr Soanes. Some of the men held onto tin buckets.

"Prisoners of war. German…" Louie whispered to Maurice as she stayed his arm. "They're potato pickers. We must wait here till Mr Soanes comes to us."

So, they waited, while the farmer set the group to their task. When he had finished, dismissing the men, turning away from the group, he glimpsed Maurice and his mother on the pathway and walked towards them.

Maurice felt shy all of a sudden, gazing at the farmer with one eye closed as Louie explained the mission, handing him a letter from her pocket: a reference written by the headmaster. The farmer listened and smiled from one to the other. He said he knew Braddy and agreed to take on the new farm labourer the following day, for a trial period, as long as he was an early riser and could be at the farm by six each morning.

Getting up at five was hard at first, but he soon became used to it. The trial spilled into a proper job and very soon he became part of the team, proud of his work and proud to be earning. He had found his ideal job. He enjoyed working at the farm with the men and then later with the land girls who came to work there. His confidence grew as he learned the tasks given to him.

It was a strange thing, so they said at the farm, that he was so good with the horse when he hadn't had previous experience with horses.

Punch was the horse who pulled the plough, a mischievous great beast when he was in the stable, and very sure of his value to the humans. Punch took liberties, trapped you there to stroke him, nuzzled pockets for treats.

The old man who had met him on that first day was called Mr Cooper and his job had been to care for Punch. He taught Maurice how to keep the stable clean, how to keep his water bucket filled, how much feed to give him and that half an apple often quietened him when he wanted attention, which he did regularly, sometimes kicking the stable door to get it.

He taught him how to mind the great horse's hindquarters, in case he jittered and kicked out and killed him dead, as he put it.

So, Maurice learned to talk to Punch until the horse would wicker and whiney at his approach and nuzzle him for strokes and scratches, gently breathing his horsey breath into the boy's face until they trusted one another.

Maurice seemed to know by instinct how to stand quietly, his hand extended, until even an obstreperous cow who didn't wish to be moved would edge forward to his fingers and sniff them with quivering nostrils, coaxed to do his bidding.

Punch was ancient but valuable. He did all the heavy work around the farm and although, like any older animal, he could be stubborn at times, he had a valiant heart and never failed to get the job done. He was as big and strong as an elephant. Soon, there was unspoken love and trust between boy and horse.

Very quickly, Maurice became part of the farm, to the point where he was invited into the big kitchen and Louie stopped making his lunch. Along with the other farm labourers he would eat whatever Mrs Soanes had made for them. This was generally hunks of bread and soup, sometimes cherry curd and cake with it.

He gave half of his wages to Louie with a feeling of pride. He was a man and he was earning money.

He learned to milk the cows, to care for the pigs and to drive the new truck, having been taught by various men on the farm, including Monty. He was a good, steady driver. Within a couple of years, when the Ministry of Agriculture roped Monty in to transport the prisoners of war from place to place, Maurice and Punch found themselves redeployed in moving the POWs themselves.

The German and Italian POWs were housed in separate barracks and worked apart because of their great loathing of one another. Given the opportunity, they would spit at each other, raise their fists in a challenge and threaten to fight. The opportunity only arose when one cart passed another on the road as they were taken to their place of work.

Maurice was a little taken aback and unnerved when he first took Punch out in the cart to collect the German prisoners. On passing the Italian men, there was so much hostility, with shouting, swearing and waving of fists, that Maurice wondered how he would quell the riot if it came.

But strangely, each and every one of the men seemed to like him.

Perhaps there was an unspoken code of conduct which they all adhered to; more probably, they didn't want to get into trouble. They wanted the war to end so that they could return to their families. Perhaps they had been through such hell that shouting abuse at each other was simply a matter of fun. They were hard-worked, but they behaved decently and gave him cigarettes when they had them, so that he learned to smoke.

He enjoyed listening to their chatter above the clip-clop of the old horse's great hooves on the road. The rapid, excited tones of the Italian and the deeper murmur of the Germans.

One or the other of them would ride up front with him, speaking English to him – for many of them spoke the language to one degree or another.

Sometimes one of them would ask him a favour, but he was always careful about these; you had to be careful about messages, which might cost lives.

But there was one man, a German, who Maurice liked above the rest, and came to trust.

He was called Felix. Quite good looking, a good ten years older than Maurice, and very easy to talk to. He wasn't what Ken would call a 'Don Juan', not like one or two of the American soldiers who chatted up the local girls at the dances. He was quiet, almost a shy character. Felix was tall, gangly, but held himself well and was interesting to get into conversation with.

It was partly Maurice's fault that the whole affair between Felix and the land girl started in the first place.

Molly, she was called. Fair-haired, small, pretty.

He was driving the cart through Forest Hill, towards the lower, muddier fields, where the Germans would be working that day. When he reached the top of the lane besides the grand old farm at the corner of the small village, they saw the land girl ahead of them. She was fluffy as a helpless chick and she was trying to lead or, rather, to coax and push a large cow back through the gate and into the farmyard.

The men watched her, some of them in hungry fascination, others in sympathy. They stared, though none called out to embarrass her or whistled either. Maurice stared, too, smiling to himself as the cart slowed at the corner and the harness jingled.

As they reached the farm entrance, Felix, sitting up beside him, turned towards him.

"Maurice, let me down. She is not going to manage. I can help her," he implored.

"I'm not supposed to let any of you down until we reach the field…"

The man shrugged. "You know I'm not going anywhere, just to help the girl," he said. "When I've done that, I will run down the lane after you."

He nodded at last, gently tugging on the reins to stay Punch.

The girl had been ignoring them until then. Now she glanced over her shoulder, aware of Felix leaping down from the seat beside Maurice.

They watched as the German got her attention.

Having spoken to her, she handed him the thick rope about the cow's neck at last. He twisted it a little tighter in his hand, walking calmly ahead through the gate, talking to the cow in a gentle voice – it was as though it was something he was very used to doing.

Maurice clicked his tongue at the horse, moving away along the lane because he couldn't be late, wondering whether Felix had also worked on a farm. He had never said as much.

After that, Maurice found himself stopping quite frequently at the gate to the farm until, before too long, he found himself stopping there himself, after his work, to deliver notes to her. It became a routine and the other men accepted it as such.

It was at the end of that warm summer that he lost his old friend. It put him against the Italians, which was irrational, but he couldn't see it then.

It happened at the close of a particularly long, hot working day. Hot as Tuscany, when the wide patchwork of greens and yellows shimmered in a heat haze and his face and neck had burned red.

The men, whatever their nationality, had grown sunburned through the summer months. Now those Italians who hadn't been collected were waiting, sweating in the heat, for Maurice to return with the cart. Their water had been used up.

They were tired and thirsty and longed for rest. Before he arrived at the field gate with Punch, many of the Italian

POWs were spread eagled on their backs on the parched earth, arms held over their eyes against the sun.

Even stoic, faithful old Punch was wilting in the heat of the day as he plodded along the road, his tail swishing from side to side to beat off the aggravating horseflies. The horse's hooves had clattered discordantly on the road as though the old horse was a little drunk, his great haunches appearing to sink heavily as he walked.

They were a little late. Maurice should really coax Punch into a trot. But today it would be too much for the old man.

As they heard the horse's hooves, the men began to rouse themselves from the ground.

When he reached the gate, leaping down from the cart, the Eyeties sat up, and the thought dawned upon them that the cart might have to make another journey yet. As they processed the thought, it was as though a bomb had fallen in the field.

A sea of men surged towards him, laughing and shouting with relief. So many chattering Italian voices as they raced, pushing and jostling each other to be sure of a place upon the cart. They clambered into it in any way they could, hoisting themselves over the sides, hands grabbing hands to be pulled up as Maurice called out, "Whoa, hold on!"

The old horse groaned, a long, deep sigh, like a sudden, distant wind, as if all air had left his lungs. His rear end shuddered and collapsed between the shafts, his strong legs buckling beneath him with all the sudden weight of the soldiers until he sat on his haunches like a dog and keeled sideways.

"Get off, you bloody idiots!" Maurice shouted, jumping down, pushing at them, shoving them backwards with authority he'd never used before until they stumbled back with surprise, staring at him until they realised that the cart was tipping and understood what had happened at last. They were unused to the changed young man who shouted at them, pushing them off the cart with punching arms.

At last, the cart emptied of human cargo, he knelt by the horse's head, putting his hand upon the strong neck to stare into the animal's frightened eyes.

"Run and get the farmer." He eyeballed a man he thought he could trust, one of the group leaders.

"Please…" he added in desperation.

The man nodded, setting off across the road. Not one of his fellow prisoners attempted to follow, instead forming a semi-circle around the boy and the horse at a respectful distance as Punch struggled to breathe, while angry tears bleared the boy's eyes.

*

Nobody could have described the heat in Egypt to him, although some of the more experienced soldiers had tried. A relentless and sometimes oppressive intensity made whatever outside task you were delegated even harder, and yet, having lived in England all his life and never gone abroad, the sunshine and bright colours were intoxicating.

The desert air made it impossible to breathe at times, the furnace blistered your skin, and the wind, which threw up the sand so that it pelted with its sharp sandstones, were new experiences to young men who had only ever travelled to the British seaside before Egypt.

You were punished if you allowed your skin to burn. A soldier must use an ample amount of sun cream and socks must be worn to the hem of a man's army shorts. These were the rules – heaven help you if you were caught sunbathing.

He'd been nervous on the great ship going out from Liverpool and after this, seasick.

At least, being seasick stopped him from thinking about Ken and his mother, and his girlfriend, too. He believed that he loved Cynthia, another Quarry girl, and hoped she would wait for him.

All he wanted was to feel better, praying to God to help him recover his stomach. The mumbling of men who moaned and groaned at the motion of the boat became a plaintive music that accompanied the early days of their journey. Most of them had never been on a ship before, or even seen the sea. Their training in Hampshire hardly prepared them for it, or for the homesickness, as the sea became their new home and their families disappeared.

Maurice didn't want to betray his feelings, something that his new friend, Alfie, found impossible. The young man suffered miserably for several days, alternately puking into a bucket and crying.

Maurice kept his feelings to himself and tried not to think of Louie or Ken or Don, tried not to think of home, though he wanted to. Ken had given him more money that he had ever seen when he left him at the railway station. He hadn't realised his parents had that kind of money, but he did understand they were proud of him as they were of Donald.

The great ship sailed through Christmas 1947 and arrived in Malta on Boxing Day, and here they were marched to a military camp for their Christmas dinner.

After this, back upon the ship to Egypt where stories were heaped upon the new soldiers with brutal relish by the old guard. Stories of the Fedayeen, of the ambush of British troops, of abduction and torture, of shootings and bombings, of knife attacks and hit and run accidents, not to mention sickness because of unsanitary conditions around the army camp.

The war might be over but it had left its problems world-wide: whole families murdered, displaced, and with nothing to their name. The Jews, clamouring in their thousands for refuge in Israel – but kept out because of politics – the final insult that they had to drink their own piss on board the refugee ships for want of fresh water. At least the army had water.

When he had lined up with the others for his medical, the doctor had asked him, "Are you Jewish, Jacobs?"

"No, sir," he said.

Both Ken and Don had been asked this question over the years. Ken's advice was to stay calm and simply deny it. They were Christian, always had been. There were Jacobs buried in many churchyards in England just as there were people called Jacobs sent to the horror of the concentration camps. Hitler's mob wouldn't have hung about to check who was Christian and who Jew. The name would have damned them if an invasion had happened.

The war had ended at last but the recent riots in Manchester and protests in Liverpool made life precarious for Jews even now; perhaps it wasn't the Nazi's alone who wouldn't hesitate to attack you if your surname was Jacobs. Maybe there were those people, even among his own countrymen, who wouldn't fail to damn you if your name sounded anything but Anglo-Saxon.

The Daily Express had been full of it. How the Jewish insurgents in Israel had kidnapped and then hung the two British soldiers in retaliation for the execution of two of their own men. Then, after the hangings, some British troops and policemen attacked Jews in revenge.

The newspaper article had helped to spark anti-Jewish riots in British cities. Ken had worried about their safety and the safety of their younger son, no less so that he was being sent to Egypt, a place where he might come under attack, a place with its own anti-British insurgents.

Ken, who had lost his big brother in that first war, had succeeded in keeping his fears to himself, but had prayed for Don every day and now prayed for Maurice.

Gradually, as the seasickness passed and he made friends with other young men who would be in his unit, Maurice grew resigned. There was no way out; he might as well make the best of it.

He had joined REME: the Royal Electrical and Mechanical Engineers. Their job was to repair and maintain all vehicles for the army. 'Arte et Marte' was their motto: by technical skill and warfare. Meaning that they would deliver the goods no matter how difficult the task. They would be based in the district of Ismailia and his days would be spent repairing tanks and other vehicles, or so he believed.

When the great ship docked in Port Said at last, Maurice had his first taste of excitement for some while to come. Everyone agreed that they were sick of the ocean and most were by now relieved to have arrived in Egypt. For the first time, excitement overruled anxiety. The port itself was a thing of beauty and interest.

Gently jostling one another on the gangplank, loaded down by their kit, Maurice twisted about, hand on rail to see the ornate white building with arches and blue marble domes on the very edge of the water, just like something from the film *The Thief of Bagdad* which he'd seen at the pictures with Louie. There were ships larger than any he had seen in Portsmouth or even Liverpool. Cargo ships, naval ships, small fishing vessels, all contained in the same port. For a brief while, the bright sunshine and colours and smells of oil and sea made him forget the reason that he was in Egypt and there was a holiday mood about the place.

In that moment, he forgot about the dangers they had been warned of, not just attacks by resentful nationalists who wanted them gone; not just the harsh climate which could be hot by day and freezing by night, but 'jippy tummy' and rabies and a whole collection of vicious diseases.

The punishment if you left the compound without a permit was severe, they had been told. A REME soldier, an older man, told them of the soldier who had overstayed his curfew time. When the man returned, naked apart from his underpants, clutching his arms across his chest, shivering and drunk in the dark and begging to be allowed back inside, he told them of the Egyptian men who had robbed him of his money before stripping him and sending him on his way. He was court martialled.

Lesser punishments were for sunbathing, which happened, especially when new recruits had some leave from their duties and no idea of the strength of the Egyptian sun so blistered their skin. This was punished by repeated marching: left, right, right turn and then a half salute, again and again until the recruit lost the will to live.

And now, waiting for the Egyptian train to take them first to Ismailia and then to a place called Shandur, jostling for a place on the crowded train along with the other soldiers, he could believe that this was a merciless land and yet he was fascinated. Such a clamour and noisy racket on the platform. Men and women tried to sell things to the soldiers – goods and drinks, mostly. They'd been warned about pickpockets and people who would trick a person into parting with too much money. He held tightly to all his possessions, gazing for a moment in appalled fascination as an older brother of thirteen or thereabouts lifted the front of his small sister's skirts in an effort to make money out of anything, even his little sister.

There was no ventilation on the packed train, which stank of unwashed bodies and sweat-encrusted leather. They sat shoulder to shoulder in the carriages, with the impression of endless sand –sometimes flicking away the flies and mosquitos with gradual lethargy caused by oppressive heat, often nodding off. When they reached the next town, they were given a sandwich and the chance to climb from the train to stretch their legs. They talked and smoked cigarettes, mostly nervous, but keeping it to themselves.

At last, they got their first glimpse of their barracks in Shandur. Their first glimpse of imprisonment and of two years of military service; they could only write to their families and receive letters.

He gazed upon the sprawling collection of tents, marquees and buildings of all shapes and sizes which included the Nissan huts which would be their dormitories.

Surrounding this compound were impenetrable rolls of barbed wire. No way out and no way in. In front lay the wide expanse of desert, and behind it the Suez Canal which reached to the camp and which they were in Egypt to protect as a trade route.

He followed his friends into one of the Nissan huts, his stomach rumbling, which temporarily overcame any other feelings. Army-style, the floor concreted – a single lamp swinging from the ceiling.

There were two iron-framed beds left. Maurice took one and Alfie the other. The mattress was well worn and it and the pillows smelled stale from its previous occupants. They made up their beds with the two pillowcases and two sheets folded there, finally pulling up the three rough woollen blankets and arranging the mosquito nets.

Then, they made for the cookhouse together.

*

They had all done their basic military training, which gave them confidence, although they were yet to realise how basic that training was for what they were about to face.

Maurice quickly settled into army life: the gratuitous daily routine of keeping their quarters clean, laying out kit for inspection, the drills and the engineering work; and when he could, he dreamed about Cynthia and his family far away.

There was a private beach for the army, at Ismailia, just a few miles away from Shandur where their barracks lay. Here, they could swim in a pool, for there were sharks in the sea and crocodiles in the Nile. Or they could bathe in areas of the Suez Canal where the boats came in. The private beach was the most exotic place that Craftsman Jacobs of REME had ever seen.

All the men had done their basic training in engineering. Maurice found that he had more skill than most. He was used to tinkering with engines and had been responsible for the upkeep of the new tractor on the farm after Punch died. For the Ministry of Agriculture, he had driven a range of lorries and heavy vehicles, delivering supplies to various farms and collecting their harvests. Not long after his arrival he was recruited as a driver.

Being RSM Daniels' driver was one of the most enjoyable jobs that Maurice ever had. Yet again, he felt that he had landed on his feet.

He carried on with his work as a mechanic, but if Daniels required him to drive him to a meeting at some other place, this took priority. As a result, he got to see much more of the country than he might have done, and with a man who was easy to talk to and who he liked.

He enjoyed driving, was cautious and careful, but never a nervous driver. Even when traversing the Canal Road, which was a hotspot for sudden hostility directed at army vehicles, Daniels trusted him to ensure that nothing could go amiss with the jeep. They kept handguns beneath their seats in case they should break down on a desert route.

There were still the routine tasks, like the sentry duty by day and by night. The local Egyptians were poor for the most and didn't want the British in the country. They would take anything that they could. Food from the food store, petrol, vehicle parts, whatever they could get their hands on. So, these things were guarded.

His least favourite sentry duty was the one near to the canal. Although protected by barbed wire, with the banks of the river steep and difficult to traverse, the land between the wire and the canal was dangerously narrow.

One evening, taking his turn to do sentry duty, he took his watch alone through the dark. The khaki brown battledress kept the dry, sandy wind at bay. Sometimes he stamped his heavy boots on the ground, looking forward to his bed as he stared out across the dark water; he'd grown used to the uncomfortable mattress by now.

He allowed himself to think of his mum and dad, wondering what they were doing.

He started to compose the letter to them in his head and his thoughts drifted to Cynthia, the girl he had known for a short while but thought beautiful. They had met at a dance and she said she would wait for him. He felt sure he wanted to marry her.

The sudden noise to the side of him brought him back to the present. He tensed his body at the snuffling whine coming from the top of the bank. He lifted the rifle, drawing in a deep breath and holding it, aligning his sight with the point of the rifle and turning it towards the sound. A shadow emerged beneath the moon.

A red dog appeared from the Nile grass. Part small Alsatian, part fox; thin, rangy and no doubt mean. A jackal, perhaps. He was supposed to shoot it instantly; he'd get into trouble if he didn't shoot it. Dogs carried all kinds of disease including rabies. Wild dogs would attack in an instant, especially when hungry – and this one looked hungry. The army insisted that if a wild dog came close, you must destroy it.

The dog looked towards him, sniffing the air. For a split second they stared at each other, the dog and the man, so close he knew he should shoot quickly, but the dog stopped snarling. He, she perhaps, seemed to be waiting.

And then, the first of her pups emerged, plodding through the tall reeds behind her, and a second to follow.

"Bloody hell!" he muttered to himself, worrying about the possibility of court martial for misappropriating army equipment, remembering the words, "You must shoot a prairie dog if it comes within thirty feet of you."

This one was less than fifteen. He raised the pistol, but couldn't do it.

Gritting his teeth, he held the pistol above his head and fired it at the bright stars above.

Her pup yelped at the sudden whiplash sound, while the dog reeled about immediately, disappearing into the reeds once more, followed by her two children.

He let the gun down, cursing himself for being an idiot as footsteps ran towards him from behind. He knew the two soldiers, one a friend, the other who liked to taunt his fellows, someone they all tolerated but who would easily provoke a fight if he had the chance.

"Just a dog." He shrugged. "I missed…"

He stared at them, smiling, wondering whether his story should be more elaborate.

"Only injured it? You'll have to do better than that if there's a riot and the shit hits the fan," the troublemaker mocked.

He laughed and thought of Sandy.

*

About six months after arriving in Egypt, Maurice developed the kind of nagging pain in his back tooth that couldn't be ignored.

At the BMH, the army hospital, he was told that they couldn't deal with the kind of dentistry required for difficult wisdom teeth. He would have to visit an army dentist in Ismailia.

He had to make the journey alone, even though it was unwise to do this. He didn't like the idea. He thought about increasing attacks on lone soldiers. But if it was the only way to get some relief from the pain, that was what he would have to do.

They gave him a hand-drawn map of how he should find Main Street, where the dentist had his surgery.

At the bus stop, on the main road, he stood for about forty minutes with local people, waiting for the old banger of a bus to arrive.

There were several people in the queue; the most interesting of them was a pretty Egyptian girl in a green and white dress, a little matching hat perched upon her dark hair.

Before the bus came, Maurice smiled at her once and she smiled back. He lit a cigarette, smoked it for a while and looked at the canal waters shining beyond the scrubland. When he dropped the cigarette butt and extinguished it with his boot, a small brown snake slithered from the cornflowers growing nearby. He gave an involuntary gasp of surprise and the girl turned and giggled.

"Harmless," she explained.

The bus came at last. A rattling, bone shaker of a thing, spray painted green and in need of urgent repair. He climbed aboard, parted with his money, giving it to the near toothless driver and sat behind an old lady with a basket on her lap and a crocheted hat.

He wondered, nervously, what the dentist would do.

The bus took them to the centre of the town, though it took a while. There was no order about the traffic, which moved as and when it pleased. He stared from the bus window marvelling at the chaos as battered cars and rickety carts lugged by mules crossed the road, higgledy-piggledy before them. He gaped at the pedestrians fighting to cross the street, dodging horse-drawn carriages and the carts carrying various wares from fuel to vegetables. Buses, bicycles, civilian cars, the tooting of horns and shouting added to the confusion. For a while he forgot the pain in his tooth.

When the bus stopped, he got off and followed the girl in the white and green dress, nervously touching her arm. She had spoken English after all. He held out the hand-drawn map, pointing to Main Street.

The girl held up her four fingers. "Four streets." She smiled, then stabbed her forefinger towards the first of them. "You go that way."

Beggars tried to stand in his way, holding out their hands for money: old men and children, mostly, with pleading upon their faces and outstretched hands. Maurice shook his head dismissively and kept walking, staring at the street signs in confusion.

When at last he found the building, it resembled a private house. A white picket fence surrounded a carefully tended front garden. He walked along the path, rang the bell and waited.

The dentist was a large cheerful man who seemed to enjoy his work, which made him rather nervous from the start. He asked Maurice to sit back in the chair and he took two

X-rays of the back of his jaw. There was no messing about after this. He received two injections, certainly numbing the pain, but the tugs and tearing of his mouth as two roots were drawn left him gripping the arms of the chair, fearing the large man might pull him from it.

He closed his eyes throughout, refusing to see the blood.

Four of his back teeth were drawn that day, without any consultation. He was grateful that they were back teeth only. Cynthia wouldn't think him so handsome without his front teeth.

When the dentist had done, he gave Maurice antibiotics and cotton wool buds to staunch the blood until the wounds had congealed, then returned him to the army. Dizzily, staggering at times, he found the bus stop and prayed that all insurgents were busy elsewhere, that day.

On the bus back to the barracks, people stared at his swollen face and the dried blood caked at the corners of his mouth. He ignored them, falling asleep with his head against the window, hating dentists and missing Louie.

*

He was happiest when driving Captain David Daniels around Egypt.

Daniels was in his forties, unmarried as yet, and from a comfortably off family who lived in Hampshire. He enjoyed playing golf, which Maurice had never played. They enjoyed conversations about cars and the countryside and quickly discovered other interests in common.

Daniels treated Maurice with respect, and when they hit upon the subject of the first and second battles of El Alamein, Maurice was hooked.

Daniels had been a soldier at the second battle of El Alamein, the decisive battle that marked the beginning of the end for the Axis in North Africa. He was lucky, he said, having emerged unharmed from the thick of it, unlike so many men who had lost their lives. It was REME which enabled Field Marshall Montgomery's men to keep up the pressure that broke the Afrika Korps and the Italian army, repairing tanks before sending them back into the battle.

Captain Daniels said that this was where he had really learned to think on his feet, and after this, Maurice regarded his senior officer as a bit of a hero.

After they had talked about the battle, Maurice said, "The war makes my work seem insignificant, I suppose, here in Egypt, I mean."

Daniels grunted with good humour.

"Don't underestimate your role, Jacobs. The British Army are loathed by the Egyptians. The only difference is that it's never clear who your enemy is or when they might strike. We're at threat from the Zionists as well as the locals. There's even talk of insurgency amongst the local police. We need to be vigilant all the time."

As a rule, Maurice drove Daniels to various military appointments in a Vauxhall truck.

Twice a week, he took him to visit the Timsah Grand Hotel in Ismailia. The elegant hotel was regularly used as a meeting place for high-ranking army officials.

It didn't take Maurice long to appreciate that the officer had another good reason for going there. He had become engaged to a young woman who had a clerical position at the Ministry of Defence.

Maurice had glimpsed her at the steps of the hotel on a couple of occasions. She was trim, attractive, with chestnut hair and long legs. Most interesting was her preference for trousers.

Today he waited alongside other jeeps and private cars at the front of the hotel in the dazzling afternoon sunshine. He never minded waiting, even when Daniels took a few hours over his meetings.

It was rather a luxury to think his own thoughts, sometimes picking up the atlas to familiarise himself with maps of the surrounding area. He had rapidly learned the layout of major cities like Cairo and Alexandria, even though he hadn't been to either place. Maps appealed to him, stored themselves in his brain so that if he closed his eyes against the dazzling sun, he could see not only the roads but the Nile River and the deserts.

Occasionally he turned to look at the hotel, glimpsing the porter in his red and gold uniform. He wondered what it was like inside, imagining himself entering the reception with Cynthia at his side.

Into the busy life of the street wandered a little girl of eleven or twelve, he guessed. She wore a patterned yellow dress beneath the blue hijab that covered her hair; she carried a heavy bundle of books to her chest. The dark eyes glanced up at him briefly as he sat in the driver's seat and he smiled at her, watching as she made her way through the distant market, bright with its colourful awnings and the varicoloured fruits.

From a window at the hotel's ground floor, silken white curtains rippled like water in the movement of a fan within. It was just after midday, the sun fierce and bright. He heard distant Arabic voices in the background beyond the car window.

Nails tapping on the window made him jump.

It was Julia, Captain Daniels' young lady, smiling at him cheerily then trying to mouth a message. He'd never spoken to her directly. Hastily, he opened the door, climbing out of the car, hoping she hadn't thought him asleep on duty, for his eyes had been half closed.

"Hello. Jacobs, isn't it? Care for a cold drink, Jacobs?" she asked with a smile.

He hesitated, smiling a little uncertainly at the small snub nose, the pretty face, the fashionable, cat-like sunglasses that framed her eyes.

"I'm not allowed to drink on duty, miss," he started. "I'm not even supposed to leave my vehicle…"

"No, of course not, but I'm not talking about beer. Wouldn't you like to step out of that hot car for a few minutes and drink a glass of lemonade? It's alright," she added quickly, "David, Captain Daniels, says I can invite you, and we won't keep you for long."

He nodded then. "Well, if that's the case… thank you."

"Come on, Jacobs. It's a small reward for the many times you've had to wait in this hot car!"

She waited while he took the keys from the ignition and locked the truck. Then she took his elbow lightly and he followed her into the hotel reception, feeling a little self-conscious, as though he were on eggshells, as he walked across the chequered floor and past ornate green marble pillars and potted shrubs which led towards the courtyard at the rear of the hotel.

Captain Daniels leaned back in a cream wicker chair in the shade of an orange tree, seeming to belong to the place in a way that he never could. He threw a broad, friendly smile at them and indicated a vacant chair beside him.

Self-consciously he sat. Julia sat down, too, having asked a waiter to bring a jug of iced lemonade to them.

He noticed that there were one or two other uniformed men in the courtyard, a couple of them also accompanied by women. No one appeared to notice his low rank. He dropped his shoulders and relaxed a little.

Julia sat opposite them and smiled at him over the rim of her glass.

"David tells me that you have a brother in the Royal Navy?"

"Yes, miss. He's older than me. He fought in the South Pacific. I haven't seen him for a few years; he returned a month or so after I came here."

It felt a little like an interview, but he could see that they were both trying to put him at his ease.

"You come from Oxford, yes?"

"From the outskirts of the city, miss – more the countryside, really."

After this, the conversation became easier. She told him about family friends in Woodstock and they all progressed to the subject of favourite Oxfordshire pubs. After a short while he stopped thinking about the discomfort of rank and chatted with them easily enough.

They were laughing about a famously grumpy landlord when he glimpsed the small black-haired boy in a striped robe. He entered the courtyard by a side gate which he pushed with his shoulder and closed with his foot as he carried a heavy box of oranges in a wooden crate. He had a wizened little face, like a man rather than a child. They watched his progress from the courtyard to the reception desk where he set the box down with a little difficulty on a counter that was almost a head higher than he.

He took some coins from the manager in his outstretched hand and turned at some speed from the desk, crossing back to the street.

Julia was laughing, her head thrown back, when the sudden explosion launched her from the chair while Daniels' shout as he hurled himself towards her was muffled through the buzzing in Maurice's ears.

The blast, so sudden and loud, seemed to come from everywhere at once, forcing everyone to the marble floor and, split seconds later, there was a shattering of glass from within.

The explosion stopped as abruptly as it began, followed by crying and moaning and, bizarrely, the unanswered, ghostly ringing of the undamaged telephone in the lobby.

Maurice dragged himself from his knees, dazedly gripping a leg of the upturned coffee table. There was blood dripping from a small wound on his cheek and tiny shards of glass embedded in his hand from the shattered glass jug.

Across from him, Captain Daniels lifted himself from the floor to examine Julia who he had protected and who now stood slowly amidst chess pieces scattered about her. There was groaning, but a quick examination of those in the courtyard said that no one was seriously hurt.

Julia mouthed something to them, though the buzzing in their ears had not subsided and he couldn't hear what she was saying. Then she pointed towards the hotel lobby.

It was clouded with grey, foul-smelling smoke which choked and sickened the air. Rising from the sinister silence came the moans of people who had been in the lobby, some injured, some simply traumatised.

The porter in his red uniform was lying upon the steps beneath the archway to the hotel. He was covered in plaster and his feet were shaking uncontrollably.

It was Daniels who went into the lobby first, through thick, toxic clouds of smoke, to call the army ambulances. The uninjured who had been in the courtyard outside began to help the victims inside. It was made much harder because of the debris around them: fallen masonry, glass from the chandelier and furniture that had been thrown in all directions, but the survivors managed what they could.

It was the first time he had heard Daniels speak in Arabic, as he ordered uninjured staff to fetch water and sheets to clean or bandage, then directed his attention to a woman, her body twisted at a cruel angle as she lay back against the foot of the spiral staircase. She was unconscious but alive, pinioned by stone, bleeding from her mouth, a horrific gash at her temple.

A doorman, still upon his feet but clutching a wound to his head went to her aid, attempting to push the stone urn away from her, while on the floor lying on his side and groaning, lay the young bell boy, his wounds harder to detect – perhaps internal.

Much of the entrance way lay in broken plaster pieces upon the fine marble floor. The windows had been completely shattered and as they moved their feet crunched against the fine shards of glass. They went from one person to another, loosening clothes, using anything they could find – napkins or towels – to staunch blood. Then, when the sheets came, tearing at them to make bandages.

They moved quickly as they could, doing what they could. Maurice, who hated the sight of blood, plucked pieces of glass from the arm of a young Egyptian girl and tied cloth about the wound as tightly as he could in a Tourniquet. Anger and shock made bile rise in his throat and he went outside once, just to spit, as though spitting would take it all away.

A new bomb, a bomb made from glass and nails and razors. An underhand war with home-made bombs.

As they stood together outside, waiting for the army ambulances, Daniels stubbed out his cigarette and rubbed his face wearily while Maurice wondered about the little boy with the box of oranges.

"You don't know who your enemy is or where and when he will strike… and it will get worse," Daniels said wearily. "The war is over, is it? Not here in the Middle East. Those who think we have it easy are imbeciles and this is only the start. Egypt doesn't want us here; we aren't wanted in Israel. You can't trust anyone, not even the local police. The sooner we are given the order to withdraw, the better."

The few words returned to him, heard long ago in church as he stood beside Louie on a Sunday morning, bored and reluctant; yet something had made him remember it.

"Oh Lord Almighty, help deliver me from traps and diseases…" A soldier's prayer.

A photograph of Ken as a young marine, probably taken
before he was sent to Russia. Ken is the figure kneeling
at the far right of the group

25th September 2020

Marion is back at school, taking Covid tests every day and I'm caring for Dad once more. Every day he asks, "Where's my lovely wife?" or "Where are all the others?"

By the others, he means everyone he loves, although he can't remember that they have died.

My mother, his mother and father, his brother Don, and Paula and Amy and all of those friends he had. I never want to be like this, in a world where I don't know who is alive and who is dead.

We have stopped going to lay flowers on Mum's grave, pausing to reflect upon Uncle Don by his grave; it is too upsetting for him.

I get the album out, the one Nan bought which has a picture on the front of the Queen at her coronation. Then I kneel beside his chair and go through it with him, photographs of Nanny Lou and Nanny Edna, of Grampy Ken and Ron, of Dad and Mum, so young then, giggling in a photo booth in Margate.

He asks, "Where's Mum, my wife, Cynthia?"

I feel tears coming and turn away. Loving him is a joyful thing, but loving him makes me think so frequently of death. I'm so glad that I have a family, grandchildren… If I was alone with Dad every day and without them, I would never be able to think of the future, of what we will do next, plan next.

When he has a nap, I phone the surgery and ask if his doctor will give me a call. Dad's doctor was also Don's doctor; he has been so supportive. He's gone the extra mile even through Covid.

So, I ask him whether it would be wrong to lie to him. I honestly don't believe Dad will realise that I'm lying, even after all this time, even after Mum's funeral which was attended by about one hundred and fifty people: family, friends, so many old customers from the White Hart. I don't believe he'll remember even though we walked along the path at the crematorium trying to greet and shake hands with everyone.

"I think he will trust you, and you're doing it because you feel it will be reassuring for him. I've known others do it…" He paused. "Some people write a card with a message on it, saying that they are staying with friends, that kind of thing…"

That evening I put the idea to Marion, who was less than keen at first. I understand why because I had the same reservations. What if he said, "But you told me she's dead!"

He might never trust us again. He is anxious about everything but he does trust us.

"I don't think he will say that. He doesn't remember he's eaten five minutes after he's had a full plate of fish and chips. I took him to Cornwall twice and he forgot he'd been there ten minutes into the journey home. I think we should take the risk because it might make him happier. He's constantly scared without her; he might not be if he thinks she's coming back."

I bought two greeting cards, and two stamps so it would be authentic, then copied our mother's writing from her old notebooks and did my best to write in her style, calling him 'Maur' as she had done, or 'my duck'. I told him that I was staying in a hospital in Plymouth to look after an old Cornish family friend (who had died not long before Mum had died). I said, "Don't sit under the apple tree with anyone else but me…" and gave him lots of kisses.

"Dad, you have a letter," Marion said, picking it up from the doormat.

He opened it and read it slowly, carefully, as we watched him. "What's she doing in Plymouth?" he asked, a perplexed frown upon his face, although a reason had been given within the letter.

"She's looking after Rhona. Rhona is very ill and she promised to care for her!" I shouted across the living room.

We both shout without thought now, he's so blooming deaf.

"When's she coming home?"

I panicked a bit, then. "She will, Dad, soon as she can, but she wants to thank Rhona for all the things she did for us."

"Arr…" he drawled, stroking the picture on the card, a red rose. He was content. We could see that. He must have read the card at least a dozen times before bedtime.

26th September

The month of October is big for birthdays. Lauren's is the day after tomorrow when she will be thirteen. I didn't have a clue what to buy her so yesterday I took her to the New Westgate centre as she wanted to buy some jeans and tops, complaining that many of the things in her wardrobe are hand-me-downs from her big sister.

She wanted Jess to come with her. So, the three of us parked in the humongous underground car park that I hate (despite the lettering of aisles, I always lose my car and inevitably end up wandering around for ages calling "Where are you?" as though it might answer me).

I followed my beautiful granddaughters at a suitable pace, chaperone like, because they are always embarrassed by me. I don't know why; it isn't as though I walk around picking my nose or scratching my bum or something. I think it's because I am almost sixty-three (October 4th) and sometimes guilty of talking too loudly, which may have something to do with so many school trips and having been a teacher for much of my life.

They seem to have had a good time. They bought several things, including bath bombs and a ridiculously priced ice-cold flavoured milkshake, all at my expense.

Lauren bought two pairs of jeans and some tops and Jess bought a new bra. (I discouraged her from black lace, bit early for that, I thought.) I almost said, "Over my dead body," which is something that both Mum and Nanny Edna said on occasion. Aunty Steph told me that she still says it.

"You can't go to school with those big holes in your tights and your skirt hitched up, over my dead body." Or, "You're not staying out until that time, over my dead body."

Saturday 3rd October

Today, Lauren's actual birthday, Louise had a small family party for her and invited two of her friends.

Beforehand, she had asked me to 'take Lauren somewhere', so that she could set up a yurt in the garden and decorate it with flowers for a little tea party. So, Lauren and I drifted about, first for a coffee, then to buy a few things from the supermarket until she said a little impatiently, "Nanny, what's this all about? Can we go home now?"

Lou had decorated the yurt with posies and birthday cards and colourful bunting. It looked lovely, and when Lauren's friends came, Marion and Ruby joined us and we had tea and cakes and played silly games before singing 'Happy Birthday' to her.

While sitting on the floor of the yurt, I discovered a rather large red lump on my arm. Marion suggested it was an insect bite. I didn't say anything, but occasionally the cats go inside my cabin. I think it's a flea bite. Now I'll have to move all of my paraphernalia out in order to fumigate the place.

In the evening I babysat for Harry's girls, who asked to watch *Mamma Mia* yet again. This is the fourth time. They now join in with the songs and the dancing, prancing about in fancy dress. Three-year-old Delia singing 'The Winner Takes it all' is very funny, especially when she's wearing a Snow White dress with Mickey Mouse ears on her head and when she imitates all of the dramatic, romantic gestures.

4th October

My birthday and Freya's, too.

Woke to 'Happy Birthday' messages on my phone from Tim and Debbie and Louise and presents on the cabin doorstep from James and Inna, which was a nice surprise.

I am sixty-three. Good God. I can't get to grips with it. I can remember being four years old, so how can I possibly be sixty-three? Please, God, let me keep my memory; it's the essential tool for staying positive through everything.

At Harry's, Freya was wearing her new party dress over her pyjamas, leaping about like a ballerina through the discarded packaging. Harry promised them pancakes with chocolate spread and was busy in the kitchen, beating the flour, eggs and milk. This was impressive, because he is the only one of my children who fought against cookery lessons. He spent his teenage years trying to avoid cooking, asking for pizza instead.

I did try to get him interested and involved, but he moaned so much, or messed about so much, that after a considerable time I gave up. Consequently, although he is a very kind and attentive Dad, he only learned to cook after his girls became his sole responsibility as a single parent.

This morning, after two attempts at making pancakes with shop-bought batter, he groaned, "Would you tell me why these aren't working?"

I showed him how to thicken the batter with more flour (ready-made bottled batter is never very good in my experience), then retrieved a better saucepan from the cupboard, as the saucepan is very important. Eventually we had some very fine pancakes.

At about eleven o'clock, we gathered for the annual, 'Mum and Freya's birthday walk' and ploughed through the rain and mud once again to the rope swing that hangs from a tall tree on Shotover Hill. The kids all had a go, quarrelling about who goes next. Freya made us gasp with her daring. Ned has always been daring, but Freya used to be such a timid little thing. This morning, her sixth birthday morning, she swung higher than anyone, giggling her head off and making Ned wait for some while.

At four o'clock, we met again at Louise's for Freya's birthday tea. It's so lovely to be together after having to be apart for so long cos of the Covid thing.

10th October

Woke very early, about five thirty in the morning. I'd dreamed that I was driving a tiny car along a road in Cornwall when I reached a wide brown river without a bridge. I knew that I had to get over the river to reach the castle on the other side, so I started to drive into the river. God knows what happened then, because I woke with Jack pushing his large black nose into mine. He must have been desperate for a wee, because he isn't that keen on rain and it was bucketing down, throwing itself against the wooden cabin walls with a fearsome resonance. I let him out and he came back inside in less than a minute.

I'd told Harry that I would collect the girls at about ten past eight so that he could go to work.

I'd promised to take them to the local park, so was relieved when the rain stopped later in the morning. I made the kids jam sandwiches to take with us, carrying a large towel to dry down the swings and slide. Freya rode her bicycle.

When we got there, it wasn't so much the rain that was off putting, but the many bottles and cans that littered the place after the previous night's teenage party. Mercifully, it's a small park, and I do have some sympathy for the young. There are no youth clubs around and there's precious little to do, even after the lockdown's been lifted, but where did they get the money from for so many bottles of Archer's Schnapps, of De Kuyper, cans of lager and bottles of whisky? Perhaps the country isn't so hard up after all.

I had a lot of cleaning up to do before we could play there.

18th October

Louise had a little party at her house to celebrate her birthday (actually on 15th). Any other year, we would have gone out for a meal, but presently there are a number of restrictions in restaurants, of course – so we gathered at her house, which was once my house and the house she grew up in.

It's quite a large house compared with the others on Sandhills and Louise and her children are very happy there. It needs a lot of work, though. The attic needs attention; the frost comes through in winter and it gets very hot in summer. The massively tall fir trees that overshadow the garden need chopping back.

A couple of years ago when there was heavy snowfall and the lights in Burdell Avenue all went out because of a power cut, several branches fell into the garden, some of them knocking the guttering from the back of the house and one threatening to smash the large rear window.

In order to examine the damage, I had to don warm clothing because it was absolutely freezing. I remember trying to pull a large branch away from the window, which eventually I managed to do, but not before one of the heaviest branches high above me had split from the trunk with a terrifying crack, falling towards me from the heaven's above. I escaped, tripped in my heavy boots and ended up face down in the deepest snow, narrowly avoiding the heavy branch.

I remember lying there with ridiculous intrusive thoughts in my head. "This would never have happened if you hadn't got divorced," was one of them. I got up, laughing to myself in the end. A lot of good things wouldn't have happened if I hadn't become divorced.

As Louise says, "You make new memories."

The party was fun; we played silly games in the living room, ordered pizza and sang 'Happy Birthday' to Lou, then finished by dancing in the kitchen. Marion and I left at about eleven to walk the dogs around the estate before bedtime.

20th October, Zoom meeting

I've never zoomed in my life, except for the times that Mike and I went to Saint Helena and used to zoom the family, but although he knew what he was doing, I did not.

This evening, I gave a zoom talk to Wheatley Women's Institute about my second novel and about the island of Saint Helena. Both of my first novels were written at a time when Mike and I were going through a very difficult time before our divorce, but tragic and disappointing as our marriage break up was, had it not been for that, I might never have found myself lonely and unhappy and able to express myself through writing, at last.

I have talked about these books at Headington Library and to WI groups, so far.

I'm still nervous, no matter how nice people are; sometimes I can hear myself gabbling a little, but this time, as an inexperienced zoomer, my nervousness was primarily about using the computer to reach the people. Luckily, Ruby made herself available to give me a hand. We went to the top room of Dad's house and she lay on the bed, occasionally laughing or grinning at me, but making me feel a whole lot more confident with her presence.

They were a very tolerant audience, and I sold quite a few copies of my novels afterwards, which is the point. This time no one in my audience fell asleep, which was the case with one elderly lady when I spoke to Headington Quarry Women's Institute.

21st October

Two things have happened. In an effort to make a little bit of money, rather than spending it, I've applied for a Christmas market stall in Bury Knowle park. I've been busy painting flowerpots with a scene of foxes in the snow. When the girls aren't here, I kneel on the floor in Louise's attic, a large attic, until the point where I develop cramp or need the loo.

Nobody knows I'm up there. Perhaps I could write there sometimes, be the caged tiger that a writer is supposed to be.

I'm going to put Poinsettia in the pots I'm painting. I am also making Christmas stockings, which I am filling with inexpensive but fun toys. I've got lots of really cool things I have collected to sell.

I don't know why I've chosen to paint foxes, except that they have played a part in my life and they are possibly the most interesting British mammals. In our old house, I used to feed foxes with the Sunday lunch chicken carcass, striding out into the fields to leave it by the fox hole on the hill.

A couple of times I've come very close to a fox. On one occasion, the year after my ex-husband left, I had a November 5th bonfire night for the family and afterwards I sat in front of the flames on a garden chair, mulling life over. Suddenly, a large fox appeared through the smoke to stand only a metre away from me. Heaven knows where it found an entrance, as the garden was an average size one and surrounded by a high wooden fence.

The fox simply appeared there, ghost-like. We stared at one another, neither of us confident about moving away. He had a cleft lip which appeared as a snarl, but I don't think he was snarling, just watching me. Maybe he was one of the foxes I'd fed and thought himself welcome there. He moved when I rose from the chair, running away across the lawn. The odd thing is that I couldn't see where he escaped to. He left just like a ghost. In many cultures the fox is meant to be a spirit; this fox made me think of my father-in-law who passed away not very long before our divorce. I was very fond of him; he was a highly intelligent and, very probably, wily as a fox.

We aren't going to Wales after all. Bummer. The first minister of Wales (who reminds me of one of my old teachers) has imposed a lockdown, so the places we planned to go to will all be closed.

The house I had rented looks lovely. It's by the sea and once belonged to a sea captain. The people who own it were very understanding and my money was immediately refunded. I have booked it again for next Easter.

24thOctober, Half term holiday

So, knowing that we would have to amuse the children over half term, Louise and I set about booking Warwick Castle and a theme park. We booked the Coach and Horses for a meal on Sunday (one of Amy's favourite eating places) although we had to book two separate tables with six people on each because of the Covid restrictions. I said I would cook on Tuesday, Marion said she would cook on Wednesday and we decided to have our bonfire night and Hallowe'en combined on Friday 30th October, breaking with tradition because of the announcement that a British lockdown would come into place on 5th November. We also had quite a few walks across Shotover and on Port Meadow, so the week was fun after all. Perhaps we should just stay at home in future.

Our Hallowe'en firework display was definitely the highlight.

The garden is perfect for family garden type activities, but when Louise asked, "Any chance you could decorate it like the haunted walk at Warwick Castle?" I felt a little challenged. In the end, though, I did decorate the garden and it looked good.

I tore up an old sheet and stuffed the centre of each piece with material, drawing eyes and a mouth on the limbless heads, then dangled them from the trees. I filled the garden with as many lanterns and pumpkins as I could find. I took two mannequins from the shed (Lou used to have a shop and the mannequins are the only 'stock' we couldn't ger rid of), then dressed one in spooky clothing and partially hid it behind the bushes and dunked the other upside down in the pond, a witch who has tumbled from a dunking stool. Possibly not very politically correct where witches are concerned.

It was scary enough without scaring Delia out of her wits, though she did initially hide behind her father, peering out from behind his legs.

Jack disgraced himself, though really it was my fault for placing a plate of cooked sausages on the floor while I unlocked the cabin door. It must have taken him seconds to eat all sixteen of them and I had to send people out to buy frankfurters instead. Marion helpfully brought more cooked sausages with her so, eventually, there was plenty to eat and drink.

James let off the fireworks because he's extremely health and safety conscious (which is sometimes a good thing; he occasionally verges on OCD). He did a great show and actually, I was very grateful, because fireworks have always scared me a little, even though we've been celebrating this act of terrorism since I was young.

I can still remember standing with my family as a child and singing, "Build a bonfire, build a bonfire, put Harold Wilson on the top…" which says a lot about the family politics that I grew up with.

Finally, Ned's dad happily set off a large multi-blasting finale firework that I had bought believing it was a box containing eight fireworks. If I had I read the instructions properly I'd have realised it said 'eight blasts', but Delia was doing newly learned cartwheels in the supermarket aisle at the time, so it was difficult to think.

Trusting Patrick with the finale was a risk – a few years ago he sent a rocket into the air, miscalculating the angle he'd set it in the ground. We were sent running, grabbing children as it hit a wall, then it rebounded, then knocked off the guttering until finally it spun wildly in the grass.

We gave both James and Paddy a hearty clap at the end. The children went home to bed and Marion, James and I sat in the dark garden drinking wine and watching the flames die down.

2nd November

Had to take Dad for a heart scan at the hospital today. Apparently, when he was admitted in the summer months, they detected a blip in the blood flow.

I sat in the waiting room holding his hand, while he asked a million times why we were there at all. When they called us, making us a priority on the waiting list (I suspect because his questions were driving the receptionist crazy), he was asked to take off his upper clothing and lie upon the bed beside the heart monitor. At ninety-one, he's very skinny and frail. A narrow chest, sagging, paper-thin skin, none of this would surprise others at his age, but I remember him in middle age, when he was of a healthy weight. To see him lying there like that brought out the greatest tenderness in me, at least until the questions started again.

Fortunately, the Australian doctor had a good sense of humour.

The examination was quite long although it was fascinating to see the blood pulsating through his arteries on the screen above his head. He couldn't see it, which is probably just as well.

"Why am I here? What are you doing?" Then after twenty minutes, "Can I put my clothes back on? It's cold as buggery in here."

The doctor had a great sense of humour, snorting with laughter every time Dad threw out his questions. In the end he asked me whether I could keep Dad quiet for a while because he needed to listen to the sound of his heart.

Gently I placed my finger over his lips to shush him.

"When can I get my clothes back on? It's cold as buggery in here." He repeated it several times around my finger.

The results should be back in a week or so.

3rd November

Disappointingly, there's not going to be a Christmas fair, now. All those pots with foxes painted on them. Ah well, have to turn them into presents, I guess.

The government is imposing another lockdown. Everything will be closed, yet again, and just before Christmas, too. My lovely friend has been made redundant from her job at Debenhams. This is a terrible situation for so many people. Another friend has decided to retire now that their furlough has ended; he's seventy and he's worked hard all of his life.

I thought about writing to Prince Charles; it looks like we are losing the battle to keep our fields. Maybe Prince Charles might get on board.

I do have sympathy for young people who can't afford homes, though. If homes in Oxfordshire and elsewhere are expensive as they are, what hope is there? Perhaps we should be thinking about a different kind of home, maybe the kinds of cabins used for holiday homes that might not impact on the environment in the same way. It isn't just the homes, it's the blessed roads that must be built.

Becky (my distant cousin in America) replied to my email, saying that Aunty June is recovering from illness and is going into a Memory home. Mum and dad, June and Bill were the best of friends and had a lot of fun when they came over from the USA and stayed in West Virginia.

Sadly, Dad knows her face in photographs, but doesn't remember her name, now.

November 4th

Today is Wednesday. I have to look after both Dad and Delia together. This is made less troublesome by the fact that Delia is a three-year-old girl; consequently, Dad never attempts to smack her around the back of the head as he did Ned when the dementia set in; he didn't do it when his own children were small. Smacking boys around the back of the head was habitual in our fathers' day, or so it would seem. Howard says he can't remember Dad doing it to him, so it's a tendency in dementia to regress to your far past. It says a lot about Dad's anxiety.

I take Ned to school, he on his scooter. The wind whips our cheeks. Autumn again, the months have been swallowed up by the Covid calendar.

When Ned is safely in class, I go to Dad's to coax him out of bed with promises of tea, porridge and a trip out. Don't have a clue where to take him at this point. I just know he's happiest in the car, where he can imagine that it's any one of the times throughout his life, and that all of the people he loves and remembers are still here with him. A kind of Lala land.

Beneath his duvet he is snug, warm and happy with his dreams and memories. He doesn't look like a man who wants to get up.

I smooth his short grey hair, which was cut at the hairdressers in the lull between lockdowns. Then I draw back his heavy curtains to see two or three seagulls hovering on the wind.

The trees around the house are very bald, now, except for the tall fir trees; their branches dangle crisp orange or with olive-green leaves which are torn away in the wind. Limp, dead leaves; Dad also feels a little limp and dead, perhaps.

"I'm not getting up. I don't feel well," he says.

"Aw, you'll be okay." I stroke the dry skin of his forehead. Sometimes during the day, I grow irritable, but rarely when I sit on the edge of his bed.

Where shall I take him? No pubs or coffee shops or places to visit today. It has to be somewhere where Delia can run around and enjoy herself. The beautiful garden centre managed by our cousin, Uncle Don's son, will be open. I'll take them there. I need to find out how Aunty Dorothy is. After that, Dad can sit inside the car, wrapped up warmly, looking at his paper while I play with Delia in the park. He often has a bemused expression on his face when he flicks through the paper, as though he has found himself catapulted into another world.

So, we go to Waterperry Gardens to walk amidst the plants. Delia tries to pick a leaf from a rather expensive plant then runs about happily while Dad asks repeatedly, "Shall we go home, now?"

My cousin is busy, somewhere, so we head off to the park.

Later in the day I collect Jess from school. A young person in her 'bubble' at school has Covid. She will have to stay at home for two weeks and her GCSE programme managed online. Moreover, this means frequent texts, asking me whether I can get her take-away food.

I suppose it will be time to write Christmas cards soon.

Friday 13th November

Something really dreadful has happened. I've told Lou that I can't babysit this evening. I never say I can't babysit, but I'm so upset for Ruth.

Ruth is a librarian. She works at the city library but lives in Abingdon. I've known her since we were at college together, where we shared a room for a long while. Although we don't see one another very often, I value her friendship so much, and we call each other frequently. Because of the virus, we have seen each other even less over these past months, but she is emotionally intelligent and great to talk to if I have a problem, she is also down to earth and extremely funny. I love her.

We meet for lunch a few times during a (normal) year – although not this complicated Covid year. She lives alone and has one son, Simon, who lives close to her. I'm his godmother.

They are lovely, both Ruth and her son. He is a popular teacher in a primary school, a gentle soul – perhaps a bit too kind for this world.

About five years ago, Simon married Tamsin. Tamsin's parents are divorced as Simon's are. In his case, they separated long ago when Ruth was a young woman. Tamsin's mother lives in Wallingford. Tamsin has had a troubled past, but Simon only knows some of it and hasn't told Ruth very much about it, only that her mother suffers from bipolar episodes. They married after a very short courtship.

They had a little girl three years ago, Lilly May. Ruth adores her and wants to see more of her granddaughter, but it seems that Tamsin is a bit resistant and Ruth puts this down to the trust issues Tamsin has with her mother. I know how lucky I am when I talk to Ruth. I may have missed out on some things over the years through caring for my grandchildren; but really, I wouldn't have it any other way.

I've loved that I can play with them, teach them a little, watch them grow, I've loved just being with them; but Ruth has been kept at arm's length from her granddaughter, or so she feels.

Tamsin sounds a little neurotic. Simon is prevented from taking Lilly May to the park on his own, the child's own father, but Ruth shows a lot of sympathy when she talks about her daughter-in-law. Ruth is a sympathetic person but, truthfully, it sounds as though the young woman is a bit of a control freak who has been hard to live with.

The last time that we spoke, Ruth hadn't even been allowed to babysit, which she desperately wants. I may have had my grandchildren a lot over the years, but at least I don't have to beg to see them.

Last night, at about half past ten, I was just settling to sleep with my face lathered in cream when the phone rang. I almost ignored it, but I'm glad I didn't now, because it was Ruth and she sounded so upset, not at all like her usual self. I could tell that she was trying so hard not to cry.

Tamsin had not only left Simon, taking their little girl, but had gone to Abingdon police station to report that he had slapped her about the head.

The police arrested him.

I knew, knew in my heart he would not do such a thing.

He isn't that sort of a person, and he loves the girl, doing everything she says and all she asks. What I did know, because Ruth had told me, was that not so long ago, Tamsin had hit Simon with a spatula, marking his cheek.

He wouldn't do anything about it for many reasons, principally because he is afraid of losing Tamsin and the child.

I also know that Tamsin wanted her own home, rather than the rented flat close to Abingdon town centre where they live now, and that Simon had asked Ruth whether she could help with a deposit.

To hear Ruth having a breakdown over the telephone was dreadful. I just wanted to put my arms around her and comfort her.

"He would never do such a thing, never; but I'm so afraid that they won't believe it. There's been so much domestic violence this year. They have to believe her, don't they? But it isn't true."

Try to stay calm, I don't believe it either, I told her. I didn't believe it, but it was a dangerous accusation.

"A policewoman called me from the station; she said I should get him a lawyer, that they wouldn't let me speak to him until he'd spoken to a lawyer… I've tried to call a duty lawyer, but no one has been able to visit yet, a busy night, apparently. What I don't understand is that it happened this morning before work, according to the police. She didn't go to the police until the afternoon, and they arrested him… actually arrested him! Put him in manacles while he was still in the playground after the class had gone. I'm terrified about his mental state and I can't speak to him. He's been confiding in me that she has changed towards him."

I tried to calm her although, truthfully, I was beginning to feel worried myself. I didn't want to call him but he is a great lawyer and this was no time for putting my pride first. I told her to get off the phone so that I could chase up my ex.

At first, he didn't answer; he hasn't had to take duty calls for many, many years.

When he answered, his voice was crusty and a little suspicious; perhaps, because I never call him. But he knows Ruth and likes her and I think, like me, he wouldn't believe that Simon would have behaved in this way.

He took her number, saying that he would call a criminal lawyer who he works with and I felt a rush of gratitude, a strange emotion after all this time.

I chucked some things into a bag, called to the dog who would have to come with me, despite Martha's soppy old cat, and drove to her house. When I parked outside, she opened the door and grabbed me in a fierce hug.

We sat, drinking tea for several hours. She told me that Tamsin had left the flat, taking Lilly May with her. She assumed she had gone to stay with her mother.

At last, at about two in the morning, the police called to say that Simon had spoken to a lawyer, but that his telephone had been confiscated, so Ruth would be permitted to talk to him on the station telephone.

He sounded dreadful, of course. He told her that they might release him on bail the following day and that the police had confiscated both their phones, as both parties had claimed coercion and violence. He was extremely worried about Lilly May, and he wanted to know her whereabouts and to have her back. He won't be permitted to return to his job until he is cleared of the accusation. I didn't tell Ruth about the backlog of cases at court, cases delayed because of the virus. Ruth will find the waiting hard – they both will.

14th November

Ruth has now collected Simon from the station. He was broken and shaking. He denied everything said in Tamsin's statement, except to admit to an argument they had about money and Ruth's future involvement in their financial affairs. He spoke about the coercion he would have been better to have done something about long ago; also, to being hit with a spatula and having a photograph (a wedding photograph) broken over his head recently.

The marriage is quite clearly over. Now, he has to clear his name and get custody of their child or at least part custody. In the meanwhile, until his bail ends, he can't contact Tamsin, can't talk to his little girl. It will be a dreadful time, a terrible Christmas for them both. I am so sad for them and must call Ruth every day.

It makes Christmas shopping seem trivial, but I suppose that I'll have to start soon. Life goes on, as they say.

17th November

The idea of having a doctor is becoming a joke. I get it that teachers and doctors are rightfully worried about Covid but what is the country coming to?

Having not booked an appointment for myself for over a year, I decide that I have been limping about on a verruca that I have tried and tried to treat myself for too long. I simply can't get rid of it. It is like walking about with a piece of glass in the ball of my foot. I know it isn't cancer, or covid, or something life threatening, but if not for sympathy with the inundated NHS, I would have booked an appointment long ago.

Also, I've been driven mad by the large, itchy area on my back which may, quite frankly, be caused by sleeping in my day clothes in a freezing cold cabin. There again, Dad has eczema, so it might be that. I don't know what it is, but I've been using a long knitting needle to scratch it with and have now made my back sore.

So, I've been waiting a few days for a phone consultation with my doctor, because that's the way we do it now. No face to face. She called me today and asked me to send a photo of my foot and my back! I suspected this might happen, because a friend who's a receptionist told me that they are receiving photos without any explanation or identification, just random photos of unidentified anatomy. Plus, how many of the over eighties have a camera phone to do this with? Really, not that many.

Anyway, I am certainly not going to photograph my foot or my back. I'm just grateful to the nurse who was prepared to give me a cervical smear recently and who didn't ask me for a photograph of my fanny beforehand.

No wonder so many people don't bother to see a doctor.

18th November

Not sleeping very well. Don't know why this is. Perhaps it has something to do with worrying about children and grandchildren. Maybe it's just my age.

I'm not worried about Covid, which I should be. I'm not complacent, it's just that there's too much to do to worry about that. I do worry about the impact of Covid on people who can't work or can't find employment. I find the perfume adverts on telly distasteful because few people I know can afford those perfumes. I have friends who are struggling now, even without the purchases they feel compelled to make before Christmas.

What kind of a Christmas will it be? Will there be midnight mass as usual, school performances of the nativity? Christmas fairs?

I must start writing Christmas cards. I'll buy the gifts that have to be sent, first, and call people I've not spoken to in ages.

Last night I fell asleep at ten thirty, then woke again at midnight and couldn't get back to sleep. I made a cup of tea and listened to the shipping forecast; it's always very reassuring, unless you are in a ship in the midst of a storm, I suppose.

I haven't been to Cornwall for a whole year. I miss it so much. I may have to watch re-runs of *Poldark*.

20th November

We can't feed him, no matter how hard we try and what we do. I don't mean literally, because he has an excellent appetite and eats like a horse considering his age. I mean emotionally. No matter how many hugs and cuddles and kisses we give him, it's not enough love. He doesn't know who's left to love him back. If we aren't there, he forgets.

He misses Mum every day, sometimes staring at the living room door as though he is waiting for her to walk through it. We have given him three cards 'from Mum' now. He reads them frequently as we leave them on the coffee table next to his chair. He misses his brother, and when we are passing Don's house – now sold, he says, "Haven't seen Don for a long time…" Which is because Don died three years ago. He is so insecure and lives every day with ghosts.

He doesn't want to be left alone, even for five minutes.

"Where are we going?" he asks, again and again; at least with the desire to be entertained.

After a long time, it becomes impossible to protect oneself against his constant and repeated questions. His vulnerability, the necessity to reassure him all the time causes a stress that's difficult to explain, except that it can make your body tense, causing headaches and a feeling that you have to get away; and then the guilt comes, because he is loved so much.

He has said two things that were funny but made us sad, too, in the past couple of weeks. Comments or questions that came out of the blue.

"Has my wife left me for another man?" He looked from me to Marion as we prepared him for bed.

"No, Dad!" I cried, desperate to reassure him. "She's looking after Rhona in a hospital in Plymouth, do you remember Rhona?"

Interesting that he didn't ask whether she had left him for another woman, perhaps.

"Oh arr… When's she coming back?"

"As soon as she can, Dad," Marion says cautiously. She doesn't find this world of make-believe as easy as I do. On one occasion I even convinced myself it was the truth. It's just that he is happier when you tell him these things. I can see him relax.

On another evening he asked, "Who is looking after me?"

"We are… always… Me and Marion." I kissed his cheek.

"Good," he said, then, "What if you two get married?"

We both laughed – dryly, darkly, sincerely – finally grinning at one another.

"No chance, Dad. We've done with that. We're very happy with what we've got," Marion said, adding, "I could do with a holiday in the South of France, but I don't need a man to take me there."

27th November

After two weeks of nursing Tiger, the cat, at Harry's house (Harry has no idea that he has a cat in his spare room because he's hardly been here, working overtime to make some more money for Christmas to purchase the many things requested by Freya and Delia on their Christmas list), I am going to have to take Tiger back to the vet tomorrow.

Poor Tiger. I think the vet thinks he has something wrong with his liver. Every day I have tried to get him to eat and I spoon feed him water through his teeth, but he's not eating anything. He can't even make the effort to bite me. He poohed yesterday, which was a mercy, although I had to open the window of the spare room and spray it with air freshener. But he's hardly moved from the place I set him down, several days ago, now.

If anything happens to him, Rose will be devastated. She's recovering from an operation at the moment, so I don't want to give her bad news.

Jess and Lauren asked me to bring him to their house to nurse him, so I did. Louise didn't know about that either; she isn't a fan of cats. The girls looked after him for a couple of days, until he got stuck under Lauren's bed and when we tried to get him out, her bed collapsed. Louise was very cross with me and Tiger refuses to go under the bed, now.

On the plus side, I was in my cabin this evening watching old comedy re-runs and sewing up two school skirts that had been Lauren's but will now do for Freya. I decided to open one of the bottles of Prosecco that I've bought for Christmas. I also decided to make a Cup-a-Soup, tomato flavour, and accidentally poured Prosecco into the kettle. If you've never tasted tomato Cup-a-Soup flavoured with Prosecco, I can recommend it. Delicious.

Monday 30th November

Had to have Tiger put down. Very sad indeed. Because of Covid, the vet wouldn't let me stay with him, but various treatments haven't improved his health. Have now buried him beside the old pug in my garden. James is concerned that it's very close to my vegetable garden. I told him it would be good for the vegetables and that he shouldn't worry.

I keep thinking I'm seeing him coming around the side of the house, abundant tail flicking from side to side. I've made him a gravestone and, when the weather is warmer, I'm going to paint this eulogy on it:

Slow tread around the house, searching for rat or bird or mouse.

1st December

Went to see Aunty Steph, long overdue. The Mason's pub doesn't do food, so the pub has been shut down for a long time during Covid. They are looking forward to being able to open again. Boxing Day, especially, is one of the highlights of the year in Quarry village, when the morris dancers gather outside the Masons and the other pubs to re-enact the drama of St George and the dragon and perform their dances. Everyone gathers there, people from Headington and Woodfarm, Barton and Risinghurst.

Steph has so much energy and is still vivacious in her eighties. She cares for all of her grandchildren as I do. She is still very, very beautiful. The closest person we have to Mum.

Chris, her middle son, is a comic. By which I mean he is a performer who has been on stage in London. Once, some of the cast of *Not going out* came to the pub to be filmed in an episode of the programme. I think this may be because Chris is friendly with Tim Vine. He organises comedy performances in the pub. I went to watch him once with a group of girlfriends; he didn't want me to, saying he might be inhibited. If that was inhibited, God knows what his language is like as a rule.

They've worked so hard to keep the pub going through the restrictions that have been made during the virus. Changing the layout of the place, putting marquees in the garden, new furniture, a new cleaning routine etc. They are still going, thanks to their planning and determination. Elsewhere, many Oxfordshire pubs are closing and being sold.

It's so sad. Pubs are second only to the church in village lives. A place where you are warm and welcome. I hope they can open soon.

It was really good to see Aunty Steph. She made Dad and I a bowl of soup with crusty bread and made me laugh with tales about things that had been going on in the Quarry. As we drove away, Dad said, "There's Don's house."

I didn't remind him that Don is lying in the churchyard, that the house has been sold and repainted, all white and modern.

"I wonder how he is?" he asked, as though he wanted to see Don.

"He's fine," I said, patting Dad's hand. "You saw him last week; we went for a drink at the Six Bells, remember?"

"Oh arr, so we did." He smiled.

5th December

Other than nursery rhymes, Freya and Delia can be quite particular about the songs I sing to them. We've started singing Christmas carols again, mostly as we travel in the car. Singing carols seems especially important if there aren't going to be any school nativity performances this year. Mostly I've been singing "Mary had a baby, yes Lord!" and 'In the bleak midwinter', the poem by Christina Rossetti. Proud to say that both girls have caught on, even if Delia sings 'In the beak midwinter, fosty wind may moan...' But the really touching thing is that they've caught on to the pity and compassion within the poem-turned-carol and they sing it with such love in their voices... until they start poking each other irritably, that is.

Sometimes I wind down the car window to amuse them, shouting, "Get off the roof of my car you silly reindeers!" Which caused two drivers to stare at me in confusion at the Wolvercote roundabout but which they think is a hoot.

I keep thinking that I've got everyone's presents until I remember someone else. I've sometimes made my own, the painted flowerpots, for example. Sometimes I've recycled, as in the case of the cute pink handbags for the little girls that I filled with chocolate. I've done whatever I can to save money and have tried to put a cap on spending. Some hope.

I recycle what I can, keeping last year's wrapping paper and nailing a plastic swimming pool that I'd cut up to the back of my cabin to keep out the rain and frost.

16th December

Nearly the end of term. Flowers and chocs for the teachers. Louise invited me and the girls to see Father Christmas at a farm near to Chipping Norton. Of course, I'm going; not very many opportunities to do anything, what with closures due to Covid.

Last Christmas, Louise paid for my ticket to go to Iceland with her which was very generous. We had such a lot of fun, swimming in the hot waters of the blue lagoon at Grindavik and standing beneath the vast night sky on a white plateau of ice in search of the Northern Lights (although Lauren got very cross and cold and ended up listening to music on the coach). Iceland's not going to happen this year for several reasons, so 'Fairy tale Farm' will do instead.

Ruth called me. There will be an emergency court hearing in February. They can't keep the little girl from her father on the basis of an accusation, but CAFCASS are now involved. It will feel such a long time to Simon and Ruth. Christmas won't be much fun for them. I suppose Christmas isn't necessarily fun for a lot of people for many reasons, especially all those who lost loved ones in Covid wards.

19th December

All three of the younger children were so excited. The older two didn't come, too old and too snooty for Santa now. I don't think Ned really believes in Santa any more, but is defiantly wanting him to be real, if you see what I mean.

Before visiting Father Christmas, we wandered along the illuminated fairy trail to admire the vision of Snow White in the dwarves' garden and listen to the mermaid singing her song.

The children bashed the interactive buttons, chasing ahead of us, until we arrived at the house of Grandma and peered through the window at the wolf in her quilted bed.

Delia's screams of terror echoed around the place as though she had suddenly found herself in the London dungeons.

She wailed, she yelled, until I had to pick her up to calm her; obviously she found the wolf to be very real. I was dummy-less and helpless for several minutes, until suggesting a drink and a biscuit in the café. She perked up then.

Santa was extremely authentic and jolly. He resided in a crowded cottage with a roaring (simulated) fire surrounded by toys. We were taken to him by a pixie. So, they liked that and chatted quite confidently to him. When he asked whether they had all been good, Ned said, "Well, mostly, but Freya put her middle finger up at Nanny last week…"

"That's enough, Ned," I said swiftly, though it was true; she said she'd learned it from her friend at school.

It wasn't the last I would see of Santa, though.

As we left Lou's house, Dad had banged on the window like a demented woodpecker, which he does frequently. When I went over to him to explain that we would be back shortly (Marion was there by the way) he asked, "Where are you going?" A thing he asks even when you are in a dressing gown and pyjamas or have only just climbed out of the bath and are shivering in a bath towel.

"We're taking the children to see Santa," I explained, expecting his interest to wane because it wasn't the pub.

"I'd like to see Santa," he said.

I smiled. "Do you mean you'd like to see Santa or that you want to come for the ride?"

"I want to see Santa," he said, with so much conviction that I faltered. He'd told me that the last time he saw Santa was in Woolworths when he was about eight. That would have been in about 1937. He's ninety-two. It could be the last chance he'll get.

"Okay. I'll try to get you a ticket for tomorrow, Dad, I promise but you have to book to see him, and with the virus, it's tricky."

"The what?" He stares blankly at me. We have explained a million times. Even with the mask on, he forgets.

They were very nice, saying they'd be very happy for Father Christmas to see an old man of ninety-two who has dementia. I told them he wouldn't be needing a unicorn ping-pong gun that shoots soft rubber balls, but I would bring two chocolate Santas and little Delia as a cover, in case he felt awkward of a sudden. But somehow, I knew he'd meant it. He really wanted to see Santa.

It wasn't a bit awkward, after all.

Santa said, "Hello, Maurice, I hear you were a publican?" And off they went; they hardly needed me there at all.

I hardly ever cry, now, about silly things, but I had tears in my eyes on the way back from Chipping Norton, while Dad and Delia stuffed their faces with chocolate Father Christmases.

When we reached Woodstock, he asked, "Where's Mum?"

I think he thought of her then because Fairy tale farm was something she would have loved. She loved celebrations, holidays, family treats and cooked a mean Sunday lunch. She loved life. For the most part, so do I.

24th December, Christmas Eve

Had no time to write. Busy wrapping presents, visiting people, writing cards, buying food, taking dogs to the vet, etc. Christmas always gets me like that. It's probably the same for everyone else, but women especially.

I remember, once, a school inspection that happened the week before Christmas, unbelievable!

I recall getting up at five in the morning to ensure that all my presentations, and facts and figures were in order for the inspectors. I was the only one in the school when I heard Eric the lollipop man walking along the corridor. I stuck my head around the door to say good morning and there was nobody there.

When Mary Walker, a senior teacher, arrived an hour or so later, she told me the sad news that Eric had died from a heart attack in the early hours of the morning.

"No. I heard him put on his coat and pass my class," I argued. "He can't have."

Spooky, but true. Anyway, back to now.

Jess asked me to take her to a sleepover in Thame. I have many texts each day from her.

"Nanny, can you bring my PE kit to school?" or "Nanny, can you buy the ingredients for millionaire's shortbread?"

and so forth. As her mum was still working, I took pity on Louise.

Before I arrived to collect her, her new text read, "Nanny, can you buy two of those alcopops drinks, please?"

She is almost sixteen. I checked with her mum for permission and she said, "Okay, then."

I have spent the past two days mostly driving about. Often, admittedly, as in the case of Inna and the Moldavian champagne which was wonderful, as is her Ukrainian hospitality, the driving had a happy ending.

I listen to radio four, mostly, and drove about mulling over Boris Johnson's declaration of another lockdown and the cancellation of Boxing Day. What are we meant to do? Take all the shopping we bought back? Leave people on their own, come Christmas? I know this is very serious but I certainly used the 'F' word a lot at the news. Now we are in tier four, apparently – undeniably bad.

As I drove in the dark with Jess and her friend, enchanted by the pretty coloured lights of Christmas in Thame, I couldn't help but think how sad it all was that the pubs, normally filled with happy, excited people at this time of year, were in darkness. So sad and terrible.

Last year on Christmas Eve, we went to the Christingle service with the children at Holy Trinity Church in the Quarry. It's a tradition. This year there was a Zoom service. I don't know whether God would approve of this distancing.

Suddenly, I remember my two old neighbours.

Harry would normally go to stay at his sons in Birmingham for Christmas, but can't this Christmas, of course. Walter lost his boon companion, his little dog this year, and appears to have been very lonely. I have two packs of sausages and carrots spare and a couple of boxes of biscuits, so visit Harry, first.

"Arr," says he, "I got plenty of carrots but I'll take the rest. Thanks."

"What are you doing for Christmas dinner? Would you like me to bring you some?"

Louise has suggested I invite him to dinner, but we are already two over the normal 'bubble'. She has suggested we invite several older people, but I had to point the Covid out and veto it in case the Covid police turn up and fine us all.

"Oh no, I'll be all right thanks. Already did m' vegetables and I got two nice bits of turkey."

After that I skedaddle to Walter's house. Several knocks and a tap on the window later, and he opens the door. He looks a little irritated at being called away from the television; I might have been a mugger, after all. But he casts a smile at me after I have explained.

"Thanks for asking, my duck, but the people opposite already asked me."

When I get to Marion's with the presents, she has had a battle with Dad who keeps turning the Christmas tree lights off to save electricity.

She's going to sell him on eBay, apparently. Don't think there'll be any takers.

I give her a stocking, filled with a beer and chocolates to put outside Dad's door before he goes to bed.

At Louise's, Lauren gives me an excited hug and I hug her skinny little body back.

"You give the best hugs, Nanny," she says.

Ah, bless… what's she after, I wonder?

I say goodnight to them all and head for James' house. No longer Lancelot in the wild woods, he has had a shave and a bath and is wearing a rather nice shirt and jeans.

I make a pretty good three course dinner for James and I, after which we sit down to play chess, so that he can thrash me for the umpteenth time.

5th January 2021

Christmas? Well, it went very quickly, that's all there is to say. Most of us have been unwell since Boxing Day, which puts us in the same situation as most of the rest of the nation, according to the new figures. But we are very lucky not to have lost anyone.

I sent a Facebook message.

"Sorry not to have sent any messages for some while, but we are thinking of everyone out there. Marion and I have been pretty tied up and pretty unwell, actually. Now almost at the end of our track and trace isolation."

Dad was so unwell on Boxing Day that he collapsed. As he came to stand next to me at the kitchen sink, his face turned white and he mumbled incoherently and then fell on the floor before we could stop him. He lay very still in a faint and I thought for a moment he was dead. It was horrible. After a few seconds he came round, but he couldn't speak; his mouth opened and closed like a fish gasping for air.

We called the paramedics who examined him and took him to hospital. About four hours later, they called us to take him home again, no doubt inundated by Covid and fooled by his charm. They failed to give him a Covid test.

We spent a true night of the long knives trying to deal with him as he couldn't sleep. He stumbled about the bedroom trying to breathe, couldn't settle and was really off his head, talking incoherent gibberish. No one slept before three in the morning.

In the morning we called the paramedics again. They took him back to hospital and this time tested him and discovered he had Covid.

Somebody up there loves him. Aged ninety-two, they gave him oxygen and put him on a drip.

He spent a week in hospital, recovering.

On the day before his release, a nurse at the JR said they were concerned that he would be too difficult to nurse and that he could have a place at a hospice near to us; but that we wouldn't be allowed to visit him until the end of February.

We knew, in that time, he would be very lonely and probably forget everything about his life; so, he is now sleeping in the living room because he cannot manage the stairs very well. He is suddenly older, frail, thinner, but eating well and at home with us. We are very lucky that he is alive.

Very grateful to the REME personnel. Dad hasn't done anything like good old Captain Tom, but they have sent him a lovely card with the REME insignia on it and a beret badge and stripy socks. The card says, 'We are so sorry to hear that you are unwell and we send our best wishes. You will always be a part of the REME family and your service to the corps helped to make us what we are today.'

He keeps picking up the card and stroking the spine.

He is as loving and demonstrative as ever, but he needs help with everything, now, and constant supervision. So, I have moved in with Marion to help look after him.

His command of language has deteriorated so that he forgets simple words and stutters for a while as his brain struggles to retrieve words.

"Pull the... the... things," he will say, gesturing at the curtains.

"Who's at the... there, there!" he says, pointing at the windows.

Sometimes at night, he has hallucinations. When we asked him why he had risen to use the loo in the middle of the night, rather than his familiar, en-suite bathroom, he answered, "There's a young woman in there..."

He has seen the young woman three times now, but is never able to describe her. So, whether it is Mum when she was younger, or Paula, or Amy, or indeed, his own mother, we can't be sure.

When he came home from the hospital, he fretted so much about Mum.

"Where is she?" he asked repeatedly; and tired, I cried and felt so guilty about everything, then pulled myself together.

The next day he received another letter.

'My Dear Maurice,

Marion and Chris say that you are worrying about me. You mustn't worry. I am fine and looking after Rhona who is unwell. Marion and Christine will take care of you. Howard will come to visit you. I promise that you will see me soon. I love you with all my heart. Cynthia X'

Happiness was instant, he was so relieved. He smiled, knowing that one day soon, they will be together again. At least that much is true.

Ghosts
Bletchingdon and Wantage

I asked our mother, once, why she'd had four children. Her answer was that there was little else to do in Bletchingdon, the little village in Oxfordshire in which we lived. I don't think she was very fulfilled then, which is why she changed things. She admitted to ramming a spoon into Marion's mouth once, when she wouldn't eat, and coming to the decision that she needed something else.

When I asked her what she did in the day, other than looking after us while Dad worked at the Cowley car plant, she said, "Well, I washed the chicken's eggs beautifully and kept the house clean." There was a twinkle in her eye as she said it; across the years, she had read Germaine Greer.

I don't believe that she was very interested in us as younger children, but came into her own when we were teenagers and at our most difficult.

I know, because she confided in me when I was a young woman, that she had more than her fair share of amorous advances, including the man whose name I don't remember who chased her around the kitchen table in Bletchingdon and who she repelled with a kitchen knife.

I think I recall the man she was talking about, a friend of our father, someone who had brought us four cute and motherless black rabbits which we kept in a hutch for a few weeks. We could never touch or hold them because they were totally wild, scratching and biting us. In the end, we set the kits free, releasing them into the fields, just as, in the end, our mother was released from the fields.

As for her children, well, we had a lot of freedom in Bletchingdon. Paula and I went to Mrs Heinz nursery and then to the village school. My closest friends were Lorna and Sally Anne. Sally Anne's father worked at Kirtlington Park stables. We went there sometimes in the summer, to play with the puppies who were born there.

Younger than eight years old, we made camps in the woods where we would romp about for hours on end. Paula, two years younger than me, was always there. When I look back, I needed her to make me brave. She was more confident and courageous than I was, standing up to people, and at that young age, climbing the tallest trees in the wood.

She was thin, wiry, brown-skinned and from an early age she wore round national health glasses. She insisted upon shorts and short hair. She competed with my brother constantly. As far as she was concerned, she was a boy. When I was young, I accepted that.

We were happy at Bletchingdon school. I remember few difficulties. There was the time I was told off by the head teacher for accidentally kicking a football into a window and breaking it. Paula came straight to my defence, telling the teacher that I hadn't meant to do it and that she mustn't punish me.

Then there was the day when the little boy next to me pulled out a pen knife and threatened to cut my throat. I don't think I felt fear, it was surprise really. I think I thought he was pretending to be a pirate and I grinned at him. The teacher took it away from him with little fuss and we carried on with our work.

Two things happened on my seventh birthday that I have never forgotten.

I took the brown satchel I'd been given as a birthday present to show to my teacher. When we trooped to the village church for Harvest Festival, another teacher thought that it contained harvest produce, gifts for the altar. She took it from me and placed it with the tins and vegetables, until my howls of grief spoiled 'We plough the fields and scatter' and she returned it to me.

Having made an excellent recovery from that, I told my friends in the playground later in the morning that I was having a birthday party and that the Beatles were going to perform in my house.

These are the days before parents were supposed to collect their children from school. I was followed home by a stream of excited six and seven-year-olds who arrived on our doorstep, eventually tracked and followed by their parents. Mum, mortified, sent me to my room while she made her apologies. I narrowly avoided a smacked bottom. To this day, I know that I believed in my own story. I'd been expecting the Beatles to come all day.

On the plus side, the Rotherwick family of Bletchingdon park invited the village children to their son's birthday party. The Beatles weren't there either but, of all the children, I was chosen to be Cinderella to Robin

Rotherwick's Prince Charming. We had a real horse-drawn carriage covered in silver foil, brought inside the grand house, pony and all.

The only thing I resented about Bletchingdon were the 'flat foot' lessons I was forced to take with a nurse and a small group of children in an annex to our classroom. Repeatedly picking up a rubber mouse by its tail with our curled toes was deadly dull. The knowledge that I had flat feet almost scarred me for life. I've always been self-conscious about my ugly feet.

Howard was a toddler, then, and Marion just a baby.

As the eldest, I was supposed to mind our little brother, Howard, but I don't think I did a good job of it. I failed to watch him during the village cricket match when he climbed to the top of the marquee. Failed to mind him in the park next to our house that time he climbed onto the massive rollers used to mark the turf and fell headlong into a tank of white lime.

Once, deliberately and without forethought, apparently, I opened the goose pen gate to retrieve a ball, forgetting to close it, allowing four-year-old Howard to wander inside in his little black duffle coat. Fortunately, Howard fell onto his face or, as they later told me, the gander might have pecked his eyes out. His little body was covered in bruises despite the thick duffle coat and Dad raced to the rescue having heard my yells, fearlessly grabbing the gander by its neck and swinging it through the air so the neck snapped without a sound. We had the gander for dinner.

Howard had a talent for getting in trouble without my interference and he had a sense of adventure all of his own, which tested our parents over the years.

Our Dad had a large piece of land beyond the vegetable garden. Here, he kept chickens and geese. Here, too, was the shed with the hot lamp where chicks were incubated and reared. We would squat on our haunches in the heat from its lamp while the small yellow squawking things scuttled in the sawdust around our legs.

"Move carefully. Slowly..." he told us, in case we crushed them beneath our shuffling feet, reminding us to pick them up gently while their soft feathers tickled our hands. When a chick became poorly, he would revive it with drops of brandy.

I think we would have remained in Bletchingdon if not for the combination of Mum's restlessness and his own dislike of the long journeys by motorbike to Cowley factory, especially as he had to work overnight. In most cold weathers – ice, sleeting rain or snow – he would return home in the morning to sit in the kitchen with chilblained feet in a bowl of hot water.

Before he left us at night, he would lie upon the bed inventing wonderful tales of the countryside. My favourite was the one about the brave little mouse and the cowardly fox who preyed on him, his snout twitching at the end of a broken pipe.

He mistrusted foxes with the same passion that I admire them, probably because he saw at first hand the barbarous way a fox dealt with chickens. He spent many hours sitting high up in the branches of a tree with his gun, trying to catch a particularly daring fox, but never succeeded in getting anything other than angry and frustrated.

In the end, the old fox was killed by a car.

Mum and Dad went away somewhere. Later, we found out that they had been on a course, something about becoming publicans, but we didn't know what that meant, really, and living from day to day, we probably didn't care, didn't know we would be saying goodbye to Bletchingdon. Nanny Lou came to take care of us. Marion was only a baby, then, because she was in a pram when Nanny Lou took us for an evening walk to wear us out.

It was a summer evening, still light, still warm, and we walked beside her as she pushed the pram. We stopped when we saw it lying in the ditch beside the road, the beautiful red fur thick with blue bottles that buzzed in the warm air above the large, dead fox. An early science lesson in what happens to animals when they die.

We left the house in Bletchingdon a month or so after that, leaving for a very different kind of home. Dad always smiled and joked with us, no matter how he felt, but he didn't really want to leave the village. He was content in the countryside, an old country boy at heart.

Different adventures, different environment, no longer the fields, the park and the swings. Perhaps that's why Dad took us to the White Horse hills almost every day. Once the territory of King Alfred of the Saxons, now a stamping ground for the racehorses and trainee jockeys who thundered past us as we exercised our fat golden retriever, Brandy. It became our own vast garden.

The Post Office Vaults – a Victorian post office that had been converted some while ago into a pub – was a vast, tamed, indoor garden of Aspidistra and spider plant, with dark passageways which were excellent for hide and seek. There were also many landings and spacious rooms in which you could become lost for hours. Mum became hysterical on one occasion, believing that Paula had left the building, aged six, when in fact she had screwed her little gymnast's body into a cupboard.

There were large urns to hide behind, and stuffed owls and foxes to pull faces at: Victorian memorabilia of every kind. We hid messages in the base of the black lacquered clock and took the medicine bottles from the leather case to contain our home-made potions – until we were stopped as the medicine bottles proved to be old and valuable.

Only the light from the long, box sash windows illuminated the drawing room by day. This room was deathly quiet and Paula and I were made to learn our times tables there at the weekend. She learned them more quickly than I, even though she was younger, and I remember crying over them in despair.

A Victorian kitchen stood above the stairs that led to the bar; above the stairwell was a glass roof. I've loved the sound of rain beating upon glass ever since we lived there.

We had a spectacularly large living room which Mum called the nursery, although I don't know if it was ever intended to be a nursery, but there was a rocking horse in front of the tall windows overlooking the town square. A short spiral staircase led to five bedrooms.

We children viewed it as 'our house'. Of course, our parents didn't own it, but we didn't understand that.

The pub came with a lodger: a tall, genteel, white-haired old gentleman whose name I can't remember. If not for the fact that he greeted us when we met him in the corridor, he might have been a ghost. Mostly, he kept out of our way, which was sensible as, when not at school, we careered about the corridors as though they were our own personal playground. Sometimes he gave us sweets, or as Marion pronounced them, 'Thweets,' because she had a lisp.

We were rarely allowed into the bars, especially not when we first arrived there.

Our parents drastically changed the reputation of the pub, but this took a while. It didn't take long for them to realise that some of the rougher customers thoroughly enjoyed their poor reputation. In particular, the group of road builders who believed that they owned the place and who frightened other customers away with their swearing and sometimes, fighting.

The brewers who owned the place hadn't warned them, and neither Mum nor Dad had any experience of dealing with ruffians. The behaviour and reputation of this group of men was so bad that Mum would lock us away from them when we were in our beds at night. She told us stories about how difficult life had been for them when we grew older. I imagined Joss Merlyn in Jamaica Inn and his evil band of smugglers, and I wasn't far off the mark.

It was Mum who had the spirit to deal with them, or perhaps she felt responsible, having orchestrated the move to a pub. Maybe she believed that none of these bad boys would hurt a woman. Dad was brave, though. On one occasion, one of the men lifted a fist to Mum and he thrust out his hand to stop him. When he told the man to leave the building, he broke a glass bottle on the counter and thrust it towards Dad's face.

Our parents broke the group gradually and with sanctions, because eventually, their peer leader apologised like a teenager who needed his youth club. He agreed they would stop being rowdy and abusive, and they did, and after that, the pub increased its custom.

Paula taught me how to escape from the building via the Drayman's hatch at the rear of the pub while our parents were busy at weekends. We had a great time exploring the town square with its statue of King Alfred. But it didn't take long for our adventures to come to an end. We weren't allowed to wander the town unaccompanied. The hatch was locked and bolted when they found out and, eventually, we were sent to our grandparents on a Friday after school.

It was on a rainy Saturday that Paula dared me to enter the forbidden territory of the attic. This was loosely sealed by two criss-cross planks of wood that had been nailed together, but it was relatively easy to crawl beneath them and up the dark, cobwebby stairs.

We were not disappointed, finding a vast attic filled with old packing cases. The packing cases were filled with old files, but there was a desk with a lid and a wooden chair before it and piled upon the desk were dozens of old, black-and-white photographs of soldiers in white uniforms, sprawled upon rattan chairs, while in the distant landscape, palm trees grew.

We lifted the photographs in innocence, musing half interestedly at the unknown soldiers and we were there for some while before Mum's voice called from the foot of the staircase. Her voice was studiedly calm, but we heard the tremor of panic beneath it.

"I told you both you were to keep away from the attic. It's unsafe, the floor is unsafe. Come downstairs."

I was old enough to have heard the fear in her voice. It wasn't until many years later that she explained about the ex-soldier turned licensee who had hung himself in the attic. I knew she'd been scared to visit it herself as much as she was frightened that we might come to some injury.

It was adventurous Paula who suggested visiting the empty warehouse opposite St Mary's school one Saturday morning, having been told by a classmate that it was a whole city of wild cats. It was relatively easy to push through the unlocked warehouse door. Easy to enter the dark, smelly emporium of stray cats. It didn't occur to us that there were tigers lurking inside.

Crate upon open crate of mother cat and her kittens, every colour, tiny bundles of fur – some of the kittens were just days old, their eyes still closed. It was a cat zoo.

The air was thick with their disgusting smell, but it didn't bother us. We reached into the crates to pick up the blind and helpless kittens, cradling them to our chests and crooning over them as we had cradled the chicks reared by Dad. Each, silently wondering whether Mum would let us keep one or two of them.

Many of these little families appeared to have been abandoned by their own mothers.

Then, "Ow!" I screeched, as a pitifully thin tabby mother flicked her claws at my arm from the depths of her dark crate to warn me away.

Alerted, other adult cats climbed from hiding places and started towards us, staring at us with gleaming, narrowed eyes. We fled through the warehouse door, running fast for home as we imagined an army of mother cats chasing after us. It must have made an impression on me, because I had nightmares about being attacked by cats for a long time after this.

After about a week at Garston Lane School, I wanted to return to Bletchingdon village school. We renamed it, 'Ghastly Lane School' as I recall.

Suddenly, the old-fashioned structure of a village school, which made me feel safe, was replaced by sixties, open-plan chaos. I didn't have a clue what was going on, either guessing or copying other people.

Lessons became entirely confusing. I remember sitting at a desk before a pile of coloured rods which were something to do with maths, but not being able to understand what their function was. In the end I built towers from them.

The open-plan classes were huge, the playground, also, and the teachers remote from me. Eventually I did find a friend, Hillary, who allowed me to join in with her playground staged performance of *The Sound of Music*. What I will never forget is when the teacher who caught me talking to Hillary in class asked me to put out my hand. I had no idea what was going to happen, even when she produced a wooden ruler. I was in shock when she lifted it and thwacked the ruler across my palm.

The only thing I remember liking was assembly time. I enjoyed singing and was allowed to sit next to Hillary.

One Saturday morning an old gentleman, or so he seemed to me, a round, heavily-built, balding man who, preferring to sit at a table in the window with his newspaper, came to the Post Office Vaults. He became a regular visitor. The pub was quiet at this time and as long as we children were quiet, we were allowed to come there to speak with Dad, usually to ask him for our pocket money.

I remember staring at him, not knowing who he was, but just a little interested. It was very early in the morning, only just past opening time; this man was the first customer of the day. Dad took me aside to tell me that he was a famous poet. If he had been a pop star, I suppose I would have been a little more interested. The name Sir John Betjeman meant nothing to me at the time.

I suppose Dad thought I might like to know because I'd made it clear that I wanted to be a writer one day; specifically, I wanted to be Enid Blyton. A couple of years later and I wanted to be Elinor M. Brent-Dyer of the *Chalet School* fame. When I wasn't messing about with my siblings I sat with my nose in a book or scribbled stories which were heavily inspired by these writers.

When they wanted to pull the old pub down, it was Sir John Betjeman who saved it with a petition.

Our bedroom, Paula's and mine, overlooked Wantage town square. Sometimes at night, when we were supposed to be in bed, we would watch the busy life of the town with King Alfred's statue at its centre.

Most thrilling was the fair which arrived once a year. The heavy glass windows managed to block out much of the noise but couldn't mute the music and the squeals and the excitement of the waltzer and bumper cars. When our mother came to check on us, we would fly to our beds at the sound of her heels on the carpet, then lay panting beneath the blankets, unable to muffle our excited breathing. After she left, we would lie quietly, staring at the luminous strips of colour that flew from the rides and onto our bedroom ceiling.

Almost as exciting was the hunt meet on Boxing Day.

We loved the pageantry: the patient horses bearing their red-coated riders, the excited but biddable beagle hounds who milled about the horse's legs, sniffing and whining but rarely barking, a seething mass of wriggling bodies and wagging tails. We watched from the tall windows of the drawing room as our parents drifted through the melee with silver trays bearing the Christmas cup.

That's where Paula and I fell in love with the hunt, understanding nothing about what happened to the poor fox until many years later. That's where the desire grew to learn to ride ourselves. Our favourite book became *The Ballad of the Belstone Fox* and our favourite artist, Norman Thelwell.

Wantage was the place we said goodbye to Nanny Lou. We didn't understand that she had cancer, or our father's sadness at the time. He had lost his father, Ken, by the age of twenty-eight and he was only thirty-six when he lost Nanny Lou.

That last Christmas, she came to stay in Wantage.

We placed our letters to Santa under Nanny Lou's supervision in the great, black marble fireplace which was never lit, but by teatime, the Santa magic still hadn't drawn the notes up into the chimney. So, the next day we went with Dad and Nanny Lou to the little woodland copse close to Uffington and the White Horse hill. Carefully, she placed our notes into an envelope and laced string through it. With Dad's help, she tied the letters to the lower branches of a tree.

We received most of the things we had asked for on Christmas Day so were confident the letter had arrived safely at the North Pole.

In January, after a short spell in hospital, she died. She had lung cancer, but we hadn't known that.

After her death, we went back to the little copse with Dad. He took us there often, but perhaps he needed to visit the place more than ever. With careful movements he reached up to the branches of the tree, removing the letters that still fluttered in the wind. There were tears in his eyes as he placed the envelope inside his jacket pocket then turned away from us to hide his face. It was as though he had known the letters would still be there.

Mum and Dad in the pub

Home is where the Hart is

We moved from Wantage to Old Headington, a stone's throw from Headington Quarry. I was ten, Paula, eight, Howard six and little Marion only four. It was a good move; we recaptured that lovely freedom we had in Bletchingdon.

A fresh world of adventure and possibilities; even though, at first, one or two of our new friends confided that they had been told not to play with us because we were pub children. We were confused. Mum was furious, understanding snobbery rather more than we did, but thankfully, they have been our friends ever since.

Bluebells grew in the lane behind the old pub on the tiny triangle of green beneath the high yellow walls of crumbling stone. It's a place unchanged over centuries. We could feel that history and imagine the ghosts walking back and forth to pub and church. The high walls of lane and garden are yellow and sturdy. We played there and walked home from the school and library through the maze of lanes.

The huge iron bath with its black eagle's feet at the White Hart bears the mark of all of the bums of the centuries, an impress in the iron which cannot be removed no matter how well Mum scrubs at it. These were the beginnings of a love of history. Paula and I wandered from the library with our noses in books by Leon Garfield.

It must have been May when we moved there. I was ten, which means it was 1967 and the jukebox in the pub would no doubt have played Tallahassee bridge, the lyrics of which would have been lost to me, and Windy; the lyrics of which are so simple that I remember them and can still sing them word for word.

There was sunshine and a wind tugging at my home-made dress, which Mum had made in the style of Mary Quant. We were turned outside the moment we arrived with the removal van, forbidden to enter the old public house until they had installed our things, all except for Marion, who was only four and had to stay at home.

We made good use of our time, exploring the long Victorian pub garden with its ancient yew tree, then wrenching open the door to the stables where, so Dad had told us, coach horses had once rested overnight.

We swung from the high, iron hay rack fixed to the stable wall and took turns to leap from a mounting block. Then we went into the maze of lanes behind the pub, turning the corner by the Victorian gas lamp now turned electric, which was just like the lamp post beneath which Mr Tumnus meets Lucy.

And, just as suddenly, I was alone. My siblings had escaped their bossy older sister. Just the sound of birdsong now. Just the quiet. Nice to be rid of them for a while, to be alone with my own thoughts, being watched by the ghosts as they made their way back and forth.

I started to pick the bluebells, singing to myself all the while.

But I wasn't alone for long. As I yanked at the thick green stems, Paula reappeared on top of the old, ivy-clad wall. She had climbed it to get a view of the ancient chapel on the other side, half covered in ivy. It is still the chapel, in my mind, where Galahad found the Holy Grail.

Paula and I knew all about the Holy Grail. We had a beautiful copy of Sir Lancelot of the Lake, by Roger Lancelyn Green; and we were both in love with the text and the gorgeously romantic illustrations.

I was always half worried that Paula would fall, knowing as the eldest that it was my duty to stop that kind of accident. But she was eight by now. I just wanted to be Guinevere picking bluebells for a while, but twice in her life, Paula had fainted and the doctor hadn't resolved it; one of these occasions had been when she was walking along a high wall imagining she was a tightrope acrobat.

A couple of weeks prior to this day, she had been stung almost to the point of death by a dense jungle of nettles in an old quarry after walking along a low wall in Headington Quarry. One minute she was walking her tightrope and the next she went all wobbly and fell.

Neither Nan nor I could pull her out. She had fallen a distance of about ten feet and was lying very still in the nettle leaves. A few seconds later she opened her eyes. Every time she moved she was stung afresh, but she refused to cry. Paula always refused to cry when she was little, though I cried buckets over any mishap.

Thankfully a young man came walking along the lane to our rescue. He leapt down, pulled her up in his arms and pushed her onto his shoulders so that Nan could pull her out. She was covered in red welt marks and had to be coated in thick layers of calamine lotion.

"Get down before you fall," I said, imitating Mum. Then, "Where's Howard?" I asked.

"We've found two boys," she said. "Christopher and Graham. They've got bikes."

They joined us minutes later. Chris, stocky and blonde, about my age, and his younger brother, red haired and with light freckles. Howard ran after them, trying to keep up with their bicycles. They skidded to a halt and stared at me. Their faces were full of friendly mischief. I dismissed them snootily, resenting the fact that the others had found them first.

"We've made a gang..." Paula added from the top of the wall.

I was annoyed, then. How had they made a gang without me? Anyway, it was an all-boy gang, if you discounted Paula, who spent her life being a boy. There again, if there was a gang, I wasn't going to be left out.

"What are you going to call it?" I asked. If a gang, it had to have a name.

"Don't know. The White Hart Gang?" Paula suggested, leaping deftly from the wall to land a few feet away from me.

Then she came around the corner, the girl with short brown hair and the smartest school uniform I had ever seen. I stared, holding the fast-wilting bluebells to my chest. She must have been between Paula's age and mine. Competition from someone in a smart school uniform bothered me a little.

"Do you want to come and see Mr Pickwick?" she asked, seeming to ignore me in favour of Paula.

"Who's Mr Pickwick?" Paula asked.

"The horse in the field at the end of the village."

Her name was Helen. She was mad about horses. She was also the brains behind many of our adventures and because of her we became the Pickwick Gang and the old stables at the foot of the garden became our headquarters.

We filled it with our treasures, the relics we dug up in the old garden: rusted spoons, broken pottery and the white clay bowls of pipes once smoked by old men. We wrote on the smooth, uneven walls and the black lacquered, wooden door with chalk: 'Tresparsers will be Prosecuted.' Our chalkings remain to this day.

We fought with the indestructible spears of the Yucca plants, which we would pull up to attack each other in sword fights, whipping each other without mercy in our own Arthurian games. Sometimes, before we were stopped by the adults, we intimidated children who were visiting the pub with our Yucca swords. This was our garden, after all.

We had many adventures. Sometimes we constructed them ourselves, playing at King Arthur and Robin Hood. Our torture chamber was the Aunt Sally post, where we would bind our victim by the wrists with a skipping rope. The victim was generally Marion as she grew older. Howard and Graham would sit on her legs to prevent escape while we older ones turned the Aunt Sally post slowly to stretch her body. We never succeeded in helping her to grow. She remained tiny all of her life.

We took down the nineteenth-century swords and pistols that hung from the pub walls at afternoon closing time, a time when our parents rested before the second bout of the day; but we were discovered by Dad before we could finish our pirate game, and our weaponry was screwed safely to the walls.

Hanging over a third of the garden were the dark green fronds of the ancient yew tree. Only Paula ever made it right to the top to sit on the highest branches, swaying in the wind with the rooks until Dad told her to come down. He kept his voice steady, but threatened to take the club furniture out of the old barn and to lock it up so that the Pickwick Gang couldn't use it anymore.

"You can see Oxford up there!" she called to us on her descent, as though she had climbed Mount Everest, confident as a small, skinny monkey but not wanting him to ruin our new club house.

That was how we met the family next door over the high stone wall, four boys who were about our age and their collie dog. Paula made friends with them while climbing the yew tree. Only the friendship didn't last long. We quickly set about warring with them, although they were fiercer than we were. We only threw crab apples; they threw stones. In the end, we made peace because their mother and grandmother invited us all for tea and cakes in fear for their windows.

We were sent to St Andrews School in the London Road, where Mum's sister Stephanie was a teacher. We older ones liked it there, though Marion ran away twice because she didn't get maths either and when she didn't produce many answers she had to sit in the corner of the class. But for the first time in my life, I started to understand and like maths – which I hadn't at Ghastly Lane.

But I think my greatest achievement aged ten was becoming the girlfriend of the most popular boy in the school. Andy, whose Dad was our window cleaner, always took the part of Captain Scarlett and chose me as Melody Angel. My confidence grew and grew after that.

At first, we were scarcely aware of the customers unless we met them in the garden. There were one or two that we liked and bumped into on a Saturday morning, when Mum insisted that we all do jobs to keep us out of trouble. Equally she would give us a job if one of us even mouthed the word 'bored', so we rarely did.

We liked Farmer Brown from Elsfield, a quiet old gentleman who always wore a tweed jacket over his clothes. We liked Old Will, who had worked on the railways and talked enthusiastically in his monotone voice about Cornwall, specifically St Ives. We smiled at Coke Tony who came from miles away to drink Coca-Cola but we didn't know, then, that Andre was referred to as Andre Previn because he resembled the famous conductor. Neither did anyone know that the peace of this lovely old pub was about to be shattered by the building of the John Radcliffe Hospital, and that our parents would become licensees of one of the busiest pubs in Oxford.

We were allocated various jobs at the weekends and during holiday times. Fetching the bread from Mr Berry's bakery was a favourite, because the bread was always warm and we would tear off the ends of the loaf as we walked. Picking up the dog poo with a shovel and throwing it behind the laurel bushes (my job as a rule) was the least favourite.

Paula and I had to polish the great eighteenth-century brass measuring jugs before the bars opened. We didn't much enjoy this, but it gave us a great lesson in history. All of those artefacts have since gone, I don't know where to, they ought to have been destined for a museum. I can see them in my mind. The swords and pistols, the brass jugs, the black, marble clock, the majestic stag's antlers, the stuffed foxes head and eighteenth-century tankards – most of all we loved the original eighteenth-century print of the barmaid reaching out a hand to a young man for payment as he turns his pockets inside out. It had the words beneath it, "Pay now, drink later."

The handwritten, framed pages of a play written by an Oxford student in the nineteenth century quickly drew our attention and imagination. The story of a landlady who ran a brothel from the pub, though I don't think we knew what a brothel was until we began to read teenage novels and listen to radio four. Equally, maybe Mum explained at a later stage, as she never balked at discussion about sex in the way that Dad did.

Chris and Graham told us that the White Hart was haunted and in the play, Joan is hung from a beam in the pub by one of her customers.

"Rubbish, no it's not," Mum said, after we had been there some months without a hint of a ghost and because Howard in particular suffered sleepless nights. We wasted no time in hunting for beams that weren't attached to ceilings. All were worn thin with age, varnished black and firmly fixed to the roof, bar one. That was in Howard's bedroom. What's more, there was a deep groove at the centre of it that, we decided, could have been caused by the friction from a rope.

We spared no time in telling him that she must have been murdered in his room. He told us to get out and threw things at the door; then, for the following months, he slept with his white bedsheet wound about his head.

Mum getting ready for work in the evening was a right palaver; it was also a time when we could talk to her quietly as she applied her make-up in the mirror. Firstly, there was the outfit, then the face and hair in place and finally the long nails that could, on occasion, dig into your arm like a cat's claw when you had annoyed her. She was more glamorous than any landlady had a right to be and wouldn't descend to the bar until she felt ready to meet her people; she was a sixties babe.

She also, as Dad would say, "wore the trousers", or "was the boss".

Dad rarely scared us in the way that Mum could when she felt challenged. He would threaten to smack, but never followed through. He might say "My eyes are flashing," but that only made us laugh.

He smacked me only once in my life, when I ran into the lane between the Post Office Vaults and my school, hiding because I wanted some free stick insects that the teacher was offering to anyone who brought a jam jar. Mum said she didn't want crawly things in the house. So, angry and disappointed, I ran away for a short while to sulk. When Dad caught up with me, he caught my arm, gently leading me home. He was my friend, had never hit me, so, I was in ignorance about what would happen next. When he closed the door behind us, he sat on the bottom stair and lifted me across his lap. I still didn't understand the gravity of the situation, but I got the slipper across my backside with some force and howled, then cried for a long time. That was the only time Dad ever hit me.

That we loved creepy crawlies was a dad thing. He often asked us to do little chores in the vegetable garden with him and generally we didn't mind. He had a plot of land once more, this time a little orchard behind the White Hart, hidden amidst the lanes. It was assumed that it belonged to the old pub and he was certainly given permission to use it, although years later we discovered that its ownership was under dispute. Anyway, it was a life saver for him, as it did much for his relaxation and happiness. Mum's temper was quick, a lightning bolt that could strike at any time but vanished within seconds. Dad was a slow burner who took things on the chin for a long time and then blew up and said a lot of things he later regretted.

He no longer had the time to keep geese or chickens, but he enjoyed growing vegetables in this peaceful place surrounded by tall trees. He liked that old Mrs Coggins and Miss Salt, who lived in the nearby cottages, came to ask his advice about gardening and that the doctor chatted with him across the stone wall.

He showed us how to hold the tiny seeds in the nest of our palm, measuring the holes in which to plant them with a finger, so, in the garden we met creepy crawlies galore, observed them, put them in jars, had snail races and amused Marion by sticking a snail on our nose with its slime. We learned about woodlice, earwigs, beetles and spiders. Mum loathed these things, but we were very much interested in them.

We often joined him in his garden and only ever made him cross on two occasions. Once when we rescued one of the moles – who were his enemies – by lifting it in a kitchen colander in case it bit us. (Arthur, the fat white cat we had inherited with the pub later killed it – Mum was even more angry about the colander.) On the second occasion when he hadn't found the time to return to his vegetables for a few days and discovered a massive hole, big enough to stand in, right in the middle of a freshly dug area. There were a lot of discussions going on about a possible nuclear war at the time and the hole was the foundation for Howard's nuclear fallout shelter.

Paula and I rarely argued in the big outdoors, but as we grew older, we argued rather a lot. I suppose this is quite normal for sisters, but in some ways, we were anything but normal.

Gradually, we began to enjoy adult programmes as much as *Thunderbirds* and *Captain Scarlett*. Mum disliked *Till Death Us Do Part*, but Nanny Edna loved it, so I watched it at Nan's house. Mum, meanwhile, let me stay up later to watch historical plays and dramas. I loved *The First Churchills* with Susan Hampshire and later, Glenda Jackson as Elizabeth I.

Paula was a big fan of *Columbo* and *The Persuaders*. So, our interests often clashed and we would have arguments

– those arguments were minor compared to the rows we had about Paula's noises. Others rarely heard these noises, and it wasn't until much later that I understood she was copying Dad who has made them all his life, usually when he is stressed or anxious.

I do remember looking up at him once when we lived in Wantage and asking him why he made them. He just looked crossly at me, frowned, but said nothing. I remember being told that children should be seen and not heard, but the truth was that we talked noisily all of the time, even through mealtimes. I got a strong feeling from his frown that I should never, ever ask him about the noises again, and I didn't.

The noise was the gentle, sonorous murmur of a distressed animal; that's the only way I can describe it, low in his throat, distressed. Things were okay when he did it; my child's emotions were manageable, then – but my younger sister copied him in everything, which Mum believed was her fault for wanting a boy when she carried Paula in her womb. So, gradually, Paula aged eight or nine started to copy him, making the same noise, only by the time she was ten she made it so frequently that it began to drive me utterly bonkers.

Today, my reaction would be called misophonia, I suppose. Certainly, it was bad enough to make me highly irritable, even want to flee the room with my fingers in my ears; but when it came to a choice of leaving the room or being able to watch the Monkees or Top of the Pops in peace – well, Paula and I would physically fight about it. Once, I slapped her on the arm and she punched me in retaliation, until Howard got out of bed, woken by the shouting and stood at the top of the staircase to bellow down to the bar.

"Mum! Chris and Paula are fighting about the noises again!"

But it was after a particularly bad bout of the noises in the rear of our grandparents car on the way back from Bournemouth, when Paula and I had been confined to a small space for some while and our loud row shattered the peace of Elizabethan Serenade from the car radio, that Mum made the decision to send me to a child psychiatrist in Oxford.

Truthfully, she may as well have sent me to talk to a supermarket manager for all the good it did. The man spent most of my session with him trying not to laugh and asking mild but nonsensical questions about my brothers and sisters. The interview didn't last very long and ended with a short report, the gist of which was that I felt responsible for my siblings. I really didn't, at least not to that extent; I just felt so angry and distressed whenever I heard these noises.

Now I know that misophonia is a sensory disorder and not a matter of preference, but I reached the age of sixty before I understood this. As a child and a teenager, everyone in my family viewed it as silly behaviour and yes, I thought it was pretty silly of me too if truth be told.

Our escape hatch was the big outdoors. We were the best of friends outside. The noises disappeared completely; Paula's learned tourettes and my suffocating misophonia seemed to vanish to nothing as we escaped from our emotional shackles to ride bikes and horses, to swim and wander. Another route to happiness was the privacy of our bedrooms and reading, or writing, or to paint, for we all loved these things, accompanied by the music we listened to on the radio or our small, boxed record players.

A moustached man came calling one Saturday morning before opening time. Mum came down to drag the heavy bolts across the door, letting him inside.

At the time, Paula was inspecting the seat cushions for loose change dropped by customers.

She had a jar, in which she saved the shillings and sixpences to boost her pocket money. When the man arrived, she hid in the back bar and listened to their conversation. It wasn't particularly interesting until he mentioned the ghost of Joan.

"She's been seen going about her business in the cellar, often floating through the wall where the door's bricked up," the man said.

Mum laughed, the kind of laugh which says you don't believe a word of it.

We believed it. We'd only been down there once with Dad; cos the ancient stone stairs were dangerously smooth and slippery with all the feet going up and down over the centuries. But we had seen the shape of an arched door in the white plastered wall of the cellar that her ghost was supposed to pass through.

The arched door was a half door, as though the floor had swallowed it up until it could swallow no more. They, the various customers, the draymen, the vicar who came to our school to do assemblies, told us the door had led to a tunnel which went to the church across the road.

Perhaps, Mum suggested, it was to take the communion wine across without being seen by the villagers or, maybe, when King Charles I made his parliamentary headquarters in Oxford, the tunnel was used by Headington people to get food to his soldiers. In any event, the impress of a door said there had to be something on the other side.

They laughed a lot, our Mum and the man from the brewery, while Paula half listened. He told her there was a particular pewter tankard, taking her to it and lifting it down from the highest dusty shelf above the colourful array of bottles. He said that previous landlords had believed the tankard was haunted, that sometimes, across the years, it appeared to have been moved by an unseen hand. It had been found upon the bar in the morning, or on a different shelf, and once, standing on a barrel in the cellar. It was very old, so he said, dating back to the time of Oliver Cromwell.

As the two examined it, turning it over to look at the imprint of its maker, Dad came downstairs to get ready for the day. He joined in with the conversation, asking the man about some of the other artefacts in the pub.

I don't think I remember the strained atmosphere between our parents during the morning, as they were both working and we were upstairs; but that atmosphere spilled into the afternoon. He was unusually impatient, a little distanced from us. He made the little noises emanating from his chest so frequently it was as though a small, stressed animal sought escape from his body.

Then, in the afternoon, the argument between our parents began. It started in the kitchen, with Mum telling him he was a silly bugger, then with him following her down to the bars until the two ended up in the cellar, locked into their own battle that we knew nothing about.

There was shouting. We believed it had something to do with the haunted tankard. Only many years later did we understand. It was the first of several rows they had. Dad always followed Mum's lead, but jealousy lifted its ugly head on many occasions after that.

Our own peaceful places tended to be our bedrooms. We didn't have to share bedrooms any more as there were five of them on different floors. Being an old pub, which dated from the middle of the seventeenth century, some of the floors and walls sloped, giving the rooms their own individual character. My room was on the second floor, immediately above the bars but away from my parents and siblings on the top floor.

The wide, irregular, wooden-framed windows overlooked the churchyard. There was a window seat, from which you could watch the church weddings at St Andrews Church on a Saturday, although I gradually grew tired of doing that. It was, I thought, as lovely as Maria Merryweather's bedroom at Moonacre Manor, even though it wasn't a circular room.

In the winter, the gentle sound of the White Hart inn sign which hung just beside my window swinging on its frame lulled me to security and sleep.

Over the years I read many novels in this room, cried over boyfriends, learned to love radio Luxembourg and then radio four, learned about classical music from Richard Baker and listened to it on a record player after a Bernard the communist, who became locked in many conversations with Dad, but who was slowly dying from cancer, gifted Dad all of his classical records.

From my bedroom window, I watched the snow fall until it covered the churchyard to the sound of Winter from Vivaldi's Four Seasons. I snuggled up to our poodle, Suki, and wrote stories that no one would ever read. I loved my bedroom at the White Hart and it loved me. When I fell out with Paula, I banged the door shut in protest, locking myself away.

By day, the pub did a reasonable trade, but the evenings were by far the busiest time. Then, the university students would arrive from Headington, Oxford and Ruskin College, which was just along the road. We didn't really have a lot to do with them until our teenage years, but one advantage to growing up in a pub is that you learn to chat with a wide variety of people, which we did.

You rarely feel lonely in a pub, because of the almost constant sound of happy chattering below you.

It was the opening of the John Radcliffe Hospital that had the greatest impact on the White Hart and on our lives. The pub became the meeting point for doctors and nurses who, especially at lunch times, packed the place in their droves – their bleepers, calling them back to the hospital punctuated everything.

Mum made the decision that we would have to provide food as well as drink. What she did provide was so simple, but so popular, that the pub became famous for its hot beef sandwiches, hot ham sandwiches and ploughman's lunches. The latter consisted of a very large wedge of bread, a hunk of cheese and pickles with butter and Branston pickle. The orders had to be taken quickly as hospital staff usually had little time to spare.

Before long they had to take on extra staff, employing Mr Gammage and his wife to work behind the bar and in the kitchen, then more and even more staff. For us children, it was often like having a party in the house, even though we weren't invited until we were older. Both our parents were popular with their customers, but Mum was undoubtedly the beauty and the brains behind it all and was never bored again as she had once been in Bletchingdon.

We had many famous customers, mostly because of the proximity of Ruskin College. Paula was over the moon when the composer John Williams came into the pub and Mum called her into the bar to get a peep, knowing what a fan of his music she was.

Dennis Waterman and Rula Lenska visited, and Legs Larry Smith of the Bonzo Dog Doo-Dah Band became a customer, once inviting our parents to a party at his neighbour's house in Henley; his neighbour was George Harrison of the Beatles. It was late and they had no one to look after us; besides, I don't believe Dad would have enjoyed it half as much as Mum.

Mum was quite competitive, no less so when it came to her children.

When we were young, it was Dad who fuelled our imagination, except that Mum bought the materials for that outlet, the paints, the writing pads, and she loved to visit castles on holiday. We went to so many castles. It was Mum who encouraged us to use the local library.

But Dad was the one who acted the fool with us, who shouted, "You're it!" and ran away for us to chase him, whether it was in the house or outside. It was Dad who took us on walks and talked about wild animals and what plants and trees were called and it was Dad who made up stories about animals at bedtime.

Mum was constantly driven by the need to be a success, whether that was making money or giving us work ethic.

I think she often felt guilty about Marion. She once said to me, "I used to leave her in the cot for longer than the rest of you..." By which she undoubtedly meant that life became so much busier when they moved us to the Post Office Vaults and that running a pub at the same time as caring for four young children was sometimes exhausting.

So, she did all that she could for Marion in order to make amends. She probably came into her own as Marion's mum when all four of us were at St Andrews School in Headington. This was the school where Aunty Stephanie taught and where Mum's great-aunt had also taught. The four of us had differing experiences. Paula, Howard and I liked our school, generally, but Marion wasn't always so keen.

For a start, aged six, she ran away when a teacher made her sit in the corner for not doing enough maths. She hadn't understood the maths. When playtime came around, she ran away across Bury Knowle park, duping the lunchtime lollipop man into believing she was going home for lunch. She cried when she reached home and Mum marched her back to school to remonstrate with her teacher about her humiliation and demand extra maths homework.

On another occasion, a dinner lady who was much loathed by the children stood over her until she ate her cooked liver (as I remember, a pretty grey and disgusting dish) and semolina, hated by most children. She wouldn't leave the house the next morning.

So, when she complained to Mum that Margaret Johnson had been chosen to play Mary in the nativity; she who always took the register; she who was always the teacher helper; she whose father was a doctor at the John Radcliffe Hospital and whose mother was a school governor; she who lived in the little house in the lane behind us, our mother started a rather competitive campaign to get one up on Mrs Johnson.

One of the ways in which she did this was through sewing elaborate outfits for her youngest daughter.

Mum was good at sewing, but she hadn't taken up her sewing machine since Bletchingdon. No time. She didn't let that stop her. If Marion was going to be an angel in the nativity, she would be a humdinger of an angel, with silky white voluminous skirts and wings that would knock the rest of the cast over.

In the spring, the Singer sewing machine came out again, this time for a National Costumes of the World dressing-up day. She was determined that Marion's costume would out stun everyone else. She spent days working on the red with white polka dots material, turning Marion into a Flamenco dancer complete with flowers in her hair, colourful fan and tap shoes.

It was the third 'out-do Mrs Johnson' costume that won Marion first prize at the St Andrews School fete and a rosette, pinned onto her costume by the vicar. This time,

Mum had really gone to town, with shimmering green material bought at Debenhams that she turned into a mermaid's tail and a blonde wig pinned over the mermaid's dark hair.

Margaret Johnson went as Alice in Wonderland. I think our mother had a smirk on her face when she was presented with a rosette for third place.

After St Andrews School, I went to Bayswater with my three friends. Bayswater school stood at the edge of the Barton estate. I grew in confidence, discovering that I was quite good at English, history and art. My spoken English suffered a bit, but that's a common, temporary way of fitting in with others.

It had its fair share of intimidating pupils and teachers. Frequently, a small queue of boys waited outside the headmaster's office, exhibiting bravado as they awaited the cane. It didn't occur to us that as they were always the same suspects, the cane wasn't working, or that girls didn't get the cane. The girls could be as tough as the boys. We had been protected at our primary school; at Bayswater we quickly learned who the leaders were and kept out of their way unless they spoke to us directly.

A couple of the teachers smoked while teaching. I loved the music teacher's lessons; she played the piano with a fag hanging from her lip, ash falling onto the keys.

The staff were male in the majority and generally kind, but there was one in particular who would pat girls on the head, laugh at his own jokes and snap without warning...

Andrew was a mild person, a bit of a scaredy cat. He was quiet, kept himself to himself, kept out of the way when there was any argument at break time, always on the periphery of things. Mr Williams was the science teacher whose moods were fickle and who was possibly heading for a nervous breakdown.

Having gone from very little basic science at primary school to experimenting with roaring blue flames on Bunsen burners, we were still a little naïve about dangerous stuff. I don't remember what Andrew did to his Bunsen burner, but absolutely nothing that Andrew did was ever daring or deliberate. So, when his Bunsen burner surged upward, threatening to singe the blonde hair of the girl beside him, we gasped in open-mouthed shock as Mr Williams, in his white lab coat, sped through the aisle of heavy wooden benches to yank Andrew by the neck of his jumper, dragging him over a desk so his head bumped against it, then shaking him hard at first and then dropping him onto the hard floor.

There wasn't a sound in the room as we watched, shocked into a more fearful silence than usually existed in the science lab. We watched as Mr Williams lifted Andrew off his feet again, this time by his ear which tore and bled profusely, dripping red onto the floor like blobs of thin paint.

Even the harder pupils amongst us stared in shocked silence, as though we were waiting for something even more terrible to happen. Mr Williams sent Andrew to the school first aid lady, sent him to walk alone, although the boy must have been reeling with the pain. It was the first time that most of us had witnessed real violence. The poor lad walked silently, cupping his ear with a hand. No one asked to go with him; we were all afraid to.

The Pickwick Gang came to an abrupt end when I reached the age of thirteen. Boys and pop music were more important to me by then, along with Jackie magazine, my yellow hot pants and novels by Jean Plaidy. I added David Cassidy to my poster collection along with Gary Glitter; neither was as good looking as Paul Newman, but my friends liked them, and I wanted to be the same.

Paula and Helen became best buddies, still bombing around the Croft lanes in search of mystery- finding lost dogs and climbing walls while I stopped noticing that Helen had taken my place. My latest fights with Paula were over the telephone because we could listen to pop music on the 'Dial-a Disc' telephone service, much to Mum's irritation. When she found out, she tried to stop the practice, saying it was too expensive; so, we would sneak from our rooms when our parents were working to fight over the receiver, putting the blame on one another when the bill came in.

The Pickwick Gang now mostly consisted of Howard, Chris and Graham. Paula had started at Cherwell School. Being smarter than I, she passed her eleven plus. She was popular and made her own friends at Cherwell, both male and female. Mum was very kind about my eleven plus failure. I don't think Dad even understood that the eleven plus exam was important. Paula was a lot better at studying. I would start to read an assignment about the Enclosure Act, get halfway through the page and then imagine I was married to Max de Winter.

I suppose it was Howard's fault that the Pickwick Gang ended in drama, but he hadn't intended any harm. Although Paula and I could be quite vicious towards him at times, we came down on his side firmly... after a lot of teasing.

The fire took a long time to take hold of the old stables. It would have smouldered, igniting the dry wood of an ancient beam, glowing and burning like amber through the long evening and through to the early hours of the morning until it grew, eventually devouring the rafters.

The barn was at the end of the long pub garden, so far away from the pub itself that the fire wasn't noticed until the middle of the night, until poor, kindly, white-haired Miss Salt woke to the fumes as they drifted inside her own cottage. She came to the pub door in her dressing gown and shawls at about the same time that Dad got up to use the toilet, smelling the distant smoke through the landing window.

It was Paula who shook me awake as I lay with Suki, the apricot poodle, who lay in the crook of my leg.

"The stables are on fire; Dad's called the fire brigade!" She told me, "Mrs Salt's cottage might burn down!"

I leapt out of bed, following her to the little window on the landing where Howard and Marion were now kneeling upon the window seat. Through the dark garden, I could see the distant flames as they licked at the barn roof like golden orange ghosts.

"My bike's in there," Marion said anxiously – then, "Can the fire spread to us?"

Mum reassured her with a hug.

"I wonder how it started," she said, in abject innocence.

We all had our theories. Only Howard remained silent.

"Where's Dad?"

"He's outside the front of her cottage, waiting for the fire engine to come."

I imagined Miss Salt, swathed in Granny shawls, staring up at her home as the flames encroached. She had given us apples and biscuits as we played in the stable. We all felt sorry for her.

Then, Paula turned to Howard.

"You were playing in the barn with Graham!" she said, remembering. It wasn't actually an accusation, more of an observation.

His cheeks burned as red as if he had been standing in the glow of the fire.

"That was ages ago, this afternoon; it wasn't me, I didn't do anything!"

We all stared at him now. His face crumpled and his eyes filled with tears.

Mum twisted her lips thoughtfully; she stared at him for a long time, it seemed, in the way she used when she was suspicious. She was a formidable interrogator. She kept a stick on the top of the kitchen cabinet. She had never used it on us, but at times she would take it down and point it at whoever she believed to be the liar or instigator of a crime.

"Let's not start blaming people before we know," was all she said, releasing Howard from the narrowed blue eyes.

We implored her to let us go out into the Croft to watch the firemen when they came, but she packed us all off to bed, so we saw none of it, but had to lie in bed and imagine the water cascading over the flames.

It was a surprise to us, the next morning, to find that nothing was really changed after all, but for the hiss of smoke rising from the roof, and a narrow, jagged, blackened hole in the stable roof that hadn't been there before. We watched from the window again. A few firemen were still drifting about the pub garden, some of them yawning, needing sleep. They removed their helmets and sat upon the grass. Dad was deep in conversation with one of them.

Mum took them mugs of coffee, pausing to speak to him. He jerked his head up towards the window, as though he were saying something about us.

It was Saturday morning. Paula and I went out into the Croft to investigate. Word spread quickly through the village, just as the smoke had.

Helen turned up a little while later on her bicycle. Howard, Chris and Graham were conspicuous in their absence.

"Who started it?" Helen asked.

We shrugged.

"Perhaps it was started by an arsonist," she suggested. "I know." Her voice was eager with the plan forming in her head. "Let's investigate, let's be detectives and find out how the stable caught fire!"

There was no time to find the word arsonist in the dictionary just then, so we followed her on our bikes, madly pedalling about the Croft for a long time, with no real idea about where we should start and who we should interview.

After about half an hour, we returned to the stable.

There was a fireman standing outside, inspecting the damage.

"We're going to find out who did it!" Helen assured him confidently.

He looked from one to the other of us, running a hand through his matted hair, a little grey and powdery with ash. His helmet was held in the crook of his arm.

"We know who did it," he assured us.

"Who?" We waited eagerly to know the criminal's name.

But he wouldn't answer, even though we pestered him, followed him with our endless questions.

Our parents wouldn't tell us either, not for a long time.

In the end, we heard it from Howard himself.

He and Graham had got hold of a box of matches from the bar and decided they would have a real fire in the barn. They climbed the old wooden ladder to the rafters. They had, they said, put out the fire when they had finished. Both boys were home for tea by half past five, but the fire hadn't been properly extinguished and had smouldered all evening.

He hadn't confessed under torture, in the end, his own conscience tormented him.

The matches were hidden afterwards, and our stable den denied us. Dad placed a large padlock on the door.

We were so excited. Our annual holiday and this time it would be in Cornwall. Excited and then arguing in turns. All of us packed into that old estate car.

Nanny Edna, squashed but uncomplaining, tried to keep us from fighting by singing music hall songs from her teenage years.

"K,K,K Katie, beautiful Katie, you're the only little girl that I adore..!"

We drove into the dark, finally leaving the pub and the dogs in the capable hands of Mr and Mrs Gamage and their children.

We stopped for fish and chips and kicked each other under the table until Dad lost his temper, which rarely happened; threatening to turn around and go home if we couldn't pipe down. When we got back into the car, Marion fell asleep on Nan's lap and Howard dozed between Paula and I.

Coming off the motorway, we followed narrow, windy roads beneath a roof of dense, green branches and through the trees, the occasional cottage light. We were enchanted.

At last, the winding tarmac met with the estuary which followed us all the way to the sea. Meandering, following us, re-kindling our excitement until, before us, lay Looe harbour with its fishing boats bobbing upon the black water beneath strings of fairy lights. All nestled below the higgledy-piggledy houses and hotels peering down from the steep cliffs.

Mum woke my sleepy brother and sister who stared out of the car windows with the thought of two whole weeks away from home; the joy of ice cream, sunshine and swimming in the sea, and all of the while the Beach Boys sang in my head.

Mr Maggs' hotel was perched high up above the town with no access by car. We parked beside the harbour to drag our suitcases and bags to the hotel. They bumped behind us on the stone steps that wound up and up like the spiral in a fossil.

I shared a room with Nan, my co-conspirator and confidant. I never had to ask for her permission to do anything. She always agreed with me.

Lovely, leisurely days of exploration. I've been to so many places in the world but will always be fondest of that holiday, always love sea gulls and blue skies.

We took a boat out to Looe Island and saw the seals keeping cool beside the long, dark rocks. We dug a channel beneath Nan's deckchair so she slipped backward into the sand. Paula whistled the bars of "Devil Gate Drive" and begged Mum for a mock leather jacket.

I had brought my oil paints with me, painting the harbour from our hotel bedroom in garish colours. We returned from the beach one day and I accidentally knocked the painting from the dresser. Nan attempted to sponge the oil paint from the carpet with her flannel and soap. This didn't work, in fact it made things worse. So, she pulled a rug across the mess, hoping that it wouldn't be spotted by the cleaning ladies.

I woke early each day; how could I not with that sunshine and sea smell and the sound of gulls?

The gulls could be savage. The day after we arrived in Looe, a gull swooped down from a roof and, noticing our ice creams, it tore Marion's cone from her hand. It might have scarred her for life, but Mum bought her another ice cream and a halter neck top from a seaside boutique.

I began to creep out very early in the morning whilst Nan and everyone else was sleeping. I loved the feeling of independence that it gave me- to sneak from the hotel in the early morning before the air warmed up, while the thin, grey mist floated about the fishing boats. Crossing the bridge to East Looe, I wandered through the empty streets.

One morning, a young man- about nineteen perhaps, and good looking- stood on the deck of his fishing boat. He was winding some fishing tackle, I think.

He watched me as I wandered along the harbour wall, smiling all the while, and winked at me.

I felt empowered as I went onto the beach to fill my pockets with shells.

Paula and I paddled in the shallow, muddy water when the tide went out, trying to catch sand eel and other tiny fish in our nets. We did not quarrel, not once. We had space and fresh air and security and fun.

One day we watched two boys throwing stones at a grounded gull. Paula, always the brave one, got into an argument with them. They shouted at her rudely, but Paula was never intimidated as I was. In the end, they left the harbour.

She crossed the river to pick up the gull, but even Paula was in some awe of the razor-sharp beak.

"I'll get a towel," I said. "We could pick it up in that and take it to the RSPCA. There must be an RSPCA."

I raced back to the beach. Our nan slept in her deckchair while Mum lay sleeping on her stomach in her new costume so that the sun could turn her back brown.

Dad was the only wakeful adult. Through black sunglasses, he watched Marion paddling in the sea. Howard had made a castle from sand.

Dad looked at me with one eye closed behind the glasses. He asked what I was doing and where Paula was. I told him about the seagull, said I needed a towel. Carelessly, he picked the nearest free towel from the sand, a rather gorgeous and expensive one. Later, we'd get into trouble for that.

The exhausted seagull had almost given up the struggle as Paula crouched next to it.

"It's got a crab hook in its mouth," she said, showing me a short length of nylon crab line dangling from its beak that I hadn't noticed before. Nervously, I threw the towel over it as though to catch a small tiger, but left Paula to pick it up in her arms.

It kept quite still after a small struggle, so we climbed the stone steps from the harbour to ask the lady at the ice cream counter where the RSPCA was.

The streets were packed with tourists as we passed the fish market and the car park, making our way toward the railway station. The ice cream lady said that the RSPCA was in the street opposite.

At last, wilting now in the bright sunshine and the heat of the day, we found the tall building with a sign on the door. I knocked several times as it was closed. Then, at last, a window opened above and a woman with dark hair and plump, brown shoulders stared irritably down at us.

"What do you want?"

Her voice was harsh, irritable. But we weren't put off. When she realised our mission, she would understand, or so we believed.

"We've found a seagull; it's got a hook in its mouth."

"What do you expect me to do about that?" she yelled- "Dirty, smelly thing! Go and put it in the harbour with the others."

With that, she banged the window shut.

We stared at one another in disbelief that anyone from the RSPCA would say such a thing.

Paula shrugged. "I suppose if it was a snake, we wouldn't have rescued it," she said sagely.

Sometimes, Paula's wisdom could be extremely annoying; even more annoying was that she was probably right and I was desperate for an ice cream.

Morosely, we wandered back to the harbour. I cared about the seagull and was depressed that our mission had failed.

We sat together on the top step, staring down at the brown water.

Paula lifted a corner of the towel to look at the bird. From the shadow of the towel, it stared back at us with one black eye, limply clacking its powerful beak.

We didn't know it, but we were being watched. I think the man had been waiting for the tide to come in. He was an older man, perhaps once a fisherman, but now his job was to ferry tourists across the Looe River. He stood a few feet away from us, his elbows resting upon a barrier as he smoked a cigarette. Tanned skin, lined face, frowning at us.

"What you got there, then?" he asked.

We told him. He squashed his cigarette butt with the toe of his boot and joined us on the steps.

"Budge up..." he said.

We got up to let him sit in our place.

He uncovered the gull. Resentfully, I told him about the RSPCA lady.

"That weren't the RSPCA," he assured me. "There's people living in the flats above the office. You're supposed to call the number on the door. She were probably annoyed that you kept knocking."

Fascinated, we watched on either side of him as he held the gull tightly beneath his right arm, clamping his hand about the bird's head. Then, with his left hand, he took a penknife from his pocket and, as his hands were full, he asked me to open it for him.

Slowly and with great care, he prized open the reluctant beak with the knife blade. Then, he set the blade on its side so the gull couldn't shut its beak. In one swift, although probably very painful twist, he removed the hook and threw the bird out towards the river.

The gull took off instantly, stroking the air with its long, strong wings.

Over the two weeks we turned lobster red first and then brown. We used all of Dad's spare change in the amusement arcade. Nan taught us how to use the fruit machines and we developed her addiction.

Every evening we ate out, often fish and chips and pasties on the quay but sometimes in a restaurant. Once we ate at a pub restaurant in a village close to Looe.

As we returned to the hotel, giggling about something, a white owl flew from the dense, dark woodland, crossing the road ahead of us.

"The white owl of doom..." Nanny Edna proclaimed solemnly; "Someone is going to die!"

Mum turned to us, her plucked eyebrows raised in an arch at this gypsy nonsense.

"Not on my watch," she said dryly.

Before the holiday came to an end, I persuaded my parents to buy me an ornamental cast-iron ship and two fishing floats in bright colours with which to decorate my bedroom, so far from Cornwall. On the morning we had to leave, despite being the eldest, I cried silently all the way to the Tamar Bridge, missing the pastel blue sky above the sparkling silver sea, missing the gulls and the green water rippling over the rocks.

But money didn't grow on trees, as our mother always remarked, and they needed to go home to earn some more.

When we finished at our primary schools, Mum sent us all to different secondary schools. I don't really know why but can only speculate. Perhaps she was trying to protect me, as my younger sister had proved herself the cleverer one; maybe we simply followed our friends.

Paula went to Cherwell School, Howard to Oxford Boys School and Marion to Northway Middle School, then later to Milham Ford. Each of us found the subjects that we liked and did well in, amongst other strengths. I think Mum had it in her mind that I would be a teacher when I reached teenage. I had other ideas, of course.

Paula knew what she wanted to do with her life from the time she watched the mounted police controlling the crowds at the Oxford United football games at the Manor ground in Headington. Howard became a skilled artist under the tutelage of his art teacher, a well-known local artist called Bernard Hickey. He also learned the skill of a stonemason, becoming interested in sculpture.

Marion had no idea what she wanted to do, being very young then; but she was artistic, loved drama and was highly sociable.

Both Paula and I, who had begged our parents for a long time, learned to ride at Mrs Shepherd's stables in Forest Hill. It wasn't terribly expensive – in part we paid our way by helping out. She was joint master of the South Oxfordshire hunt, an incredible lady who rode horseback into her old age. Dad knew Mrs Shepherd and her son from the time he had worked on a local farm during the war. Her methods could be a little unorthodox. We learned to ride on a Thelwell pony called Mousey, who was stocky and black but who galloped fast while our feet almost touched the floor. She was kind to us and especially to her horses. We learned much from her, not simply the method and practicalities but about understanding animals, that animals have individual characters, just like human beings.

I joined Oxford Ladies as a runner while Paula excelled at swimming. I was a fast sprinter at school but quickly learned that I was one of the slowest at this dedicated sports club.

On horseback or on our bikes or walking to the library, the two of us were relaxed and happy in one another's company. Wind or rain, sunshine or snow, it was as though she forgot to make the weird little animalistic noises in her throat and I stopped being aware of them. We were friends in the great outdoors, just happy sisters.

Much of the time, Paula wasn't happy in herself. She hated clothes and wore jeans and sweatshirts. Dresses confused her. If we had a family event or a party to go to, Mum grew rather anxious, suspecting family pressure to see Paula in a dress. She often suggested a trip to Oxford to buy a skirt and blouse. Paula would give in and comply in the end, but inevitably, her bedroom floor would be piled with things while she emerged wearing something rather badly, as though she had put it on in anger and her whole body hated it. We knew, I knew, that she was right. Trousers simply suited her better. Neither did it help that she developed a large bosom early on. She hated her bosoms, especially in a swimming costume – unless it was a bog standard sports costume.

She went from being a skinny, wiry girl to a rounder woman within a short space of time. It was as though her metabolism changed drastically. Perhaps this was something to do with her teen age, but she began to steal into the kitchen for more food: comfort eating.

I think it was during this period I woke up to the fact that she ought to have been born a boy. God had made a terrific mistake, but we didn't talk about gender issues, then. She had no choice; she had to be a woman and there was no going back.

In 1972, aged twelve, she saved someone from drowning at Temple Cowley swimming pool. Her class were about to start a swimming lesson and were sharing the pool with other children with various disabilities when someone spotted the boy, sinking down toward the bottom of the pool. He had either fallen or climbed into the deep end unobserved.

Every minute counted. In a panic, the class teacher sent Paula to find the swimming teacher before attempting to bring the boy to the surface herself. One or two attempts were made in the following minutes, and when even the swimming teacher failed to pull him from the bottom, Paula got into the pool of her own accord. At first, she too failed, coming to the surface for air; but on her second attempt, she dragged him upward, saving his life.

The boy was eleven. His parents were so grateful to her. They came to her school and presented her with a gorgeous paperweight with tiny flowers set in glass. The local paper took her photograph. Our parents were so proud. We enjoyed basking in her glory for some while, having children confront us at school with the words, "I saw your sister in the paper!"

A letter arrived to say that Paula would receive an award from The Royal Humane Society. The award was presented to her by Lord Longford at the Town Hall in Oxford. Mum and Dad attended and took me with them. Mum cried silently through her presentation.

For a while after, Paula was happy again. The experience had perhaps made her feel loved and accepted for who she really was.

Prudish denial didn't exist in Mum, or if it ever did, it mattered less than her love for Paula and her great need to protect her, but there was still a huge stigma attached to homosexuality and Mum was very aware of it. As for Dad, he didn't understand at all, or perhaps chose to bury his head in the sand, or worried about what others would think.

Aged fifteen, a group of friends came to the White Hart to visit me. We sat in the garden around one of the pub tables. As we chatted, Paula strode into the sunshine to join us. She sat down and a young female friend of mine began talking to her. After several minutes, Paula went back to the house.

"Your brother is really good-looking!" The girl smiled.

I think I felt a kind of amused pride at first, until I remembered and had to explain that Paula was my sister. After this, I wasn't always happy for her to join us.

There were times, however, when I knew how much I loved her. That time when she was eleven and had to go into hospital was a Beth March moment.

She said she felt unwell during the evening, unusual for her. She had a pain across her belly and Mum sent her to bed with a hot water bottle and disprin. I knew it was genuine, because Paula never made a fuss and because she was prepared to miss *The Benny Hill show*.

Mum asked me to check on her, which I did at first; then I forgot for rather a long time as I watched TV. On my third visit, I panicked. She had got much worse. Her normally healthy skin had turned milky white and sweaty. She lay very still, as though ever movement hurt her, only her hazel eyes moved slightly and her lips, as she whispered, "Get Mum, my belly really hurts."

I went to the bar. Peering through a gap in the door, I searched for Mum through the veil of smoke and the noisy conversations.

"Who do you want, my duck?" asked Bert's wife, Joan. She beckoned to Mum, who came instantly, pushing her way through the human barrier to reach me.

Within minutes she returned to the bar, calling above the noise, "Is there a doctor in the house?"

There were several, fortunately – Doctor Elliot being the best known of them. He examined Paula and said that she should go to hospital immediately. He believed she had appendicitis. She was in hospital for several days.

I remember missing her, and, for the first time in my life, imagining life without her. When she returned from the hospital she had to stay in bed for a while. How I had missed her was soon forgotten as the anxious, caged-up little noises grew more frequent, haunting me with a vengeance.

In the house in the deepest hollow of the Quarry lived Dad's brother, our uncle Don, his wife Dorothy who was a nurse and their four children who were similar in age to us. Susan was the only girl and close in age to Paula and I while Will, Robert and Oliver became Howard's good friends.

Mum and Dorothy were very different people, but they grew close over the years. If there was any serious health issue involving us, Mum would reach for the phone to ask her advice.

The tale of the Christmas morning they came to pay us a visit has become a bit of a family legend. The story of how Dad plied both with drink as the adults sat talking and laughing in the living room while we played together in the house; we were brought back to them by a tremendous crashing noise; to find Uncle Don had fallen backwards on his chair like a large, rounded bird, frozen in winter, his feet pointing to the ceiling as he lay chuckling on the floor. And Aunty Dorothy, so kind and wise, temporarily floored by sherry, who went to bed when they reached the Quarry, failing to cook the Christmas turkey.

Our Grandparents home in Headington Quarry was a second home to Paula and I. From a young age, we were sent there at weekends so that our parents could manage the pub. When I close my eyes, I can travel around it as it was, before fir trees were planted in the front garden, now grown so tall they eliminate the light. Once, the house was filled with light.

It stands in New Cross Road within a (now crumbling) high wall of light-coloured stone. Built by Grampy Ron in the very late 1940s, it was then a thoroughly modern show home built of stone and marble and Nanny Edna was justifiably proud of it. After Kiln Lane, they brought up their four children in this house: our mother and her siblings, Stephanie, Christine and Geoffrey.

Behind the house lay a beautiful rose garden and behind this an apple and plum orchard with a concrete pigsty where we used to play and carry out experiments, making perfume from the roses, finding out whether worms could swim and if ants could be confused by chalked circles – that sort of thing. In the summer, Nan and Gramps had the whole family there for dinner or tea. In the afternoons we would play rounders with our cousins and hang upside down from the trees.

Our grandfather always projected good humour and authority and he liked Dad enormously, although Dad was far less assertive than Grampy Ron. Both men had kindness and goodwill at their heart.

As a fine stonemason, he worked on the repair of Oxford colleges as well as for the Duke of Marlborough at Blenheim Palace. Nan kept a telegram from the old Duke to our family when Gramps finally passed away.

He was taken on to do repair work at Boarstall Manor and he created beautiful monuments like the one to the memory of Ian Fleming in Swindon. Paula and I often went with him as he supervised work.

But his real passion was football.

He had been a young player for Headington Quarry, which joined with Headington United, and later contributed his own earnings to develop the club after it moved to the Manor ground. He became chairman of Oxford United in 1957, the year of my birth. His passion for football, specifically for Oxford United, was enormous. He was generally impassive, but his excitement and joy became apparent when Oxford United won.

On a Saturday evening, he would allow Paula and I to stuff as many Jaffa cakes as we liked, so long as we let him watch *Match of the Day* in peace.

He formed close relationships with other managers and directors, especially Arthur Turner, perhaps, who he took on in his capacity as chairman of the club after he had been manager of Birmingham City. In turn, Arthur Turner recruited young players such as Maurice Kyle, Cyril Beavon and Graham Atkinson. Gramps was photographed with many famous managers, chairmen and directors of the time for the local newspapers; Sir Matt Busby and Eric Morecambe amongst them.

We loved him, were sometimes a little in awe of him, and were so very proud of him. School friends who followed Oxford United knew about Gramps. I'll never forget the rush of emotion I felt when my ten-year-old boyfriend of the playground, who was seated in the supporters' area, turned to grin at me as Paula and I sat with Gramps in the directors' box.

After a game, we would join Nan in the Ladies' room, bribed to be polite with fairy cakes and lemonade until we grew bored and were finally sent outside to run about the empty stadium where we made nuisances of ourselves, or chatted with the kindly stewards.

For a while, we had free range to run about the stadium, slamming down the wood and metal seats which made a lovely clanging noise that echoed around the entire grounds – until whichever sports presenter who was trying to interview our Gramps, Jimmy Hill on one occasion, asked us to stop, and then we would be returned to annoy Nanny Edna.

We were taken to away matches on a coach with the players. When the coach stopped, Maurice Kyle bought us bars of chocolate and packets of crisps. We sang football songs to ourselves all the week, chants to egg on the players, "Jimmie, Jimmie Baron..." was our favourite.

Gramps was a smoker, had smoked since he was fifteen. He had also worked as a stonemason before masks became compulsory, breathing in the fine stone dust which gave him Silicosis.

Firstly, he suffered the gradual slowing down of the energy he always had, then the breathing difficulties that finally left him gasping for air, stripping him of his strength and confidence. He was forced to use a gas tank and oxygen mask in the end.

By the time he met Eric Morecambe in the board room, he was at the stage where he needed the services of an oxygen tank and mask around the clock. They were heavy, clumsy, cylindrical things, provoking the comment from Eric, "By golly, sir; that's a big pipe you have there!"

We had been on so many lovely holidays with our grandparents, to Bournemouth, Yarmouth, to Cornwall and Wales. Wales was our last holiday with him. He had to use a wheelchair and he hated that, hated the indignity of being pushed around Betws-y-Coed instead of being able to walk. He hated being dependent upon other people.

So, he was forced to retire as the chairman of the club, which must have been hard for him; he'd devoted most of his adult life to it.

Aged fourteen, I stayed with him for a couple of hours each Saturday afternoon to give Nanny Edna a break from nursing him; either drawing, writing, or doing my homework while he watched the television, occasionally helping him with his oxygen bottle and mask. This was some small return for the things he had done for us. I didn't resent it but think he was embarrassed at times. It was nothing compared with the care our grandmother provided, giving him oxygen, medication, food he could eat; lifting him from chair to bed, feeding, washing him, and in the end, it took its toll on her.

At school, in my art class, I made the clay torso of an Oxford United supporter as a present for him. I still have it.

He died in January 1972, about a year after giving up his chairmanship of the club. His coffin was laid out in the living room that Nan was so proud of, close to the marble fireplace he had built. I asked to look at him and Nan took me into the room. It didn't look like him; his face was fixed and stern, like a figure made from wax.

My favourite photograph of him was taken in the long garden of their house. He is seated in the wheelchair with the roses he had grown in the background. Nan's little poodle, Bonny, sits at his feet.

Nan had nursed him for a long time; she was tired, but I don't think anyone realised the impact his death would have upon her. Perhaps, at first, his death was softened by Aunty Steph, Uncle Dave and their boys moving in with her. That, at least, prevented her from being lonely. But when they left to live in their own home, anxiety took hold of her.

She worried about bills, about the future, about us. She missed him so much and she was exhausted. She had begun to decline. This large house where they had lived together with children and grandchildren, had hosted Christmases and all kinds of family events, this place in which we had so much fun and laughter began to trouble her.

Bayswater school was on the edge of the Barton Estate, which had a negative reputation. Once, it was a tiny village. During the war, fifty temporary council houses were built; then between 1945 and 1950 a further thousand. Perhaps it grew too quickly, because it had its problems across the years. I had several good friends at Bayswater school, most of them lived on the estate, all good people whose families made me very welcome. I made my first black friend, Juanita, a girl with an incredible, quiet sense of humour.

After that first day in the large playground, where I shivered with Janet and Kim and was more nervous than I had ever been before, I was happy at Bayswater.

I got on well with several of the teachers: the history teacher, Mr Brown, who had a little beard and resembled King Charles I, and Mr Awde, the English teacher, who tolerated my love of Jean Plaidy and explained to me that Sir Francis Drake may have circumnavigated the globe but he didn't circumcise it. Then there was the geography teacher, Mr Castor, who loved cricket and tried hard to encourage me to love geography. I think the good outnumbered the bad.

Both Paula and I were swots. I produced a number of essays for Mr Brown, one about the Tudors, another on the subject of Elizabeth I and one about the history of a variety of Oxfordshire pubs. It began with the history of our very own pub. I learned that the emblem of the White Hart was originally the badge of Richard II which he had taken from his mother's coat of arms, but may have been a pun on his name, Rich-hart. I learned a lot of things.

One day in spring as we were talking in the front playground at school about whether we would be allowed to go to a

David Cassidy concert in London, a group of students gathered beyond the large school gates. They held cardboard boxes in their arms. We watched them, assuming they were giving out free bibles.

I can't remember which of us broke away from the group first. A few pupils had started moving cautiously towards the high fence like curious cows.

The students were from Oxford Polytechnic, newly built on the edge of Headington; after a while they started to take the little red books from the boxes, handing them out from the gates.

The books passed down the line until one came to me; it was the size of a small diary.

That's how I got my copy of the Little Red School Book.

I didn't get to read it until I went home on the bus. I remember giggling with Janet at some of the sexual references. The book didn't worry me at all, but when they had been handed out, the students told us we were invited to walk out of the school on the following week.

I hadn't a clue about the significance of the book or why it had been given to us, then, but if there was to be a party, I wanted to go. More than this, I was afraid not to go. Several of our friends had said they would walk out, following the polytechnic Pied Pipers.

I climbed down from the bus and wandered through the Croft, my nose in the book, past Dad's big vegetable garden, through the stable block and down the garden path.

The pub was closed at this time. Our parents were tidying up the bars and the kitchen and waiting for us to arrive home.

As I walked through the back door, I handed the little red school book to Mum.

"Some students gave me this," I said, waiting.

She held her head back a little, frowning as she looked at it. Both parents read the same daily newspaper, even though their politics varied to some extent. Tales about this book had been in the newspaper, but I was fourteen, addicted to *The White Horses* on TV, imagining I would ride my own Lipizzaner one day. Then naïve and politically unaware, I only understood that the students' behaviour had been furtive.

Both Mary Whitehouse and Margaret Thatcher disapproved of it, because it was believed to normalise 'licentious behaviour'.

On the bus with my friends, I had giggled at the text about masturbation. I had no idea that it was 'Essentially a manual for kids on how to challenge the authority of the school system.'

I watched our mother flip back and forth through the pages as I hopped from foot to foot, wondering what was for dinner rather more than caring about the book. I saw her expressions change, sometimes frowning, sometimes biting her lip in thought, sometimes amused. Finally, she handed the book back to me.

"Have a read of it," she said. "Tell me what you think."

"They want us to walk out of the school next week…"

"Who?"

"The students who gave them to us; they were telling us we should walk out at lunch time."

"Oh. What do you want to do?"

I remember being impressed. I thought she would tell me not to break the school rules, but she didn't.

I shrugged. "I don't really want to walk out, but if my friends do, I suppose I will."

"You don't have to do something just because your friends do it. Perhaps you should have a talk with them," she suggested, then adding, "If you do walk out, you're to come home straight away."

It bothered me all week. Some of the pupils were undeniably tough and it was better either to keep away from them or at least not to argue with them. I hated having to make the choice; hated the peer pressure I would feel, but I really didn't understand why I was being asked to walk out.

When the day, the morning, the very lunch break came at last, I still hadn't made up my mind. We stood together in a huddle after lunch, waiting in the playground. The students watched us from outside the gates, waiting for the first pupil to leave.

For some of the older pupils it was an easier decision. A large group of them strode briskly past us, confident, their bags swinging from their shoulders. A few of the younger boys left, noticeably and understandably perhaps, some of the frequently caned who had a real cause to hate the place.

Close by, teachers were waiting behind the glass doors at the front of the school, watching and waiting, but doing nothing as yet.

My hand flew to my lips as I saw the car.

Our car, a battered silver hatchback, parked across the road beside the modern church. My mother sat in the driver's seat, waiting for her moment, watching the students – long nails tapping agitatedly upon the steering wheel.

"Shit, it's my Mum," I hissed, seeing her before she saw me.

My friends gaped, all eyes upon the car. Juanita giggled at my dismay. I dreaded what she might do next; she had never been afraid of voicing her opinions.

My friends were all laughing at the situation, now, grinning at me, waiting for this new drama to unfold.

Suddenly she got out, shut the door behind her – she crossed the road with purpose, walking briskly. She wore her smart coat and high-heeled boots. The boots that meant business.

I froze as she stood before the student's ringleader, the tall young man in the denim jacket. For a moment I imagined her with the stick in her hand, the one she kept on top of the kitchen cabinet for our benefit. Maybe she was hiding it behind her back ready to wave it about in the air like Zorro. Even worse, perhaps she intended to hit him with it.

As if to shield him from the possibility of attack, his girlfriend and several of the other students stepped towards him. "Oh no…" I hissed silently, my mouth gaping wide in horror.

But she only hit him with her words.

I heard the angry rise and fall of her voice across the distance as I hid behind my friends. My heart thumped then, and I turned, half walking, half running back towards the school as her words snapped through the air. Something about intimidation, an accusation of privileges they didn't deserve… My mates were riveted by her performance, seemed not to notice my going.

"Haven't you got anything better to do with your life?" I heard her screech. "No better cause than this?"

I pushed the swing doors to enter the school, my shoes clumping on the shiny, linoleum floor. My long fringe swung down over my face, a veil to cover my embarrassment.

Hardly noticing anything, blindly reaching for the stair rail, I found myself staring into the face of the history teacher, Mr Brown.

He smiled. I smiled back, but it was a tense smile.

"She's amazing," he said, nodding his head towards the students outside. "She ought to be a school governor."

There was no sarcasm; he meant it. I didn't agree with him at the time.

"You shouldn't be embarrassed." Mr Brown smiled.

I was embarrassed, but no one teased me, and that was the end of my interest in The Little Red School Book. The students disappeared, never to return.

Our Mum would have been good under a Totalitarian Regime.

We had several cousins. Apart from our Jacobs' cousins, there were Aunty Steph and Uncle Dave's children: Andrew, Christopher and Mathew. We went on holiday with them sometimes. Andrew and Howard were very good friends, but Andrew wasn't used to having a bossy older sister as Howard was and tended to keep out of my way, then.

We had Aunty Angela and Uncle Geoff's children, Michelle and Tammy, who had been brought up immersed in Irish culture as well as English, for Angela came from Ireland. I was very jealous of their ability to do Irish dancing which they performed at a birthday party.

Our aunts and great aunts were inspirational role models, all very different in personality, but in their individual ways, all as beautiful and charismatic as Mum.

When I was a teenager, Angela gave me my first food for thought about politics. She was very loyal to her home country, as Irish people are, although perhaps most impressive of all to me was that she was friendly with one of the dancers in Pan's People, the group that appeared weekly on *Top of The Pops* and that she was a glamorous blonde.

Her lesson in politics and Ireland came after the bomb scare, although Mr Brown had taught me quite a lot.

I don't remember Mr Brown teaching the class specifically about the IRA at a time when they were being held responsible for bombings in London and Birmingham. Neither did he talk to us about the transportation of Irish people to the Caribbean islands in the seventeenth century. But I recall him speaking about the harassment of Roman Catholics by the numerous restrictions imposed upon them after the Tudor period, and about the Penal Laws.

As a young teenager, I was more aware of racism against the Irish than against black people. There were only a few young black pupils at Bayswater compared with white; it wasn't the multicultural setting that schools are today.

But we were exposed to passive-racist doses of anti-black and sexist television programmes in large dollops, in the form of programmes like *Love Thy Neighbour* and *Bless This House*; the kinds of insidious racism we watched and absorbed in our veins. After all, the adults laughed at these programmes and made their own jokes afterwards.

Racism against the Irish may have been a part of our life in another way.

"Don't get in a Paddy," was term used without compunction, anti-Irish jokes went around the playground at school frequently, portraying Irish people as dull witted.

The antidote to this racism was Dave Allen. Paula and I loved him. He made Benny Hill look like a child with a finger up his nose. Dave Allen was handsome, clever and his humour was always darkly funny.

It was late at night and I was propped on my elbow, reading in bed to the familiar hum and chatter of the voices in the bar beneath me when the telephone rang. I heard Dad's footsteps creaking upon the long landing outside my room. He answered the telephone with a couple of words, replaced the receiver softly and went back to the bar.

His voice rose above the innocent conversations while I was only half aware of it; neither did I register that the voices were suddenly stilled to silence. There was a lull. People seemed to be leaving the bars and entering the street.

Both parents came back upstairs. Dad used the phone once more while Mum's feet pounded along the corridor towards my room.

"Get up," she said. "Put on a dressing gown and come down to the bar."

Then she was gone, no explanation. I wondered whether there was another fire. I pulled my shoes over my socks and listened to her mounting the stairs to my sisters and brother; then I scooped Suki the poodle into my arms and left the room, just in time to meet the others at the top of the staircase; Mum was leading Marion by the hand while Paula and Howard stood behind her.

She gave us a frenetic and rather distracted explanation; in an obvious hurry she failed to press the mute button so that Marion stared at her in open-mouthed disbelief.

"Now, there's no need to worry; it's probably just someone fooling around. A man called Dad to say he's planted a bomb in the pub – so, the police say we all have to go outside and wait in the street." She pulled Marion's coat on and snapped Delly onto her lead, handing the dog to Paula as I was wrestling with the poodle.

I think we all said, "A bomb?" with various degrees of incredulity and fear.

Howard's voice was animated, however, slightly excited at the prospect of telling his friends. Bombs to him, at that age, were something Wile. E Coyote might use to destroy the Road Runner, although he had attempted to build a nuclear fallout shelter in Dad's vegetable garden.

Paula and I, at least, had seen the news items about the pub bombings in Birmingham for which the IRA had been blamed. My embarrassment as I appeared in my dressing gown in front of a crowd of strangers soon nullified my fear of bombs. The four of us were hustled through the bars and past the empty tables with abandoned glasses of beer.

In the street outside, the road between the White Hart and the church was filled with the ejected customers, now shivering in the darkness. Many of them had carried their drinks outside. There was a strange hush about it all, broken occasionally by the sound of nervous laughter. Some stamped their feet against the cold while others were clearly vexed at having to leave the warm bars. They waited as though they expected to go back inside at any moment, shivering beneath the light of the Victorian streetlamps.

The customers made a respectful alleyway for us, the only children present, so that we could reach the cobbled pavement on the other side of the road. Joan and Bert, frequent customers in the evening, stood protectively beside us while some loudly denounced the IRA for ruining their evening. Motherly Joan opened her coat to cradle Marion within its folds while Howard disappeared behind the church wall to have a pee.

After a short while the police cars arrived along with a large police van. Our parents spoke briefly with them, after which the bomb squad explosives officer went inside with a German shepherd at his heels. Suki, the miniature poodle, wriggled in my arms to get down, yapping at the Alsatian to warn him off.

Mum bit the side of her beautifully manicured thumb nail and looked up at her pub, wondering whether it would explode at any minute.

Gradually, disgruntled customers began to move away, deciding they would get no more beer that evening.

When the officer emerged much later, it was to talk to Dad. They had searched the entire pub for bombs, but found nothing.

It wasn't until the family gathering, a few weeks later, that Angela gave me a different perspective on Ireland. I was young, the subject was complicated; she kept it simple for me. An impromptu history lesson without passion or favouritism. Influenced by adults and the friends that I'd heard in the playground after the hoax bombing, I'd told her the hoax itself was probably the IRA.

In her home community, in Ireland, the ordinary people held a Ceilidh or a disco to raise money for the IRA, she told me. The IRA had meant a very different thing to the Irish. Thousands of Irishmen of both denominations had fought and had been killed with the British in the First World War. It was after the war that so many of them pushed for Independence from Britain. Police forces around the world were used to defend British interests, and so the police in Ireland had become a target of the IRA, and recently, police in Ulster had behaved with brutality towards peaceful, civil rights campaigners.

It was probably the first time I saw things as less than black and white.

The seventies were a time of upheaval and rebellion. Despite the presence of secret police who visited the pub – because, after all, we were close neighbours with Ruskin College where the Trade Unions sponsored working people from all over the world; at a time of bombings and miners strikes, picketing protest and rebellion – our parents maintained a peace at the White Hart. Dad had a bit of surveillance paranoia, nevertheless.

Our Dad didn't like to be spied upon or singled out; although there was only one discussion that I remember about a visiting man who had never been to the pub before who he tried to draw into conversation. The visitor remained impassive all the while he lodged on a bar stool close to a large group of miners from Yorkshire, refusing to be drawn into the most basic conversation, listening all the while.

When we became aware of Dad's political anxiety, Paula and I teased him cruelly with an ungrateful and mischievous sense of humour. We would wander into the bar after closing time to play songs on the jukebox. Part of the Union by the Strawbs and Marc Bolan's Children of the Revolution, which gave him little peace.

When some of the miners came to Ruskin College, where they remained for a few weeks, they moved in and out of the pub in a glorious band of brothers, making such a cacophony and bringing such energy with them that it was as though the world had been taken over. Dad tolerated the invasion for a long time, until the neighbours on either side of us protested about the noise which carried on late into the evening. Their singing was so infectious, so much louder than the jukebox and I welcomed the break from studying for exams.

"I've been a wild rover for many's the year

And I spend all my money on whiskey and beer

And now I'm returning with gold in great store

And I never will play the wild rover no more

And it's no, nay, never..."

(Thump, thump, thump, thump on the wooden trestle tables)

"No, nay never, no more

Will I play the wild rover;

No never, no more!"

A victorious male voice choir, always a beating heart inside their songs.

I swotted for my exams with their noise beneath my room, smiling and enjoying the distraction.

"I tell you, that chap is a Special Branch Officer, the police are watching them..." Dad said one day after another visit from the moustached stranger who told our parents that he was a businessman.

Mum frowned. "And how do you know that?" she asked irritably, not wanting to be spied on by the police, not wanting to believe it and knowing how anxious Dad was.

"He wears a suit and he keeps himself to himself. Tells you nothing about his life. He's cagey. He's watching them..."

This conversation, overheard by me, was exciting. Real smugglers and red coat soldiers, four and twenty ponies, trotting through the dark. A bit like *Poldark*, I imagined, and it had arrived at the White Hart. I had no idea that the government feared a revolution, were worried that Britain might become a communist state before too long, or that radical protest groups were being infiltrated by undercover cops. In my cosy world, I'd no experience of what revolution would entail or understanding of why anything needed infiltrating in the first place.

Aged seventeen, they transformed my school into a Middle school, so I went with a couple of friends to Milham Ford girls' school after that.

I started to demand my rights, too. Having worked in the pub kitchen at weekends for some while, I asked Mum for a raise in pay. She said no, almost immediately.

In defiance, I got a job at the Black Horse Hotel in St Clements. Here, I made beds, cleaned rooms and on one occasion, almost choked a vicar's wife with a poached egg through lack of concentration (her husband said that under no circumstances must I bring eggs, as they made her sick). I needed money to compete with some rather entitled young women at my new school. I bought impossibly long, swishy dresses from Laura Ashley in Oxford, frequently tripping over the long hems.

I had my first sexual encounter, or rather clumsy grope, with the boy along the road. This was interrupted by his savvy mother, who banged heavily on the door and called out to him in a high, shrill tone.

I spent long hours in the eagle-footed bath, carving things out of new bars of soap, listening to Steeleye Span, Jethro Tull and Free on an old cassette player until Mum pounded upon the door to tell me that other people had a right to use the bathroom, and in the case of Steeleye Span that I should "Turn off that monotonous zeetar music." She had no soul for folk music.

Denis Healey, the then Chancellor of the Exchequer, came to the White Hart with a group of people from Ruskin College and left his black briefcase in the bar. Mum brought it upstairs to the kitchen and contacted the college; so, Paula and I had a quick look through it, but it was filled with boring although no doubt essential paperwork. We snapped it shut before her return.

I went on a school trip to Paris, the first time I had ever been abroad. I went with my friends under the supervision of the French teacher. One evening, we escaped her and wandered into the Parisienne streets to find a bar. A French man with good English chatted us up, but his intentions were dishonourable and we had to run away, giggling but slightly nervous. When we arrived back at the hostel, we were all very tipsy, having not drunk much alcohol before. The poor French teacher was distraught. She had been searching the streets of Paris all night. But she didn't punish us, which was more than kind in the circumstances. I think she may have been sympathetic because I rambled on about my 'difficult life'. I didn't have a difficult life; I had a splendid life. I've felt guilty about the poor woman ever since.

This was also the year when Paula and I, having witnessed an enactment by the Sealed Knot society of a skirmish between the Roundheads and the Cavaliers at Brill in west Buckinghamshire, wrote to them applying to be cavaliers. They wrote back, saying that we had to have our own horses, which we did not, and that they only had spaces for Camp Followers, which we turned up our noses at, feeling more than a little insulted.

Paula had long wanted to apply to become a policewoman, not just any policewoman, but her love of horse riding and experience of watching the mounted police in crowd control situations at the Manor football ground had inspired her to want to be that. She worked much harder than I to get good results in her exams, taking the exam to get into the police force and passing with flying colours.

Not one, but four police people came to the White Hart to interview her. They came upstairs to sit in the living room while the rest of us had to keep out. Mum was very tense; she so wanted Paula to achieve her dream.

I didn't understand how much this ambition meant to my sister until later. Perhaps, fearing failure, and because we could be quite competitive, she didn't confide it to me; but she had to our Mum. Mum knew.

They must have asked her all kinds of questions. They spent at least an hour with her in our living room and when they emerged, Paula was smiling.

I had kept out of the way, thus far, but saw one of the policemen follow Mum into the kitchen. Apparently, he had said that he wanted to have a quiet word.

He told her that Paula had been an excellent candidate – great exam results, confident in her answers, pleasant to talk to but that they were concerned that her little habit, the barely discernible sound she made in the back of her throat, might be a sign of anxiety, and that he didn't think she would be accepted into the police force.

We knew – we all knew – that Paula was the bravest of us all. She would climb the highest tree, leap from the sloping roof of the White Hart by climbing out of the window above the back of the bar, save people from swimming pools when a teacher failed to do it. But nothing my mother could say would change their decision.

Paula the unstoppable, Paula the brave, Paula the maverick had been crushed for a while. Quietly, she retired to her bedroom to cry away from us, one of the few times she allowed herself to cry. She would talk to no one. Mum worried while I missed her.

I suppose that in my selfish, teenage world, I didn't notice the changes in Nan for a long time. She was my second mother, had taught me to sew and knit, to make pastry, to press flowers, all of the small but interesting things she knew about and I loved her very much.

When I was born, she filled my head with stories about the Christine who had died and who I was named after. She used to lie upon the bed with me when I was very small, gazing at the stars beyond my curtain to tell me that the brightest star was Christine, that Christine was brilliant at athletics and swimming, telling me how gentle and kind she was. So that in a way I was probably a bit in awe of my dead aunt and vaguely worried that I would never be able to live up to her.

Her daughters often teased her, about her lack of political knowledge, her cooking skills and her knitting, which sometimes resulted in one cardigan arm a little longer than the other. But Nan had something that they didn't, a way of listening to you and telling you that everything you did was amazing. She had the time to listen. She had time to spare for us, teaching us the Lord's prayer, telling us wonderful tales about the Quarry and about her upbringing in the Cowley Road. She had time for other people, too. Everyone liked her.

She also had premonitions. Some of these were about important events; more often than not, they were almost insignificant. Like the time she came to Cornwall with us, along with our parents' friend, a teacher from Fort Myers in Florida. She had a dream one night that a brown mouse leapt from some orange flames and ran over her shoe. She told us about it at breakfast time, hating rodents as she did.

Later that morning, we visited Tintagel. Ed Symms, the lecturer from Florida was a fan of John Steinbeck and I had read *The Acts of King Arthur and his Noble Knights,* which was written while Steinbeck stayed in England and which I bought at an old book shop in Padstow.

We were all walking along the narrow path towards the sea at the foot of Tintagel Castle when Nan gave a scream and we turned, just in time to see the little brown mouse leaping from the tall, orange tipped flowers to run straight over her shoe.

Several years before this, while Gramps had been alive but at work, Paula and I stayed with her in the Quarry and saw her cry: a very rare thing indeed. We hadn't understood why she wasn't her usual self; as a rule, she was very jolly around her grandchildren. But she had been subdued that morning until the point where she told us that she was taking us home to Wantage on the country bus.

We sat behind her, looking out at the countryside while noticing that she was trying hard not to cry. When we arrived at our home, Mum sat her down in the kitchen to explain that her favourite nephew had been killed in a car crash. This was the first time she had heard the news, and yet she had experienced overwhelming feelings of dread all morning.

She wasn't pretty in the way her girls were; she used to try to cover her little snub nose with foundation, but she had such lively eyes, so mischievous and full of fun, I could see why Grampy Ron fell in love with her at St Giles fair.

We visited her often after Aunty Steph and Uncle Dave moved out. She always said that she was fine but the house with its emptiness started to swallow her up. It wasn't like her to be so still, so withdrawn and inactive. She began to worry about things. Much of this was kept from us, although she shared her worries with her children. Worries and loneliness are a bad mix, so, gradually she grew thinner until she could no longer be bothered to cook for herself. She may not have been a great beauty, but she had always dressed with care; perhaps this was the most obvious indication that something was wrong. Nanny Edna ceased caring about her appearance. The lively eyes became dull, the skin around them bruised by fatigue as she stopped sleeping.

We, her grandchildren, were sheltered from the truth of it for a long time and were slow to understand the fear and anxiety which had gripped her for so long. She became so silent, so thin, almost electing to be mute.

In the end, her children sold her house, the place that Gramps had built and which now swallowed her up. They purchased the little house directly opposite her old home and for a long time she was happy there, making a recovery. She made it her own with her ornaments and photographs, tended the garden to her liking and struck up friendly conversation with her neighbours.

But a breakdown suffered once can occur again. Despite the visits that we made to her and the visits she made to her children, something unseen, some terrible loneliness that she felt inside gradually returned, devouring her spirit.

Once again, she fell quiet, became disinterested in the idea of holidays, disinterested in the life around her. She grew sad; it was impossible to make her smile. All of the old symptoms of depression returned but this time, they were far, far worse.

Nan came to live with us for a while. Marion slept in the single bed in our parent's room, while Nan had Marion's room.

It must have been so difficult for Mum to run a busy pub, to stay on top of four lively young people, to cook for us all and maintain her relationship with Dad, all while caring for our grandmother, too. Sometimes she failed, becoming snappy, occasionally sitting with her head in her hands at the kitchen table. No one could criticise her for a lack of determination and her love was strong, but it wasn't the easiest of times for her.

She did her best to coax Nan to eat; she took her to the doctor; she took her out with us on Sunday afternoon trips. When Nan failed to brush her hair, which grew flat and wispy, Mum brushed it into shape. She dressed her and stood over her to ensure that she ate. But after a long while, she knew that Nan wasn't improving.

I don't recall the month, but it must have been late on a summers evening, about an hour before closing time, when the pub and its garden were still busy with groups of customers. Our mother sent me to Nan's room to check if she was all right. If I had not gone there, I'm not sure what might have happened.

When I peered around the door, Nan's bed was empty but for the imprint of her shape upon the mattress and the smell of talcum powder. She was spending more and more time on her bed, now.

I called her name as I trailed downstairs, looking into the other rooms and the bathroom as I went. She was nowhere to be seen.

I went upstairs again.

There was a window in Marion's room, so we will never know why she chose Howards, except that the window in his room was taller. She would have had to climb onto the dresser to reach the sill.

Later, recalling the scene, I would think of the Wendy bird in Peter Pan.

I stared up at her, believing that it was some kind of joke on her part. Really, when I first saw her, I had no idea that she was contemplating the end of her life. I don't know what I believed exactly, perhaps that this was the old Nanny Edna having a joke.

She stood very still, looking downward at the cobbled street, a small, thin figure in her white nightdress – the only thing that moved in the evening breeze. It was as though she was on the point of flight, just pausing with her hands held either side of the window.

At first, I actually laughed; a little nervously, but I laughed. Then I understood at last, but it was too incredible to be the truth. People in my family didn't commit suicide…

"What are you doing, Nan?" I asked in a hushed voice.

She half turned – I can see her face, still. Her hair, still dark, her chin turning to her left shoulder blade; the lack of any expression on her face, as though she didn't know who I was.

"Come down…" I pleaded.

She said nothing. She turned back to the cobbles far below her, keeping her body very still.

Then Howard came into the room. He was still young, then. It was a shock for us both.

"Get Mum," I said without looking at him.

I waited, while she stood like a statue clothed in white, framed by the tall window.

She came quickly and quietly, afraid perhaps that any movement might make Nan lose her footing. At first, her face crumpled in pity. Next, she hitched up her skirt and climbed onto the dresser to stand beside Nan. She touched her thin arm gently.

"Go downstairs," she told us. "Don't let anyone come up here."

She persuaded Nan to come down. After this it was impossible to guard her actions around the clock.

Nan went to the Warneford Psychiatric Hospital in Headington. It was some while again before she recovered.

I had to make my mind up about what I was going to do after my A-levels. Mum and I had very different ideas and frequently argued. Dad either viewed it as Mum's domain or felt that he didn't really mind what we did.

She felt that I should go to teacher training college as her sister Steph had done and several aunts before her.

I thought that I was destined to work on a kibbutz in Israel. I had talked myself into believing this without considering any of the practical issues; frankly, my ideology was weak.

The seed of this idea began years before.

Both Paula and I had a keen interest in history and so, when a remarkable programme which was brutally honest and shocking was aired on a Sunday afternoon, showing footage of the war including of inmates in concentration camps, we watched it, at first scarcely comprehending it. It was called *The World at War* and was narrated by Sir Laurence Olivier

When he found out that we were watching it, Dad joined us, which was just as well as there was much that we didn't fully understand. It was our first awakening to barbaric atrocities against Jews. One particular film clip I will never forget was of a naked young person immersed in icy cold water, shivering uncontrollably, as an experiment into the kinds of temperatures that soldiers might be able to endure.

It didn't give us nightmares, though we were only about twelve and fourteen when we watched it; but the images went around and around in my head as though I had my own problem to solve, even if I didn't understand what that problem was. It gave me a life-long interest in the history of Judaism. I geekily pursued my own studies, borrowing library books about Israel, tracing maps of Israel, even doodling the Star of David in my lessons.

Then, of course, I read the novel *Exodus* by Leon Uris. I must have read it four times at least, until it became dog-eared and covered in teacup stains. I probably identified with the character Karen, who joined the Zionist cause.

Mum was genuinely concerned that I might join a kibbutz in Israel. The truth was, the more I thought about what it would actually mean, the less sure I became, but it didn't stop me from blaming Mum for at least a year. "It's your fault I didn't go to Israel!" I would snap, when the truth was that I didn't have the confidence to do it. Instead, I applied to go to teacher training college.

Paula, in the meanwhile, came out of her bedroom and decided upon two courses in life. If she couldn't join the police because of a slight tourettes syndrome that no one but the police and her older sister ever noticed, she would go to agricultural college and win tractor driving competitions; and if Dad and some members of the family believed she ought to behave more like a girl, then she would begin dating young men to serve them right.

There were two sides to this. On the one hand I was impressed with her efforts; on the other, she appeared to be competing with me and I was hard put to keep up with it.

First there was the young man from Iran, a student at Brookes. She dated him for some while, seemingly with the intent to wind Dad up as much as she could. There followed many lengthy, hissed conversations in the kitchen between our parents about my sister going to Iran and being forced to wear the hijab; even worse, having children, having few rights over those children and never being allowed to return to Britain.

Then there was the American soldier from the Bicester Garrison who was actually great fun. It seemed that Paula, too, had ideas about leaving the country and was far more confident in her approach than I, having fallen at the first kibbutz hurdle.

But in the end, these relationships came to nothing, and having made some kind of point to our father, she moved out to begin the agricultural course at a college in Buckinghamshire.

Not very long after this, I went to teacher training college. I didn't really know what else I wanted to do with my life but knew that I had to earn a living.

Leaving the pub with Dad as my driver, I felt as though I was travelling to the end of the earth. In fact, Culham college was about thirty minutes away by car.

I stood within the now almost bare walls of my room for ages, staring at my forsaken posters, remembering so many things. Feeling both nostalgia and nervous anticipation.

God knows how I would have felt had I been going to Israel.

I visited Paula several times. She seemed happy, having made friends. They plied her with drink one night and pierced her ears.

She introduced me to Saul, the black boar that none but Paula could coax, and she won a tractor driving competition.

Howard and Marion had a few more years of schooling. They did well, especially in art and design. Howard became a fine stonemason like Grampy Ron and an artist, too; he took a year out in Australia when he was still young. Marion became a teaching assistant after experimenting with various jobs. She, too, is an artist.

Nanny Edna survived the ordeals of the mental health system in the eighties, which included the cruelty of electric shock therapy. She lived into her late nineties to tell us risqué jokes about nuns and bananas, inspired by her friend, Doris. She also turned a wild squirrel into a pet, hand feeding him nuts from the windowsill of the home she lived in.

Mum and Dad supported us through good decisions and through bad, through most of our emotional highs and lows, in fact. They ran the White Hart for thirty years.

Sometimes, when we are finding it hard to cope and need inspiration from those people who guided and advised us, we watch an old holiday movie of ourselves in Great Yarmouth. We were very young. We smile at the film of us playing cricket with our cousins in Nan's long and beautiful ghost garden that no longer exists.

We watch Marion buried up to her neck in the sand on a sunny beach, her chest rising up and down as though she can't breathe, but with a happy smile upon her face. Howard, aged six, fielding a ball to his cousin in a game of cricket, his arm whirring backwards rather than forwards. Paula and I, leaping up and down on trampolines aged ten and eight. She, so skinny and wiry, experimenting with overhead flips that I was afraid to try.

Our youthful, handsome Dad, sporting dark sunglasses and grinning at the camera from his deckchair. Mum, eternally young, flirting with the camera as she lifts the hem of her sixties dress to paddle in the sea.

The colours in the film have faded but the sun shines strong behind our silhouettes, highlighted with a golden edge, as though we will cavort on a beach for eternity.

Lightning Source UK Ltd.
Milton Keynes UK
UKHW010847310123
416239UK00001B/201